THIS
IS NOT
A GAME

THIS
IS NOT
A GAME

A NOVEL

Kelly Mullen

DUTTON

DUTTON

An imprint of Penguin Random House LLC
1745 Broadway, New York, NY 10019
penguinrandomhouse.com

Title page illustration by RedHead_Anna/Shutterstock

LIBRARY OF CONGRESS CATALOGING-IN-PUBLICATION DATA

Names: Mullen, Kelly, author.
Title: This is not a game : a novel / Kelly Mullen.
Description: New York : Dutton, 2025.
Identifiers: LCCN 2024024528 | ISBN 9780593854471 (hardcover) |
ISBN 9780593854488 (ebook)
Subjects: LCGFT: Detective and mystery fiction. | Novels.
Classification: LCC PS3613.U4464 T48 2025 | DDC 823/.92—dc23/eng/20240809
LC record available at https://lccn.loc.gov/2024024528

First published in 2025 by Century, an imprint of Cornerstone. Cornerstone is part of the
Penguin Random House group of companies.

Printed in the United States of America
1st Printing

The authorized representative in the EU for product safety and compliance is Penguin
Random House Ireland, Morrison Chambers, 32 Nassau Street, Dublin D02 YH68, Ireland,
https://eu-contact.penguin.ie.

For my grandparents,
Leatrice, Edward, Reta, and Harry

ONE

An Invitation

Mimi wheeled her canvas shopping cart behind her as she walked briskly into town. She had to hurry and get to Doud's for a sourdough before they closed. It was a chilly autumn afternoon, and Mackinac Island was humming with bicyclists and sightseers. Walking had always been her favorite stimulant. Even on days when she didn't have a particular destination in mind, nothing felt more liberating than a bracing constitutional around her little island home in the Great Lakes. She cherished how Mackinac's ban on cars (strictly enforced since 1898) kept away codger types who drove around in Cadillacs and droned on about their sleep apnea and hip replacements.

"Rosemary, hey! Wait up. Rosemary!"

Mimi quickened her pace as she walked past the hardware store. Anyone calling her by her given name, Rosemary, didn't know her very well. There was no need to look back, anyway. It was Herb. The smells of floor polish and paint thinner hovered in a cloud around him wherever he went.

"C'mon, Rosemary! Wait up!"

She rolled her eyes as she halted and spun around. "I can't, Herb. No time today." *Why did people always try to wheedle themselves inside her quiet little world?* That's why she liked her bridge group. They respected her privacy. None of that "sitting around drinking wine and baring your soul" kind of nonsense.

Herb caught up to her, huffing and puffing. His chambray shirt, emblazoned with a *Hi! I'm Herb! How can I help?* name tag, was stained with little continents of sweat.

"Just wanted to talk to you about your geraniums. Before it's too late for them."

Mimi heaved a sigh. "I understand the concept of deadheading, Herb."

Herb laughed nervously and held up his hands. "Hey now, no need to snap *my* head off." He paused to give her a wink. "Just wanted to remind you that since it's been a mild fall, the geraniums are still going strong, so be sure to keep that deadheading going until we get a hard freeze." He pushed his glasses up on his nose. "And, should you require a new pair of gardening shears, they happen to be fifty percent off this week, but I'm making it sixty percent off for friends."

"Okay." She nodded. "I'll stop by tomorrow and get a pair. For fifty percent off."

Mimi continued down Main Street, her shoes brushing through a confetti of autumn leaves on the sidewalk. Their earthy aroma reminded her that the thousands of visitors who flocked to Mackinac for seasonal events like the Fudge Festival would soon be gone. Only a few hundred islanders, who stayed year-round, would remain, and the price of a cup of coffee would drop by half.

When she reached the familiar sign above Doud's—*Welcome to America's Oldest Grocery Store*—she hustled inside and headed toward the bakery. There was one solitary sourdough waiting for her in the display case, next to a box of glazed donuts. She reached out to take it just as another woman's hand reached for it too, bumping into hers.

"Oh!" said the owner of the hand.

Mimi gave her the once-over. A young tourist with a bouncy ponytail.

"Didn't see you there," Ponytail added, with a shrug.

Mimi stepped in front of her, seized the loaf, and placed it firmly into her cart. She smiled brightly, then turned around and headed for the deli meats. Ponytail would be fine. She had decades of warm sourdoughs ahead of her.

On her way back down the street, Mimi turned onto the wooden walkway that led up to the colonnaded entrance of the Mackinac Island Public Library. Her footsteps matched the rhythmic click-clack of her shopping cart as it bumped along behind her. The jingle of the door announced her arrival, and her friend Pam looked up from her post behind the circulation desk.

Mimi paused to admire the latest display of books. *Classics That Will Make You Weep.* Kleenex boxes with *Boo-hoo!* and *Sniffle!* written on them were being used as bookends.

"Did it catch your eye? I was proud of that one."

"It's another Pam original," said Mimi, approaching the desk and placing her return in the drop slot.

"Are you coming to bridge next week? I'm going to host it here after hours. We can bring wine. I got special permission."

"It's in my appointment book," said Mimi, waving goodbye and heading for the exit. Pam was a good egg and a stalwart friend. Their relationship was straightforward and honest. She wasn't concerned with petty town gossip or tiresome obsessions with social status and beauty. They could talk about books and sip coffee together in easy silence. Plus, she was a damn good bridge player.

As Mimi headed home, she checked her Fitbit: 10,008 steps. Good, but she could do better tomorrow. She took a left turn onto her cul-de-sac, and her lakefront cottage, a postcard-perfect Victorian, came into view. The sun was now an orange disc slipping below the distant tree line of mainland Michigan, casting warm sparkles on the water's surface.

"Evening, Joan," she said to her lavender snowmobile, Joan Rivers. The vehicle was parked inside the portico attached to the side of the house. Mimi went in through the side entrance to the mudroom and wiped her wet shoes on the mat. Joan would need a good washing and waxing before her first ride of the winter season.

She went into the living room and pressed play on her portable speaker. Miles Davis's velvety trumpet floated into the air as she walked over to the Art Deco bar cart by the fireplace. A Gibson at dusk was a ritual that she and Peter had begun in the early years of their marriage. More than five decades later, this savory-sweet cousin of the martini was still her drink of choice.

"One, two, three," she said to her favorite onions, the tipsy kind that came bathed in French vermouth, as she impaled them onto a metal cocktail stick. After a gentle stir of the ingredients in a small crystal pitcher, she strained its contents into a chilled martini glass and took a sip. The gin's icy botanicals rolled pleasurably over her palate. Any concerns always seemed to melt away at this time of day.

Sure, occasional intrusive thoughts crept in. Like that salesclerk at the makeup counter last weekend. The one who had offered her unsolicited advice on teeth whitening while she was trying on lipsticks. She ran her tongue over her teeth at the memory of it. They *had* looked kind of yellow in that ridiculous magnifying mirror with LED lights. Perhaps she did drink too much coffee, like the woman said. But when did arctic-white Chiclet teeth become such a thing?

"What do you think, Big Phyllis? Should I whiten my teeth?" asked Mimi, turning to the large Kentia palm behind her.

Big Phyllis looked a little droopy. Mimi set her glass down and walked over to check her soil.

"You're a bit dry. Have a drink with me."

Reaching into the broom closet for the watering can and plant mister, she gave Big Phyllis a heavy pour and spritz.

She took another sip of her Gibson and felt the gin tingle her synapses as she headed into the kitchen. With a quick sawing motion of the bread knife, she severed the heel from the sourdough loaf, and its tangy essence wafted out. She tucked some Gruyère in between two slices and gently lowered them into a skillet bubbling with melted butter. As the grilled cheese sizzled to a golden brown, she heated some tomato soup in a pot and poured it into a small bowl. Pleased with the results, she sat down at the table and set to work on the newspaper's daily crossword:

A maneuver in a game or conversation

P-L-O-Y

She heard a rattling sound.

It was coming from the screened-in porch. She got up to investigate and found the outer door leading to the backyard had swung open. Odd, but not out of the ordinary, given the occasional gusts of wind coming in off Lake Huron. The door clanged against the frame and swayed open again in the breeze.

Walking over to close it, she could see something lying on the mat. A bright blue envelope. Strange that they hadn't simply used her mailbox. She picked it up and took it into the kitchen. It was addressed to *Rosemary Louise MacLaine,* her full legal name, which appeared to have been typed on an old-fashioned typewriter. Using her silver-handled letter opener to fillet the envelope, she removed the contents. On top was an invitation printed on thick nine-by-nine cardstock with embossed lettering:

Your presence is requested at the home of Jane Ireland
for an auction benefiting

The National Arts Foundation

COCKTAILS AND CANAPÉS

JAZZ AGE ATTIRE

SATURDAY, NOVEMBER 5TH

7:00 P.M.

LILAC HOUSE

1 LILAC LANE

MACKINAC ISLAND, MICHIGAN

Please read the two enclosed documents and follow
the instructions precisely.

Mimi frowned. *Jane Ireland?* Her wealthy socialite neighbor? Who was rumored to be dating her own son-in-law, thirty years her junior?

Unlike the jaunty nine-by-nine invitation, the other documents were "we mean business" letter size. She unfolded the first one, which had also been typed on a typewriter:

Dear Rosemary,

I know your secret. Perhaps you're thinking of
declining this invitation. Unfortunately, that's not an
option. Purchase Kimiko Mitsurugi's manga, Memento
Mochi, at the auction and pay the required amount in full.
Further details, including wire transfer instructions, are
in the second document.

Jane

Mimi's necklace felt heavy and tight around her throat. She clutched its small emerald pendant between her thumb and forefinger as the refrigerator's low hum buzzed in her ears. Holding her breath, she unfolded the second page. Everything was there. Names. Dates. Astonishingly precise details. She let the papers fall to the floor.

How could Jane possibly know what she had done?

Her mind wandered to the spreadsheet of various investment accounts and passwords that Peter had meticulously kept. She'd been living comfortably off their savings for over twenty years, but this could change everything.

Mimi went to the cupboard where she kept a pack of Pall Malls, a cut-glass ashtray, and her Dunhill lighter, a gift from Peter after he'd returned from a business trip to London. The engraved letter *R* was almost rubbed away now. She'd given up smoking in her thirties, but she always allowed herself one cigarette per year on her birthday. Today was not her birthday, but this development demanded it. She sat down at the kitchen table and lit up, savoring the first puff as it seared her nostrils. The soothing rush of nicotine flooded her brain.

Like everyone else on the island, she knew Jane's late husband had been obscenely wealthy. *So why would she need blackmail money?* Perhaps he hadn't left her enough to subsidize her decadent son-in-law-shagging lifestyle. Mimi exhaled and a cloud of smoke curled around her.

Unless this wasn't about money at all. Perhaps she had hurt Jane's feelings by consistently rejecting her social advances over the years? There had been suggestions of coffee or a cooking class, and she could faintly remember Jane once inviting her over for a luncheon. But the woman was a frivolous ding-a-ling whose cord didn't reach the outlet, so she always declined. They lived in different worlds. *Had her curt "no, thank yous" driven Jane to exact revenge?* No, that made no sense. What social capital could Jane Ireland possibly acquire from her? She was just an ordinary seventy-seven-year-old woman.

The grandfather clock chimed, startling her from her thoughts. It was ten p.m. After going about her bedtime routine in a daze, she slipped between the cool bedsheets and stared at the ceiling. Soft rain pattered on the leaves outside as a deep ache settled in her chest. Over the last twenty-three years, she had built a life for herself on Mackinac and settled into the comfort of her daily routines. Now those foundations could crumble. She was living minutes away from a blackmailer. Perhaps she would have to sell her beloved home.

She lay awake for hours unspooling her thoughts. Finally, anger steamrolled over her fears, and a decision clicked into place. She would go to Jane's wretched little party and bid at the auction. And then she would take the same approach she'd taken her whole life whenever she encountered a bully: clear-eyed confrontation. *Listen to me, you succubus cow. Who the hell do you think you are?* Yes, that sounded good. *Did Amazon sell bulletproof vests?*

Mimi rolled over on her side. She relaxed and closed her eyes. *But could she handle this all by herself?* Attending this swindler's shindig alone was a paralyzing thought. Her eyes fluttered open.

Should she bring Addie? Her granddaughter loved the intricate work of solving a problem. Addie's brilliant mind thrived on this kind of stuff. If only they hadn't had that terrible fight last Thanksgiving. Despite feeling guilty about it, Mimi hadn't made an effort to clear the air, and they had only exchanged a few perfunctory emails since.

Who was she kidding, anyway? She'd have to tell Addie about all this at some point. She was her only living descendant and the beneficiary of her will. What would happen if she died suddenly? Or if Jane contacted her again? Would Addie just show up one day to clear out her house and discover a stack of unopened blackmail correspondence? No dusty old box of wartime love letters in the attic for her to find, just the remnants of an extortion plot against Grandma. Knowing Addie, she'd use it as material to spice up the eulogy.

She would call her in the morning. No, a call was too easy to ignore. What if it went to voicemail? She couldn't leave a message. She didn't trust her voice to sound okay. An email would be better.

She could not do this alone.

TWO

No. 30702

*She was the kind of person you were just drawn to. You know?
When she walked into a room, it lit up. Everyone paid attention.*

Addie rolled her eyes at the TV and gave Edgar's soft black fur
a stroke. Why did every murder victim's best friend feel the need
to say that? It was doubtful that many people were capable of lighting up rooms. She hit pause on Keith Morrison, who was nodding
his head along sympathetically, and got up to get a pint of ice cream.
She shut the freezer door to find Edgar staring up at her plaintively
with his yellow-green eyes. He yowled.

"Ah, sorry, boy," she said. "I forgot your lunch, didn't I?" She
opened a pouch of cat food and filled his dish.

She sank back into the couch. The TV went dark for a moment
before cutting to a commercial, and Addie caught a glimpse of her
reflection in the blank screen. She was wearing a stained *Buffy*
T-shirt, surrounded by unopened moving boxes, and watching
Dateline, the murder-mystery equivalent of empty calories. A far
cry from five months ago, when she was toasting her engagement

to Brian over a Michelin-starred dinner. Though she was pleased that she was letting her hair go back to its natural state: red and curly. For the last three years, she'd been straightening it and dyeing it auburn because Brian preferred it that way.

She switched from *Dateline* to an episode of *Poirot*. From empty calories to comfort food. David Suchet was just what she needed right now. The undisputed GOAT. Branagh, Finney, and Ustinov all paled in comparison. She selected "Appointment with Death" and hit play.

Her watch buzzed with a text message from her friend Sarah:

> What time are you seeing Martin? I took the
> day off too.

Addie checked the time.

> Yikes, didn't realize it was already noon.
> In an hour.

> Want to meet at our spot after?

> Sure, see you soon.

Switching off the TV, she got dressed and then walked downtown in a rush of anxiety. As she took in the confident geometry of the Chicago skyline, she felt a deep loneliness. It struck her that the sense of ownership she once felt for her city was now gone.

Arriving at the Law Office of Martin Statler, she double-checked the address. She had envisioned an enormous glass skyscraper, but this was a narrow nineteenth-century row house, an anachronism wedged between two high-rises. It looked almost whimsical.

The reception area was cozy and filled with plants. Natural light streamed in through a large bay window. A tall man resembling a weathered version of Martin Statler's LinkedIn photo appeared in the hallway, wearing a rumpled suit.

"Ms. Paget?"

"Hi, yes," she said, standing up to shake his hand.

"My sixteen-year-old is going to be jealous that I'm meeting the creator of his favorite game."

Addie looked down, embarrassed. "Well, co-creator," she replied.

"Aha. Precisely the issue we're going to fix," he said, guiding her into his wood-paneled office.

They sat down in a pair of pleasantly worn leather club chairs. A tall plant sat on the table between them, partially obscuring their view of each other.

"Zanzibar gems are my favorite," said Addie, peering through its shiny leaves to get a better look at Martin. *Was he dodgy or paternal?* She couldn't decide.

"Aha," he said warmly. "A fellow plant enthusiast. I knew I was going to like you."

Cynicism bubbled up inside of her. Was he faking the plant connection to lure her into a raft of exorbitant legal fees? Was his son really a *Murderscape* fan? Did he even have a son? It was hard to trust anyone anymore.

"I do have a green thumb," she responded flatly, "although I left most of my plants behind at Brian's."

Brian. Saying his name squeezed her throat. *Why had she believed him when he said he loved her? How could she have been so brainless, so gullible?* Bitterness clenched her heart.

Martin furrowed his brow as if he were about to respond with a profound botanical metaphor, then jumped up. "Aha! Before I forget . . ."

He went behind his desk and pulled out a *Murderscape* hoodie from a clear plastic bag. It was from the first merch collab they'd done, with Adidas. The brand's logo had the game's iconic stiletto dagger slicing through it. With a broad smile, he held it up and plucked a Sharpie from the pen cup on his desk.

"Would you do me the honor? His name is Eric," he said, tapping the marker on a framed photo of a toothy teenager.

"You bet," said Addie, suddenly ashamed for having doubted his sincerity. Martin handed her the sweatshirt and she flipped it over. Brian's logo for his company, Closed Casket, was stamped on the back.

"Feel free to cross that out," said Martin, pointing at the logo with a wink.

"No, he deserves half the credit," she said, uncapping the Sharpie and drawing a large ampersand next to the two stacked C's, then signing her name.

"Thank you," he said, carefully folding the sweatshirt and placing it on the desk. He sat back down across from her and narrowed his eyes thoughtfully. "You know, business relationships often mirror failed marriages. Highly emotional situations. I just want to prepare you . . ."

Addie's chest tightened. She looked around. "It's a bit stuffy in here, isn't it? I think I need some air."

"Of course," he said, jumping up again to open the window.

The noise of the bustling avenue outside momentarily invaded the room as a cool breeze wafted in. Addie closed her eyes and breathed deeply as the street sounds gradually subsided into soothing white noise.

"Let me start over," Martin continued. "I noticed you rescheduled this meeting a few times. It's okay if you're not ready to do this."

Addie shook her head. "I was struggling to decide what to do before, but then I saw this," she said, handing Martin her phone with a *Fast Company* article pulled up:

MICROSOFT ANNOUNCES GAME STUDIO ACQUISITION

Today Microsoft announced its plans to acquire independent game development studio Closed Casket, founded by newcomer Brian Perry, for an undisclosed sum. The studio is behind the beloved multiplayer episodic game *Murderscape*, which has over 85M monthly active users.

Murderscape features "crime traveling" detectives who solve mysteries in different eras, from belle epoque Paris to hard-boiled 1920s San Francisco and pharaonic ancient Egypt. The gameplay blends breathtaking action and puzzle-solving with nostalgic Easter eggs from classic whodunits sprinkled throughout.

The acquisition is seen as part of the tech giant's wider strategy to develop more exclusive originals in-house. "Brian is a visionary, and the immersive worlds he crafts attract players of all kinds," said Microsoft in a statement.

"I am so deeply honored and excited to join the Microsoft family," said Perry.

Martin handed her phone back. "I'm sorry."
"I have a feeling 'undisclosed sum' translates to 'piles of money.'"
He gave her a small smile.
"Until I saw that, I was still holding out hope he might have included my name somewhere. Stupid, I know."
"It's not stupid. Just means you believe in the goodness of people." He tilted his head slightly. "Can you take me back to the beginning?"
Addie spent the next hour dissecting the anatomy of her relationship with Brian. She outlined the creation and launch of *Mur-*

derscape while Martin listened with attentive care, asking so many insightful follow-up questions that Addie had to remind herself that he was a litigator, not a therapist. She reached into her bag and took out her laptop, turning it around to show him the screen.

"I don't have records to show my work versus his. But see this email chain?" she said, pointing to the screen. "I wanted *Murderscape* to have the best story possible, so I handpicked writers from *The Last of Us* and *Red Dead Redemption*. And I made sure the narrative team collaborated with everyone, from the art team to the dev team, from the very beginning." She pulled up another email. "This exchange happened when I brought in a big television writer who used to work on *Poirot*. You can see Brian fights me on it in his reply." She read aloud from Brian's email: *"No way, that guy is in his sixties. Too old. He won't understand nonlinear writing."*

Martin followed along, squinting at the screen.

"Anyway, I held my ground and insisted on these specific writer hires, and we ended up winning a BAFTA for the game's narrative design. It was always a tug-of-war between us. He was obsessed with the mechanics and I was obsessed with the story."

"Did you ever have any kind of employment contract with him?"

"No. That's the thing. I didn't want a contract. I didn't want to work with or . . . for . . . the guy I was dating. At the time I'd just been promoted to senior art director at the ad agency I work for, so I wasn't going to leave my job for a side hustle. And anyway . . . I trusted him."

Martin took off his glasses and polished them on his tie. "In terms of the origination of the idea, when did that happen?"

Addie fidgeted with her wristwatch. "Well, it's a bit of a cliché, but it happened in a bar."

"Some of the best ideas in the world are hatched in bars."

Addie smiled. "Brian and I were still a new couple. I was already working on the *Murderscape* concept, and he had just started

Closed Casket. Our shared passion for gaming was what attracted us to each other in the first place. We ended up writing down some ideas on a little spiral notepad I always carried around. It had this abstract drawing of a raven on the cover, with *Quoth the Raven* printed on the top of each page. I'd found it in a gift shop when I visited Baltimore. We even sketched out a company logo together. It was this intertwined signature of two *P*'s. We were going to call the company Paget & Perry."

Her mind fast-forwarded to months later, when she'd asked Brian to change their company name to Paget & Perry, as they'd discussed. He'd dismissed the thought immediately. *It doesn't matter, Addie. The Closed Casket logo is already designed. We don't have budget for a new logo. Murderscape's dagger is what people will recognize anyway.*

After the game became a success, he'd presented her with a big *Murderscape*-themed cake for her birthday. The Closed Casket logo was emblazoned in blue frosting across the middle, with a marzipan stiletto dagger plunged into the center and red icing "blood" dripping down the sides. If there was ever a symbol of the power imbalance in their relationship, it was that dagger cake.

Martin shifted in his seat. "Do you still have the *Raven* notebook?"

Addie swallowed and shook her head. "I don't. There were pages and pages of ideas in there. I'm pretty sure I left it sitting out on my desk. Once things picked up with the game, it was just gone one day. He must have taken it."

"Well, I probably don't need to tell you that having the notepad would be helpful. It's the only evidence that firmly cements your authorship."

Addie nodded. She was brimming with frustration and self-doubt.

"How about text messages?" Martin asked.

"I have some. But I've been looking them over, and I'm worried that out of context they don't fully reflect what I actually did. A lot of my contributions were just conversations. Sometimes it was only the two of us working together late at night. Talking or brainstorming on a whiteboard . . . nothing permanent. Honestly, I have doubts myself sometimes. Everything is such a blur."

"What about the other people involved?"

"Everyone else is on his payroll at Closed Casket. They might diminish my role to protect him. What's in it for them if they back my story, anyway? Who knows, maybe he gave them equity to keep them quiet."

"Do you think you can share all the records you have with my office?"

"Okay."

Martin rose from his seat. "Well, I'm honored to work with you, Addie. I know this is hard, but I'm going to do everything I can to make it as painless for you as possible."

He walked her back to reception, helped her with her coat, and opened the front door. As she descended the steps, she turned around to see that he was still standing in the doorway, smiling sweetly and waving. Like he was sending her off to school for the day. Definitely paternal.

She walked up State Street toward Roosevelt in a daze. The thought of never seeing Brian again was bad enough. But seeing him in a courtroom would be terrifying. They hadn't spoken a word since the breakup three months ago. It had all been so sudden and shocking. Well, maybe not totally shocking, but she hadn't paid attention to the warning signs. Things were fine-ish, and then, one night, while they were making a pizza together in their kitchen, he just ended it without explanation. *I think you and I both know this hasn't been working for some time.* His tone was cold and mechanical. It felt more like he was firing her than dumping her. The moment had replayed in her brain on a loop ever since, like a cutscene in a game.

As she approached the commanding facade of the Field Museum, she could see Sarah waiting for her at the entrance, her long hair a chestnut wave flowing in the breeze.

"You doing okay?" she asked as Addie came up the steps toward her.

"I don't know," Addie responded as they approached the ticket window. "I think I'm still in shock, or denial, or something."

"Did you like Martin? My uncle says he's the best litigator in the city. Very underrated."

"He's great. But I'm still not sure I can go through with it."

Sarah put her arm around Addie and gave her a side squeeze. They took their tickets and entered the museum's vast, light-filled atrium.

"So. Plants or mummies?"

Addie turned to her with a look that said, *Do you even need to ask?*

"Right," said Sarah as they wended their way through the crowd toward the Ancient Egypt section. "I should have known the dead would cheer you up."

"They're not dead. They're vitality-challenged."

Addie's phone buzzed. It was an email from Mimi. She stopped in her tracks.

"What's up?"

"It's an email. From my grandma."

"Your grandma on your mom's side? The salty one?"

Addie nodded. "Peppery too."

"Hey, look," said Sarah, gesturing to an unwrapped mummy lying in an ornate sarcophagus. "I think that one's new."

Addie frowned down at her phone screen. "It's strange. She sounds . . . cheerful."

"Didn't you guys have a falling-out over Brian?"

"Yeah. Thanksgiving last year. We've always had our little explosions, but this one was nuclear."

"She hated him that much? What does the email say?"

Addie read it out loud:

Addie,

I know you're busy and have a lot going on with the breakup. Listen, I need to see my only grandchild. Would you please come visit? The last time we were together didn't end well, I know. Here's my idea. I've been invited to a party the first weekend of November, and I thought you could come with me. The island will be nice and quiet with tourist season ending, and I promise to keep the I Told You So's to a minimum.

Love,
Mimi

P.S. I'll treat you to all the fudge you want at Ryba's!

Sarah nodded. "Sounds like she feels bad. You should go."

Addie paused to think. Mimi was being uncharacteristically needy. The same woman who once explained to her *We aren't a hugging family* was now begging her to visit. She had to admit, it felt nice to be needed by her grandmother. Other grandmothers were not like Mimi. They showered their grandkids with affection and kept photos of them in their wallets. Mimi was unsentimental. Feisty. Maybe something else was going on.

Sarah read from a placard on the wall: "*A CT scan of this female mummy, No. 30702, revealed that she had curly hair and likely succumbed to tuberculosis.*"

"Curly hair, I like her."

"*The heart was often left in place during mummification, but in this particular specimen, the heart is gone. She was eviscerated completely through an incision in the left side of her abdomen.*"

Addie nodded. "Sounds about right."

THREE

Pen vs. Pencil

As the horse-drawn taxi turned onto Main Street, Addie called out to the driver, "You can drop me off here." The familiar clip-clop of the horse's hooves came to a halt. She hopped down and paid the fare.

Her phone buzzed with a photo from Sarah, sitting next to Edgar and holding up a glass of wine:

> We've fired up Netflix! Edgar wants to watch
> Labyrinth. Have a good time on Mackinac. You
> deserve an escape from all this. 🖤

She looked around. Despite the cold temperature, the sky was bright blue. It was a Friday afternoon, but no one was in sight. Anywhere else, the sense of isolation might be eerie, but on Mackinac, the solitude of the six-month offseason was peaceful. She switched her bag to her other shoulder and turned onto the stone path that led up to Mimi's cottage, taking a moment to appreciate its charm. The paint looked fresh, the curtains were open, and a layer of white frost covered the trees and shrubs out front. It was a scene straight out of a snow globe.

A wave of apprehension mixed with affection flooded over her. Maybe this time they could just keep things simple and try to enjoy each other's company.

She raised her hand to knock, and the front door swung open. Mimi was standing before her in overalls and a flannel shirt, holding a soft cloth and a bottle of Turtle Wax. "Hello, dear," she said, smiling.

"Hi, Mimi," she replied, stepping inside and setting her bags down. The air was thick with the smell of lemon floor polish and glass cleaner.

Mimi gave her a pat on the shoulder. "It's good to have my curly redhead back."

Instinctively, Addie touched the top of her head. "Yeah, I wanted to let it go natural again. Couldn't fight the curls. They insisted on a comeback."

"Was just giving Joan her second coat of wax," said Mimi, wiping her forehead with the back of her sleeve. "I'm going to change out of these overalls."

She left the room as Addie took off her coat and hung it over the back of a chair, surveying the cozy living room filled with stacks of books and magazines, calcium supplement bottles, and Mimi's collection of old cameras and binoculars. Or "clean clutter," as she preferred to call it. The only thing that seemed out of place was the faint odor of cigarette smoke hanging in the air, underneath all the astringent smells.

Wandering over to the bookcase, she paused as her eyes landed on an old hand-tinted sepia photo of Mimi and Grandpa Peter. Mimi looked glamorous. Flame-red hair with soft waves, like Rita Hayworth. A contrast to the stick-straight bob she now sported, with its faded shade of copper. Grandpa was so handsome, with water-blue eyes like Paul Newman's. He'd only been in Addie's life until she was ten years old. What would it have been like to spend time with him as an adult? Was it possible to feel nostalgic for something that never happened?

Her mom's old set of the Boxcar Children books lined a shelf next to the photo. She smiled and ran her finger along their spines, pulling out one of her favorites, *Mystery in the Sand*. She opened it and inhaled the book's familiar, musty smell. Its aging pages were an instant gateway back to her childhood. She thought of the summer her parents had taped together a bunch of cardboard boxes in their backyard, a makeshift boxcar for her to play in and re-create the neighborhood mysteries from the book. If only her parents were still here to help tape *her* back together. She felt tears come to her eyes.

"Want to have a Gibson with me?"

Mimi's voice pulled her back to reality. She blinked and closed the book, inserting it into its place on the shelf. "I actually had some wine on the plane, so I'm good."

"Suit yourself. I'm having one." Mimi headed toward the bar cart.

Addie looked at the grandfather clock. "Isn't four p.m. a little early in the day for a drink that's basically pure gin?"

Mimi paused and turned around to face Addie. "You know, one drink to celebrate my granddaughter's arrival does not make me Peter O'Toole."

"Fine. I guess I'll have a little something. How about a vermouth and tonic?"

Mimi's eyebrows shot up.

"What? It's refreshing."

"Sounds like a drink that's missing the point." She walked over to the small bar refrigerator and wriggled a bottle of Moët from the back. "Let's open a bottle of bubbly."

Addie sat down on the sofa and sniffed the air. "Have you been smoking?"

Mimi kept her back to her as she expertly popped the cork and filled two flutes. She turned around to hand her a glass. "Must be from the last time the bridge group was here. Pam likes her Pall Malls."

"Didn't realize Pam's a smoker. How's the rest of the group doing? How's Marie?"

"Marie's dead."

Addie paused. "Wait. What?"

"Yep," said Mimi, taking a seat next to her. "Cancer. At my age, you can't count on people sticking around."

Addie stared into her champagne. "That's a dark thing to say."

"It's not dark. Just reality."

"Well, I'm sorry to hear about Marie." Addie looked over at Big Phyllis, whose leaves were a sickly shade of brownish green. "What's been going on with Big Phyllis? It's horticultural homicide over there."

"I've tried everything," said Mimi. "I think her time might be up."

"Don't say that. I'll have a look at her later and see what I can do." She set her flute down on the coffee table. "So, tell me about this party we're going to."

Mimi reached for her iPad and handed it to her. "This is our illustrious host."

Addie began to read the article on the screen:

SEPTUAGENARIAN SOCIALITE DATING SON-IN-LAW

Page Six can exclusively reveal that Jane Ireland, once described as the "Queen Bee of the Manhattan Jet Set," is dating her own son-in-law, Matthew Reed. Reed is 44 and still legally married to her daughter, Alexandra. Tongues wagged earlier this year when Ireland and Reed were seen frolicking on picturesque Mackinac Island, where Ireland owns an enormous compound.

Once upon a time, Ireland was wed to hedge fund manager Nelson Ireland, whose grandfather was a director of U.S. Steel. They were an "It Couple" until Nelson's death in 1997. Ireland, who also owns a five-bedroom penthouse at the San Remo, went on to date a string of B- and C-listers in the early aughts and even had a cameo, as herself, in an episode of the original *Gossip Girl*.

In a terse email statement to Page Six, Alexandra said: "Matthew can do whatever he wants with his life. Sadly, my mother is a grade A narcissist and her betrayal does not come as a surprise to me."

Should make for an interesting Mother's Day card this year . . .

Addie set the iPad down and raised an amused eyebrow. "She sounds like a hoot."

"She's not. She's completely hootless."

"Then why are we going to her party?"

"I already told her I'd come," said Mimi, clasping her hands together. "Besides, I wanted to see you after our little kerfuffle. I thought, if we went to a party together, it would be a nice way to . . . reconnect."

"You thought if we went to a party with people you don't know or care about, I'd forget that you refused to accept my fiancé into our family?"

Mimi drew in a long breath through her nose. She reached for the newspaper and folded it open to the crossword. "Want to take it for a spin?"

Addie smiled. "Of course. Do you have a pencil?"

"You don't still use pencil, do you?"

"I like to understand what's going on before I commit to an answer."

Mimi handed her a ballpoint pen with *The Chicago Gazette* imprinted on it. "Here, give it a try."

"Fine," said Addie, begrudgingly clicking the pen as she began to work her way through the first few clues. "Did *The Chicago Gazette* have a crossword?"

"No. It would've cost us too much space that could otherwise go to a local advertiser."

Addie frowned at a clue. "Do you ever miss working?"

"Not really. There was always a deadline looming. It was high pressure."

"I forget—you were the copy editor?"

"Copydesk chief," corrected Mimi. "It wasn't hard-hitting journalism. Mostly stories about city council or school board meetings. But it was interesting work. And it kept me sharp. Like eating razor soup for lunch every day."

Addie paused. "Okay, how about this one. 11 across: *Italian opera from 1892.*"

"Hmmm," said Mimi. "RIGOLETTO."

"Nice," said Addie, filling in a couple of squares, then stopping. "Actually, that might not work because it looks like the last letter is going to be an *I*."

"Well, PAGLIACCI, then," said Mimi.

"Ugh. See? This is why I prefer pencil," Addie grumbled as she tried to convert her *R* and *I* into a *P* and *A*.

"Give me another one."

"I think I'll fly solo for a bit. I need to concentrate."

"Crosswords are supposed to be collaborative, you know."

Addie slid the paper and pen across the table. "You drive, then."

Settling her reading glasses on her nose, Mimi studied the puzzle. "Here's a good clue for you. 29 down: *Bamboozled.*"

"Very funny," said Addie. "How many letters?"

"Six, second letter is *O*."

"FOOLED . . . although, you know, it could also be CONNED. I would wait before you fill it in."

"I'm going with FOOLED."

"It's probably a mistake. Better get a pencil."

Mimi set her reading glasses down and looked up at her. "Pencil is fear, Addie. You know, there are two types of people in this world. Overthinkers and doers."

"Are you seriously telling me that because I prefer the option of an eraser, I think too much?"

"I'm only saying that you need to toughen up. If you're going to face Brian in court, you need to be decisive."

Addie set her flute down, sloshing champagne over the rim and onto the table. "If you must know, I haven't decided what I'm going to do yet." She dabbed at the spill with her cocktail napkin. "I'm working with a lawyer, but we haven't filed anything."

Mimi looked up at the ceiling. "I can't believe you would even hesitate."

"Have you considered how hard this is for me, Mimi? I still have feelings for him. I can't just bulldoze over people like you can."

Mimi swallowed hard. "He was an arrogant jerk, Addie. And he had a weak chin."

"Yes, I remember your thoughts about his chin."

"Receded straight into his neck. Can't trust someone like that."

"You say that like it's the most obvious thing in the world. You know, I need *someone* in my life. I get lonely."

"Lonely? You have a nice life."

"Being orphaned after your parents die in a car accident isn't exactly a 'nice life.'"

"You weren't orphaned. A twenty-one-year-old is not an orphan."

Addie shot her a sharp look. "Orphans don't have to be minors."

Mimi closed her eyes and pinched the bridge of her nose

between her thumb and forefinger as the weather forecast played softly on the television in the background.

Temperatures are still plummeting, folks. We're looking at a low-pressure system coming in from the northwest . . .

Addie shifted on the sofa. *So much for enjoying each other's company.* She decided to change the subject. "Do you know about this snowstorm that's coming?"

"Yeah, they've been talking about it all morning. We've got Joan Rivers, though. She'll get us anywhere we need to go." Mimi placed her flute on the coffee table and turned to face Addie as if she were beginning an interview. "I didn't mean to upset you, dear. Can we start over?"

Addie nodded.

"How's Edgar doing?"

Addie smiled. "He's good. Getting old."

"Aren't we all," said Mimi, rubbing her knees. "Listen, tomorrow before the party, I was thinking I could make your favorite Elvis waffles, and we could watch that *Godfather* reunion special they keep promoting everywhere. Pacino must be in an iron lung by now." She patted Addie's leg. "And on Sunday, I'm going to take you for fudge at Ryba's. There's something I want to talk to you about."

Addie noted the strain in Mimi's voice. "Is everything okay?"

Mimi's eyes flicked away. "Of course." She lifted the bottle of Moët and topped up their glasses. "I'm happy you came to visit, dear."

They clinked their fizzing flutes together in agreement. Addie lifted her glass and took a long sip of champagne as she studied her grandmother. Everything seemed normal on the surface, but she felt unsettled as they sat together in silence.

She closed her eyes. Martin had been pressing her to send over the documents and texts they'd discussed in their meeting, but she hadn't done it yet. Going through all of it would mean facing her fear: that maybe she hadn't played as big of a role in *Murderscape* as she thought. So many of her ideas were shot down or altered or developed into something else. *What if the evidence didn't back up her memories? Was the game even really hers?*

FOUR

Where's Jane?

Addie appeared in the portico, and Mimi took a moment to appreciate her granddaughter's natural beauty. The family resemblance between them was obvious in her wide-set green eyes. Her champagne-colored silk dress with glass beading was perfect for the Jazz Age theme without overdoing it. She looked like a silent film star. *Addie had everything. Talent, brains, beauty. Where had her signature moxie gone? Why had she allowed this bossy-pants gamer guy to redesign her life?*

Her thoughts went back to that grievous day when Addie's parents had died in the car accident. Mimi had made a silent promise to them: she would devote her remaining time on earth to guiding her only grandchild toward a successful, productive—perhaps even remarkable—life. Brian did not fit into this plan. From the moment they were first introduced, alarm bells went off. He hardly acknowledged her. She knew his type. Women of a certain age were invisible. What could he gain from making small talk with her? His self-importance filled her with disgust. She'd fretted about their relationship ever since. *What if she couldn't keep her promise?*

Mimi gestured to Joan Rivers. "Your chariot is ready."

Addie smiled as she walked toward her. "Love your dress, Mimi. Very Helen Mirren." Her eyes traveled to the shapeless leather bag slung over Mimi's shoulder. She raised a disapproving eyebrow. "The carryall, really?"

"What? It's practical. Some dinky little clutch can't handle everything I need." Mimi slipped on her fuzzy Uggs and put her satin pumps in the carryall. "You want to wear my other pair?"

"No, thanks," said Addie, buttoning her coat. "Uggs make me look like a Clydesdale."

Mimi hiked up her gown and threw one leg over Joan. She patted the passenger seat behind her. Addie approached Joan cautiously. With a nervous little hop, she landed squarely on the seat.

"Don't worry, Uneasy Rider—she's street-legal," said Mimi, gunning the engine to life. "Ready?"

Addie gripped Mimi's waist tightly. "I'm thinking."

Mimi hit the gas, and the snowmobile lurched forward. It was a serene winter's night, and the falling snow sparkled under the streetlights as Mimi expertly maneuvered the roaring machine. The ride over to Jane's would only take five minutes. Mackinac's small surface area, just under four square miles, meant every islander was a neighbor.

A tornado of worries in Mimi's brain spun to life. *Why hadn't she told Addie about the blackmail when she arrived yesterday?* She sighed as a sharp, painful thought entered her mind. She knew why she was putting it off: because she couldn't bear to tell her granddaughter the deep, dark secret behind all of this. If Addie couldn't understand and walked out of her life forever, it would be . . . Well, she wasn't capable of contemplating that right now. It was time to get to the auction and confront Jane. This assault on her peace of mind could not continue. Everything else would have to wait until Sunday at Ryba's.

After traversing a steep, winding path lined with fir trees, they arrived at the long driveway of Lilac House. The imposing wrought iron gates parted, and a stately Tudor-style mansion came into view in the distance. Perched atop a hill, it practically glowed as the white winter moon filtered through the clouds, casting eerie reflections on the snow. Surrounded by hedges and geometric topiaries in every direction, it had a dramatic cliff's edge to the left, dropping off into glistening Lake Huron.

"Wow and wow again," said Addie. "This isn't a house. It's a manor."

Floodlights came on and washed them in light. A security guard waved them through, and they approached a snow-covered drawbridge spanning a wide moat. Mimi trimmed the engine as they crossed. The moat's water, dark and deep, appeared ready to swallow them up.

They parked Joan at the front of the house. Addie offered her arm as Mimi changed out of her Uggs, and together they ascended the stone steps, which had been cleared and salted for guests. The house loomed over them. Spotlights illuminated the exterior from the ground, presumably to make the house feel inviting, but they had the opposite effect. The place looked like a vampire's lair designed by Henry VIII.

Addie turned to Mimi and smiled as she reached for the gargoyle door knocker. Mimi's stomach clenched. The growing chill in the air sent a shiver down her spine.

Then, the front door opened.

A housekeeper with rosy apple cheeks, wearing a crisp uniform, beckoned them in. "Come inside, ladies. You must be freezing."

They stepped into the foyer, which featured a broad empire staircase and a spectacular crystal chandelier. Recessed arches displayed classical statues and candelabra sconces flickered on the walls. The air was a heady mix of candle wax and incense. Party conversation and the gentle tinkling of glasses emanated from somewhere farther inside the house.

"What a magnificent home," said Addie.

"Thank you, madam. I'm Barb."

"Nice to meet you. I'm Addie, Rosemary's granddaughter. I'm here visiting from—"

"Where's Jane?" Mimi stepped forward and handed Barb her coat.

Addie shot Mimi a furtive glare. "That was brusque, Mimi."

"Oh, she's still getting ready," said Barb, smiling pleasantly. "Everyone else is in the library. Come this way."

She led them down an arched hallway, her footsteps echoing on the black-and-white-checkered floors. They passed a grand ballroom that glittered with gilt-framed mirrors.

"I'm afraid the weather might be turning against us tonight. But we've got the fireplaces going and plenty of whisky and hot chocolate to keep you warm. Most of our guests came in from out of town, so they're staying with us over the weekend."

They entered a dazzling, two-story library lined with leatherbound books. Another grand staircase curved upward to a wrought iron balustrade encircling the second floor. A pair of deep-burgundy chesterfields faced each other in front of a green marble fireplace roaring with blazing logs.

Several people stood around, clutching cocktail glasses. Everyone seemed to have taken the interwar-period theme seriously. The women were dressed glamorously in satin and lamé gowns and the men in tuxedos. In the corner, a man with an angular face, wearing a white tuxedo jacket, was playing a grand piano. A few guests turned in their direction as they entered the room. No one made an effort to welcome them.

Barb lifted a coupe from a tray. "Champagne?"

Addie took one and smiled. "Thank you."

"Do you have anything stronger?" asked Mimi.

"Yes, madam, although it's just myself and the cook tonight. No bartender on duty."

"I'll have a Gibson. It's just gin with a little dry vermouth and three cocktail onions on a stick."

They wandered over to a long table arranged with hors d'oeuvres and tureens brimming with fresh flowers.

Mimi surveyed the room. No Jane or her *son-in-lover*, Matthew, in sight. Such a small group. *If this was an auction, where were all the people?* Her eyes landed on a tall man with an upright posture and narrow shoulders. She recognized him instantly. He had ignored the Jazz Age dress code entirely and was wearing a short-sleeve button-down collared shirt and khaki trousers. A limp necktie dangled from his neck, accentuating a prominent Adam's apple. She frowned. "What's Jim Towels doing here?"

"Who?"

"Jim Towels. I think he's the only islander here besides me. Strange."

"His name is *Jim Towels*?"

Mimi shrugged. "The guy's lucky he has a silly name. It's the most interesting thing about him."

"Who is he?"

"Owns the island print shop. Lives in a nice house with a big rose garden."

"Why's he dressed like an IT consultant?"

"He's always been a bit of an odd duck. Has all the charm of an actuary."

Addie tugged on her arm and nodded toward a man in a top hat with bronze skin and perfectly coiffed hair. "That's Sebastián Palacios, the host from the *Godfather* reunion!"

Mimi nodded absently. "Where's Jane?"

"He's a game show host too." Addie plucked a stuffed olive from a platter. "He's on *Battle of the Extroverts*. You should see some of the wild stuff he gets people to do. I wonder how Jane knows him."

"Who?"

"Sebastián Palacios." Addie turned to Mimi. "Are you okay? You seem distracted."

Mimi opened her mouth to respond, and a piercing dog bark came out. They both looked down in unison. Two plump dachshunds stood at their feet. The brown one was barking, and the blond one was quiet, wagging its tail excitedly.

"Barnabas! Binky!" called a sturdily built man wearing chef whites. "So sorry, ladies," he said, running over and picking up the barky one.

Addie crouched down to pet the quiet one.

"This one hasn't been behaving at all tonight," said the man, patting the head of the growling dachshund in his arms.

"I know how you feel," said Addie, looking up at Mimi. "Love their names."

"Thank you. Barnabas here is named after my favorite TV character. And that girl there is named after my ex-wife, aren't you, baby? God rest her soul."

"Oh! Goodness, I'm sorry," said Addie.

"Don't worry. She's not dead. Just dead to me," said the man. He was a classic aging Beach Boy type with a SoCal lilt to his voice and the weathered complexion of someone who had spent his life outdoors.

"Well, you have great taste. I'm a *Dark Shadows* fan too. I'm Addie, and this is my grandmother Rosemary."

"I'm Gus," he said, balancing Barnabas in the crook of his arm while extending his hand to offer a weak handshake. "Jane's brother. Nice to meet you both."

Mimi's face changed. "You're Jane's brother?"

"Guilty as charged. Lending her a hand for a few weeks while she finds a new chef. I used to cook at the Drake Hotel."

"Gus!" called a Hitchcock blonde with pouty red lips, from the other side of the room. She wore a sapphire-blue dress and a chignon so tight it pulled at her temples. Approaching them in a huff, she shot Gus a fierce look. "Can I talk to you for a moment?"

"Of course," said Gus politely. "Then I've got to get back to the kitchen. Ladies, this is Lillian."

She offered Addie and Mimi a thin smile as they introduced themselves, then turned back to Gus, taking him by the elbow. He gave them a little wave as she led him away.

Barb reappeared and presented Mimi with a Gibson, garnished with two onions, on a mirrored tray.

Mimi looked down at it disapprovingly. "I asked for *three* onions."

"Oh. Sorry, madam. I'll—"

"It's fine," said Mimi, taking the drink.

Barb offered an apologetic bow and walked away.

"Mimi, what is going on with you?"

"Two onions is bad luck. It's the rule of the Gibson."

"You need to loosen up," said Addie, taking a sip of champagne. "It is an odd mix of people here tonight, isn't it? Everyone seems to be looking at each other out of the corners of their eyes."

"Yeah. Like those retail-loss-prevention cops at Walmart."

Addie dipped a shrimp puff in rémoulade and offered it to Mimi. "Will you please eat something?"

"Okay," Mimi complied, helping herself to Addie's plate.

A man in his forties wearing a double-breasted tuxedo and a floppy velvet bow tie entered the room. Mimi froze. It was Matthew. She had met him a few times in passing when he'd been out with Jane on one of her power walks. He had an appealing boyish quality. *Was he aware that his seventy-something girlfriend was a conniving grifter?* They made eye contact, and his face brightened.

"Hey, neighbor!" he called out as he approached them.

Mimi gave a half-hearted wave. "Hello, Matthew. I've been looking for you. Well . . . I mean, I've been looking for Jane."

"Ah, yes, she should be here any minute. You know her. Always has to make an entrance."

Mimi noted how the corners of his mouth were turned up in a smile, but his eyes weren't smiling. "This is my granddaughter, Addie."

"Oh!" he said, taking a step back to look at them side by side. "I should have seen it sooner. Of course you two are related."

Addie exchanged a look with Mimi.

"It's not just the red hair. You both have the same . . . *je ne sais quoi*. It's behind the eyes," he said, pointing at his own.

Mimi studied him. *How did this innocuous-looking puppy dog end up in a tabloid scandal with his mother-in-law?*

They stewed in a long, strange silence.

Addie shifted her weight from one foot to the other. "I love old houses like this. The smell of old books, the art, the furniture . . ."

"That is my room spray," said a slender woman with deep ebony skin and microbraids arranged in an elegant bun, turning to them and setting her half-finished appetizer plate down on an end table. "*Bouquiniste.* It evokes the romanticism of wandering among the dancing motes of dust in an old bookshop." Her thick French accent coated each carefully selected word.

"This is Veronique Loubatier," said Matthew. "She's a world-famous nose."

"I create scents that elevate your sense of wonderment and offer nostalgic echoes from the past."

Barb passed them, carrying an elaborate tray of crab legs on ice, arranged in a kickline.

Addie followed the tray with her eyes. "All the food here looks so delicious."

Veronique sniffed. "I do not eat food that does the cancan."

The sound of a fork clinking against glass silenced the room. Heads turned toward Matthew, who stood holding a raised coupe, his fork in the air like a maestro brandishing a baton.

"Good evening, everyone. The auction is about to begin. But first," he said, gesturing to a group of glass cases and an elaborate wall display of fencing suits and swords, "I want to draw your attention to an array of items that will be auctioned off tonight. Jane's late husband, Nelson, was a collector of many things, but antique weaponry was his one true passion."

He walked toward one of the cases and lifted the lid. "Jane hates guns, so this is the only one she'll let me keep in the house. It's an 1874 Colt 'Open Top' Pocket Revolver," he said, holding it up. "It was once owned by the famous sharpshooter herself, Ms. Annie Oakley. Her initials are engraved on the cylinder."

"It's tiny," said Lillian. "Is it loaded?"

"No, but we keep the bullets in that drawer over there, if you want to try it out." He winked at Lillian and gently handed her the gun. "Here, have a look-see. Rumor has it, Ms. Oakley slept with it under her pillow."

Mimi's eyes traveled around the room as Matthew gestured to the display, explaining the history of each item to the group. At first glance, people appeared to be enjoying themselves, but upon closer inspection, the smiles seemed forced. Jim Towels was fascinated by a mace, while Veronique fiddled with a crossbow. It felt performative. *Could all of these people be in on this blackmail scheme with Jane somehow?* Mimi's molars ground back and forth as she considered the possibility.

Addie nodded toward Veronique. "I want that crossbow she's holding. It's just like the Arbalest from *Fire Emblem*!"

Mimi rolled her eyes. Of course a place like this would make Addie's childlike imagination run wild. Meanwhile, she was living her own personal nightmare. *What could her blackmail payment possibly cover in a place like this? The water bill?* She just wanted to get through this ordeal and find an opportunity to talk to Jane.

She looked at her wristwatch. "It's 7:41. Where the hell is Jane anyway? This is ridiculous. It's like we're all waiting for the pope."

"This is our prized piece," Matthew continued, walking over to the fireplace mantel. A large, shiny knife was mounted on the wall above it. "It's not for sale, I'm afraid. It's from the Kamakura era."

Mimi stared at the knife and gasped in recognition.

"It has a rather unique pistol-grip jade hilt inlaid with rubies. Just like—"

"Just like the one from *Memento Mochi!*"

Addie turned and stared at her grandmother as if she'd lost a front tooth. Mimi silently scolded herself. *No one needed to know she'd been obsessively Googling this mysterious manga.*

"Didn't realize you were such a fan, Rosemary," said Matthew, lifting the knife from its display hooks. "Here, you can hold it."

He stepped forward and carefully placed it in Mimi's hands. She looked down at it, conscious of his careful eye on her as she handled the weapon. For a moment, she allowed herself to imagine plunging the blade into Jane. She curled her fingers around the smooth hilt.

The room stirred, and everyone's heads tilted upward. A bank of bright lights flooded the second-floor balustrade. Jane glided onto the walkway above, and the piano player launched into a lively rendition of "It Had to Be You," heralding her arrival. She turned to slowly descend the curved staircase, revealing a spectacular, body-hugging gown with gold beading and an elaborate, flapper-style headpiece adorned with peacock feathers. She was punishingly beautiful. Her lithe figure reminded Mimi of a perfectly proportioned Ionic column, like the ones she'd seen on a cruise in the Cyclades with Peter. The air seemed to vibrate with electric energy around her.

Startled by Jane's sudden appearance, Mimi almost lost her grip on the knife. She fumbled to steady it, and the blade nicked her finger.

"Jane!" exclaimed Lillian, arms wide, approaching their host for a hug.

Mimi looked down at her hand. Blood beaded on her right index finger where she had gripped the knife blade. The pain signaled a warning to her brain: *This night is not going to end well.*

FIVE

Something Unexpected

"Oh no, Mimi!" exclaimed Addie, taking her grandmother's hand to examine the cut. "Are you okay?"

Mimi pulled away. "I'm fine." She set the knife down and reached into her carryall, retrieving a Band-Aid. As she placed it around her finger, she nodded toward Jane. "I see Norma Desmond is here."

Jane worked the room, confidence radiating from every pore. Mimi's eyes fastened on her blackmailer. Diamond chandelier earrings swung from her ears as she spoke to each guest, her well-modulated voice making it clear that she was the star of tonight's show and the rest of them were mere spectators. *Was this woman enjoying putting her through this torture?* The thought of confronting her was beating inside Mimi's head like a timpani. She could almost feel those manicured claws breaking through her skin.

Jane made her way toward them, and Mimi stiffened.

"Rosemary! My dear. You know, I've been trying for *so long* to get you to join the FOJ Club." She turned to Addie and winked. "Friends of Jane."

Mimi forced a tight smile. "Been sleeping in a cryochamber, Jane?"

Jane belted out a gusty laugh. "You are just the funniest, Rosemary."

"What *is* your secret?" asked Lillian. "You never age."

"Like I always say," she said, leaning in toward them conspiratorially, "just enjoy life, and don't look in the mirror!"

"I'm surprised you can see yourself in a mirror at all," muttered Mimi.

Addie gave her an elbow between the ribs.

"And who is this?"

"This is my granddaughter, Addie," Mimi replied, lips pressed tightly to her teeth. "She's the creator of a popular game you might know, *Murderquest*."

"Murder*scape*," Addie corrected.

"Oh, wow! I love that game," Jim Towels chimed in. "It's so cinematic. What time period is the next mystery going to be set in?"

Addie smiled uncomfortably. "I'm actually not sure."

He extended a hand to Addie. "Well, it's a pleasure. I'm Jim Towels, proprietor of Towels Print Shop. I do menus, lanyards, brochures, name tags, that sort of thing. I'm also a card-carrying member of Mackinac's chamber of commerce."

"Okay, everyone," said Jane in a breathy voice, relishing the opportunity for drama. "This way!" She ushered them out into the foyer, and they all followed along like ducklings. "We want you to partake in a little tradition we have here at Chez Ireland," she continued, swanning over to a control panel and pressing a button with a flourish. The home's massive front door slowly opened to reveal the freshly salted and shoveled drawbridge about a hundred feet away, showcased by floodlights lining both sides. "We call it Drinks on the Drawbridge."

There were low groans and protestations among the group as they shuffled through the door and out into the cold night.

As they reached the drawbridge, Matthew turned around to

face them. "Now, we don't want your hands to be empty, so we're serving you some of our special grand cru from our vineyard in Santa Barbara."

Everyone lightly clapped as Barb appeared with a large tray of pewter chalices, and Matthew filled them from a magnum labeled *Growing Concern.*

Mimi squinted at the label. It featured a charcoal drawing of Jane leaning sensually against a wine barrel with the caption, *Full-bodied.*

Matthew raised his cup proudly. "This wine is not a gift from nature. It's a product of innovation, persistence, sustainable practices, and discriminating taste. Please enjoy."

Mimi reached for a chalice and took a mouthful.

"Wow." Addie grimaced after taking a sip. "Tastes like fermented NyQuil."

Mimi coughed. "I think they harvested these grapes from a wax fruit arrangement."

Matthew scanned the group as guests offered half-hearted "aahs."

"It's certainly unforgettable," said Jim Towels.

A blustery wind whipped around them as the flurrying snow-flakes increased in size and intensity. Jane clutched her headpiece with the tips of her fingers.

"Let's do this fast!" Matthew called out as he held up his chalice. "Here's to Drinks on the Drawbridge, and to all of you! Cheers!" Everyone responded in kind, taking tiny sips.

The group hurried back across the drawbridge and up the stone path, then on inside, stomping their shoes on the rug and brushing snowflakes from their clothes and hair.

"Well, that was pointless," grumbled Mimi.

"*Oui. Très* pointless," agreed Veronique.

"Just one more thing, friends," said Matthew, walking toward the control panel and punching in a code. With a variety of clanging and creaking sounds, the drawbridge slowly heaved its way up and stopped upright at a ninety-degree angle.

"Isn't that the only way out?" asked Sebastián.

Matthew smiled enigmatically. "Indeed it is." He pressed another button, and the massive front door creaked shut with a great solitary thud, the echo reverberating throughout the house. Everyone exchanged uncomfortable glances. He chuckled. "The fun begins now. You will be wined and dined like royalty before we release you."

Mimi gripped her carryall and pulled it close to her. The foyer suddenly seemed darker, smaller. They were trapped inside this moat-wrapped mansion from hell.

Lillian radiated nervous energy. "But what if someone wants to leave?"

Matthew exchanged a knowing glance with Jane and turned back to the group. "We'll treat you so well, you'll never want to leave."

"And here we have Lot #7, a Millicent Barnstable, the world-renowned dead-bird portraitist," said Matthew.

He was standing at a podium on a small, elevated stage in the ballroom. A single row of chairs formed a half circle a few feet away. He lifted a black velvet cloth covering an easel, revealing an oil painting of a dainty, pale-green bird lying on its back on a park bench, claws thrust skyward.

"Now then, who would like to start the bidding on this stunning work, titled *Tennessee Warbler in Repose*?"

Mimi checked her watch: 8:51 p.m. She felt queasy. A bundle of nerves squeezed every organ in her body. Each minute felt like an hour. She scanned the group. Most of them sat stone-faced; a few others milled around a dessert table laid out with liqueurs, chocolates, and macarons. Except for Jim, they were all complete strangers. *Why had this odd mix of people come to Mackinac? Could they all be in on it with Jane? Her co-conspirators?* Her eyes landed on Veronique, who had just entered the ballroom. She looked anxious as she rushed to take a seat and raised her hand to bid on the painting.

"Aha. Veronique!" said Matthew theatrically. "Do I have an opening bid?"

"$50,000," said Veronique flatly.

Matthew raised his eyebrows. "Ms. Barnstable has only produced thirty-five works in her lifetime. I certainly hope there is a commitment of more than $50,000 for this magnificent depiction of a fallen feathered friend."

"$75,000," called out the man who had been playing piano earlier.

Mimi looked in his direction. He leveled his eyes at her. Something about him didn't sit right.

"Thank you, Woody," said Matthew. "Do I have $100,000?"

Addie leaned over to Mimi. "I don't think that guy's name is Woody. I recognize him from somewhere, and that doesn't sound right."

Mimi dug through her carryall in a quest for Altoids. She could hear the tin rolling around, eluding her fingers among all the last-minute items she'd tossed in. She turned to Addie. "How many more lots are there going to be?"

Addie flipped through the auction program. "About ten. Everything is so expensive, Mimi. Why did we get invited? You can't afford this stuff."

"Let me see that," said Mimi, taking the program. She flipped to the page displaying *Memento Mochi*. It was misspelled *Momento Mocha* and the starting bid was listed as *100,00*. Was that a misplaced comma, or a missing zero?

Mimi turned her attention to Jane, who was seated at a table in the back corner. Lillian sat next to her, whispering something in her ear. Their exchange looked heated, angry. Mimi furrowed her brow as she watched Jane. Her head bobbed as if she were drunk, about to fall asleep. Suddenly, she pushed Lillian away and planted her hands flat on the table. Attempting to stand up, she wobbled on her stilettos and then flopped back down in her chair. Barb rushed over to help, but Jane waved her away.

A little smile came over Mimi. It was gratifying to see Jane disheveled. Everything the woman projected spelled control. Her thin body. Her perfect house. Her bright white teeth. She shut her eyes and thought of the words she had imagined saying to Jane over and over again: *Listen to me, you vacuous twit. This auction is a sham! You are not a philanthropist, you are a philanderess! You should be ashamed of yourself.*

"Okay, ladies and gentlemen," said Matthew, the deep timbre of his voice echoing out over the small group gathered in such a large room. "We have a special surprise for you. Our mystery guest has arrived."

Barb opened a pair of doors, and in walked a slender Japanese woman wearing overlarge neon-pink cat-eye glasses and a black satin dress. Her glossy, thick hair grazed her shoulders as she walked purposefully toward the stage. Mimi squinted. She looked familiar.

"I am proud to introduce you all to our dear friend, the world-famous mangaka Kimiko Mitsurugi!"

The room erupted into applause.

Mimi took in a gulp of air. Kimiko Mitsurugi. Author of *Memento Mochi.* She'd read that name a thousand times over the last few weeks and learned everything about her, knowing she was about to bid on her most famous work. Her only work, from what Mimi could gather. *Why the hell was she here?*

Matthew held up a small book and lifted his voice. "This is the first copy ever printed of *Memento Mochi*, from Kimiko's personal collection. It can now be yours."

Kimiko smiled as she approached the podium. He handed her a pen, and she signed it with the exaggerated flourish of an artist.

"Adding her signature significantly increases the value, I think. So, shall we start the bidding at $200,000?"

Mimi drew in a breath. *$200,000?* She was going to have to sell her cottage. A deep roar thrummed in her ears. Her palms were clammy. Was this a panic attack? She'd read about them in *Reader's Digest* but wasn't sure.

"C'mon, folks, Kimiko Mitsurugi signed this treasure. It's her magnum opus."

It was up to her to make the bid. She broke into a sweat as she stewed about how high she might have to go to fulfill Jane's demand. *Time to get this over with.* She slowly raised her hand in the air.

"All right. I have $200,000. Do I have $225,000?"

Addie turned to her, agog. "Mimi, are you nuts?"

"$250,000," said a voice from the other side of the room. Mimi looked around, panicked. It was Woody again.

Matthew nodded to him and cast an eye over the audience. "Do I have $275,000?"

Everyone quieted.

Addie gripped Mimi's forearm. "That is *a ton of money.* You can't afford this."

"Anyone?"

Mimi curled her nails into her palms and clenched her jaw. She thrust her hand up high.

"Mimi! Stop. This is reckless."

She felt a bead of sweat roll down the side of her face. Her eyes fixed on the hammer Matthew was holding in midair. *Strike the damn hammer.*

"Sold! For $275,000 to Mackinac's very own, very generous Rosemary MacLaine."

As everyone politely clapped, Addie gripped Mimi by the elbow as though she were a misbehaving child and steered her toward the exit.

"Let's take a break, folks," said Matthew.

People rose from their seats and mingled as Addie and Mimi scooted out into the hallway.

Keeping hold of Mimi's arm, Addie led them into the drawing room. "I can't believe you just blew what could have covered my entire college education on a fifty-page comic book!"

Mimi twisted free from Addie's grip and fished in her carryall for her Pall Malls. She walked across the room and pulled open the French doors. Addie hugged herself as the frigid night air flooded the room, blowing in flakes of snow toward her.

"So you *are* smoking," said Addie as she watched Mimi step onto the balcony and light up. "You lied to me."

Ignoring her, Mimi exhaled a plume of smoke through her nostrils.

"Carelessly throwing away your life savings is one thing, but smoking, Mimi? If you're not careful—"

Mimi laughed into the cold darkness outside. "If I'm not careful, what? It could kill me? Please. Stop treating me like I should be stoned in the town square by the American Cancer Society."

Addie placed her hands on her hips. "Are you going to tell me what the hell is going on?"

Mimi turned her back and didn't answer.

"Come on, Mimi. This isn't some heartwarming reunion. You dragged me here from Chicago so I could watch you inhale carcinogens and drop money like you're in the Rat Pack? I don't have time for this insanity. I've got my own problems." She paused and took in a breath. "Is everything always just about you?"

Mimi squeezed her eyes shut. How did she end up in this hopeless mess of blackmail, bad weather, and strange people? This was not how she had planned to tell Addie, but it was time. Stress roiled inside her body as she reached into her trusty carryall and produced the blackmail invitation and letter with the auction instructions. She'd intentionally left the document detailing her secret at home. The papers trembled as she turned around and handed them to Addie, who took them sharply and began to read. Mimi watched her read and reread them.

Addie looked up. Her green eyes were clouded with confusion. "You're being blackmailed? Is this a joke?"

Mimi studied Addie. Her mouth twitched at the corners. *Was that the ghost of a smile?* "You find this amusing?"

Addie furrowed her brow. "No, of course not. I just never thought something like this would happen to me."

Mimi frowned. "You mean to *me*?"

There was a short silence.

"I'm sorry, Mimi, but I've spent the last three months alone in a studio apartment watching *Dateline* with my cat. You're being blackmailed?! This is . . . It's just all so unbelievable. Why didn't you tell me? What could Jane possibly have on you?"

"Addie, I can't tell you about all this right now."

"Tell me. Please."

"I promise I'll tell you tomorrow. We'll get fudge at Ryba's and have a nice long talk. Can we just get through this awful night?" Mimi ashed her cigarette into the snow. "Look, I should also tell you that I'm planning to sell the cottage. I've been looking at condos in Florida."

"What?" said Addie, taking a step backward. "You can't move. Mimi, you *are* Mackinac!"

"Not anymore. It's not the same place to me."

Addie covered her face with her hands. "None of this makes any sense. I still don't understand. Why did you bring me here tonight?"

Mimi held her breath, trying to keep the panic at bay as she stared out at the whirling snow. "I invited you because I need you, okay? I can't do this alone. I need backup. This kind of situation . . . It's sort of *your thing*, isn't it?"

Addie smiled faintly. "It might be. If I knew what sort of situation we were in."

"Who else would I have called, anyway?"

Addie's smile died on her lips. "Glad I could be your last resort."

"That's not what I mean." Mimi took another drag, the tip of her cigarette glowing bright orange.

The wind was picking up, and the snowflakes were becoming denser. Mimi shivered and tossed her stub into the snow below. She turned to face Addie. "Listen, I—"

A scream pierced the air. They stared at each other for a moment, frozen and silent in shock. Another scream. This one higher-pitched and more primal.

"Let's go," said Mimi firmly. She marched across the parquet floor and down the hallway.

Addie gathered her wits and darted after her. They found everyone standing in the foyer, looking confused.

"What the hell is going on?" said Gus, emerging from the direction of the kitchen.

Hysterical cries echoed through the house.

"Upstairs!" shouted Kimiko.

Everyone clambered up the stairs together in a herd. They surged down the hallway toward the screams and stopped still. Barb was standing at the end of the hall, frozen in the doorway of the master bedroom. Wild-eyed, she gripped a quaking tea service tray, the cups and saucers clinking together loudly. As a ripple of fear and confusion set in, Matthew carved his way through the group toward Barb.

Her lips trembled as she struggled to speak. "It's horrible. I can't . . . She was just . . . The blood . . ."

Matthew took her by the shoulders and looked directly into her eyes. "Barb, calm down. Take a deep breath. What are you trying to say?"

The clinking of the dishes reached a fever pitch until she finally lost her grip and the tray crashed to the floor. She burst into tears and fell to her knees.

"It's . . . Jane. Jane's dead!"

SIX

A Dark and Stormy Night

Even in death, Jane looked glamorous. Her right arm was lying at her side, and her left was outstretched like a ballerina starting a pirouette. A deep red stab wound in her chest looked as though it had gone straight through her rib cage and into her heart. Gasps of horror and disbelief filled the room as the group gathered around the bed. For a moment, no one moved.

"Well, she's definitely dead," said Sebastián, twisting his hands together.

"Quite dead," said Kimiko.

Addie felt a lump in her throat. She took a moment to absorb the shock and unreality of the scene. Jane's arms, in the final throes of death, had spread blood up and down the bedsheet, making patterns reminiscent of snow angels.

"Somebody check her pulse!" shouted Gus.

Everyone looked panic-stricken, blank and wide-eyed with fear. Matthew's face contorted in deep horror. Addie looked to Mimi, who stood still, completely frozen.

Jim Towels edged forward with trepidation and felt Jane's wrist. He looked to the group and shook his head. "She's gone."

"How is this even possible? She was so . . . alive just a minute ago. I don't understand," said Lillian, holding her head in her hands.

"Look!" exclaimed Veronique, pointing to the bed. "There is something in her hand." She reached toward Jane.

"Be careful! Fingerprints," said Addie.

Using the very tips of her perfectly manicured fingernails, Veronique pried a crumpled note from Jane's lifeless hand.

"What does it say?"

She opened it gingerly and read it aloud. *"WE NEED TO TALK. MEET ME UPSTAIRS IN 15 MINUTES."* She turned it around to show the group. It was written in black ink, in simple block letters.

Addie squinted as she studied the paper. It was cream-colored with a gilt edge.

"What's that?" said Jim Towels. "On the duvet."

Everyone leaned in for a closer look. Resting atop the duvet was a ruby, sparkling in the folds of the silk fabric.

"That's just like the ones in the *Memento Mochi* knife," said Lillian, turning sharply to Mimi. "Rosemary, you're the one who had it."

"Yeah. We all saw you two leave the ballroom ten minutes ago," said Woody. "What exactly were you doing?"

Mimi's face tightened. "What? No. We didn't have anything to do with this!"

Addie had never heard such fear in Mimi's voice. She walked toward her and put a protective arm around her shoulders. She gave her a gentle squeeze, a small gesture of solidarity. "We were talking in the drawing room," she explained, looking to the group. "Mimi was having a cigarette. There's a half-smoked Pall Mall out in the snow if you don't believe us."

Sebastián turned to Matthew. "Is there anyone else in this house?"

"There shouldn't be," he replied, his voice cracking.

"Are you okay, Matthew?" asked Lillian, touching his shoulder.

Before he could respond, Gus broke down into gasping sobs. "My God. How could this have happened? My Janie's gone?" Veronique walked over and patted him gently as he turned away from the body.

Addie paused for a moment and looked around, every sense on alert. She directed her attention to Barb. "What do you remember seeing when you first came in? Did you see anyone in here? Did you hear anything?"

"Nothing," responded Barb, swallowing nervously. "I was only in here for a second."

Everyone went silent, eyes flitting in all directions.

Matthew took on an air of authority. "Please, ladies and gentlemen. If you can all head down to the lounge while we handle this . . . situation, it would be greatly appreciated."

"I want to stay here," said Gus. "I want to be with her!"

"Everyone, please," said Matthew firmly. "We need to secure this room. I need you all to go to the lounge and remain calm while we call the police."

Addie looked to Mimi, whose worried expression mirrored her own. "Are you okay?"

"I'm not sure," responded Mimi in a voice so low it was barely audible.

"Come on, everyone, let's go," said Sebastián. "This is a crime scene."

One by one, the group filed somberly out of the room.

As Mimi walked out into the hallway, the long strap of her trusty carryall caught on the door handle. When she tried to wrench it free, the carryall slipped from her hands. It fell to the floor, spilling its contents everywhere.

Addie squeezed her shoulder. "I'll get your stuff, Mimi. Just stay right here."

Mimi remained silent and still as Addie gathered her breath and darted around the hallway, picking up Mimi's keys, lighter, Altoids, and lipstick. Fear prickled at the base of her hairline. As she knelt down and reached for Mimi's Bicycle deck of cards, she heard the scrape of a key slotting into a lock and the click of a bolt. She looked up and caught a surreptitious glimpse of Barb, who was pulling on the door handle to Jane's room, checking to ensure it was locked. She handed the key to Matthew, and he slipped it into his pocket. They exchanged a few words in a hushed tone.

"Come on, Mimi," said Addie, rising to her feet and putting the items back in Mimi's carryall.

They slowly descended the empire staircase together, with Addie holding on to Mimi's arm. She could feel Mimi's body trembling through her fingertips.

Jane's wound flashed in her mind. Despite countless hours creating scenarios like this for *Murderscape*, the reality was far more gruesome than she could have ever imagined. The copious amount of blood pooled around Jane's torso was imprinted on her brain. *What would it feel like to be stabbed?* The cold metal slipping into your body, breaking through tissues, bones, organs, ligaments. *How long would it take you to realize you were bleeding out in your own bed?*

She sucked in a breath to steady herself. Mimi was still shaking. She needed to stay strong for her. Despite their argument just moments ago, she was relieved to be there so that Mimi wasn't in this situation alone.

No one spoke as they gathered in the lounge. The room had taken on a sinister air. They all stood for a moment in a charged silence.

The rattle of a cocktail shaker made everyone's heads jerk toward the sound. It was Woody, standing at the bar.

Kimiko glared at him. "You're making cocktails? Our host has been murdered."

"And I need a drink," said Woody. "Anyone else? I've got gin in here, but I can do vodka next."

"I'll have one," said Sebastián. "Twist of lemon."

Lillian plopped down on a chintz-upholstered sofa with tasseled pillows. "I'm feeling claustrophobic. This place gives me the creeps."

"How can you feel claustrophobic? This place is the size of the Hermitage," said Jim Towels.

Veronique crossed her legs and lit a cigarette. "'Body.' I don't like that word. You're a human being with a name. Then you die . . . and you're just a body."

"Wait a minute," said Gus, pointing to Addie. "I see what's going on here."

Everyone's heads swiveled toward Addie.

"This is a little joke, isn't it? Jane hired you to do this. You're the murder-game lady. Are you tonight's official detective too?"

Addie gasped, stunned by the accusation. "What? No."

"It's a murder-mystery party, isn't it? You're telling me it's a complete coincidence that the creator of *Murderscape* is here with us on a dark and stormy night when my sister supposedly gets bumped off?"

"Jane *would* do something like this," said Lillian, adjusting her chignon. "Fake her own death just to get attention. She'll probably jump out of a cake later."

Addie opened her mouth to continue denying Gus's accusation, but she stopped herself. *What could she even say right now to make them believe her?* She made eye contact with Mimi, who remained stoic.

"If this is a joke," said Jim Towels, looking pallid and sweaty, "or some sort of game, I need you to tell us right now. I have a weak heart."

"It's not," said Addie, taking in a breath. "This is not a game."

SEVEN

Easter Eggs

Lightning forked across the night sky, and hard sleet pelted the lounge windows. Addie could see that condensation had formed on the insides of the panes, emphasizing the warmth of the house compared to the freezing-cold temperature outside. She looked at her phone: 9:43 p.m.

Matthew and Barb appeared in the doorway, and the room fell silent.

"Oh, Matthew, I'm so sorry!" said Lillian, running up and embracing him. Addie noted how he tensed and subtly pulled away from her.

Barb's voice was low and shaky. "We've just spoken with the police, and I'm afraid we have some bad news to share."

"Oh God. I can't take any more bad news," said Jim Towels.

"We seem to find ourselves in a bit of a situation. Mackinac only has one police officer on duty tonight. It's usually very quiet here in the offseason. Turns out, he went home to the mainland, sick."

Sebastián's face reddened. "Are you kidding me? Our host has been murdered and no one can help us?"

"There are other complicating factors," said Matthew. "Tourist season has just ended, and the Grand Hotel is closed. It's just us and a few hundred other people on the island."

"Can't they send a helicopter?" asked Kimiko.

"Everything is grounded due to high winds."

A thick atmosphere enveloped the lounge as everyone took in this information.

Gus ran a hand over his face. "This is unreal."

"What about an off-duty policeman?" asked Mimi. "I know there are at least a couple who live here on Mackinac."

"We can ask them," said Barb, "but their instructions were pretty clear. They want us to sit tight."

Matthew took in a breath. "Please, everyone. We need to ask that you all continue to remain calm."

"Calm?" asked Woody. "How can we possibly stay calm?"

"I can just see the headline now: *Mackinac Maniac Runs Amok*," said Jim Towels.

"I agree with Matthew. Let's try not to panic," said Sebastián. "In all reality—"

"In all reality, what?" snapped Woody. "The killer pole-vaulted over the moat and ran off in the middle of a blizzard to hide somewhere on a tiny island where everyone knows everyone? I don't think so. No, the killer is here, among us."

"Shouldn't we search the house?" asked Jim Towels. "Just to be sure? Maybe there's an intruder."

"Barb and I are going to do that right now."

Kimiko placed her hands on her hips. "Will you at least put the drawbridge down?"

"We certainly will. But not until the police arrive. I'm the only one who knows the code to the drawbridge, and Barb and I personally assured them we'd keep you all here."

Woody sniffed. "You mean hold us captive, like prisoners."

"Are there not any cameras?" asked Veronique. Her veneer of French calm had dissipated.

"No," said Matthew. "We used to have some, but we had them taken out after Jane read how hackers can break into your system and spy on you."

"I remember that," sighed Jim wistfully. "Jane valued privacy more than anything. She hated social media too. She always sent those beautiful handwritten letters on scented stationery. Never emails or texts—she thought they were too impersonal. Jane was timeless. A real class act."

Lillian stood up. "Well, I refuse to sit here and wait for some psycho killer to pop out and impale me on a meat hook."

Mimi turned to Addie and spoke in her ear. "That was awfully specific."

"*Texas Chainsaw Massacre* reference," explained Addie.

"Ah."

"What about the guard?" asked Veronique. "Where is he now?"

"He's already gone home," said Barb. "His shift ended at nine. We don't have him stay overnight in the offseason."

Lillian walked toward the window and peered out into the snowy darkness. "I bet I can swim that moat. I practice the Wim Hof Method. Maybe I'll just get the hell out of here."

Matthew clapped his hands together authoritatively. "Listen, no one is swimming the moat. It's two hundred feet wide and twelve feet deep. You'll get hypothermia. Where would you go, anyway? Nothing's open. You'll freeze to death out there."

"Could they be hiding somewhere else on the property?" asked Mimi.

He passed a hand over his face. "Yes, I suppose that is possible. There's an observatory, a pool house, and some changing rooms by the tennis courts."

Barb took in a breath. "Ladies and gentlemen, please. We need to raise another matter."

"What now?" asked Kimiko dryly.

"Don't tell me you're out of gin," said Mimi.

"It seems that Jane's wedding ring is missing."

"The one Nelson gave her?" exclaimed Gus. "She never took it off."

"So there's a killer *and* a thief in this house," said Sebastián.

Voices broke out across the room, talking over one another as tensions rose to a cacophony.

Addie took the opportunity to speak with Mimi quietly. "I want to have a quick look around to see if there are any footprints in the snow."

A wrinkle formed between Mimi's eyebrows. "Huh? Why do you need to go? Let the police handle it."

"Have you looked outside? The snow is coming down hard out there. Footprints might get covered up before they get here. The killer might have fled and hid in one of the other buildings on the property, like you said. We need to determine whether the killer is still inside the house!"

"Fine. Just tell the castle guard over there you need to use the bathroom," said Mimi, nodding toward Matthew, who was blocking the room's entryway.

"That won't work. Look—" Addie jerked her chin toward a narrow door. "There's a guest bathroom right there. He's just going to tell me to use that. I was thinking you could help me."

"Whatever you're thinking, the answer is no. He just said that he and Barb are going to search the house. What if you run into them?"

"I promise I'll be careful. Can't you think of something, Mimi? Distract them."

"Sorry, my tap shoes are being re-soled."

"Please, Mimi? I just need to slip out for a minute. C'mon. Do it for me?"

Mimi paused, then huffed. "Fine. Go."

As Addie walked toward the doorway, she heard a loud cry. She glanced over her shoulder to see everyone rush toward Mimi.

"Rosemary, are you all right?" Lillian exclaimed. "Is it your heart?"

"No, bile duct," Mimi said faintly. "Damn gallstone. Pain comes and goes." She gasped dramatically. "This is a bad one. Help me to the couch."

Addie slipped out of the room while the group crowded around her.

"Let me get you some water," she heard Jim Towels say behind her.

"No, something stronger," croaked Mimi.

Addie tiptoed into the conservatory and cupped her hands over the cold glass of one of the windowpanes. Lake Huron was a gloomy black mass in the distance. The wind was roaring louder, making the snow fly horizontally across the glass.

Was this real? An actual murder? Her obsession with mysteries hadn't prepared her for anything like this happening in real life. She felt a shiver of excitement as she crept down the hallway. The portraits of various Ireland ancestors stared down at her from the walls. Her breath was quick and shallow. Images from the evening's events flitted through her mind. She thought of Mimi's hands touching the missing knife and winced.

Why hadn't she paid closer attention to what everyone was doing during the auction? Annoyed with herself, she took out her phone and went to her text chain with Sarah. What could she possibly type? Brian would be the perfect person to call. He'd help her strategize and come up with a plan. But that wasn't an option. She put her phone away.

She entered the dining room, its Art Deco accents echoing the Easter eggs she had included in *Murderscape* for fellow Poirot enthusiasts. Brian had fought her on those. *This game needs to have mass appeal, Addie. I can promise you there is no Venn diagram overlap between gamers and fans of 1990s British television.* But she'd held her ground, and *Murderscape* players had picked up on their cultural significance and loved them. The Easter egg victory had been one bit of ammunition she'd been able to use whenever he'd cut down her other ideas. That insecure feeling he embedded in her from the early days of their relationship had simmered inside for so long now. Whether he'd consciously or unconsciously meant to diminish her confidence, she'd never know.

The dining room was eerily silent, except for the loud ticking of an antique clock on the mantel. Scanning the pristine white lawn outside, she could see there were no footprints anywhere. She turned down the hallway that led to the kitchen area and hurried up a back staircase. It led to a semicircular room that overlooked the side yard and much of the backyard area. She was probably inside some kind of turret. The snow-draped hedge maze in the distance looked ominous. It reminded her of the one in *The Shining*. It was all clear, just a thick expanse of untouched snow in every direction. She headed back down the stairs and peeked through the kitchen windows—no footprints there either.

When she returned to the lounge, she lingered in the doorway. Everyone was huddled around the room in pairs. She studied each individual's expression. *Which one of these people hated Jane enough to kill her?* She listened to the thumping of her own heart as self-doubt washed over her. Besides footprints in the snow, what other clues could she even look for? Reality was sinking in. She had no experience with any of this. *This was a real murder.*

She walked toward Mimi. "What did I miss?"

"Towels launched into a kind of safety briefing. Suggested we implement a buddy system and sleep in shifts. But that fell apart. No one in this place can agree on anything. It's every man for himself." She tilted her head toward the window. "Did you see any footprints out there?"

"Nope, nothing."

"Has anyone been following the latest forecast?" asked Sebastián, who was standing by the window next to Lillian. "It's all over the news. The storm is getting worse."

Jim Towels heaved a sigh. "You mean it's going to get even more . . . blizzardy?"

Lillian held up her phone to show the group a news article. "They're calling it a bomb cyclone of 'historic' proportions."

Matthew reappeared in the doorway and the room quieted. "Barb and I have completed a search of the ground floor. We're going to search the rest of the house and prepare rooms for all of you." He hesitated and took in a breath. "In the meantime, Gus will keep you comfortable with plenty of food and drink. If you want to leave the lounge now, you can. But do it at your own risk. The knife is missing from its display . . . and the gun is also missing."

His comment hung in the air.

Jim turned to Lillian. "You were the one playing with the gun."

"I wasn't *playing* with it!" she snapped, straightening herself. "I was just being a good sport. I put it back."

"She's right," said Sebastián. "Anyone could have taken it."

Addie clasped Mimi's hand. "I need to talk to you. Now."

EIGHT

Suspects

What?" said Mimi. "Why are you looking at me like that?"

Addie stood with her arms folded in front of the library's enormous blazing fireplace. "This is bad, Mimi. You cut your finger on the missing murder weapon. Your fingerprints and DNA are all over that thing."

Mimi waved the thought away. "Pam's son is the chief of police. He knows me. Besides, I've been with you all night. You're my alibi."

Her eyes narrowed. "You always do this, Mimi. You downplay things whenever they get serious. I'm telling you, you're going to be perceived as a suspect, if not *the* suspect."

"Please. I'm practically ready for a Life Alert pendant."

"I hate to break it to you, but you have a motive. What if the police find out about your 'financial arrangement' with Jane?"

Mimi went silent.

Addie pointed to the trusty carryall. "Let me see the blackmail papers again."

"I knew that two-onioned Gibson was bad luck," grumbled Mimi. She pulled out the invitation and letter, handing both to Addie. While Addie reread them, Mimi considered what the police might find when they arrived. Surely Jane would have covered her tracks. *But what if they searched her cottage and came across the document detailing her secret? Or the trifold brochure for the Sunset Retirement Community in Florida? She had circled a two-bedroom condo in black Sharpie. Would she look like someone preparing to run away?*

Addie lowered the note and leveled her gaze at Mimi. "Are you going to explain to me *why* you're being blackmailed?"

"No, I told you already. Not tonight."

Addie scowled. "Not even after all this? Must be the Crime of the Century."

"It's complicated."

Her scowl deepened. "We have to launch an investigation. The first twenty-four hours after a murder are the most important, and I don't want my grandmother spending the rest of her life in the crowbar hotel. We need to—"

"Stop. This isn't your video game, Addie."

Addie's cheeks flushed, and the brightness in her eyes dimmed. Mimi recognized this tempestuous look. It was the same one that appeared whenever she told Addie no as a child. Addie's mom would make the same face when she was little too. She felt a heart squeeze at the thought of her daughter.

"How can you just assume the police won't consider your role in all this?"

Mimi gave a dismissive shrug. "The police will be too busy looking at the boyfriend to suspect me. It's always the boyfriend."

"You mean the son-in-law."

"Exactly. That woman would make Caligula blush. I'm sure blackmail was the least of the stuff she was into. Besides, the very idea of me following her upstairs to her room and stabbing her . . . It's ludicrous."

"Mimi," said Addie sternly. "You attended a party tonight hosted by a woman who was extorting money from you. A room full of people witnessed you follow her blackmail instructions at the auction. 'That woman' is now dead. Your prints and DNA are on the murder weapon. And the only person who was with you all night was your own granddaughter, who co-created a famous multiplayer game about murder."

Mimi let the words sink in. "Okay," she said tightly. "I see your point. But what can we do about it now?"

"We need a plan. Do you have anything to write on?"

"Of course," said Mimi, producing a small Moleskine notebook from her carryall.

"I don't suppose you have a pencil?"

Mimi smiled. "Lucky for you, I do." She fished into her carryall and extracted a small pouch, which held a freshly sharpened Faber-Castell No. 2 pencil and a scorepad she carried around for bridge. She handed her the pencil.

"Thanks," said Addie, who took it and drew a horizontal line across two of the notebook's pages, adding markers above it with labels like *Auction begins* and *Jane's body found*. "Now, let's establish the killer's timeline. First, we need to pin down the time of the murder."

"Well," said Mimi, looking at her watch, "I've been watching the clock pretty closely all night. It had to be between about 9:00 and 9:15, because we left the ballroom at 9:00 and Jane was still there."

Addie tapped on the page with her pencil. "This notebook is going to be our murderboard."

"Our what?"

"You know how in all the detective shows they have a board covered in pushpins and photographs and red string? It's basically our map of all the clues. We'll use this to help us stay organized as we pursue our investigation."

Mimi sighed. "And what else does a murder investigation entail?"

Addie considered the question. "In *Murderscape*, the first priority in every case is to secure the area. That's done. I checked for footprints in the snow, and as for the crime scene itself, I saw Barb lock the door to Jane's room and give Matthew the key."

"Doesn't that mean Matthew still has access to the crime scene?"

She began to pace around the room. "Yes. But there's nothing we can do about that right now. We have to focus on interviewing suspects to see if there are any contradictions in their accounts. Of course, we should also gather evidence. Perhaps we can even try a re-creation, but—"

"Dear, do you hear yourself? We're out of our depth here. We aren't detectives."

"No, we aren't. But we have skills."

Mimi stifled a laugh. "Skills? What skills do we have, exactly?"

"Really, just the same ones you need to be good at *Murderscape*. Or to piece together a solution before Poirot does."

"Nobody can do that."

"Good point. Look, we just need to analyze the facts without emotion. That should be easy for you, Mimi. Also puzzling skills— we've got those. Attention to detail."

"Okay."

"And a little healthy teamwork."

Mimi shrugged. "I guess three out of four isn't bad."

"We need to be sure we speak to each suspect alone. If we do it in front of anyone else, we could get answers that are influenced by the other people in the room. And we can't mention what we learn from the other guests either. We have to keep our cards close to the vest so we're in the best position to catch anyone in a lie."

They shared a silence, thinking. The logs in the fireplace popped and crackled.

"Everyone's stressed and scared. They might open up if we play this in a relaxed way so it feels casual. You'll just seem like . . ."

As Addie trailed off, Mimi knew exactly the words she was trying to phrase tactfully. She decided to save her the effort. "A bird-brained old busybody with nothing better to do?"

"Well, yes," said Addie, avoiding eye contact. "It's the perfect ruse. We don't want anyone to feel like they're being interrogated under a bare light bulb. We need to be tactful. When we do the interviews, I think it would be good if we played off each other. If you take the lead—"

"*Take the lead?* Addie, are you nuts? I can't just pull up a chair like I'm Dick Cavett."

"Actually, I think you can," said Addie. "You have that quality, Mimi. People let their guard down around you, even when you'd prefer they didn't. Strangers always want to talk to you."

Mimi nodded. "It's been a curse my whole life. The outside doesn't match the inside."

"Yeah. You've got Resting Nice Face." Addie sat down and flipped to a fresh page in the Moleskine. "Let's write down all the suspects and what we can remember."

1. *Matthew, Jane's boyfriend and son-in-law*
2. *Gus, Jane's brother and chef*
3. *Jim Towels, owner of Towels Print Shop and Mackinac local*
4. *Lillian, blonde in blue dress*
5. *Sebastián Palacios,* Godfather *reunion host, also game show host*
6. *Veronique, famous perfume nose*
7. *Woody, pianist*
8. *Kimiko Mitsurugi, mangaka, creator of* Memento Mochi

"I've been trying to place him all night," said Addie, pointing to Number 7. "He looks familiar. I'll have to do a deep dive on IMDb later. I think he's an actor."

"Woody?" snorted Mimi. "He's not handsome enough to be an actor."

Addie cocked her head to one side. "Well, not conventionally, no. But he's got an interesting look. Sort of like Willem Dafoe."

"Lillian and Jane were having a pretty heated argument during the auction. And I noticed Veronique arrived late," said Mimi, tapping a finger on Number 6. "Right before she bought the Millicent Whoever bird painting."

"Good, Mimi. I need you in observation mode. Keep it up." Addie drew a diagram of the seating arrangement from the auction and scribbled down other details spliced together from their joint recollections. She added *Barb, the housekeeper* as Number 9, then underlined Matthew's name. "I think we should focus on Matthew. If I were watching this on *Dateline*, I'd be screaming at the TV right now."

"It's always the boyfriend, isn't it? But what about Gus? He's got an aura of failure about him. Desperation . . . and desperation makes people do bad things."

"Would he have inherited any money after Jane died?"

"Depends on her will."

"Let's talk to Gus first. He's her brother, so he'll probably have more information than the others."

Mimi pointed to the blackmail papers. "What are we going to do about those?"

"Let's get rid of them," said Addie. She walked over to the fire and placed the papers directly onto the blazing logs.

Together they watched the papers blacken and curl as they burned.

"We need to figure out who did this," said Addie, although she seemed to be speaking more to the fire than to Mimi. "We're trapped in this place with a killer. Everything we do from this moment forward counts."

NINE

The Last Word

The butcher's knife in Gus's hand gleamed under the bright kitchen lights as he sliced into a lattice-top apple pie. Outside, the wind groaned, rattling the windows. Addie and Mimi hesitated in the doorway.

"Can we chat with you, Gus?" asked Addie, eyeing the knife.

He paused and turned to them, holding it in midair. "I suppose."

"Mind setting that knife down first?" added Mimi.

He laid it down and waved them over to a kitchen island as long as a hall carpet. Addie and Mimi pulled out two counter stools and sat down. Compared to the historic feel of the rest of the house, the kitchen was radically modern. It was fully equipped with the finest appliances and trimmed in shiny stainless steel accents that matched the stainless steel countertops. A bank of professional-grade refrigerators looked as though they could hold enough food to feed all of Mackinac.

"We're very sorry about your sister," said Mimi. "How are you holding up?"

Gus went to a drawer and retrieved a pie server. "I'm doing

okay." He looked over at them and pointed a thumb toward the pie and then at his paunch. "Stress eater."

Mimi nodded toward a large bottle of vodka next to him. "That for your stress too?"

"Oh no, no," he said as he pried a slice free and transferred it to a plate. "Vodka's just for making the crust. Keeps it flaky. Can I interest you ladies in a slice?"

Addie nodded enthusiastically.

He turned the enamel pie dish toward them, revealing an interior layered with slices of golden apple. Pointing to the flaky crust, he explained, "The alcohol allows it to stay moist without becoming chewy." He served each of them a slice.

"Nice kitchen," said Mimi. "Have you been working in here all day?"

He sighed. "Yep. Probably best if I do stay in here. Helps me keep my mind off things."

Mimi nodded in understanding.

"Mmm," said Addie, taking a big, gooey bite. "I love pie when it's like this. Not hot but still warm."

"Looks like you could use some help in here," observed Mimi, nodding toward the dirty china choking the sink. Unwashed wine, cocktail, and water glasses were jumbled in random bunches along the counters.

Gus looked wounded. "Jane has . . . *had* a house manager in the warmer months to keep the place properly staffed. But now that it's the offseason, Barb and I have to take on the household duties. It's been exhausting running this place as a skeleton crew. Not to mention hosting this damn party."

Mimi listened thoughtfully as she took a bite of pie. She studied Gus. Per Addie's instructions, she was in full "observation mode." His eyes were red-rimmed and bloodshot. His gaze unsteady. *Definitely a boozer.* She noted that there seemed to be two versions of

Gus this evening. Earlier he was reeling from Jane's death. Now he seemed rather calm and congenial. An odd shift for someone whose sister had just been murdered. "I completely understand, Gus. It's too much to expect from one person," Mimi said, scooting off the counter stool and clasping her hands together. "All right, grab some aprons and run a big sink full of hot soapy water. The three of us are going to make quick work of this."

Gus followed Mimi's instructions dutifully as Addie collected dirty glassware.

Dunking her hands into the sink, Mimi began scrubbing a plate. "Listen, we want to help you find out what happened to your sister. We can only imagine how difficult this has been for you. To carry on with all your responsibilities while dealing with her death."

"Murder. You mean her murder."

Mimi nodded as she rinsed the plate. "Can you help us create a timeline? Tell us what you remember?"

He furrowed his brow. "I don't know how I can help. I didn't see much."

"You were in here during the auction?"

"Mostly, yes. I was prepping to serve a late-night snack. Jane liked to offer one for overnight guests. I was making my pies and preparing my signature hot toddy, which I call Lullaby in a Glass. Make it with chamomile."

They had a good system going—Mimi washing, Addie drying, Gus putting clean items away.

Mimi rinsed a glass and handed it to Addie. "Did you go into the ballroom during the auction at all? Or were you in here the whole time?"

"I went in there once before the auction started, to check that the food-and-drink setup looked okay. Later I came back to top up everyone's champagne glasses. Wasn't in there very long because I heard the oven timer go off for my pie."

"What time did you top up the champagne glasses?"

"About ten past nine. Matthew was onstage doing his thing. I went back into the kitchen and started working on my second pie. Made it with some beautiful Michigan cherries."

"No better cherries on earth," agreed Mimi.

"I remember your cherry pies, Mimi," Addie chimed in. "Can't wait to try yours, Gus."

They worked together for a few moments in silent solidarity, with only the gentle sound of sloshing water and Gus opening and shutting cupboards in the background.

"Can you remember who else you saw in the ballroom at 9:10? Besides Matthew? Whose glasses did you refill?" asked Mimi.

His weather-beaten face creased even more as he considered the question. "I remember Sebastián was talking to Lillian over by the desserts. Definitely topped them up. Lillian had been drinking quite a bit, I noticed. Also Woody, because he was taking a break from playing the piano. He bumped into me and spilled some champagne on the floor. He seemed distracted. Didn't say anything. It was a bit rude." Gus put another plate away, then paused. "How about a digestif while we work?"

"No, thanks," said Addie. "I need a break from drinking."

"Yes, please," said Mimi. "I need a break from not drinking."

Gus walked toward the door with a sense of purpose. "Any preference?"

"Surprise me."

He raised his hand to his chin for a moment. "I have just the thing," he said, pointing one finger in the air. "I'll be right back." He left the room through a swinging door.

Addie shook her head. "You are really overdoing it, Mimi. I refuse to hold your hair back if you barf."

"He's the type who takes pride in making things for other people, okay? The man's sister just died. He needs to feel comfortable right now if we want him to open up. Trust me."

Addie's eyebrows shot up.

Gus returned, holding a bottle of Chartreuse in one hand and bottles of gin and maraschino liqueur in the other. "We're going to have a Last Word," he declared as he began to mix the cocktail in a shaker. He looked to Addie. "Sure you don't want one too?"

Addie shrugged. "Okay. Why not?" She noted Mimi's subtle nod of approval in her peripheral vision.

His hands trembled as he reached for the Chartreuse. "I love this drink," he said, measuring the iridescent green liqueur into the shaker. "It takes you back in time, to Prohibition, when the house was built." He held the shaker with both hands and gave it a forceful jostle. "Flappers. Fedoras. Spats. This cocktail was invented right here in Michigan. The complex flavor of the Chartreuse was used to mask the bathtub gin."

"Was it Nelson's father who built the house?" asked Addie.

"Grandfather." He paused to garnish each drink with a brandied cherry. "The Irelands were rumrunners. This place used to be an adult Disneyland of sorts. They supplied all the liquor for the island, including the Grand Hotel."

"Thank you," said Addie as he handed each of them a Last Word.

"There's a private cove where the boats came in from Canada, and there's secret passages all through the house. Jane told me there's a speakeasy too, but I've never seen any of it myself."

"Really?" said Addie, taking a sip. "You've never had a look around?"

"Nope. Only been here a few weeks. Place kinda gives me the creeps."

"Now that's a cocktail," said Mimi, raising her glass toward Gus in approval.

Addie dried a coupe with a tea towel and held it up to the light to check for streaks. "Does anyone else know about the secret passages? Barb?"

Gus shrugged. "I don't know."

She gave him a disbelieving look.

"I really don't, I swear," he said, raising his arms in a defensive gesture. "Like I said, I haven't been here that long."

"I forgot, where did you say you were working before?" asked Mimi.

"The Drake," he said proudly.

"Lovely hotel. Why did you leave?" asked Mimi.

He took a long sip of his drink. "Let's just say I got into a bad situation once, and Jane helped me out."

Addie began to feel the warm euphoria brought on by the cocktail. "What was it like working for your sister?"

"Honestly, before tonight, I was thinking about staying on the island. Jane and I were never close before, but I thought maybe that could finally change." His voice cracked and he shook his head. "It's all just hitting me now. The tragedy of it. She was so brilliant. You guys probably don't know that Jane had a PhD in astrophysics."

Mimi slowly turned her head to Addie, and they shared a look of disbelief.

"We grew up poor. In Odessa, Texas. She graduated high school two years early, got a full ride to Texas A&M, and then went to work at—guess where—NASA."

Mimi coughed. "NASA?"

"Yep. Worked as a coordinator for her bigwig boss, a creep who took advantage of her innocence. With him, she learned all about how the other half lived. She watched how the astronauts' wives dressed and then completely 'reengineered' herself, so to speak." Gus stopped and arranged the clean water glasses on a shelf. "Of course you can guess what happened next. She got pregnant, and then he didn't want to have anything to do with her, so she had to quit her job."

"So how did she ever come into this . . . lifestyle?" asked Addie.

"She met Nelson at a fundraiser. He was a kind man, and they fell in love. When she confessed she was pregnant with someone else's baby, he married her without batting an eye. After Alexandra was born, Nelson adopted her as his own. He had an observatory built here so Jane could gaze at the stars every night." Gus smiled and shook his head. "She was obsessed with it. A few years ago, she was asked to fund some special research project to study the birth of new stars. They even gave her a small piece of the project to work on. She was thrilled. Had the whole observatory redone. It's state-of-the-art now. Did you know that Mackinac is an ideal location for an observatory because there's almost no light pollution out here?"

Mimi swallowed, trying to conceal her utter disbelief as she washed the last plate, gave it a hot rinse, and handed it to Addie. "What happened to Nelson?"

"Heart attack. Alexandra was devastated. She called him Dad her whole life."

Mimi untied her apron and gave the counter one last polishing swipe with a tea towel. "Where does Alexandra live now?"

"She's in LA. She and Matthew had one of those whirlwind romances. He swept her off her feet when she was in college. They got married in a courthouse. It was all very quick."

Mimi considered asking him about the Alexandra-Matthew-Jane triangle, but it was too delicate a question for the moment. She decided to shift the focus back to Jane. "You said you were never very close with Jane, right? When was the last time you saw her before you started working here? Thanksgiving or Christmas?"

"No. Jane didn't really do holidays centered around food. It was last spring, when my band, the Large Hadron Colliders, came to town to play a show on the island. Jane came by to see us perform. We did have some nice times together."

"Did you notice anything else tonight? Even the smallest thing could have significance."

He looked up at the array of copper pots and pans hanging above them as he formed his answer. "Well, I will say that I think you should look into Jim."

"You're kidding, right?" said Mimi.

He put the rest of the clean plates away in a cabinet as he spoke. "He was kind of obsessed with Jane, and she seemed annoyed by him. I don't really know why she kept him around. He wasn't even supposed to be here tonight, from what I understand."

"He wasn't invited?"

He shook his head. "Don't think so." He glanced at the digital clock above the oven, which read 10:22. "Listen, thanks for helping with the dishes, but I've got to finish prepping the late-night snack. I'm still going to serve it tonight. In Jane's honor."

"Thanks for the beautiful pie," said Addie.

Mimi drained the last of her drink. "And I enjoyed getting to have the Last Word."

Gus turned toward the hallway. "How about I show you ladies to your room?"

TEN

The Murderbook

We need to search this house, Mimi," said Addie, pushing aside the heavy brocade curtains in their room to look out the window. The back garden's expanse had been smoothed out under a vast, undulating white blanket. Even with the exterior lights burning brightly outside, she could barely make out the outline of the marble fountain through the torrents of sleet and snow. The sprays of water had frozen midair into icy plumes. Several of the towering cypress trees that lined the perimeter of the pool had been uprooted and toppled over.

"Did you say something?" Mimi called out from the walk-in closet.

"I said I want to search the house for clues. We need to see if we can find the notepad that matches the note in Jane's hand. I'm going to look in the study."

She took out her phone—only twenty-four percent battery left. In the morning, she'd have to borrow a charger from someone. The storm was getting national coverage:

ARE WE WITNESSING A REPLAY OF THE GREAT LAKES
STORM OF 1913?

FRESHWATER FURY: BOMB CYCLONE WALLOPS
NORTHERN MICHIGAN

IS THE GREAT LAKES CYCLONE THE NEXT CLIMATE
CHANGE DISASTER?

Another urge came over her to call Brian. She pulled up their last text messages:

> Pick up your phone, Addie.

> > I've been speaking to a lawyer. He'll be in touch.

> Addie, please. This is crazy.

She thumbed at his name on the screen. Brian would help her figure out what to do. She hated this feeling of confusion and not having answers. As much as she hated to admit it to herself, she missed him. Being together, especially in those first couple of years, was an exhilarating rush of creativity and ideas. Their passionate debates inspired her best thinking. Her whole career, both as an art director and game designer, was about control. Crafting people's experiences and anticipating their choices. But Brian was the one thing she could never control.

Mimi emerged from the closet, carrying an armful of clothes. "I think Jane stored half her wardrobe in there. Go look."

Addie stared at her in disbelief. "We can't just help ourselves to a dead woman's clothes!"

"Sure we can. We both need to find something comfortable to wear. The maid said—"

"Her name is Barb. We need to remember everyone's names tonight for the murderboard. Not to mention 'maid' is an outdated term. It's classist."

"Okay, fine. Her Excellency the Right Honorable Barb told us we could make ourselves comfortable. She even set out little Marvis toothpastes for us, and one of those fancy loofahs that remove dead skin from—"

"Mimi, stop. You're doing it again. Downplaying. We have to focus on the *murder* we're trying to solve, remember?"

Mimi raised a firm eyebrow and handed a mauve cashmere sweater to Addie. "We'll be better detectives if we're not shivering."

Addie relented, taking it and pulling it on over her dress. It fit snug like a second skin, and the scent of soft jasmine wafted into her nostrils. She sighed. Whenever Mimi was in a situation she couldn't control, her protective shields went up. This emotional armor of hers, designed to deflect, downplay, and deny any form of uncertainty, was infuriating. *Why couldn't she just acknowledge her fears like a normal person?*

"If you want to snoop around tonight, you can't do it in a gown and heels. They need to turn up the damn heat in this place. Try these leggings I found. They're lined with fleece."

"Mimi, you won, okay? I put on the sweater. Can we move on?"

"Fine. But you really need to keep your feet warm. There's some cashmere socks in there."

"Okay. I'll wear them when we search the house."

"We're not creeping around this old house."

Addie huffed impatiently. Ever since her parents died, Mimi had been determined to direct how she should live her life. It was time for her to take the reins instead. Be more assertive. She wanted their relationship to be on an equal playing field where each adult respected the autonomy of the other. Mimi needed to understand that she no longer welcomed her "good intentions." Easier said than done, however. It was becoming increasingly difficult to resist shouting out, *You're not the boss of me, Mimi!*

She took in a breath. "Has it ever occurred to you that I want to help you, Mimi?"

"Why would I think that?"

"You don't think I'm trying to help my grandma avoid a murder charge?"

Mimi set the pile of clothes on the bed and looked down at them as if they might help her form her next thought. "Honestly? No, I don't think you are. Look around. We're locked in a spooky mansion with a dead body. If I didn't know any better, I'd think you designed this whole experience. It's like one of your games. A breakout room."

"Escape room. Those are pedestrian, Mimi. I would never create one of those."

Mimi picked up the clothes and went into the bathroom.

Addie shook her head and went back to her phone. "Do you really want us to sit around in here and twiddle our thumbs, waiting for the cops to arrive?" she called out. "I can't believe you're not even a little scared about this."

Mimi didn't respond.

"We can't just hide out in this fusty bedroom. The storm could let up soon and the police will be here. Then what? You talk to Pam's son, who just happens to be a cop—"

Mimi reappeared in the bathroom doorway. "Sam."

"Pam's son's name is Sam?"

"Yes. Sorry he isn't Phineas or Silas or some other name resurrected from a previous century that's part of some ridiculous trend."

Addie took a deep breath. "Listen, what I'm trying to say is we need to get serious and progress with our investigation. Just because Mackinac's chief of police happens to be Pam's Sam does not mean you're going to just walk away from this situation scot-free."

"Well, I still can't believe any of this has actually happened," said Mimi, rubbing her forehead. "I miss my old life. Back when spotting Henry Winkler at Doud's was as much excitement as I got."

Addie paused for a moment to appreciate this rare expression of vulnerability from her grandmother. She softened her voice. "Mimi, if we give up, then we're essentially presenting the cops with a gift: your motive, plus incriminating evidence. All wrapped up in a pretty pink no-alibi bow."

"I don't think that metaphor's really working for you."

There was a thoughtful silence.

Mimi gave a resigned sigh. "Shouldn't we start building out the timeline in the murderbook a bit more? And get moving on these interviews?"

Addie smiled and nodded approvingly. "Yes. And it's a murder-*board*, by the way, but I like your name better. Let's call it our Murderbook." Addie flipped to the timeline page and jotted down a few notes. "You were good back there, by the way. With Gus. The dish-washing thing. You established a relationship before you started asking questions. I'm impressed. Maybe—"

Someone knocked at the door. They both jumped.

"Urgent knocking," said Mimi. "That's always a good sign."

Another knock.

Mimi approached the door. "I'll get it. I've lived long enough." She hesitated. "Who is it?"

There was a brief silence, then Barb's faint voice squeaked from behind the door. "Good evening, madam. I thought you might appreciate having some whisky in your room?"

Relieved, Mimi opened the door to reveal Barb holding a silver tray.

Addie smiled and waved her away. "No, thank you, Barb. Have a good—"

"Speak for yourself," said Mimi, "I'd love some, thank you." She gestured for Barb to enter. "So, Barb, I've been meaning to ask you, is that short for Barbara?"

"Why yes, it is."

"I knew it!"

Addie rolled her eyes as Barb set the tray down on a table and Mimi casually leaned against the doorframe, chatting away with her. Addie tuned them out and went back to IMDb, toggling back and forth between different actor pages and a BuzzFeed listicle: "17 Shows from the '90s You Liked But Probably Totally Forgot About Until Now."

A few minutes passed before Barb finally left, and Mimi closed the door. She turned back to Addie with crossed arms and a self-satisfied grin.

"Is Barb your new bestie?" said Addie, without looking up from her phone.

"For someone so clever, I'm surprised you didn't see what I was doing. I was buttering her up. To get information!"

"Nice. What did you get?"

"Well, there are forty-seven rooms in the house. We're on one of two guest floors, the other one is directly above us. She told me who's staying on which floor. There's also a secret bunker beneath the observatory. It was built during the Cold War. Jane had it fully stocked with food and supplies. Apparently, she was one of those doomsday-prepper types. Y2K freaked her out, and she's been ready ever since."

Addie raised an impressed eyebrow. "Anything else?"

Mimi shrugged. "No. She invited us to join the others for Gus's late-night snack in the lounge. I didn't mention we already had pie with him. She looked at me blankly when I asked about the speakeasy and the secret passages. Then she tried to sell me some essential oils, one of those pyramid schemes, so I wrapped things up."

"See, you are good at this. You get people talking." Addie went back to IMDb as Mimi walked toward the window to watch the intensifying storm.

After a long silence, Addie jumped up. "Found you!" She held up her phone, turning it around to show Mimi. "Look. It's Aero! Aero Hart!"

"What?"

"Woody. His real name is Aero."

"Aero? Who is he, the lost Marx brother?"

"He was on that show *Bloody Mary* in the nineties, about the vampire bartender. He played the inept bar manager who doesn't know she's been killing all the patrons."

"Must have missed that one."

"I completely remember this show. And he had this catchphrase, 'That sucks!' It was a wink to the audience. They were in on the joke, but he wasn't. It broke the fourth wall. Now that I think about it, that show was really ahead of its time."

"You're losing me."

"Sorry, sorry. I just think there's something important here, Mimi. If he's using a fake name, he must be up to something." Addie took out the Murderbook and began writing out what she could find from his IMDb bio:

> 7. ~~Woody~~ Aero Hart, 51, from New Orleans, Bloody
>   Mary *star, plays piano and guitar, dated Heather*
>   *Graham, nominated for an Emmy*

"An Emmy?" said Mimi, looking over Addie's shoulder. "That guy? He seems so vanilla."

"Yeah. Says it was for his role playing a young Walter Mondale in a TV movie called *Fritz*."

"Oh, I see. Well . . . yeah, that's good casting, actually."

"Why don't you talk to Veronique while I'm searching the study? I saw her go into her room a while ago. It's right across the hall."

She turned to Mimi, who was back over by the window, gazing out at the snow. Her reflection blended with the darkness outside in a spectral collage. "Let's meet back in the lounge for the late-night snack at eleven. We can talk to some more suspects then."

"Okay."

The night outside lit up, and a crash of thunder shook every corner of the room.

"I remember the last time we saw thundersnow," said Mimi, stepping away from the window.

Addie smiled faintly. "I do too. It was Christmas Eve. I think I was ten, maybe? We made hot chocolate and watched *Shadow of a Doubt*."

"Most kids would have been scared. A bad snowstorm and a creepy movie. But you loved it. And your mom made my oatmeal raisin cookie recipe. You said they were better than mine because hers had more raisins."

"Ha! You remember that?"

"Of course I do. Turncoat. That was a nice time, wasn't it?"

ELEVEN

A Knock at the Door

Mimi sat down at the vanity and took off her necklace. She placed it on the soft velvet lining of the jewelry box in front of her. Relieved to have a moment to herself, she looked in the mirror. She bit her lower lip. There was fear in her eyes. Her cheeks had lost their usual pinkness. Addie was right. She was downplaying a horrible situation. *What had ever possessed her to drag her unwitting granddaughter to this nightmare island within an island?*

Sitting across from Addie at Ryba's tomorrow and confessing her sins over a plate of homemade fudge seemed a million miles away. Her pulse was loud in her ears. *How would Addie react?* She felt the urge to smoke and eyed her carryall, considering another Pall Mall.

If Peter were still alive, he would wrap his long arms around her, hold her tight, and tell her to stop fretting. *Things always have a way of working out, Ro*, he would say, resting his chin on her head, mashing down her hair. *Dial down that worry machine of yours. It's gonna be okay.*

Mimi grabbed some fancy wrinkle-plumping cream from a tray and rubbed it all over her face and neck. She dabbed on some lipstick and forced a smile in the mirror. She looked wretched. And her damn teeth were definitely looking yellow.

She got up and headed back into Jane's closet, toward a section at the back labeled *Fat Clothes*. She shook her head. Nothing was bigger than a size eight. She selected a white button-down shirt, along with a tailored black blazer and trousers. Slipping them on to form a makeshift suit, she had to roll up the trousers to her ankles, given the height differential between herself and Jane. Addie wanted "serious." This was the best she could do.

There was a soft knock on the door.

"Addie, is that you?" asked Mimi, walking across the room. "Did you forget your—" She opened the door to find Jim Towels standing in the hall, wearing plaid flannel pajamas with a matching floppy nightcap and slippers.

She took a step back. "Jim, you startled me."

"Hi, Rosemary," said Jim, blinking nervously.

"Nice jammies. Did you get the lead in Mackinac's annual production of *A Christmas Carol*?"

"Barb brought them to me 'cause I was freezing. They were Nelson's. Damned aorta's been thickening up, gives me cold extremities. Want to feel my fingers?"

"Ummm, well, sure," said Mimi, extending an index finger and touching his thumb. "Right-o, Jim. Positively arctic."

"Can we talk?"

"Sure," she said, opening the door wider and gesturing for him to enter. "We've been neighbors for over two decades, so I'm going to guess you're not the murderer."

Jim looked down the hallway in both directions before stepping inside. "Well, you never really know your neighbors, do you?"

She held up the whisky decanter Barb had left in the room. "Since you already have an actual nightcap, would you like the other variety?"

"Oh no, I've already had my one allotted white wine spritzer tonight. Alcohol gives me acid reflux. Listen, I know it's late, but there's something I need to get off my chest."

"Please," said Mimi, gesturing to the small Art Nouveau table and chairs in the corner of the room. "Have a seat."

She pulled the stopper out of the decanter and poured a finger of whisky into a crystal tumbler. "I was going to give it a rest for the night, but given the situation . . ." she said, raising her glass in his direction before taking a swig.

"I don't blame you."

"What's on your mind, Jim?"

The leather squeaked as Jim settled into the chair. "Well, I feel like you're the only person I can trust here, Rosemary. I mean, you and I are the only islanders, right?"

"Yes. Well, except for Barb. And Matthew and Gus count too, I suppose."

"Right. But I know you. I mean, you've been on this island longer than I have. You know everyone. People respect you. You're a Mackinac mainstay—"

"Jim, I wave to you once a week on my way to play bridge. Let's not act like I'm some pillar of the community. Get to the point."

He looked down. "I wanted to tell you that the note in Jane's hand . . . it was from me."

Mimi sat down in the chair across from him. "Seriously? You said you wanted to meet her. Why?"

"I was trying to warn her. You see, two nights ago, Jane called me for advice. She was scared."

"Wait," said Mimi. "Back up. You and Jane were friends?"

"Yes. I . . . She confided in me. I don't think she had many people she could turn to here. Or anywhere, really."

Mimi knitted her brow. "Don't take this the wrong way, Jim, but you and Jane don't seem to travel in the same social circles. How did you get to know each other?"

"Well, my print shop is on her morning power walking route, so she'd wave to me each day. And then we just started talking. Before I knew it, she was opening up to me about what was going on in her life. I gave her calligraphy lessons too. And sometimes we'd also . . ."

Jim hesitated.

"Go on," said Mimi, leaning forward.

". . . Sometimes we'd talk over bowls of Cap'n Crunch in my kitchen. She rarely ate sugar, so we called it 'cheatin' with the Cap'n.'"

"So . . . that's why you wrote the note in block letters? In case anyone found it, you didn't want them to recognize your handwriting."

"Yeah. But I figured someone would put it together eventually. The paper is from the notepads we sell in the premium section at the shop. The special ones that minimize ink feathering and come in a hand-stitched leather memo block."

"Listen, Jim, I need you to level with me. Did you print the blackmail invitation for Jane?"

Jim looked confused. "What blackmail invitation?"

Mimi eyed him skeptically. "C'mon, Jim, please. The nine-by-nine invitation to this party and the typewritten letter sizes?"

"Rosemary," he said, his upper lip twitching, "I don't even know what you're referring to."

Mimi considered this information while she studied Jim's body language. He'd always seemed like an honest fellow, but to his earlier point, *how well does a person truly know their neighbors?* It was probably best that she didn't push further on the blackmail topic, with him or anyone else. There was no need to draw attention to herself.

Jim shifted in his seat, causing the leather to squeak again. "Anyway, like I was saying before, when Jane called me, she asked me to come to the party and look out for her. She said she was worried that someone was out to get her, but she didn't say who."

"Okay, so you came to the party to help keep a watchful eye. What concerned you enough to write the note?"

"Well, it's probably going to sound a bit far-fetched," said Jim, scratching his earlobe. "I thought Matthew seemed to be *up to something*. He was making me nervous. I just got a vibe."

Mimi took a sip of whisky and raised her eyebrows from behind the glass.

"So I gave her the note to meet me upstairs in fifteen minutes. But soon after that, I noticed she was acting a bit funny. I figured she might be pretending to be tired so she could have an excuse to go upstairs and talk with me. I had some time to kill before we were set to meet—" He stopped and laughed nervously. "Sorry, poor choice of words. I had some spare time, so I wandered around for a bit. Went to the bathroom."

"Which bathroom?"

"The one by the dining room. Anyway, just as I left the bathroom, that's when I heard the commotion upstairs and, well . . ."

Mimi thought for a moment, rubbing her thumb and forefinger together. "May I ask you a silly question?"

"Sure."

"Why a note? Why didn't you just talk to Jane?"

His shoulders slumped. "She was mad at me."

"Really?"

"Yes. She said she'd decided she didn't want me to come to the party, but I was worried about her, so I showed up anyway. Gus gave me dirty looks all night. I think she told him I'd been disinvited."

"Why were you two in a fight?"

Jim sighed. "I'd confronted her about the Page Six article. Told her she needed to stop this thing with Matthew before it ripped apart her whole family. I suppose I came across as meddling."

Mimi nodded and swirled the remaining amber liquid in the glass. "So you weren't on speaking terms when you showed up at the party?"

"No. She was annoyed with me all night. Kept shooing me away like I was a fly in her La Mer face cream."

"Was she in a fight with anyone else tonight?" continued Mimi. The image of Lillian and Jane exchanging harsh words at the auction flashed through her mind.

"Not that I'm aware of," responded Jim. He was making direct eye contact as he spoke. "I will say, it felt like this party was thrown together very last minute. It was fine, but nothing compared to the parties that the Jane I knew liked to throw. Big, extravagant affairs. Elegant sit-down dinners for dignitaries, alfresco fundraisers in the summer, elaborate themed birthday parties for Alexandra. Back when they were speaking, that is."

"Did you ever meet Alexandra?"

"No," said Jim. "Last we spoke about her, Jane was getting fed up with being left in limbo. She'd been pressuring Matthew to leave Alexandra."

Mimi shook her head. "Mother of the Year."

"Rosemary, if I may . . ." said Jim, straightening himself in the chair and clearing his throat. "Jane wasn't as bad as everyone made her out to be. She was just a complicated woman."

Mimi shifted in her seat. "So, do you think Matthew could have done it?"

"Well, he certainly wasn't acting innocent tonight."

"How does an innocent person act?"

Jim looked down at himself, then back at Mimi. "Well, like me, I guess."

She looked at her watch. "This was good info, Jimbo. I appreciate you confiding in me. You've always been an upstanding member of the community. I can see why Jane trusted you."

"Well, I am a three-time winner of the Better Business Bureau Torch Award. They don't just hand those things out to anybody."

"I have to meet Addie downstairs for the late-night snack in a bit. Are you going to go?"

"Nah, I'm going to bed," said Jim as he rose from his seat and made his way to the door. "Thanks for listening." As he entered the hallway, he turned back. "Hey, Rosemary, can I ask you something?"

"Sure."

"Are you scared?"

"Me? Not scared exactly," said Mimi. "Disturbed, but not scared."

"Even with a murderer running around this creepy old house in the middle of a snowstorm?"

Mimi took a moment to consider the question before responding. "You know, Jim, when you've been alone for as many years as I have, you have lots of time to think about what you've done right and what you've done wrong. Believe me, that's far scarier than meeting a killer in a dark hallway."

TWELVE

Side Quest

Addie crept downstairs, wearing the socks she'd borrowed from Jane's closet. They served the dual purpose of muffling her footsteps and keeping her feet warm. As she reached the ground floor, the icy temperature of the house made her shiver underneath her dress, which had sustained a few rips and stains throughout the evening. Fortunately, Jane's sweater helped hold in some heat.

She took a moment to get her bearings and establish the layout of the ground floor in her mind. Just a few hours ago, the grandeur of the house had been enchanting. Now it felt ominous. She stopped and turned back to make sure she wasn't being followed.

Rounding a corner, she approached the study's mahogany door and pressed her ear up to its solid presence. Silence. She gripped the handle, turning it slowly and holding her breath as she eased it open. Inside, the room was lit only by the fading glow of embers burning down to ash in the stone fireplace.

Her hand searched the wall for a light switch but found nothing. From the weak light of the fire, she could just make out the shape of a green-glass banker's lamp on the desk. She carefully shut the door behind her and made her way toward the lamp, feeling around until she grasped the metal chain and pulled.

The soft light illuminated the richly furnished room, all deep hues of brown and burgundy. She waited for the flutter of nerves in her stomach to settle. A floorboard creak above reminded her she was in a house full of strangers.

She quickly checked the surface of the desk. No computer. She pulled opened the drawers. All were empty. No odds and ends, no pens or papers. Even the *Wine Down* magazines in a basket on the floor were stacked in a perfect, uniform pile. She walked over to a credenza and opened the doors. Its shelves were empty too.

Turning toward a wall of bookshelves, she took a moment to study the framed photos on display. Weddings. Childhood. College. Matthew was the constant in each picture. A teenage Matthew with his lacrosse team. Their jerseys read *Poplar Tree Academy*. Another photo of Matthew and Jane, both looking younger and blissfully happy, sitting astride a pair of mint-green Vespas under an olive tree. Matthew was holding a wine bottle high in the air. Addie's eyes wandered over to the right side of the photo, where an unsmiling young woman sat at a picnic table. Her chin rested in her hand as she looked off in the distance. *Was this Alexandra? How long ago did this Matthew-Jane thing start? Who took the picture?*

Suddenly, there were heavy footsteps in the hallway. She froze. They stopped just outside the door. From the crack of light underneath the doorframe, she could see the faint shadow of shoes.

She held her breath and considered her options. The desk looked big enough to hide under. Or maybe she could just come up with an excuse for being in there. A chenille throw draped over an armchair caught her eye. *Oh, sorry, I was just looking for a blanket. It's freezing in this old place.* Keeping a careful watch on the shadow, she tiptoed over to the chair and wrapped the throw around her shoulders.

The footsteps resumed and continued down the hall. A rush of air escaped her lungs.

She turned around and surveyed the room. It was oddly sterile and fabricated. The side quests Brian created in *Murderscape* had given her the same feeling. Side quests were challenges that deviated from the mystery and weren't required to complete the game. They'd fought about them passionately during preproduction. He liked to distract players with pointless activities that were ultimately wastes of time, in her view, feeling it was a necessary respite from the intensity of the game. She wanted players to stay focused on fulfilling their critical path and solving the mystery. But one of his side quests, from the "Nefertiti" episode, became a fan favorite. It was a challenge where players had to find all the missing statues created by one of the suspects, an artist. Brian had rubbed it in her face when a major gaming influencer, Pokimane, streamed it to her millions of followers.

Her eyes locked on to a first edition of Edgar Allan Poe's *Tamerlane and Other Poems* enclosed in its own display case. She approached it and gently opened the lid. Her eyes welled up as she reached out and lightly brushed the book's spine. She was in the presence of one of her heroes. His namesake, her black cat Edgar, came to mind. She clenched her hands together, thinking of her sweet little boy, safe at home with Sarah. Chicago felt worlds away now. She closed the lid to the case and gave the room a final check. Nothing else seemed to offer any useful insights.

Opening the door slowly, she stepped back into the hall. There was no one around, no sound except for distant voices coming from the direction of the lounge. She decided to take the opportunity and head in the other direction to have a snoop. As she turned the corner, she stopped short. At the end of the hallway was Matthew. His back was to her, and he was talking to someone in an animated fashion. He was gesticulating wildly, clearly angry.

She watched as he finally leaned to one side to reveal it was

Kimiko he was talking to. She was at least a foot shorter than Matthew, so she had been eclipsed from view. Addie strained to listen to what they were saying.

"*Why not?*" she heard Kimiko say. Her tone was edgy with irritation.

Matthew responded, but it was difficult to make out the words. Then he raised his voice. "I don't have time for this!" he shouted, throwing his hands up in the air. "I have to go help prepare everyone's rooms. My mother-in-law is dead. I'm living a nightmare. Stop being so damn selfish."

Addie frowned. Interesting choice of words from Matthew, to call Jane his mother-in-law and not his girlfriend.

"Hi there," said a voice from behind.

Addie jumped. She turned around to find Gus standing behind her. "Oh, hello." She took a deep breath, hoping her heartbeat would return to normal. "You scared me."

He nodded downward, indicating the drinks tray in his hands. "Barb likes a stiffener after work, so I thought I'd bring her one." He tilted his head to one side. "What are you doing here?"

"I was just looking for a blanket. Found this one. Now I'm a bit lost. The house is so big."

"Of course. Sorry about the temperature. This old place is hard to heat."

They fell silent and stared at each other for a moment.

"Are you going to join us in the lounge for the late-night snack?"

She nodded.

"Lounge is that way," he said, offering an exaggerated point in the other direction. "I'll be back in there to check on you shortly."

"Right. See you in a bit."

The hall was feeling drafty, so she pulled the blanket around herself. As she headed toward the lounge, she had the sense he was watching her go.

THIRTEEN

Teckels

Mimi knocked on Veronique's door and looked at her watch. She was supposed to meet Addie back in the lounge at 11:00, and it was already 10:54. Jim's surprise visit had eaten up fifteen minutes. She needed to hurry.

The door opened a few inches, and Veronique's elegant, heart-shaped face appeared in the crack. "Oh," she said blithely. "It is you."

"Who did you think I might be?" asked Mimi.

"Perhaps this Barb character. With chamomile tea and some chocolates before bed. Would have been a nice gesture. But please, come in."

Mimi nodded thanks and entered the room. The wallpaper was an intricate floral motif with complementary toile fabrics for the duvet and pillows. A settee framed by a pair of leafy ferns in the corner completed the botanical effect.

"Have a seat," Veronique said, gesturing to the settee.

Mimi sat down hesitantly, realizing that the only place left for Veronique to sit was on the bed. She watched her kick off her heels and arrange herself on the bed, like a mermaid in a side-sit position, the beads on her gown making a soft scraping sound against the duvet fabric.

"So, are you going to ask me if I killed Jane?"

"I wasn't going to lead with that, no," said Mimi, leaning back against the settee.

Veronique tilted her head to the side. "Shall we have a smoke?" Extending her hand, she offered a cigarette case monogrammed with the letters *VL*.

"Thank you, but I have my own," said Mimi, reaching into her carryall. "I'm a Pall Mall gal myself. Have Kurt Vonnegut to thank for that." She accepted a light from Veronique. "Do you think Jane would be upset if she knew we were smoking in her house?"

The left side of Veronique's mouth curled up into a smile. "I don't want to say anything about the woman now. She is dead, and I do not like to speak ill of the dead."

Mimi tilted her head slightly in anticipation. "But . . . ?"

"She was a control freak. So no, I don't think she would have been okay with smoking in her house."

"I know Jane was your client, but . . . were you friends?" An ash was beginning to form on Mimi's cigarette. She looked around the tiny room for something to tap it into.

"Here," said Veronique, hopping off the bed. She took a framed photo of Jane and Nelson off the nightstand and laid it on the table in front of Mimi. Veronique tapped her cigarette onto the glass, then laughed softly. "She would have really hated that," she said, nodding to the picture frame now lightly dusted with ash. "We weren't really friends, no. She was a difficult client. Very picky." Veronique paused, then turned to her. "You know how some smells have colors?"

"I think I do know what you mean," said Mimi, rising from the settee and pointing out the window. "That way is my cottage. I have a lot of plants, and whenever I walk in the door, it smells very green. I love it."

Veronique smiled. "Yes." She paused and looked around the room, nostrils faintly twitching. "This house, it smells gray to me. Like a graveyard at night. It's not a charming old house with character. It's a cold, dark place without any love."

Her words reached into Mimi, who became aware of two distinct threads of thought. This was a woman who intrigued her more than she had anticipated. And yet Mimi sensed she was someone you would be foolish to mess with. In another life, they might have been friends.

Mimi nodded. "May I ask, how did you meet Jane?"

Veronique took a long drag on her cigarette. "It was years ago. Paris. I had just formed my company, Sentir. She was at her annual wardrobe appointment at Maison Schiaparelli. Looking impossibly beautiful as always, surrounded by seamstresses. I was there working on a project." She paused, the smoke forming a cloud around her. "As I walked by her, I passed through a noxious wall of tuberose and stopped dead in my tracks. I said, 'Madam, pardon me, but you do not want to wear a perfume that is advertised at bus stops. Let me make you something bespoke.' And she has been my client ever since."

"What scent was she wearing?"

She waved a dismissive hand. "One of those brand-name perfumes marketed to be chic but really just licensed by the designer to some manufacturer in New Jersey. It is always in the bargain bin at the airport duty-free."

Mimi took a moment to consider where she could press further. She decided to go back to the night's events to keep things moving. "I noticed you arrived a bit late to the auction," said Mimi cautiously. "You sat down after everyone else."

Veronique ashed her cigarette onto the picture frame again. "Yes. I had told Gus I would help him with the *teckels*. He was very busy, and I have an affinity for them."

"*Teckels*? Is that some kind of salty snack?"

"No, no. Dachshunds, sorry. It is the French term."

"Ah yes, of course. Is that because you relate to them, having a sensitive nose?"

Veronique smiled and became more animated. "Yes. I also like their silly shape. They make me laugh. I told Gus I would watch them because he was busy. I fed them and then let them out to tinkle."

"Which door was this? What time?"

"The back door in the laundry room. It was probably just before nine p.m. Maybe five minutes before? They set off some kind of motion sensor, a security alarm. So I whistled for them to come back inside." She laughed gently. "The snow was so deep their little bellies got stuck. I had to dash out and carry them back inside. Then I locked the door behind me."

"The door wasn't open for very long, was it?"

"No, no. And I was there the whole time. No one could have come in or out." Veronique settled back on the pillows. "It is nice to have a cigarette with someone."

Mimi smiled. "It is."

"We have an expression in France, *Il faut bonne mémoire après qu'on a menti.* It means that a liar should have a good memory. I was not blessed with one of those, so I would not dare lie in a situation as serious as this. I will tell you everything I know."

Mimi considered this statement. *Could this just be a clever tactic to build trust?* "I appreciate that. Can you tell me, then, do you remember where you were right before Jane died? From 9:00 p.m. to about 9:15 p.m.?"

"I was in the ballroom. I was either bidding or walking around, humming along to Woody's piano."

"Do you remember the last thing you said to Jane?"

Veronique bit the side of her lip. "We did not interact much. No more than a kiss on each cheek when she arrived in the library. But I do remember one thing that struck me as peculiar."

Mimi took a deep drag on her Pall Mall.

"When Matthew saw her, he gave her a kiss and commented on how good she smelled."

"What's peculiar about that?"

"I smelled her too. She was wearing her *everyday* bespoke signature scent. It is an intoxicating jasmine with a tonka bean drydown. I designed all three of her signature scents: *everyday, special occasions,* and *feral.*"

"So you mean . . ."

"Olfactory habituation. An evolutionary trait we all possess, for survival. Matthew had not been spending much time with her. She smelled like new to him." She ground out her cigarette on the picture frame. "I guess she did not think tonight merited *special occasions* or *feral.*"

Mimi looked at her watch. "This was helpful, Veronique. Thank you."

Veronique rose from the bed and opened the door. "I hope you are able to get some sleep," she said, with a smile, as Mimi slipped out the door. "*La nuit porte conseil.*"

"Is that another illuminating French expression?"

"*Oui.* It means 'The night brings advice.'"

FOURTEEN

The TikTok

Addie stood alone by the sofa, surveying the group gathered in the lounge. Everyone had changed into pajamas or casual wear. She glanced at the mantel clock: 11:06. *Where was Mimi?*

Kimiko was seated in an armchair, drawing on a sketch pad. Despite the heated discussion with Matthew just moments ago in the hallway, she appeared calm. Addie noted how she'd hardly spoken a word to anyone all night. Perhaps she was an introvert, although her avoidance of the group seemed more intentional than that.

Lillian, clad stylishly in fuchsia silk pajamas and matching heels, had arranged herself on a chaise. Woody was playing the baby grand piano in the corner. Eyes closed and immersed in the improvisation, he lacked his usual perma-sneer. Sebastián was seated on the edge of an armchair, looking guarded and tense, with his hands clasped, staring at the floor. He wore expensive-looking paisley pants and a sweatshirt with an embroidered green spade emblem. Subdued without an audience, his silver-tongued-showman arrogance had dissipated.

Addie walked over to a pedestal table that held a tray of tulip glasses filled with brandy. She took one and had a sip, letting the sweet warmth rest momentarily on her tongue. This whole evening was starting to feel like a fever dream. *Who were all these random people? What was Brian doing tonight? Why wasn't Mimi back yet?*

She followed Lillian with her eyes as she got up from the chaise and approached Gus, who had just come in and was setting up the sideboard for the late-night snack. She whispered something in his ear. He seemed agitated as she grasped his elbow and whispered again. Despite her intensity, she was doing her best to project an air of civility. They were arguing in the constrained way people do when they're aware that other people around them might notice. It reminded her of the fights she'd had with Brian at Closed Casket in the months leading up to their breakup. When the open office space felt like a public stage where colleagues could watch their relationship crumble.

Mimi, clutching a fresh Gibson, entered the room and hustled toward her.

"Where have you been?" Addie whispered through gritted teeth.

"This is grim, isn't it?" she said, looking around. "The pajama party from hell."

Addie nodded to the Gibson. "Where'd you get that?"

"Stopped by the kitchen on the way in here. Helped myself."

"Well, you're late. I was getting worried."

"Got waylaid by Towels. But I got some good intel, from him and Veronique. He wrote the note to Jane. I'll tell you about it later. Any luck with your search of the study?"

"Nope. JDLR."

"Huh?"

"'Just doesn't look right.' It's police jargon we use in *Murderscape.* It was a Potemkin village in there. Impressive facade of lovely period furnishings but nothing in the drawers or cabinets. It's a study in name only."

"Hmm," said Mimi. "Well, I hit a dead end too. Jim said he doesn't know a thing about the blackmail. I'd figured he was only here because of his printing services."

Addie nodded. "Okay. For now, I say we focus on questioning suspects about the auction. We don't want to draw any more attention to the blackmail until we know more." Addie gestured toward Lillian, who was now seated alone by the fireplace, prodding the logs with a poker. "She was arguing with Gus a moment ago. It looked pretty heated."

"Jane too, at the auction. What's with all the drama?"

"Let's talk to her," said Addie. "Now remember, Mimi, try to be engaging."

Mimi reached down deep to retrieve her most disarming smile as they crossed the room. "Well, hello there, Lillian," she said as they approached her. "May we join you?"

"Oh," she said, perking up and placing the poker back on its stand. "Okay." Lillian smiled enigmatically as they took a seat across from her.

"We're devastated about Jane," said Addie softly. "We were saying earlier how we couldn't remember the last thing either of us said to her."

Lillian nodded. "Consider yourself lucky. Her last words to me were 'Leave me alone.'"

"Oh no, really? Did you have an argument?" asked Mimi, taking a nonchalant sip of her Gibson.

"Sort of," said Lillian. "She was my client. And I think she was mad at me for not making enough time for her. I think she wanted to be my only client."

"What is it that you do?"

She slid a business card across the table.

Lillian Powell, MA, CPC, PCC, ELI-MP

Board-certified astrocartographer and life coach

Empowering people to pursue fulfilling lives
since 2017

empowerwithpowell@gmail.com

"I'm a life coach for high-net-worth individuals."

Mimi studied Lillian carefully. She could tell she was the type of woman who brought intensity to everything she did. Her creamy complexion glowed in the firelight as though she were lit from within. It also highlighted the deep worry lines in her forehead. They seemed to indicate that while she had it all together now, perhaps she had "a past" as well.

"Can you tell us more about what your work entails?" asked Mimi.

"My services are pretty comprehensive. Social media presence. Career changes. How to carry yourself. I craft someone's persona, I suppose you could say."

"And doing this kind of work is how you met Jane?" asked Addie.

"Yes. She paid me well. Even funded my astrocartography training."

Barb arrived carrying a bottle of Growing Concern wine and offered to pour them a glass. Lillian appeared grateful for the interruption.

"I'm okay," said Addie.

"I'm concerned enough already, thanks," said Mimi.

"I'd love a glass of wine," said Lillian. "But is that stuff biodynamic? I only drink biodynamic."

"I'll have a look around the cellar and find you something else, madam," said Barb.

Lillian leaned in closer to them. "Nasty chemicals. They dull my intuitive chakra."

Mimi nodded along heartily, as though she couldn't agree more that an intuitive chakra should never be dulled.

"In my astrocartography practice, I utilize combined aspects of visualization, astrology, and geography in conjunction with a client's natal chart to plot their planetary lines in order to suggest the optimal living arrangements for enhancing their destiny." Lillian pushed a wisp of hair behind her ear, causing the bangle on her wrist to slide down and reveal a small tattoo of a fleur-de-lis. "Some might say my services are just an extravagance for needy rich people. But I like to think I help people who are unhappy."

"Was Jane unhappy?" asked Addie.

"I think she was, yes," Lillian said, after a long pause. "But what my clients choose to share with me is private." Lillian looked wistful, her finger tracing curlicues along the profile of a small statue of Venus on the table next to her. "This is beautiful. I think it's a Lalique."

Mimi continued as coolly as if she were taking a sandwich order. "Do you remember what you were doing from 9:00 p.m. to 9:15 p.m.?"

"I don't," Lillian said, straightening in her chair. "But if what you're really asking is did I kill her, the answer is no." There was a defensive sting in her voice. "I was in the ballroom the entire time during the auction. I never left."

"Do you have anyone who can corroborate that?" asked Addie.

"Not really. I was making the rounds, talking to everyone, trying to be a good party guest. So, no, I don't have one single person who can affirm I was there the whole time."

"Can you remember anyone who wasn't there?" pressed Addie. "Or anyone who got up and left?"

A crease formed between Lillian's brows. "No. But I can distinctly remember Matthew being there the whole time. When he wasn't onstage, he was talking with everyone. He's a wonderful host, don't you think?"

Mimi noted how her eyes glinted. There were definitely some romantic feelings there. "Do you remember any other specifics from the evening? Anything seem strange to you?"

Lillian shook her head and then paused. "Well, wait a minute," she said, raising a finger in the air and brightening. "We did make a TikTok!" She took out her phone and thumbed through it. "I'll show you."

Addie opened her mouth to explain TikTok to Mimi.

"I know what TikTok is," Mimi grunted.

"Here!" said Lillian. She handed Addie her phone. It was playing a TikTok featuring all the decorations and food from the party, interspersed with Lillian lip-syncing to "Party All the Time" by Eddie Murphy and Rick James. "It's an atrocious song, I know, but it's trending right now," Lillian explained. She looked over to Mimi and added, "People are using this song to show the crazy over-the-top parties they go to."

Mimi shook her head. "I miss the days when people appeared on screens to do something interesting."

"There's Jane!" said Addie. She scooted closer to Mimi so they could watch the video together. It played again: quick shots of the table of desserts, silver tureens filled with colorful hydrangeas, a shot of the drawbridge, Lillian singing along in between. At the very end, Jane popped into the frame next to Lillian as they sang the last lyric into the camera together, *"Party all the tiiiime."* She was holding a coupe of champagne with a text overlay that read, *French 75s!! Jane's fave!!!*

Mimi looked up at Lillian. "Can we watch it again?"

"It plays again automatically. Are you sure you want to? It's an awful song."

Mimi leaned in closer as the video played. "Look," she said, pointing to the background behind Lillian and Jane. "There."

Addie squinted. Standing behind them was Matthew, facing the camera, with stony cold eyes.

"He's wearing a coat. That's odd," said Mimi.

Addie watched again. Mimi was right. Matthew was wearing what looked to be a cashmere coat. Indoors, in the middle of a formal party, it was indeed odd.

"What time did you post this?" asked Addie.

Lillian took her phone back and looked at the screen. "Around 8:30."

Addie leaned forward. "Do you know why he was wearing a coat?"

Lillian considered the question as she slipped the phone into her beaded clutch. "I did see him go outside to talk to the guard at one point."

"Really? When?"

"It was around the same time." Lillian got up from her chair. "If you'll excuse me, ladies, I have to call someone." She gave them a little wave goodbye before leaving.

Addie's shoulders slumped. "That was anticlimactic."

"Matthew was definitely up to something in that video."

"I don't know, Mimi. Just because he gave a creepy look to the camera doesn't mean anything. I think Lillian knows more than she's telling us. She seemed closed off."

"Well, you can't expect her to break the sacred vow of client-astrocartographer confidentiality." Mimi downed the rest of her Gibson and set the empty martini glass on a bunch of *Wine Down* magazines stacked on the coffee table. "Maybe she's protecting Matthew? When she spoke about him, it seemed like there were romantic feelings there."

Gus came back into the room again, wheeling a cart filled with charcuterie boards, pie wedges, and cake stands piled high with fruit. It resembled a Flemish still life.

"Just what we need," grumbled Mimi.

Gus gestured to the table. "Please, everyone, help yourself to our Late-Night Grazing Table. It was Jane's signature offering for over-night guests."

An unmistakable melancholy hung in the air as everyone made their way toward the food.

Addie turned to Mimi and spoke in a low whisper. "While ev-eryone's eating, I want to search the rest of the house. There must be some real clues *somewhere*."

"Do you really want to take that risk? There's a killer on the loose."

"It's riskier to sit around and do nothing."

Mimi gave a resigned sigh. "Fine. But you're not going alone."

"Okay. I'll be right back." Addie got up and made a beeline to the Late-Night Grazing Table, grabbed a plate, and quickly loaded it up with cheeses, crackers, thin slices of prosciutto, pickles, cookies, and macarons. She hurried back over to Mimi.

"What are you doing? I thought we were leaving?"

"We are. We're just taking this to go. Do you have a suitable bag in there?"

Mimi dug down into her carryall. "See, I told you this thing is handy," she said as she retrieved a plastic bag and handed it to Addie.

"Will you hold it open wide, please?" said Addie, using her hand to shovel the plate's contents into the bag. "There. A moveable feast!"

Mimi rolled her eyes and dropped the bag into her carryall as though it were a dead mouse. "Can we go now?"

FIFTEEN

Choose Your Own Adventure

They passed by the conservatory and entered the mouth of a long, dark hallway. A ball of fear lodged in Addie's throat.

She heard a sound and placed her arm in front of Mimi, bringing them to a halt. Addie strained to listen. It was the faint clacking of dachshund toenails sauntering down the intersecting hallway ahead of them.

Binky appeared from around the corner and spotted them. She wagged her tail expectantly.

"It's okay," said Addie softly. "Binky's the quiet one."

Then came the staccato sounds of a fast trot. Around the corner came Barnabas, skittering toward them, yapping loudly.

"Barnabas! Binky!" called out Gus, from somewhere deep inside the house.

Addie grabbed Mimi's elbow and pulled her into the nearest room. She closed the door silently behind them. In the darkness, they stood perfectly still while they waited for Gus to lumber away with the dachshunds. She flipped on the lights, and they surveyed the opulent powder room they found themselves in, complete with white marble columns, classical-style busts, and floor-to-ceiling mirrors flanking the walls.

"Viva Las Vegas," said Mimi, blinking from the glare.

Addie sat down at a brightly lit vanity. "Let's stay in here for a few minutes just to play it safe." She took out the Murderbook and began writing. "After we do a quick sweep of the ground floor, I'm thinking we talk to Matthew."

"Is he our prime suspect?"

"Well, I'm not ruling anyone out just yet. But I mean, as you said, it's always the boyfriend." Addie paused, her pencil hovering over the page. "Although he is 'grieving,' supposedly. Do you think if we question him people might think we're being insensitive, or suspect we had something to do with it? Too risky?"

"Too risky?" Mimi snorted. "I hadn't noticed we were being cautious."

Addie looked up from the Murderbook. "You pointed out that Jane was acting strange right before she died. You said she looked drunk, but maybe she wasn't drunk. What if she was poisoned before she was stabbed?"

A silence passed between them as Mimi frowned, deep in thought. She looked up. "Jane's bust."

"Her bust? What do you mean? You think leaking implants may have contributed to her death?"

"No, no," said Mimi. Her eyes were far away. She pointed behind Addie in the mirror. "Jane's bust! Look."

Addie spun around. Mimi was staring at a carved marble bust of Jane, displayed on a pedestal.

"Look at the neckline," said Mimi. "There's a seam."

Addie walked over and placed her hand on the bust. She pulled on it, but nothing happened. Leaning over to study it closely, she ran her hand along the seam. Then she gripped the head and turned it like she was twisting open a soda bottle.

It snapped to the side, and the mirrored wall next to them concertinaed open to reveal an elevator.

They both jumped back.

"Oh. My. God," they gasped in unison.

A single elevator button was labeled *Back in Time*. Addie reached out and pressed it.

Mimi swatted her hand away. "What are you doing? We don't know where this thing goes."

The whirring sound of the elevator moving up the shaft was unsettling.

Addie shifted her weight and put one hand on her hip. "Don't you see, Mimi? This is a key branch on our decision tree."

"Let me guess. Some of your gaming lingo?"

Addie nodded. "Yes. Remember those Choose Your Own Adventure books that I was obsessed with as a kid?"

"Of course, but—"

The elevator dinged and the doors swished open.

Addie stepped inside. "Well, this is exactly like those books. We have to decide how to respond to this game mechanic. Are you coming with me or not?"

Mimi allowed a moment of silent defiance to pass before she followed her in. "We were just talking about risky," she grumbled. "Now we've moved on to all-out reckless."

As the doors closed, an old-timey standard played from speakers above. *Happy days are here again.* They stood in silence, facing forward for the rest of the descent as the song continued cheerfully in the background. *The skies above are clear again.* A ding sounded as the elevator came to a halt and the doors opened.

They stepped into a dimly lit entrance hall with a pair of wrought iron gates at the end. A damp stillness hovered in the air. It felt as if they had crossed the threshold into another world below the house. A sign hung above them: *Welcome to The Worst Kept Secret, est. 1920. No Unauthorized Visitors Allowed Without Prior Approval.*

Mimi shook her head. "That sign needed a copy editor."

The gates parted, opening into a vast room the size of an airplane hangar. Immediately, the lights flashed into bright mode to reveal exposed brick walls and two crescent-shaped bars stylishly flanking either side of the room. Mirrored shelves were stocked with hundreds of bottles of alcohol that glittered like jewels.

Addie looked closer and realized they were alphabetized, from Ardbeg to Zacapa. "Wow, look at this place. It's a shrine to booze."

Mimi took in the room appreciatively. "Perhaps I misjudged Jane."

Addie read a plaque on the wall above a large stone fireplace: *The Ireland compound drew luminaries and politicians from all over the United States. This site originally housed a subterranean distillery, a French restaurant, and a gambling parlor, which we have now lovingly converted into an honorary speakeasy.*

Kneeling down in front of the hearth, Addie leaned in and held her hand close to the massive opening. She extended a finger and touched the grate. It was warm and filled with ashes. She stood up and brushed her hands together.

Mimi ran her hand along the wood grain of the bar counter and rubbed her thumb and forefinger together. No dust.

"Of course!" exclaimed Addie as she walked down a narrow ramp that ended at a bank of floor-to-ceiling windows. "This is what Gus was talking about. It's the cove where the boats came in." She pressed her nose up to the glass. The outside floodlights revealed a small beach next to a rocky cove leading down to Lake Huron's icy gray waters.

She turned to a framed picture on the wall. It was a hand-drawn front elevation of the house. She read aloud to Mimi from its caption: *"Philip Ireland built this house in 1920. The Irelands and their team of rumrunners would bring alcohol from Canada down the St. Mary's River, weaving through a labyrinth of small islands to come to Mackinac. The boats would arrive at night. They supplied the island, the Grand Hotel, and the surrounding areas."*

She studied it carefully and took down a few notes in the Murderbook. Scanning the room again, she paused. In the back corner of the room was a narrow door.

As she walked toward it, Mimi stopped her.

"Where are you going now?"

"To check what's behind that door. Keep a lookout."

Before Mimi could protest, Addie turned the knob. The door opened inward, and the hinges groaned. She flipped on the lights and entered a small, utilitarian space with low ceilings. Stacks of papers covered the desk, and a row of filing cabinets lined the walls.

"Aha," said Addie. "The *real* office. Mimi, come in here!"

She approached the desk and riffled through the papers. Bills, bank statements, tax documents, letters, press clippings, charitable donations. Matthew's name was everywhere. "Mimi! Matthew's records are all here. Come look at this."

There was no response. She looked up. Mimi was standing still, staring at something. Addie moved her head so she could see what Mimi was looking at. It was an old typewriter on a credenza in the corner. Next to it was a stack of bright blue envelopes.

"I guess our instincts were right," said Mimi, shaking her head in disgust. "The blackmail arrived in one of those envelopes. Jane and Matthew were running this whole operation together." She pointed to the typewriter. "It's an Olympia. Just like the one I used every day at the *Gazette*."

Addie began pulling open each of the desk drawers. They were filled to the brim with papers, receipts, and other odds and ends.

When she reached the bottom filing cabinet drawer, it was curiously empty.

She closed her eyes for a moment to think. Rule one of *Murderscape* was: *Don't make assumptions.* She crouched down, grabbed both sides of the bottom drawer, and lifted it off its tracks, yanking it free. Peering inside the cavity where the drawer had been, she could see there was another small, hidden drawer behind it. She felt a familiar burst of excitement. The same feeling she'd gotten whenever she and her team had solved a design problem together. She pulled on the handle to open it, but it was locked.

Addie stood up and looked at Mimi, who still appeared to be in a daze, staring at the typewriter. "Can you go out and see if there's a poker by the fireplace? I want to try something."

"Why?"

"This basement lair is just like a level in a game, Mimi." She registered Mimi's skeptical expression. "A game level is like an episode of a television show. It has a beginning, a middle, and an end. As players, we need to ask ourselves what mission we need to complete. *What is this level telling us? Why was Matthew working down here in the bowels of the house and not in the beautiful study on the main floor?*"

"Dear, I thought you said this wasn't a game."

Addie shot her a sharp look. "Mimi, get the poker."

Mimi turned and went back into the speakeasy, returning with a poker. Addie took it and jammed the point into the gap between the locked drawer and the desk. There was a pop, and she pulled down hard, prying it open.

Reaching her arm inside the drawer, her fingers touched a stack of papers and a bunch of manila envelopes. She pulled them out and did a quick scan of one of the documents. *Notice of Intention to Sue for Negligence.* Checking the drawer again, she retrieved the final item that was nestled all the way at the back: a small, leather-bound book. As she opened it, her eyes widened.

It was a ledger. She ran her finger down a column of initials: *VL. SP. LP.* There were numbers listed in the second column, along with dates and other abbreviations. She flipped the page to another grid of amounts, listed in columns labeled *Projections* and *Actual*.

"Mimi, almost everyone is listed in here!"

"Huh?" said Mimi.

"Veronique, Sebastián, Lillian, Gus, they're all being black-mailed!" She flipped to another page. "Matthew definitely teamed up with Jane on this scam."

Looking stunned, Mimi tried to absorb this information. "I . . . I guess it is oddly comforting to know I wasn't the only victim in the house."

"It makes sense," said Addie, nodding as she paged through the book. "I mean, your own contribution would probably fund a few Birkin bags and a summer rental in the Hamptons, at best."

Mimi sighed. "I wonder what the rest of them did to find them-selves in Matthew and Jane's crosshairs. Were we all being charged the same rate, or were the amounts assessed individually, cali-brated on some kind of ability-to-pay scale?" She paused. "I'd like to march up to Matthew right now and break every one of his damn fingers."

Addie continued paging through the ledger. "There's so many names and numbers in here. We just need some time to go through it. These amounts, they're extortionate!"

"I think that's the point."

"And here's *RM.* I can't believe they were expecting $275,000 from you!" Addie slammed the ledger closed. "Why won't you just tell me what led to all this in the first place?"

Mimi walked toward the office door. "Addie, I can't wheel out a dry-erase board and diagram everything for you right now. We're sneaking around a blackmailer's underground hideout after a mur-der. Let's move on, please."

Addie pursed her lips as she handed the papers and ledger over to Mimi. "Okay. Put these in your carryall."

"Let's go."

As they left the office and made their way toward the gates, the elevator dinged.

Addie froze and looked at Mimi. "Someone's coming!"

SIXTEEN

Mimi Didn't Do It

Mimi gathered her wits and ran over to turn off the lights. "Addie," she hissed. "Over to the bar. Now!" They dashed behind one of the bar counters and crouched down.

Low lights still illuminated the artwork on the walls. There was a shadow of movement and soft footsteps. They could hear the wrought iron gates squeak open. A dark form holding something in their hand slouched across the room toward the back wall. Addie's heart was pounding out of her chest. Mimi peeked around from their hiding place, trying to make out who this figure could be. The silhouette was tall, with a shadowy head that seemed misshapen.

Mimi tapped Addie and whispered in her ear. "Decision tree time. Do we make a run for the elevator?"

Addie shook her head.

The figure walked directly to the back wall as if they knew exactly what they were looking for. After a moment, they took a framed photo off the wall and stuffed it into their bag. They turned and started to walk toward the office.

"Decision tree, fast!" growled Mimi.

"Okay, we're jumping them! Count of three. One . . . two . . ."

The person turned in the direction of the two-woman stampede barreling toward them and tried to run, but they were instantly tackled to the floor. Mimi administered a swift kick to the groin. A man's voice moaned in agony.

Addie grabbed the flashlight from his hand. The figure was wearing a nightcap pulled down over the face as a mask, with two eyeholes poked in it. She yanked it off and shined the light in his face.

Mimi shook her head. "Jim Towels, as I live and breathe. You better have a good explanation for this. Otherwise, you'll be taking your damaged jewels over to Sing Sing for all those lonely inmates to play with."

"Mimi, who are you, Eliot Ness?" Addie reached out a hand and helped him to his feet. "Jim, are you okay?"

Jim was still writhing. "Rosemary, why did you do that? Why are you two down here?"

Mimi went over and switched on the lights. "Why are *we* down here? You said you were going to bed!" She nodded at the bag in Jim's hand. "What's in there?"

"It's nothing."

"You better tell us. Now."

Tears glistened in his eyes. "I was upstairs in my room trying to sleep, but when I lie flat, I get sinus drainage. So I started thinking about Jane. I decided to come down here and get my favorite picture of us, a selfie she took when we made the sign over there by the iron gates."

Addie took the framed photo from the bag and saw two paint-speckled faces pressed together for a happy smile. She turned and showed it to Mimi.

"I don't like it down here. Can we go back up?" said Jim.

Nodding in silent agreement, they made their way back to the elevator and rode it up together. During the slow ascent, a look of alarm spread across Addie's face. She nudged Mimi with her elbow, indicating Jim's pocket. Mimi looked over and noted a roll of duct tape peeking out. *Why would he need duct tape if he was just getting his favorite picture?*

The elevator dinged.

"Jimbo, it's going to look a little strange if we exit a bathroom together, so you go first. Don't worry, we won't say anything about this."

Jim turned to leave. "You still haven't told me why you two were down there."

Addie looked to Mimi. "Gus was telling us about that alphabetized-booze wonderland all night, so Mimi had to go see it for herself."

Jim nodded, seeming to take the answer at face value. "Well, see you gals later."

After he left, Mimi looked to Addie. "Okay. We've done enough searching. Can we please go back to the room now? We're lucky we ran into Jim and not the killer."

Addie held up a hand. "Hold on a minute. I'm still trying to wrap my head around what just happened. You said he gave Jane the note. That means he was trying to get her alone. And then we find him creeping around down there with duct tape in his pocket? He could have been following us. What if Jim's the killer?!"

Mimi scoffed. "Jim's not the killer."

"You don't know that. This whole Eeyore act he has going on—"

"It's not an act."

"He could be hiding something, Mimi. Maybe Jane and Matthew threatened him, and this was his revenge. Revenge can drive even the sanest people to do bad things."

"I'm telling you, Jim Towels is as likely to have 'dunnit' as I am. The guy's a human doorstop. Functional. Boring. He would never do something so colorful as commit murder."

"Not even in the revenge scenario?"

"I think you need to dial down that imagination of yours. Focus on suspects who fit the profile instead of concocting some *Count of Mackinac Cristo* story for Jim Towels."

"Whatever. I'm not going back to the room yet. Can we please just go to the lounge and see who else we can talk to?"

"Fine, but are you ever going to eat this disgusting bag of buffet hash? My carryall smells like the garbage bin at a school cafeteria."

"Oh, yes! I almost forgot. I'm starving. Hand it over."

Mimi sat down at the vanity and watched Addie wolf down her bag of snacks as she sat cross-legged on the floor.

"Want a cookie? It's just a little damp with some pickle juice."

Mimi shook her head. "No, thank you. I'm still worried that seafood I ate earlier could wash ashore."

Addie took a final bite and stood up. "Let's go."

They eased the powder room door open quietly and slipped out, making their way back to the lounge. Gus's buffet had been devoured, and everyone was clustered near the fireplace, except for Woody, who was alone, planted in a fringed armchair.

"I don't see Matthew," said Mimi.

Addie nodded in Woody's direction. "Let's try him."

Mimi touched Addie's arm. "Listen, I can't do the 'sweet old lady just asking casual questions' act with Woody. He's too . . . I don't know . . . something."

"Calculating? Gross?"

"No, I can't think of the word."

"Smarmy!"

"Enough with the Murder Mad Libs," snapped Mimi.

Addie straightened herself. "Fine. Follow my lead." She approached him casually, with a warm smile. "Hey, Woody."

He responded with an uncovered yawn. "Oh, look, it's the Warren Commission."

"We just need to talk to you for a minute, okay?"

"Sure. Why not?" He settled back into his seat as though he was about to savor an entertaining experience. "You ladies seem to have assigned yourselves the role of chief snoops, haven't you? Ask your questions. I'm all ears."

They sat down in the love seat across from him. He lit a cigarette and shook the match, tossing it into a chinoiserie planter nearby that contained a vibrant orchid.

Addie got up and extracted the match with her fingers. "This is a Shenzhen Nongke. You have to be careful. It's incredibly rare and difficult to grow."

He gestured to Addie with his cigarette. "See, I get why *you're* doing this. You're the murdery gal with the video games. But *you*—" He turned to Mimi and shook his head. "Shouldn't you be upstairs playing canasta or reading *Ladies' Home Journal*?"

Addie sat back down and placed her hand on Mimi's knee, giving it a firm *Don't take the bait* squeeze. "Listen, we won't beat around the bush, Woody. We just want to know if you noticed anything strange tonight."

He took a drag and exhaled, smiling into the cloud of smoke. "As a matter of fact, I did."

Addie flicked a quick look in Mimi's direction, then turned back to Woody. "We'd appreciate anything you can share with us."

Woody glanced around, then lowered his voice. "Well, I should probably tell you—"

Matthew burst into the room. All heads turned to him as the ambient hum of conversation dissolved into silence. He paused to catch his breath.

"What the hell is this?" he said, holding up a sealed plastic bag.

Addie squinted. Inside the bag was the *Memento Mochi* knife. She could just make out its marbled jade handle, covered in congealed blood that had smeared all over the bag. She felt her stomach coil into knots.

He took a few steps forward so that he was standing in the center of the lounge. His face reddened as he spoke. "I was helping Barb add logs to all the fireplaces. That's when I walked past the bed in *their* room," he said, pointing at Addie and Mimi, "and I noticed a strange gap between the mattress and box spring."

Everyone gasped, turning sharply toward them.

His eyes bored into Mimi as he walked toward her. "You did it, didn't you? Did you really think you could get away with this?"

Addie watched in silent shock as Mimi tried to respond, but the words wilted in her throat. The group began to murmur as growing hostility permeated the room.

"Stop this," said Addie, holding up her hands and stepping between them. "Someone planted that."

Matthew shook his head as he continued to cast his unrelenting glare at Mimi. "Please. You didn't exactly hide your contempt for Jane tonight. I watched the way you talked to her. You were horrible. Angry. You hated her, didn't you?"

Addie stopped to take a breath as fear surged through her body. "Mimi didn't do it! I've been with her all night." She flinched. Her voice was throaty with emotion. Defending Mimi further was going to require a careful and calm explanation, but her brain refused to put the words together in a sentence that sounded reasonable, logical.

Woody narrowed his eyes, turning to Mimi. "Well, I'll be damned. Miss Marple did it."

"I had no idea you were capable of something like this. How could you?" Matthew looked to the group. "I say we lock them both up until the police arrive."

SEVENTEEN

Fondue

Well, this is just great," said Mimi as her eyes adjusted to the stark white walls of the kitchen pantry surrounding them. "What the hell are we going to do now?"

"Eat," said Addie, gazing in wonderment at the impeccably organized shelves lined with neatly labeled canisters, spices, and fresh produce. The place was the size of her studio apartment in Chicago. "Look at all this stuff. It's like we're inside somebody's Pinterest board."

Mimi plopped down on a step stool in the corner. "Shouldn't we be figuring out how we're going to get out of here?"

"A few nibbles from Gus's buffet was hardly a meal. Somebody's trying to frame you, Mimi. Eating helps me think."

"Enjoy having a hummingbird's metabolism while it lasts."

Addie pointed to a shelf across the room. "There's a Crock-Pot. I could make a comforting broccoli mac and cheese, or my signature smoked tomato soup with balsamic swirl."

"You sound like a Pioneer Woman blog post."

"Actually, let's do something sweet," said Addie, purposefully walking over to the produce area and lifting a bunch of bananas from a hook. She pulled down a silver fondue pot from a shelf and set it on the counter. Underneath the pot, she slid open the lid on the burner.

"So, you've decided to host an après-ski fondue party during our incarceration?" asked Mimi, watching her flit around the room, pawing through drawers.

Addie located a butane lighter, lit the burner, and adjusted the flame. "They've got little bars of this beautiful Swiss chocolate I love. Trust me, this'll be heavenly."

"Have you forgotten that we're in mortal danger?"

Addie turned down the flame as the bars began to liquefy. The melting chocolate released a rich aroma that filled the room.

"Brian and I had fondue just like this at that hotel in Saint Moritz I told you about."

Mimi sniffed. "I'll bet he didn't have to worry about chocolate dripping onto his chin. Probably fell from his lips directly to the floor."

Addie reached for a cutting board and slammed it down on the counter. "Do you ever let up?"

"My dear, you still talk about this guy like you love him. Do you think he's talking about you while he's out celebrating his millions?"

"It's not that simple. I can't just 'move on,'" snapped Addie as she started to slice the bananas.

"Why not? You've got a full life. Plenty of friends. A good job at the ad agency. And you have me."

Addie paused her slicing. "You're kidding, right?"

"What do you mean?"

Addie set the knife down. "How many times have I reached out to you over the years and asked if we could plan a trip together? Do you ever just call me to check in? I *always* call you. Half the time it goes to voicemail. You only reached out to me when this blackmailing stuff started."

"Oh, please. I have always made it clear that you do not need an engraved invitation presented on a silver tray to come and visit."

Addie dipped a slice of banana in the fondue and offered a bite to Mimi, who shook her head and began pulling the zipper back and forth on her carryall.

"I think about this all the time. You don't ever want to talk to me about anything that's uncomfortable. The minute I try to engage you, you look away and busy yourself with some other unimportant thing." Addie paused and nodded toward the carryall. "Could you stop with the zipping?"

Mimi closed her eyes and pushed the carryall away. She could really use another cigarette, but she resisted the urge.

A silence passed between them.

"You know, your mom wanted to be a mother from the moment she and your dad got married," said Mimi, taking in a breath. "But they had fertility issues and it took them a while to get pregnant."

Addie frowned. "She never told me that."

"It was a difficult pregnancy and delivery, but at last you arrived. You were colicky for the first year, but eventually you mellowed out. You definitely had that MacLaine characteristic of being very determined. You were so dang smart. You couldn't get enough of jigsaw puzzles, Scrabble, Clue. Most kids had a favorite stuffed animal. You cuddled your precious Rubik's Cube."

"Life was good," said Addie, smiling wistfully. "Until the day it all evaporated."

Mimi thought back to that horrific day, when she'd had to tell Addie that her parents had been killed in a head-on crash with a semi on I-90. The trucker had fallen asleep at the wheel. She'd been home from college for the summer after her junior year. Her adult life was only just beginning.

"You've never asked me why I love video games," Addie continued. "I got into them after Mom and Dad died because they gave me an escape. They helped me figure myself out and work through my grief. Games fixed me when I was broken."

Mimi nodded slowly. "I want you to know that I respect what you do, dear. I just wish Brian the Terrible had never come into your life. If it hadn't been for him, you wouldn't be feeling this way. He came between us and suddenly—"

"Ha!" Addie interjected. "You really don't see it, do you?"

"See what?"

She shook her head in exasperation. "It's always something with you, Mimi. Yes, it's been Brian lately. But before that it was my career. You wanted me to go into STEM and wouldn't let up on design 'not being a real job.' And before *that*—"

"Okay. You've made your point." Mimi brushed her hand over her hair and sighed. "Whether you believe it or not, when we had our squabble over Brian, my only intention was to save you from getting hurt." She paused before continuing. "We all make bad choices, and then we waste years regretting those choices. Brian was a colossal time-waster."

"Why couldn't you trust me to figure that out for myself?"

"Because I made a promise to your parents. That I'd help you lead a remarkable life."

"Stop trying to save me, Mimi."

She sighed. "As brilliant as you are, dear, you always have your head in the clouds. You're great at creating imaginary worlds, but somehow you can't ever seem to see what's right in front of your face."

Turning away, Addie resumed peeling and slicing bananas. Over the years, she had always hoped Mimi would become soft-centered and warm, just like her signature oatmeal raisin cookies. But that never happened. Fierce pragmatism and unsolicited solutions to problems seemed to be the only things she could offer. Affection, maternal support, and even simple words of encourage- ment were not in Mimi's repertoire.

"I know you have good intentions, Mimi," said Addie, rolling her shoulders to loosen the tension in her neck. "You're just not always the best . . . grandma. I mean, would it kill you to offer me a hug once in a while?"

"Fine," Mimi sighed. "You want a hug? Let's hug. I'll give you a hug right now."

"Never mind."

A painful silence pushed each of them into their own dark corners.

Addie proffered another chocolate-dipped banana. "You sure you don't want?"

Mimi relented and took a bite, closing her eyes as the thick chocolate enveloped her taste buds.

Addie speared two more banana bites with forks and dipped them in chocolate. "I'm just saying I wish it wasn't such a one-way relationship." Sitting down on the floor next to Mimi, she handed her another bite.

"How can I convince you that you are the only reason I get up each day and get on with life? I know you want me to plumb the depths of my soul for emotional displays of affection every time I see you, but that's just not who I am."

Addie drew her legs up and hugged her arms around them.

Mimi looked at her. "I remember how you used to sit like that. When you were little. You were always inside your head, dreaming of some far-off place."

Addie nodded.

"You devoured all those old Boxcar Children books of your mom's. And when they were done, you'd make me get out her Nancy Drews and your dad's Hardy Boys. Remember that Christmas I offered to get you a new bicycle, but all you wanted was a trench coat from Goodwill?"

"Yeah. That was my Carmen Sandiego phase." Addie smiled and leaned against the wall, thinking. "But I seem to recall that you and Grandpa didn't give me what I *really* wanted for my ninth birthday."

"What nine-year-old asks for a bloodhound?" Mimi shook her head. "You were always like that . . . *sleuthy*." She nodded to the fondue pot. "May I have a little more?"

Addie smiled and got up to prepare a plate of more banana bites.

Mimi forced a weary smile. "I see so much of your mother in you. Sometimes I'm so gobsmacked by the similarities in your voice and mannerisms that I would swear she was the one standing in front of me."

"Even I can see myself when I look through her old pictures."

"Dreamers. Both of you. Your mom could have been anything, a doctor or a physicist. She had the requisite IQ and talent, just like you do. But she lacked confidence. She wanted to go to a local college, marry your dad. She didn't give a thought to her amazing potential."

"I was proud of her. Best preschool teacher in Chicago," Addie said, dabbing chocolate from her mouth with an expensive-looking linen napkin. "She loved teaching young children. What could be more noble?"

Mimi's eyes grew distant. "She was a gentle soul. Your grandfather and I loved her so much. She was gifted, but she didn't . . ." Her words trailed off.

"Just because Mom didn't inherit the assertive-and-grumpy gene doesn't mean she was a timid doormat."

"Dear, listen to me," said Mimi, turning to her. "Don't ever let anyone, including me, tell you how to live your life. I'm just trying to toughen you up. You need grit. Backbone."

Addie sighed. "You know, the grandfather in Boxcar Children encouraged the orphans' creativity and imagination, but he was also very gentle and kind."

"Well, I'm sorry you can't live out the adventures of your childhood books, Addie. This is the real world, you know."

Addie pressed her lips tightly together. "Guess it doesn't get any more real than this. Locked up in a windowless pantry after being accused of murder."

"Exactly. We can't turn on each other like this. Look at this place." Mimi gestured to the shelves around them. "We're in the seventh circle of Marie Kondo hell!"

"Okay," said Addie, scanning the room. "Let's figure out how we're going to get out of here." She pointed to an air vent above them.

"I don't like where this is going."

"I could try to get it open, but I'll need a screwdriver first."

"Well, there's some oranges over there, but I don't see any vodka."

"Very funny."

"I don't want you crawling through some air duct like you're in *Die Hard*."

Addie's eyes lit up. "That's kind of why I want to try it."

"No. Vetoed. Next idea."

Addie pointed up at the ceiling. "What about that?"

It was a smoke detector.

Mimi nodded. "I like it. Let's do it."

Scraping the last drops of melted chocolate from the bottom of the fondue pot into her mouth, Addie slid the lid of the burner wide-open, causing the flame to rise higher. She looked around. "What can we use for kindling?"

Mimi picked up a stack of white linen napkins from a shelf. "Are you ready?"

Addie nodded.

Mimi placed the napkins on the flame. "Now, start yelling like you stubbed a gangrenous toe on an ottoman."

"Help! Fire! Someone, please!" shouted Addie as the napkins caught fire and smoke began to rise.

"My heart! Help! Get us out of here!" contributed Mimi.

They pounded on the door as the beeping of the smoke detector blared throughout the house.

The sound of scurrying footsteps and barking dogs approached the door.

"Fire! Please!"

Someone turned the deadbolt and the latch clicked. The door flew open. It was Jim Towels, out of breath from running.

"Are you gals okay?"

Lillian appeared next to him. Barnabas and Binky yapped at them from below.

"That stupid fondue pot just exploded!" said Addie, pointing frantically. "I was trying to give Mimi something sweet for her blood sugar. The diabetes causes her to faint, just like those goats you see on the internet." She patted Mimi's shoulder.

Lillian ran into the kitchen. She returned with a fire extinguisher and darted into the pantry to put out the fire.

"Diabetes?" said Jim Towels. "Oh no, Rosemary. Hey, I have some compression socks upstairs you can borrow."

A muffled shriek pierced the air. They stood together in shocked silence for a moment, swiveling their heads in search of the sound's source.

"Help!" someone shouted from below. Instinctively, they all looked down at the floor.

"Let's go," said Addie.

They took off toward the cellar together. Other guests came running from all directions.

"I'm diabetic now?" Mimi whispered under her breath as she hurried along.

Addie shrugged. "Best I could do."

Jim Towels took the lead and made it to the cellar door first, with everyone crowding behind him. The worn stone staircase was narrow and dark. Dank, musty air rose up from the blackness beneath them. Addie trailed her fingertips along the wall to keep her balance as Mimi gripped her other arm tightly. Ahead of them, the other guests descended in single file, their silhouettes barely visible. As everyone reached the final steps and poured into the cellar, Lillian screamed.

Gus was standing in the center of the room, looking pale and frightened. He was hovering over a dead body that was face down in a pool of blood.

EIGHTEEN

The Cellar

It's not how it looks!" Gus shrieked.

The dead body was Matthew. A viscous river of blood seeped from his head and branched into tributaries across the cold stone floor. Veronique took a dramatic step sideways to move out of its path.

Addie grasped Mimi's arm. *Their prime suspect was dead.* Panic swept through the group as Addie pushed her way to the front and knelt down to get a closer look. There was a small gunshot wound to his left temple. As she leaned in closer, the hairs stood up on her arms. His mouth was frozen in a part grimace, part smile. She shuddered as she looked into his vacant eyes, staring into nothingness.

"Oh my God. Matthew!" shrieked Lillian. She turned to Sebastián and buried her face in his chest.

"I don't understand. How the hell did *another murder* happen?" said Sebastián, pulling away from her and glaring at Gus.

Gus put his face in his hands. "I . . . I don't know! He was just . . . he was just lying there when I came downstairs."

"Poor Matthew," said Veronique quietly.

Addie felt a sudden stillness and turned around. Everyone looked aghast, stunned. But her mind was clear. She knew what she had to do. It was just like examining the initial scene in *Murderscape*. She crouched down to study him closely, noting there were several deep gashes on the palm of his right hand. "The bullet wound is tiny," she said, pointing to his temple. "Probably the antique revolver from the library. And there's—"

"Wait a minute, wait a minute," Woody cut in, pointing to Addie and Mimi. "What are *those two* doing back out here?"

Addie got to her feet and assumed a defiant stance.

Jim Towels walked toward the group with his hands up. "I let them out. They have every right to be out here with the rest of us now that"—he looked down at Matthew—"*this* has happened while they were locked up."

Gus composed himself. "I agree. As the only member of this family left, I'm now the de facto head of this household, and I say they can remain free. I'm not leaving an old woman of diminished capacity locked in a pantry with no bathroom."

Mimi frowned.

"Yeah. I can vouch for Rosemary," added Jim Towels. "Known her for years. She's our precinct captain for Mackinac's annual Run for Plantar Fasciitis. We don't allow just anyone to participate in our community fundraising events."

"I have nothing to hide anyway," said Gus. "Addie here's the only one with any kind of qualifications to help us. The designer of a detective game is the closest thing we have to a real detective."

"So what's that supposed to mean?" snapped Kimiko. "If we don't want to answer her silly fake detective questions, we're guilty?"

Sebastián looked everyone in the eye. "Everyone, calm down. We need to stick together."

"Stick together?!" laughed Woody. "One of us is the murderer!"

While everyone continued arguing, Addie busied herself surveying the cellar—a cold, musty cave with a domed brick ceiling.

There was an eerie stillness to it despite the echoes of everyone's voices in the room. Racks and racks of dusty wine bottles lined the walls. She noted the top half of a broken bottle on the floor not far from Matthew's body.

"What are we going to do now?" asked Barb.

Lillian turned toward the cellar stairs. "I'm going to try the police again."

"I'll come with you," said Kimiko.

"No," snapped Lillian, her voice trembling with fear. "I want to go alone."

"Oh, wow, look, a '73 Chateau Montelena," said Woody, holding a bottle up to the light.

"Take it upstairs. We're going to need it," said Kimiko.

Addie turned to Barb. "Is that staircase the only entrance to this room?"

"Yes."

Sebastián approached Gus, eyeing him skeptically. "What exactly were you doing down here in the first place? Why should we believe your version of events?"

Gus stiffened. "I was restocking the wine fridge upstairs. I've been working my tail off to keep all of you fed and hydrated, not to mention cleaning up the glasses and plates you've left everywhere. I can assure you I haven't murdered anybody. I'm too tired."

"Why do I smell wine, then?" said Veronique, walking toward Gus and examining him up close, her nostrils twitching.

"Well, for starters, we're in a wine cellar," said Woody. "They must really pay you the big bucks over there in France."

"That is not what I mean," snapped Veronique, tossing her head indignantly. "I mean it smells like *metabolized* wine. Seeping from your pores. Have you been drinking tonight?"

"Look, I needed a little something for my nerves, so I came down here and had a glass of '82 Latour. But it was already opened. They'd used a Coravin."

Everyone continued to eye him suspiciously.

"It's late, and I wanted a drink, okay? I'm a chef, not a chauffeur."

Addie noted that all the boxes of Growing Concern wine were covered in dust and looked poorly packed and neglected, compared to the other carefully arranged bottles. Strange, considering the way Matthew had described the vineyard as the crown jewel of their empire.

"Look, everyone. Let's stay calm," said Sebastián. "Let's stop traipsing around a crime scene and go back upstairs."

Everyone silently nodded and filed out of the room.

Addie observed Sebastián as the group followed him up the stairs. He had assumed a sort of leadership role among them and exuded a sense of superiority she didn't like.

Mimi waited until they all had turned their backs before grabbing Addie's arm.

"Addie, the key! Didn't you say Barb gave it to Matthew and he put it in his pocket? Take it."

"Seriously?"

"Yes. Hurry."

Addie quickly weighed her options. Leaving it for the cops to find would make sense under normal circumstances. But what if the killer came back to clean up the scene and took the key? She drew in a breath and reached into his pocket. She grabbed it and handed it to Mimi, who tucked it away in her trusty carryall.

They headed back up the stairs.

"I can't believe it," sighed Addie. "I really thought Matthew did it."

Mimi paused as they reached the top of the stairs. "We need to be careful. The gun is still missing, and the killer might not be done yet." She took Addie by the shoulders. "We need to ask everyone about their role in the blackmail. Get them to tell us the stories behind those numbers in the ledger."

Addie gave an approving nod, feeling a renewed sense of

strength and determination. Mimi was finally taking this seriously. "Yes, ma'am."

They entered the lounge. Everyone was seated except for Lillian, who was standing in the middle of the room looking confused.

"Where's the Lalique?"

"The what?" asked Sebastián.

"The Lalique. The Venus statue. I was admiring it earlier. It was sitting on that table over there, and now it's gone."

Everyone looked at one another, then went back to sipping their drinks indifferently.

Addie glanced around. *Which one of these people had the means, motive, and opportunity to murder both Matthew and Jane?* Underneath the surface of civility and polite conversation, one of them was waiting, watching. Calculating their next move.

The lights flickered, pulling her back from her thoughts.

Mimi turned to Addie, and they shared a look of concern. *They weren't really going to lose power now, after all this, were they?* Addie looked around the room as every light strobed. The conversation in the room halted.

She blinked hard, focusing on a Tiffany lamp in the corner, its bulb flashing on and off.

"You've got to be kidding me," said Woody, looking up at the flickering wall sconces.

The lights turned back on brightly. Addie sensed the group's collective sigh of relief as the room returned to normal. But soon the lights began to blink again.

Wind howled through the chimneys of the mansion. A tense silence blanketed the room while the entire house seemed to tremble in the midst of the worsening storm.

Everyone screamed as the power went out and they were engulfed in pitch-black darkness.

NINETEEN

Cocktails and Accusations

arb's shaky hand lit a candle on the mantelpiece. It flickered to life, dwindled for a moment, then flared again into a confident flame.

Addie's mind churned. The candlelight was vaguely comforting, but it cast murky shadows on anything beyond its range. How could she even begin to unravel all her swirling thoughts about the two murders? It was overwhelming. They were trapped inside this ghoulish place with no power. She thought about the labyrinth of dark rooms that surrounded them. The house felt suffocating, oppressive. *What were they going to do now?*

She walked over to Mimi, who was smoking by the window. She pressed her forehead against the glass to peer out into the night. The snow was still plummeting from the sky in thick, blurry puffs.

Barb wheeled around a cart packed with lanterns and flashlights, doling them out to the guests. "I know we're all frightened, but unfortunately this happens on Mackinac more often than we care to admit because we rely on power from the mainland. Hopefully, this one won't last too long."

"Should we all just stay here in the lounge?" said Gus. "We can't have people blundering around this house in the dark. There's expensive antiques and artwork everywhere."

"We'll be able to see well enough. Most of the wall sconces are the old kind that use candles or burn oil. I'm going to light up the rest of the house now."

"Thank you, Barb," said Jim Towels, who was standing in front of the fireplace. He took a poker and stoked the logs, sending sparks up the chimney into the cold night air. "This weather is only getting worse. How are the cops ever going to get here in this?"

Addie folded her arms and turned away from the window to face Lillian. "Did you talk to the police again?"

Lillian sank into a chair. "They answered right away, but it was the police in St. Ignace. Calls are being forwarded. They said the snowstorm is slowly moving eastward and to sit tight until the wind dies down. Choppers are still grounded. We talked about trying someone local who's off duty, but they wouldn't be able to get to us either. The damn drawbridge is still up."

"Quite the crack team of Yooper police we've got," sniffed Jim Towels.

Veronique frowned in confusion. "What is this 'Yooper' you speak of?"

"It's what we call the folks on the Upper Peninsula," explained Mimi.

Gus shook his head and sighed. "Even if the power comes back on, Jane and Matthew were the only ones who knew the code to the drawbridge. There's no way to get anyone here right now."

"What if it gets colder and the moat freezes?" said Lillian brightly. "The police could just walk across it?"

"Unlikely," explained Jim Towels. "The laws of thermodynamics dictate that a body of water that size wouldn't—"

"Never mind," snapped Lillian, rolling her eyes.

Gus circulated with a bottle of cognac. Addie could see that two family deaths in one evening had understandably traumatized the man. His hands quaked as he concentrated on delivering the golden liquid into each glass without too much spillage.

"Gus, please," said Veronique, waving away the bottle. "We can help ourselves."

"No, no. I want to fulfill my duties," he replied.

"You're serving booze, Gus, not helping the war-wounded," said Mimi, lifting the Pall Mall to her lips. "You should get some R and R."

Lillian looked around, sniffing the air. "What is that lovely smell?"

Veronique gave a small smile. "I did the scent design for the house. This is my *Cozy Sweater Weather* candle. It is a resinous vanilla amber that envelops you like an oversized cardigan."

"Is anyone else thinking what I'm thinking?" asked Woody.

"That the Upper Peninsula's power grid is a disgrace, and we should write a strongly worded letter to the local government?" offered Jim Towels.

Woody sat down at the piano and started playing. Addie recognized it instantly as the theme from *Psycho.*

"Please, Woody. No more piano," said Kimiko.

"Fine," he said, banging on a bunch of discordant keys and rising angrily from the bench. He walked over to the backbar and filled a balloon glass with brandy. "I'll tell you what I'm thinking. Two murders in two hours. Who's next?"

"Never two without three," murmured Veronique.

"Come again?" said Jim Towels nervously.

"There have been two murders, and bad things always happen in threes. We are all in danger."

Woody held the brandy in his mouth for a moment before swallowing. "Well, this killer, whoever the hell he is, isn't going to get far tonight. It's apocalyptic out there."

"I'm sorry," interrupted Lillian, accepting a refill from Gus. "Can we please stop using the blanket pronoun 'he' for the killer? It could be a 'she' or a 'they' for all we know."

"That's great, Lillian," said Kimiko. "Gender equality where it matters."

"Everyone, please. The police will get here soon enough," said Sebastián. "Let's sit tight."

"Yeah. Sit tight until Mackinac's Barney Fife arrives and finds two corpses and a house full of suspects. Do you think he's ever handled a serious situation like this before?" said Gus. "Any one of us could be wrongfully accused."

"You seem to be extra concerned," said Lillian dryly. "Funny that you're also worried about the 'expensive antiques' in the house. Is Jane leaving you this house in her will?"

"Don't you dare make insinuations about me!" shouted Gus. His eyelids crinkled shut as he massaged his temples with his fingers. "Barb and I have been working all night trying to take care of everyone and clean up after all of you. I've already said it: I wouldn't have the time or energy to harm anyone."

Veronique brushed off bits of dachshund fur that clung to her trousers. "Interesting that you are pointing fingers, Lillian. You and Jane barely spoke a word to each other all night except when you were arguing in the ballroom. What was that about?"

"Well, I'm glad I stayed for the cocktails-and-accusations portion of the evening," said Sebastián, who rose from his chair.

"Yeah. You're all stimulating company. It's like being in a Parisian salon in the 1920s," said Woody, setting his drink down and walking toward the door. "But I'm off to bed."

Mimi's cigarette sizzled as she took a long pull. Addie leaned over to speak with her quietly. "You need to slow down with the smoking, Mimi. You're going to look like Willie Nelson."

She didn't respond. A vein of bright lightning flashed in the window behind her as she took another drag.

"*Insolence,*" said a voice nearby.

They both turned to find Veronique standing beside them.

"She does have a bit of an attitude, doesn't she?" said Mimi.

"No, no. *Insolence*, by Guerlain. This is your perfume?" asked Veronique, looking at Addie with a raised eyebrow.

"Oh," said Addie, embarrassed. "Well, yes. I'm surprised you can tell. I sprayed it on before I came here tonight, but that was hours ago. And I'm wearing one of Jane's sweaters, which has its own—"

"Oh, yes, I can smell that too. It's *everyday*, her custom scent," Veronique said, gently taking Addie's wrist and lifting it to her nose. "But *Insolence* is a boisterous violet. I can smell it layered underneath. It's unmistakable."

"I'm impressed. Although I don't really think of myself as boisterous."

Veronique leaned in toward them. "I want to offer you my theory. I think the murders are somehow connected to the things that have gone missing tonight."

Mimi looked to Addie, then back to Veronique. "You mean Jane's ring?"

"And the Lalique figurine. In France, we have an expression, *Qui vole un oeuf, vole un boeuf.* It means 'One who steals an egg, steals an ox.' If someone is willing to commit even a small crime, it means they have the mindset."

Addie looked around. They were huddled far enough away that no one else was within earshot. Time to seize the opportunity. She lowered her voice and leaned in to speak. "We know you're being blackmailed, Veronique. If you talk to us, we won't repeat anything you share."

Veronique lit a cigarette and leaned back to blow a cloud of smoke into the air.

"We're not here to expose you," added Mimi. "We just want to identify the murderer so the rest of us don't have to spend whatever time we have left on this planet disentangling ourselves from this mess."

"I told you I would not lie," said Veronique, looking to Mimi. "What do you want to know?"

"Why were you being blackmailed?"

She paused to take another drag. "That is a long story."

"Well, we're not going anywhere."

TWENTY

Étienne

A stream of smoke escaped Veronique's nostrils as she began to speak. "My husband, Étienne, was, rather conveniently for me, a chemist. He had access to many things in his company's laboratory that were useful when I began to dabble in the artistry of perfume. He would bring home various ingredients and compounds for me to work with." She paused. "Until one day he came home acting differently. My scents had taken off. They had gotten a . . . how do you call it . . . a cult following. They were becoming commercially successful. And he did not seem to like that."

"What happened? Did he sabotage your products?" asked Mimi, intrigued.

"No, worse. He began copying my most successful formulas and selling them on the black market. They were 'smell-alikes.'" Veronique shook her head in disgust at the memory of it. "Such a betrayal."

Addie nodded in understanding.

"We were not compatible. He was completely absorbed in his research and had no instruction book on how to deal with the creative spirit that lived within me. We should never have married, but who makes good decisions when one is young and does not understand the consequences?"

The three women fell silent. A row of candles lined the window ledge, illuminating the hypnotic swirl of white flakes outside.

"Addie's been dealing with a similar situation," said Mimi.

Addie bit her lip. She looked at Mimi. Volunteering her personal business wasn't appreciated, but it was a smart choice. She was building a rapport with Veronique, getting her to open up.

"Oh, I am sorry to learn of this," said Veronique sympathetically. "Were there any early signs your husband might be deceiving you?"

Addie cleared her throat. "Fiancé. Yes, there were a few clues. I've played them over and over in my head so many times now." She stopped. Her eyes instinctively flitted to Mimi, expecting to see judgment or *I told you so* staring back at her. But there was something else behind her eyes. What was it? *Softness? Strength? Empathy?* Mimi seemed to be telegraphing all of those things. It was a relief. Addie breathed in a deep lungful of air and continued: "The thing that really sticks out is how I always led the discussions about our future. He was probably plotting how to leave me for a while before he pulled the plug. Then he sold the game we created together and cut me out of the deal. I'm angry at myself that I couldn't see it coming." She paused, willing herself not to get emotional. "Game design is supposed to be about predicting how people think. What does that say about me?"

"We sure argued a lot about him," sighed Mimi. "I never liked him. He had a huge ego."

"Ah," said Veronique. "Perhaps it was your not liking him that pushed Addie further into his arms."

Mimi winced.

Addie decided to shift the conversation back to Veronique. "So what happened with Étienne?"

"I was blind with rage. He was allowing these criminals to not only simulate my scents but fill them with toxins and other chemicals. So, one day I filled his cologne with a toxin." She took a long drag, and the rest of her sentence came out in a cloud of smoke. "And he was no longer a problem for me."

Mimi's eyes widened at the admission. She met Addie's gaze.

"How did the blackmail start, then?" Addie continued gently. "How did they know what you did?"

"No mystery there. Jane and Matthew came to visit me when I was developing her scent wardrobe. The three of us ate and drank our way through Paris. After so many hours of conversation, believe me, there wasn't much we didn't know about each other. It was stupid of me to tell them, but they had this way of getting you to open up and talk about anything." Her face tightened. "Maybe they decided to blackmail me together. I don't really know. We stopped speaking after I started receiving the letters. I only came here this weekend because I had to buy that ridiculous bird painting."

"What did you think of Matthew?"

"He reminded me of Étienne." The leaves of a plant rustled behind Veronique as she turned to Addie. "Why don't you create another game? Make it a wild success and rub it in his face? I would recommend taking this route, and not the one I took."

Addie looked down. "I don't know. He always positioned himself as 'the brains' of our operation. I was just 'the creative one.' Sometimes I believe it. He's taken the joy out of game design for me."

"No, no," said Veronique. "Never let a man take your passion from you." She took a moment to look each of them in the eye, smiled faintly, and walked away.

"I can't decide what to think about her," said Addie thoughtfully.

Mimi nodded. "The French are always difficult to read."

"Why do you think she's being so forthcoming? No one else has been this helpful."

Mimi thought for a moment, then nodded. "It might have something to do with the cigarettes."

"How do you mean?" Addie asked, confused.

Mimi shrugged. "Hard to put it into words. After I quit the first time, there was really only one thing I missed. Smoking creates a sense of connection. There's an unspoken intimacy among rebels."

Addie shook her head disapprovingly. "What happened to shared interests? Sense of humor? Kids at the same school?"

"You sound older than me." Mimi stubbed out her Pall Mall and brushed her hands together. "What's next?"

"Let's keep moving with the interviews. Woody's gone to his room. Now's our chance to finish talking to him. Feels like he's going to be our biggest boss battle."

Mimi stared at her blankly.

"A boss is a major opponent for players in a game. Getting past a boss is a challenge that gatekeeps the game's progression."

"Whatever you say, dear. Listen, I've had too many Gibsons. I need to go winky tink."

"Okay. Please be careful."

Mimi left, and Addie looked around. Most of the room had cleared out, with others deciding to go to bed as well. Barb and Gus were talking in hushed voices in the far corner. The mood felt sullen.

Addie took out her phone: 1:07 a.m. She rubbed her forehead. Suddenly she felt overwhelmed. There was so much to do. So many questions to ask. If only she could tell Brian she was in the middle of a real murder mystery. He would understand exactly how she was feeling. The strange mix of fear and excitement. She pulled up his number on her phone screen.

He'd certainly have a thought or two as to who did it. Her finger hovered over the call icon. It was late, but he was a night owl. She only wanted to hear the familiar deep bass of his voice for a second. She hadn't heard that voice in three months. They could brainstorm different approaches to the investigation. Just like in the early days of *Murderscape*, when they spent hours theory-crafting new mysteries and all the different paths players could take to solve them.

But what would she even say if he picked up? *Hey, it's me. I'm taking a momentary break from hating you because I'm caught up in the middle of a double homicide, and I need you to help me solve it.*

Actually, he'd probably love that. Impulsively, she hit the call button.

Two rings. She grew anxious as the third ring passed and still no answer.

Voicemail. *This user's mailbox is full.* She groaned and hung up. Probably full from all the congratulatory messages on the deal. Now he had her missed-call notification to feel smug about too.

"Ready for our boss battle, dear?" said Mimi, returning from the bathroom.

She avoided eye contact, knowing Mimi would be disappointed in her for calling Brian. Nodding, she put her phone away. "Let's go."

TWENTY-ONE

Bloody Mary

Outside his door, Woody had dumped a tray full of half-eaten food, as if he were staying at a hotel. An ashtray overflowing with cigarette butts rested atop the pile of dishes.

Mimi shook her head in disgust as Addie knocked on the door.

Almost instantly, he opened it and stood with folded arms in the doorway. "Well, if it isn't Harriet the Spy and Angela Lansbury."

"Hey, Woody," said Addie. "We just wanted to finish our conversation."

He waved them in. "Be my guest."

They entered a small bedroom with a fireplace at one end and a window overlooking the hedge maze at the other. Wax dripped from several candles lining the mantel. The place was in disarray. A broken crystal vase lay in pieces on the floor in one corner. The bed was unmade and clothes were strewn everywhere.

"Jessica Fletcher," said Addie.

Woody frowned. "What?"

"You said 'Harriet the Spy,' a comparison that I personally find flattering. But Angela Lansbury is a real person. You should use her character name, otherwise your little joke doesn't work."

He took a seat in an armchair by the window and shook a cigarette from a pack of Marlboros. "I tried not to overthink it," he said, placing it between his lips and lighting up. "I was just working with the vast age difference."

Mimi bristled.

"Well, I did put a *little* thought into it," he continued. "You see, Harriet is precocious, clever. Jessica . . . not so much. She's just a pudding-faced curtain-twitcher with yellow teeth."

"You really know how to sprinkle a little insult on top of injury, don't you, Woody?"

Addie cut in. "You were going to tell us something earlier. In the lounge. You said you noticed something strange?"

Woody's face twisted into a snarl. "Yeah. Just that somebody stole my damn cuff links."

Mimi cocked her head. "Are you sure you didn't simply misplace them?"

"Who are you, my mother? I would never lose them. They're my diamond saxophone cuff links. Each little key is a diamond. I showed them off at one point and told everyone the story of how my mentor gave them to me. Set them down on a table to roll up my sleeves. Shortly after that, they were gone."

"Hmm," said Addie, exchanging a look with Mimi. "We'll keep a lookout for them."

Mimi scanned the room as Addie spoke. Her eyes fell on the broken crystal vase. Some of the pieces had been picked up off the floor and were lying on the night table by the bed. Woody caught her eye as he blew smoke out of the side of his mouth.

"I think it was a Baccarat," he said. "Shame."

"When did that happen?" asked Mimi.

He tapped the ash directly onto the floor and gave them a condescending smile. "Before the party started. I was getting ready and bumped into it coming out of the shower." He ran his long fingers through his hair and stared down at the shards.

"Expensive accident, huh?" said Mimi.

A flicker of amusement danced across Woody's face. "Anyway, to answer Harriet the Spy's question, I remember Jane acting a little funny before she went off to bed. Odd for our host to go to bed early at her own party, don't you think? Kinda put the kibosh on the whole anticlimactic shebang."

"And what time would you approximate this was?"

"She said good night to everyone right after nine p.m. I remember because I looked at my phone to check the time and realized I was going to need to go up to my room to plug it in for a charge. Unfortunately, I didn't get the chance before the power blew, and now the damn thing's almost out of battery."

"What is it with everyone and their phones? It's like you've lost a limb," said Mimi, shaking her head. "This is why I still have a landline."

"*Landline?*" Woody laughed. "You know, you should try to be less judgmental. It makes you seem old and pickled, like those onions in your drinks."

Addie looked to Mimi and said *Don't provoke him* with her eyes, then turned back to Woody.

"Did you notice anything else? Anything out of the ordinary?"

Woody knitted his brow. "There was something, yes."

Addie and Mimi both leaned forward intently.

He took a deep drag of his cigarette, his cheeks concave. "What's in it for me if I tell you?"

Addie's shoulders slumped. "Helping us solve a double murder. That's what's in it for you."

Woody let the smoke escape from his mouth.

"Doesn't the fact that two people have been murdered bother you at all?"

"It's certainly an inconvenience. Just like this storm."

Lost in thought, Mimi scrutinized Woody, sprawled in the chair with his tiresome *To hell with all of you* attitude radiating from every pore. *What was it about this guy that got under her skin?* In spite of his obvious talents, he was cloaked in anger and bitterness. She didn't like him one bit. But she understood him. Something bad had happened to him in his past to make him this way. He probably wasn't rotten to the core, but whatever good was left in him was buried way down deep. Unlikely that it could be brought back up to the surface now.

Addie pivoted away from Woody, tapping her cheek in thought. "I have something else I want to discuss. It's not about the murders." She turned and walked back toward him, stopping directly in front of his chair. "You might have noticed I'm a pop culture buff."

Woody nodded. "It seems to be your only point of reference for anything. Don't you have any hobbies?"

"The man has a point," said Mimi under her breath.

Addie shot Mimi a sharp look, then continued: "I recognize you."

His facial expression didn't change.

Addie smiled knowingly and folded her arms. "C'mon, Woody. *Bloody Mary*? I've seen every episode."

"I don't know what you mean," he responded flatly.

Addie raised her eyebrows and continued, nodding. "Well, we don't have to talk about it if you don't want to. But I don't know why you wouldn't be proud. In seventh grade, I had a T-shirt that said *That sucks!*"

Woody stretched his legs out, crossing one ankle over the other.

"I particularly loved the penultimate episode, the one with Skeet Ulrich. I recorded it on my VCR and rewatched it so many times the tape wore out. Your performance was—"

Woody held up his hand. "Enough." He took in a deep breath. "Skeet Ulrich," he grumbled, shaking his head. "I always got compared to that guy. They called him the poor man's Johnny Depp. What does that make me?"

"The utterly destitute man's Johnny Depp?" suggested Mimi.

Woody sneered at her.

"Look, Woody, we're not here to expose you," continued Addie. "For whatever reason, you don't want people to know you're Aero Hart. Fine. We'll keep your identity secret. We just want to know what you observed."

"Changing my name doesn't make me a killer."

"Okay, if you're not the killer, then tell us what you remember."

Woody leaned back in his chair. "I heard a strange noise a little while ago, before I went down to the lounge for the late-night snack. About 10:45, or maybe a little later."

"What kind of noise?"

"It was a clunk. Like maybe some metal hitting another piece of metal."

Mimi furrowed her brow. "Wouldn't that be more of a clang?"

Addie shot Mimi a look. *Cut it out.* "Please continue, Woody. Where do you think the sound was coming from?"

"It sounded like it was coming from the direction of my bathroom. I don't know, it could have just been the plumbing. This place is so old," he said, looking directly at Mimi. "Things that are old can be fussy and inconvenient."

"Anything else?" continued Addie. "If you help us, maybe we can help you find your cuff links."

Woody shrugged. "I do have one final little nugget for you. Matthew was two-timing Jane. With Lillian."

"These people make a Greek tragedy look like a Hallmark movie," said Mimi, shaking her head. "Wasn't Lillian her image consultant or life guru or whatever-you-call-it? Did Jane know?"

"Last I asked, she was still working for Jane. But Jane had a feeling that Lillian had started offering her 'services,' so to speak, to Matthew as well." Woody took a swig of water with an audible gulp. "They've been off and on for the last year, as far as I know. All the while, Matthew is supposedly getting engaged to Jane. And divorcing her daughter. That's not even a love triangle, that's a love . . ."

"Shitstorm," said Mimi.

"Look into Lillian's past. She's got all kinds of reasons to kill someone." He reached for his phone. "My phone is about to die, but because I'm such a nice guy, I'll use the last of my battery to show you this." He pulled up an Instagram post and showed them his phone. "It's from Lillian to her 7,561 followers, announcing her divorce from her husband."

The post was simple white text over a black background: *Today we are announcing our decision to separate. This 18-month union was not a failure. Our hearts remain joyous and full. The truth is that we've each met someone whose astrological profile is more perfectly aligned to our individual romantic needs. In this process of letting go, we have come to believe that there is still something very special here between us. Our love for one another will endure forever.*

Mimi shook her head. "Can't anyone just get divorced and say good riddance anymore?"

"But why would Lillian kill Matthew?" asked Addie.

"Jealousy. Revenge. Who knows? Maybe he dumped her again."

Mimi squared her shoulders and crossed her arms. "Wait a minute. How do you know all this?"

He took a long drag on his cigarette. "He's dead now, so I guess it doesn't matter so much if I tell you. I was a fixer. For Matthew. It's a complicated line of work and I don't like to talk about it, so I'm just going to leave it at that."

"What does being a fixer have to do with Lillian?" asked Addie.

"She needed to be . . . fixed," he said, shrugging, "Pardon the expression. She was having some problems with her past. Reputational stuff. Bankruptcy. Bad credit. Rap sheet from a little embezzlement scam she was running at her last job. I helped her out for a short time because Matthew asked me to. He was covering the fees and making sure that I did everything perfectly, so I figured he must be having an affair with her." He paused to take a drag. "I didn't like working with her, though. She had a lot of opinions."

"That must have been terribly inconvenient for you, Woody," said Mimi. "You know, we can vote now too."

"Lillian seems to be clean nowadays, though," said Addie. "Her life coaching business is going well."

Woody snorted. "Anyone can reinvent themselves as a life coach. The other 'life coach' I know? Did eight years at San Quentin."

"Do you know any of the other guests here tonight?"

"No," said Woody. "Strange group of people, if you ask me."

"We just have one more question for you," continued Addie. "What do you know about the blackmail scheme that Jane and Matthew were running?"

Woody began a snicker that turned into a smoker's coughing fit. "Is this some kind of joke? *Blackmail scheme?*" He paused to finish wheezing and catch his breath. "What are you even talking about? I think I'll try to find my cuff links on my own."

Addie sighed and looked to Mimi. "Let's go."

"Talk to Lillian. She's your killer," he said, giving them a condescending little wave as he led them to the door. "Bye, Harriet. Bye, Jessica."

They walked back down the corridor together in silence.

Addie shook her head. "Woody's a griefer. A player who intentionally provokes other players. He's messing with us. I need more time to look at the ledger." She ran her finger down the list of suspects and made an asterisk by Woody's name. "We're just mashing the buttons with him."

Mimi shifted her carryall to the other shoulder.

Sensing her irritation, Addie looked over at her. "Listen, I'll make you a deal. I'll cut down on the gamer jargon if you cut down on the Pall Malls."

Mimi didn't respond. She seemed far away, lost in thought. "Mimi?"

"Do you really think my teeth look yellow?"

TWENTY-TWO

Reading People

Mimi splashed her face with cold tap water and examined herself in the bathroom mirror. Her eyes were bloodshot from a few broken capillaries, and her skin looked dull and weary. Perhaps Addie was right. Maybe she did need to cut down on her vices.

"There's so much in this ledger, Mimi," said Addie, calling out from the bedroom. "I also realized something else—"

"Can you hold on a minute, dear?" said Mimi, looking around the antiquated bathroom. It was making her feel old and outdated too. Her stamina had always been a source of pride, but the evening's tribulations were wearing her down. Barb had lit a trio of scented candles along the counter. She lifted one, feeling its warmth on her fingertips, and read the label. *Moonflower by V. This otherworldly combination of marigold and gardenia will send you on a lunar mission up through a shimmering sky of flowers and then right back down to earth with a base note of grounding oakmoss.*

She set it down and looked around, noticing another bunch of *Wine Down* magazines in a leather storage basket by the toilet.

The worry started in again. *Would they ever make it out of here? Let alone to Ryba's for fudge and the Big Talk?* Her jaw tightened.

"Can you come out here?" Addie called through the half-open door. "I think I have something."

Mimi emerged from the bathroom, smoothing lotion all over her hands and forearms. "Okay. But after this we need to sleep for a *little* bit."

"All right. Listen, Gus said there are secret passages. Plural," said Addie excitedly, sitting up in bed with papers strewn around her. "Remember the front elevation of the house I found in the speakeasy? I took some notes on it. On the second floor, there's seven windows on the east side of the house, where Jane's bedroom is, and six on the west side. But when we walked around earlier, I could only count six windows on the east side. So, I'm thinking another passage must be adjacent to Jane's room."

She paused. Mimi suddenly looked stricken. She was hovering over the nightstand.

"What's wrong?"

Mimi did a double take. She frantically started opening and closing the nightstand drawers, then crouched on the floor and looked under the bed.

"My necklace," she said, holding her hand up to her throat. "It's gone."

"The emerald? You love that thing."

Mimi's eyes narrowed. "*That thing* is important to me."

Addie went quiet. Mimi's entire demeanor had shifted. "Is it possible you left it somewhere?"

"Huh?" said Mimi. She looked dazed. Her eyes were deep pools of worry.

"Let me help you look."

"No, I'm telling you it's gone," snapped Mimi, placing her hand on the tender part between her collarbones where the pendant usually rested. She walked over to the corner sitting area and sank down into a chair. "Someone's been in our room. I know I left it on the vanity when I was changing clothes earlier, because I didn't want it to catch on anything."

Addie embarked on a search of the room. She opened every drawer, prodded the duvet and pillows, and got down on her hands and knees to look under every piece of furniture in the room. The necklace was nowhere in sight.

She walked toward her grandmother and gently placed a hand on her shoulder. "We'll find it, Mimi. Your necklace is tangled up in this chain of events. Somehow, we'll unravel it all together."

"Metaphors are not your gift."

"Let's think about who could have done this. Maybe whoever's behind the murders could be planning to kill someone else and plant your necklace to try to frame you . . . again."

"You have a lovely way of offering comforting words to a wretched soul."

Addie went over to the bed and picked up the ledger. "Let's keep going, Mimi. We're onto something, I can feel it. The initials in here match up with all the guests tonight except for Woody. He's the only one not being blackmailed. He must be their number two."

Mimi heaved a deep sigh. "Why did Jane have to bring this mess to Mackinac? Our lives normally revolve around lilacs and fudge."

Addie plopped down on the bed. She tapped the pencil on the ledger while she thought.

"So, is Woody officially our prime suspect?" asked Mimi.

"Tough to say. We still haven't established a clear motive for him."

"Maybe he wanted to break away from Matthew's scheme and launch his own operation?"

"Yeah. Like a start-up for blackmail." Addie sat up resolutely. "Let's just play this out for a minute. Woody briefly stops playing the piano. He sneaks out of the ballroom and grabs the knife from the library. He's in decent shape. It would have been easy for him to run up the stairs to Jane's room. By then, she could have been fast asleep. He plunges the knife into her chest and checks her pulse, confirms she's dead. He smiles down at her cruelly. Then—"

"'Smiles down at her cruelly'?"

"I'm riffing. Making it into a story helps me think."

"I'm a fact-checker, Addie. If you want my help, let's focus on the facts instead of getting creative."

"Fine," she said defensively.

They fell silent as Addie went back to sifting through the pile of documents taken from Matthew's office.

"What about Alexandra? I can't stop thinking about her. How awful this whole situation must be. Are we sure she isn't somehow pulling the strings?" asked Addie. "What if she and Matthew never really separated? They could be a secret couple in cahoots. Like in *Death on the Nile*. Actually, that device is used in *Evil Under the Sun* too, now that I think about it."

"But . . . why? It just seems incomprehensible. To fake all that."

"For the inheritance? I don't know," said Addie, studying the Murderbook. "Is Alexandra here with us in disguise? Barb has those blunt-cut bangs. That helmet hair could easily be a wig."

"This isn't an episode of *Scooby-Doo*, dear," said Mimi. "Trust me, I've looked into her eyes. She's definitely an essential oil sales consultant."

Addie nodded. "You've always been good at reading people."

"Really?" said Mimi, taken by the thought. "You've never told me that before."

"It's true," said Addie, smiling. "You saw Brian's faults long before me."

As Addie went back to writing in the Murderbook, Mimi reflected on how indifferent and, yes, unkind she had been toward her granddaughter over the years. Addie was her only and her everything. *Why was she so hard on her? Why couldn't she be more*

*loving to this amazing young woman? Was she missing an essential
gene that was supposed to automatically kick in when she became
a grandmother?*

In waging the constant battle of Mimi Knows Best, she'd forgotten to see Addie for the brilliant, imaginative soul that she was. The silent promise she had made to Addie's parents on the day they died remained in effect: Mimi would continue to honor the hopes and dreams they—and she herself—had for Addie. She would not stop until her granddaughter found her place to shine. She could even be heading toward that remarkable life right now. If only they could claw their way out of this terrifying place.

"Is it possible Nelson Ireland had other heirs?" asked Addie, tracing a finger over the list of names. "There could be other Ireland offspring trying to get at the estate. I wouldn't rule out someone like Lillian. She seems like an NPC to me."

"NPC?" asked Mimi, blinking.

"Non-player character. It's a term for scripted characters in a game. You don't have real interactions with them. Lillian seems stiff, practiced."

"But if someone else is the rightful heir, why wouldn't they just come forward and make their claim? Why go to the trouble of flying to an island and killing Jane among a group of strangers?"

"Good point. Now that I think about it, Gus is kind of an NPC too. Always eager to say how busy and tired he is, jumps straight in with it whenever he has the chance. Like it's a prepared statement."

"Yeah, it gives me an uneasy feeling. Like when you order food in a restaurant, and it arrives in less than five minutes. Disconcerting."

Addie's gaze fell on the pile of papers she hadn't yet combed through.

Mimi turned to her. "You know, something else occurred to me."

"What's that?" Addie asked, looking up.

"The cellar stairs were old and worn, slippery. And that staircase was dark. It was hard to navigate if it was the first time you were going down them. But someone had very confident steps. It was Lillian. I heard her heels because she was wearing those ridiculous stilettos. It certainly wasn't the gait of someone who was descending those stairs for the first time."

"Very good, Mimi." Addie scribbled more notes in the Murderbook.

"I'm doing my best, dear." Mimi yawned. "What do you say we turn in?"

"Okay. What time is sunrise?"

"This time of year, about 7:30."

"Let's plan to get up at 5:30, then. Before everyone else, so we can search the house."

"No. It's too dangerous. The killer could be hiding around any corner."

Addie heaved a sigh. "I don't want to keep arguing about this. It's like a murdery *Groundhog Day*. Besides, if someone wanted to kill us, they would have done it by now. Right?"

"Dear, this is a dangerous situation. We're trapped inside a murder manor with no power. What happens when your phone dies? Then we'll have no access to the outside world."

"My phone is useless anyway, Mimi. Helicopters can't get here 'til the wind dies down, and the island police can't get here 'til the drawbridge comes down."

Mimi considered Addie's reasoning. "Can you at least explain to me what we're searching for that makes it worth leaving this place in body bags?"

"I want to find the secret passage by Jane's room," said Addie. "Although I don't trust myself to wake up that early without an alarm. I need to turn off my phone to preserve the battery."

Mimi tapped her head. "Not to worry, kiddo. I'm a Swiss watch up here. I can wake myself up. 5:30 it is."

"Seriously? I never knew that."

Mimi managed a smile. "Guess there's a lot of things you didn't know about me before tonight."

Addie lifted one of the chairs from the sitting area and placed it under the doorknob at an angle, just like she'd seen done in hundreds of scary movies. She looked at Mimi for approval.

"Not enough," said Mimi, nodding toward the vanity table.

Together, they lifted it and moved it across the room, placing it firmly against the chair and door as a makeshift barrier.

"That'll buy us thirty seconds or so," said Mimi, walking over to the heavy crystal decanter Barb had left in the room and placing it on the nightstand next to Addie. "Here you go."

"I don't want any whisky."

"For bludgeoning."

"Ah, thanks." Addie crawled into bed. "I'm worried, Mimi. The planted knife, your missing necklace . . . It's all so—"

"Let's get some sleep," said Mimi, busying herself with pounding and propping several pillows into position to elevate her head and torso. "Things will look better in the morning."

From the other side of the bed, lying on a single, flat pillow, Addie watched the shadows cast by the fireplace flicker and dance across the ceiling. Brian's face appeared in her mind. It stirred something different from the usual heartache this time. She thought of Veronique's words. *Never let a man take your passion from you.*

More than anything, she was worried for her grandmother. Unlike the orderly grids and lists in the Murderbook, her mind felt chaotic. A jumble of thoughts, clues, and theories swirled in her brain. As much as she wanted to turn everything over in her mind again, she was exhausted. She closed her eyes.

TWENTY-THREE

Inner Sanctum

Addie's grip tightened on the flashlight as they crept down the upstairs corridor that ran along the east wing of the house. It was just past 5:30 a.m., and the only sound was the wind whipping the trees outside. Only a few hours' sleep meant she was wired on pure adrenaline. Her mind felt gauzy. If she were on a mission in a game, she'd need a power-up right about now.

Mimi, by contrast, had sprung out of bed and gotten dressed faster than she had. Addie had always admired her grandmother's stamina, how her physical energy seemed to reflect her mental resolve. She hoped that she would have the same level of strength when she was Mimi's age.

"Mimi!" she whisper-shouted over her shoulder. "Are you still back there?"

"Yes. Pick up the pace!"

Farther down the corridor, shutters swung on their hinges and banged against the house. *Was this storm ever going to let up?*

"We're almost there!" Addie said, directing the flashlight toward the large archway ahead of them that led into Jane's bedroom. As they approached, Addie paused to reach into her clutch and pulled out a pair of yellow rubber gloves.

"Where did you get those?" asked Mimi.

Slipping them on, Addie gave her a playful smile. "I took them from the kitchen when we were doing the dishes. Key, please."

Mimi delved down into her trusty carryall and tugged on a zippered side pocket, producing the key. A rush of cold met them as they entered the room. Jane's body lay covered with a paisley sheet on the carved rosewood four-poster bed several feet away. They stopped for a few moments, taking in the scene once again.

There was a profound stillness in the room. Being in the presence of death seemed to mute all sound. A creeping feeling of finality cast a pall over Mimi. Wrapped up in her own worries, she had not considered the consequences of pulling Addie into this hell. Rigid, unforgiving guilt was settling into her bones. She squeezed the strap of her trusty carryall to ground herself.

Addie cast the flashlight's beam toward the bathroom. "Let's check in there."

They crossed the room and entered Jane's en suite. Gleaming white marble covered every surface. It was expansive and luxurious, with polished nickel fittings that contrasted with the antique fixtures of the other bathrooms in the house.

Mimi shook her head. "This place is a skating rink. It's a health hazard!"

"What's that about?" said Addie, pointing the flashlight at a bald mannequin head displayed on a mirrored dressing table.

"Oh dear," said Mimi. "Did Jane wear a wig?"

They tiptoed back into the bedroom and over to Jane's body. Addie took a deep breath for courage and pulled back the sheet. Jane was looking a bit wilted but surprisingly good, all things considered. Gently, Addie nudged her headpiece. It shifted to the side, exposing a bald area above her ear.

"Yep," said Mimi. "She's a Baldilocks all right."

Addie covered Jane back up with the sheet. "Maybe she had cancer, Mimi."

"It's possible. She did look very thin. Or could be alopecia."

"Last night she seemed ageless . . . immortal. Look at her now." Addie took in a breath. "I'm sad for her."

Mimi nodded. "I know what you mean. I don't know what to think anymore. This has all been so confusing."

"C'mon," said Addie, patting her on the shoulder. "Let's go try her closet."

Deep pile carpet squished beneath their feet once they entered the closet's expanse. The roving flashlight beam illuminated a treasure trove of designer clothes, bags, and shoes.

"Look at all this stuff," muttered Mimi. "Probably worth the gross national product of a small country."

Addie panned the light. It fell on a Botticelli-style nude fresco of Jane covering one of the walls. She gazed down at them knowingly, a smile hovering at the corners of her lips.

"Good grief," grumbled Mimi.

"Keep looking!"

"Her left nipple looks big enough to be a doorknob."

"Focus, Mimi."

They scanned the shelves. A large center island with various compartments. An elaborate shoe rack. Nothing seemed amiss.

"Look for something that doesn't belong. A hinge or a lever or something."

Mimi's gaze followed the wandering searchlight. "I don't see anything. What do we do now?"

"I don't know."

Suddenly, Mimi froze. Her eyes narrowed as she began to walk toward the shoe rack.

"What is it?"

Mimi pointed at a middle shelf on the rack. "Those. Look at those shoes."

Addie came up alongside her. "The sequined Louboutins?"

"No. Next to them. The beige mules."

Addie studied them. "Okay. So what?"

"Look at every other pair in here," said Mimi, gesturing to the rack. "Designer labels. 'Look at me' sky-high heels. That mule is not the shoe of Jane Ireland. That is the sensible block heel of a frump-adump."

Addie's eyes widened in realization as she turned to Mimi, impressed. She crouched down, placed her hand on one of the mules, and pulled. It didn't feel like a normal shoe; it was heavy and bolted to the shelf. She pulled harder, then pulled downward, and suddenly it snapped back like a lever.

There was a metallic ratcheting sound and then a single click, followed by a squeaking hinge as the shoe rack began to turn and open. It swiveled ninety degrees and stopped to reveal a large, two-story space behind it.

"C'mon!" said Addie.

They stepped carefully over the threshold and entered a room with an arched ceiling painted in rich hues of blue. Addie looked at the floor, which was covered in mosaic tiles. She directed the flashlight downward and realized the tiles were the periodic table of elements. *He. Ne. Ar.* The room appeared to be enclosed, with no other way in or out besides the shoe rack. On a small side wall to the right was a fringed-edge window shade with a beautifully restored gramophone sitting below it. Addie reached over and raised the shade just enough to confirm that it was the window she had seen in the drawing of the house.

Mimi was studying the bookcases that lined the walls. *Advanced Stargazing. A Cosmologist's Atlas of the Universe. Everything You Always Wanted to Know About Astrophysics But Were Afraid to Ask.* Occasional glamour shots of Jane were tucked in among the decor.

"It's hard to make sense of all this," said Mimi.

"I know," said Addie, reaching past a half-naked photo of Jane and picking up a book titled *Turning Back the Clock: The Possibility of Time Travel and Staying Young Forever.* "She was such a curious blend of narcissism and eccentricity. Like a Marie Antoinette and Howard Hughes . . . smoothie." Addie walked toward an antique rolltop desk in the corner of the room and gripped the handles. "Shall I?"

Mimi nodded. Addie pulled up on the rolltop to reveal a neat stack of papers, a Montblanc pen, and a crocodile-leather appointment book.

Addie examined the papers on the desk. "There are two handwritten letters here."

"Read them aloud."

Dear Woman Who Birthed Me,

My father, who was not my real father, kindly adopted me and gave me more love than you ever did. When I asked you why you couldn't show me more affection, you said my presence brought back too many bad memories of how you were forced to give up your dream career. What a load of guilt to put on your child.

When I fell in love with Matthew, you were happy to make me miserable then too. After we married, you, my mother (through DNA only), had an affair with him. Who DOES that? What mother competes with her daughter for the attention of other men? You told me it wasn't true and that I was imagining things. All the while you and Matthew were planning to move in together at the Mackinac estate.

I've been advised not to get a divorce, due to our lack of a prenup. It would be too messy, they say. Ironically, that was the only wise thing you ever said to me—to get a prenup. But I didn't trust your advice. So now I'm stuck in a sham marriage, to a man who is clearly a sociopath. Is this the kind of life you envisioned for your only child?

I won't waste another precious minute trying to figure out what a messed-up piece of work you really are. I never mattered. I was always just a tiny, insignificant star in the constellation of your much bigger universe.

I'm writing this final letter to you to ask you to please stop contacting me.

Alexandra

P.S. I hate you.

Mimi's eyebrows shot up. "I admire the straightforward way she expresses herself."

Addie picked up the other letter. The handwriting was elegant and fluid.

Dear Alexandra,

I hope, before you sever all communication with me, that you will read this final letter.

Motherhood was never in my plans. When I became pregnant, I lost my way. I lost my career. I lost my common sense. And you, beautiful Alexandra, were the aggrieved victim of this deplorable defect of mine. But I do love you. That's why I gave you the most beautiful name I could think of. A name meaning "from the heavens" because that was . . . and is . . . how I truly feel about you. It always broke my heart that you chose to

*go by your middle name. It seems, from the very
beginning, our stars did not align.*

*I will go to my grave full of regret for the way I
treated you. There is so much I've wanted to tell you
over the years, but the sharp sting of guilt has been too
painful. The most essential thing I must tell you now is*

Addie stopped.

"What? What's the final thing?"

"That's all there is. It cuts off."

"Oh, for criminy's sake," said Mimi. She tugged on Addie's arm. "Listen, we need to get out of here. I don't have a good feeling about this place."

Addie took the rest of the papers and the appointment book and gave them to Mimi, who slipped them into her carryall. She swept the flashlight around the room one more time, pausing the beam on a small rug in the corner of the room. "Wait, I think I see something."

Mimi sighed and raised her eyes to the ceiling.

Addie moved closer to it and focused the beam where the rug's corner was flipped up. She pulled it back farther to reveal a gap between the floorboards. "It's a trapdoor!" she said, getting down on her hands and knees. She put her ear up to the joint and ran her finger along the planks. "I don't hear anything. Maybe it's one of those panic rooms."

"Good," said Mimi. "I need a place to panic."

"There's a hasp," said Addie, releasing the latch, causing the trapdoor to swing down into the cavity below. They both peered down at a narrow spiral staircase descending into darkness. Addie directed the flashlight's beam around, but the curvature of the staircase made it impossible to tell how far down it went.

"I'm going down there. Can you stay up here and keep a lookout?"

Mimi swallowed. "No. I'm coming with you."

TWENTY-FOUR

Possibility Space

Blackness seemed to thicken around them as they descended the winding steps together.

"Hold on tight to the railing, Mimi!" Addie called back over her shoulder, noting the fearful tone in her own voice.

"Don't worry. I know you'll break my fall."

They maintained quiet footsteps for what seemed like a hundred stairs. Addie felt a tingling in her muscles, her senses coming alive. This was surreal, just like being in a game and unlocking a new area. The "possibility space" of the house kept increasing. Every discovery opened up new paths and choices. She had known there were secret passages in the house, but this one, wherever it went, meant the killer likely was able to access Jane's bedroom surreptitiously. Her feeling of pride in this finding was unmistakable. Something within her felt restored.

She thought of the oft-repeated mantra among her design team: *We don't dictate the experience, we just set the stage.* Brian used to tease her about it. He felt that any video game was ultimately a contest between designer and player. *Who was smarter?* But she saw it differently. A good game was about stimulating the hypothalamus of the player. Making them feel joy, pride, empowerment, victory, self-determination. She viewed players as participants and co-creators in the experience.

She hadn't gone anywhere near game design in months. Not since her last day at Closed Casket. Her day job in advertising had been key to keeping herself together as everything else in her life was falling apart. But now she felt the urge to get back to game design. To try it again.

Finally, they reached a stone floor and entered a room that smelled dank and earthy. The rustic brick walls were covered in framed photographs. The flashlight illuminated a sign above them that read *The Ireland Family Boozeum.*

Mimi shook her head. "There's a small part of me that wants to like Jane."

The beam lit up a section of polished wood floor that looked freshly waxed. As they crept closer and cast the light around, a bowling alley came into view. There were three lanes, along with a pair of leather booths next to shelves stocked with bowling balls and shoes.

Mimi peered into the darkness in the other direction, hoping her eyes would adjust. She could just make out the shapes of what looked like stacks of storage crates and wooden barrels lining the walls.

The flashlight began to flicker.

"Damn," said Addie, smacking it with her hand.

It flickered again, then went out. They were plunged into darkness.

"Oh my God. Give me your lighter!"

Mimi reached into her carryall and fumbled for her Dunhill. She rubbed her thumb along the etched *R* initial. "Don't lose it, please."

Addie flicked on the lighter and cast it toward a wall to their left. "I saw some candles over there, on the sconces."

They crept toward the wall and Addie pried two candles out of a fixture. She carefully lit each one, then handed a candle to Mimi.

Addie walked along the wall. It was hard to see with only the candles, so she flicked the lighter on again, illuminating a man's face.

A squeak escaped her lips. She regained her composure. It was only a photo. Black-and-white. The man was staring back at her like a ghost. He was wearing a three-piece suit and a fedora, holding a bottle of liquor. His arm was around the shoulders of a rotund man with a thick mustache.

Addie looked closer. It was captioned: *Al Capone with Philip Ireland, 1929.* "Mimi! Here's a picture of Nelson's grandfather with Al Capone!"

"Is this entire family one big crime syndicate?" Mimi huffed.

Addie made her way along the wall, studying the captions engraved on the gold-plated plaques beneath each framed photograph. She read one aloud: *"The secret passages in this house were used to smuggle rum and keep famous bootleggers and gangsters like Mr. Capone away from prying eyes. We have converted them into a museum dedicated to our family history and the Prohibition Era."*

They entered a winding hallway flanked by what looked to be a series of shadowy storage rooms filled with more barrels and crates. Addie paused to study one of the rooms more closely. From what she could see, everything was labeled *Growing Concern.* At the end of the hall, they reached a cavernous room. The air was stale, and it was plainly finished, but everything was clean. The walls were lined with vintage Temperance posters. *Dethrone King Alcohol. Please Vote Against the Sale of Liquors. Drinking Leads to Moral Degradation.*

"Wait. What's that?" said Addie, moving the lighter's flame closer to read the sign above a metal compartment: *"This dumbwaiter was used for moving firewood. However, its secondary use was for guests upstairs to hide their illegal drinks in case there was a raid during one of the family's legendary parties."*

Addie ducked her head down and crawled into the dumbwaiter.

It was a tight space, big enough to fit one normal-sized person, but certainly not two.

"What are you doing?"

Addie took hold of the cable. "I'll go up first, then send it back down for you, okay? I'll pull you up."

"Are you crazy? You don't know where this thing goes!"

"Mimi, it's a ride in 'this thing' or a journey back up all those stairs. You pick."

Mimi went quiet. "Fine. I've enjoyed knowing you."

Addie began pulling on the cable, hoisting herself upward until the dumbwaiter stopped in front of a dark space. She crawled out into it and pushed on a pair of wooden double doors that opened outward. Stepping onto the floor, she realized she was exiting a giant antique armoire in the anteroom adjacent to the ballroom. She turned around and looked closer. It was a large mahogany piece with the back removed that had been pushed against the wall. A perfectly convincing disguise.

Mimi's distant voice called out from down below. "Hello, re-member me?"

Addie crawled back inside the armoire and sent the dumbwaiter back on its downward journey. She called down into the shaft. "Hop in!"

She could hear Mimi grumbling as she blew out the candle and loaded herself in. The cable rattled in the shaft as Addie pulled on it and the dumbwaiter rose.

Mimi arrived and wriggled her way out of the armoire, stepping onto the parquet. "Seventy-seven-year-old bodies are not supposed to be doing what I am doing."

"Isn't this cool, though? Don't you feel like we're in *Indiana Jones* or *The Da Vinci Code* or something?"

"Yeah. It's exactly like that," said Mimi, brushing herself off.

"Mimi, we're getting closer to solving this, I can feel it. I went to this GDC keynote once—"

"GDC?"

"Game Developers Conference. Anyway, it was called 'Villains Are People Too.' The speaker was saying how you have to think of the villain as a whole, three-dimensional person with goals and motivations."

"And your point is . . . ?"

"That secret passage means the killer knew this house. Up until now, I was assuming it must be someone who simply hated Jane and Matthew because of the blackmail, but I think it's more complicated than that." She paused. "And rule one of *Murderscape* is: *Don't make assumptions.*"

Mimi straightened herself and adjusted her carryall. "Well, listen, we need to talk to Barb. She knows more than she's letting on."

"Why Barb?" asked Addie, furrowing her brow.

"The secret passages are all perfectly maintained. Not a speck of dust. You think Jane was going down there every day with her Dyson? Or running her feather duster along all those pristine bottles in the speakeasy?"

Addie smiled. "Good, Mimi. Look, I want to go back to the room. I need to finish going through all the documents and the ledger before everyone wakes up."

"Okay." Mimi tilted her watch toward a candle sconce on the wall. "I think we should divide and conquer. Barb told me she's an early riser and it's nearly 6:30. I'm going to have a coffee with her."

As they made their way up the stairs, they passed an ornately framed wall mirror. Addie slowed down to catch her reflection. Somehow, even though she was on very little sleep, she didn't look tired. Or like the dejected, left-behind person she had become over the last few months. Her skin was glowing and her cheeks were rosy. A part of her that Brian had stolen was now back.

TWENTY-FIVE

Driver's Ed

Barb's room was small and snug. She'd decorated it in her own version of shabby chic, with needlepoint pillows and distressed wood furniture. A kitchenette anchored one side, and an antique chest by the bed, covered with an array of flickering candles, gave the space an inviting glow.

"May I?" asked Mimi, gesturing toward a duck-egg-blue armchair.

"Please," said Barb with a warm smile. She was wearing a purple dressing gown that flowed behind her as she walked over to the sink and filled a kettle.

"Nice robe. Purple's my favorite color," said Mimi.

"Mine too. My mother used to say, 'Purple has pizzazz.'" She turned around to wink at Mimi. "Coffee? I have a French press."

"Yes, please."

"I love the first cup of the day," said Barb, setting the kettle on the gas stove.

"What a comfy spot," Mimi said as she sank deeper into the soft-cushioned seat. "I'm feeling as toasty as a marshmallow in here, Barb."

Barb scooped coffee grounds into the French press. "Thank you. I think I have an innate instinct for making spaces cozy."

"So, how are you doing?"

Barb's voice trembled. "It's just been so awful, hasn't it?"

Mimi took a tissue from her carryall and handed it to her.

"Thank you," said Barb, wiping her nose.

"Did you and Jane get along well?"

The kettle whistled.

"Jane was a real tightwad. She spent a lot of money on herself. But she didn't hire enough staff. Didn't pay us well. Bad tipper too. But all in all, she was okay. Matthew, now he was a creep." She poured the boiling water over the coffee grounds.

"You must have seen a lot around here."

"No . . . not really. They were cautious about how they presented their relationship publicly. Even though it was an open secret, he never escorted her upstairs to the bedroom. In fact, they slept in separate rooms."

Barb depressed the plunger and then poured the coffee into a pair of pink mugs that read *BABS* and handed one to Mimi.

"That your nickname?" said Mimi, indicating the mugs.

"No. It's my company name. Barb's Aroma Bliss Shop. Took a while to come up with that one. Acronyms are a real pain in the ass."

Mimi blew on her coffee and watched its surface ripple. "Can we go back to what you were doing before you found Jane?"

"Why are you so curious?" asked Barb, her tone changing. "How do I know you aren't the killer?"

Mimi squirmed. "Would you have invited me into your place for a cup of coffee if you really thought I was capable of killing anyone? Do I honestly seem dangerous to you?"

Barb considered the question. "Dangerous? Not really. I'd call you ill-tempered or testy. No offense, of course."

"None taken. Listen, I noticed Jane and Lillian seemed to be arguing in the ballroom. Do you know what that was about?"

She shook her head. "I don't. She seemed upset, yes. Kept saying she wanted to go to bed, which was so out of the ordinary for her. She could party with the best of them. I helped her upstairs, but she didn't want to brush her teeth or do her nightly skincare regimen, which was always an absolute religion with her. She just shooed me away."

"Did she say anything at all?"

"She said, 'Please leave.'" Barb's voice cracked. "That was the last time I saw her alive. I decided to go back downstairs, and I brushed against the bamboo plant in the hallway. The leaves had gotten too long and they kept hitting against me when I walked by, so I got a pair of scissors and gave them a quick trim. That's when I saw Lillian sneaking out of Jane's room—"

"Wait a minute," said Mimi, sitting up straight. "You saw Lillian leaving Jane's room right before you found her dead? Why didn't you say something sooner?"

Barb lifted the steaming mug to her lips. "I was too scared. Didn't want to say anything to anyone until the police arrived. But now, I mean, who knows . . . Feels like they're never going to get here. Feels like we're all stranded on some lost planet."

"Tell me exactly what you saw."

"It was strange. She was tiptoeing out of Jane's room, looking tense, so I waited. I didn't want to interrupt whatever was happening. Figured it was a business meeting of some kind. Or maybe a confrontation. I didn't know and I didn't want to know. 'The help' are supposed to be seen and not heard. That's what Matthew always said."

Mimi sniffed. "What a jerk."

Barb blinked and took a sip of her coffee.

"So, then what happened?"

"I headed back downstairs because there was so much work to do. But I couldn't shake the feeling that something was off. That's when I made the tea for Jane." Tears welled up in Barb's eyes. "It was chamomile. Her favorite."

Mimi handed her another tissue.

"Thank you," said Barb, dabbing at her eyes.

"Barb, if you don't mind my asking, how did you end up here on Mackinac, anyway?"

"Oh, well . . . I ran into a bit of a buzz saw about six years ago when I lived in Chicago. I was a driver's ed instructor. You would not believe how stressful that job was. Sitting for hours in a car, always ready to grab the steering wheel or pull the emergency brake. Students crashing into parking meters and pedestrians. It gave me migraines." She paused to reach for a plate. "Would you care for a snickerdoodle? They're my signature cookie. I make them with cardamom."

"I'd love one, thank you," said Mimi, accepting one and taking a crumbly bite.

"I don't mean to toot my own horn, but I was good at my job. Even received an award for heroism for pulling a student from a burning car after he ran over a barbecue grill."

"Quite laudable," said Mimi, popping the last bite of snickerdoodle into her mouth.

"But it all came to an end when I got pulled over at a traffic stop one day with a thermos of . . . Well, let's just say I'd added a little Baileys Irish Cream to my morning coffee."

"Oh no, so you lost your license?"

"Yes. And my job. A DUI is a career-ender in that industry. I lost my car too. It was too expensive to keep up with the payments." She refilled Mimi's coffee. "So, a few months later, I saw an advertisement for a housekeeper on Mackinac. Salary plus room and board. And I'd never have to worry about driving a car again."

Mimi nodded. She was still considering what Barb had said about Lillian coming from Jane's room. Something about that didn't click. She would have to ponder it later. "What were Jane and Matthew like as a couple?"

"They'd been fighting a lot lately. He had some debts. Wanted to rent out the house as a wedding venue. Start his own events business. Jane thought that was humiliating. It was tricky between them." She paused. "He thought she was stingy with her wealth, even though it seemed to me that he was having a great ride."

"So to speak," said Mimi, raising the mug to her lips. So many more questions she wanted to ask, but she had to prioritize. "What about the secret passages in the house? I overheard Gus talking about them. Are you sure you don't know where they are?"

Barb bit her lip and frowned. "What secret passages?"

Mimi watched her over the rim of the mug before taking another sip. "Never you mind, Barb. This has all been very helpful." She set the mug down. "Just one last question, and sorry if it's a bit delicate, but did you know anything about this blackmail scheme that Matthew and Jane were running?"

Barb sniffed and dabbed at her nose and eyes. "Blackmail? No, I don't know what you mean." She clasped the ring on her right hand and fidgeted with it, turning it around and around on her finger. Her face brightened. "Do you think I could interest you in my essential oils? One of my signature formulations? I've got your namesake. 'Rosemary for remembrance,' you ever heard that expression?" She reached into a pouch on the table next to her and produced a pair of glass tincture bottles.

"From *Hamlet*, I think," said Mimi, looking down at the dregs of her coffee.

"You know, a rosemary-and-fern blend would be nice for you."

"I didn't know fern had a scent."

"Oh, yes," said Barb. "I just completed level two of my

aromatherapy education. Soon I'll have my diploma. These oils, they're really something. They improve brain function and cardio-vascular health."

Mimi smiled at her. Barb didn't smile back. "You know what? Sure. Put me down for some."

"Great. I'll order you a case."

Mimi's eyes widened. "Okay, sure. A case then. Do you mind if I use your bathroom first? Sorry, small bladder."

Barb stiffened slightly. "Certainly."

The bathroom was another of the antique variety. A claw-foot tub stood in the center. Water dripped from the faucet into the sink, which was covered in a mess of face masks, cotton balls, and lotions. Mimi went to the linen closet and peered inside. Only folded-up towels and maid uniforms, all crisp and clean. She paused to think. Searching through a strange woman's bathroom was not something she had ever expected to find herself doing. But she wanted to make Addie proud.

Mimi's eyes went back to the countertop. Several cosmetics bags lay open with the contents spilling out. She peered inside one and saw the familiar orange plastic of a prescription pill bottle hidden underneath some makeup. Mimi extracted it. Vicodin. She rummaged around and found two more. Xanax. Klonopin. After putting the bottles back, she walked over to the toilet and flushed it, then briefly turned on the water in the sink.

When she came back into the room, Barb was looking out the window at the landscape, all blanketed in white.

"We aren't out of the woods with this storm yet, are we?" said Mimi.

Barb turned to her. There was a distant look in her eye. "Rosemary, I need to tell you something. Woody . . . he's a bad man. You need to be careful."

"What do you mean, exactly?"

"He's no fan of yours. He's been going around saying things.

Things like, 'I don't like that geriatric hound sniffing around my business.'"

Mimi shook her head and went to the door. "That guy's got a real problem with women, doesn't he? I'll watch my back. Say, Barb . . ."

Barb looked at her intently.

"You mentioned that Matthew didn't sleep in Jane's bedroom. Can you tell me where he slept?"

TWENTY-SIX

A Decision

Addie was seated on the floor with the ledger open in her lap and the documents from Matthew's office fanned out around her. Her mind was swirling. A pile of unopened envelopes, which she still needed to go through, lay to her right. She'd been poring over everything, hoping a clue might reveal itself and set them on the right path.

Mimi opened the door and shut it quietly behind her. "I got some good intel from Barb."

"Great," said Addie, perking up.

"She's got a pill habit that makes Sunny von Bülow look like Mr. Rogers, but she told me where Matthew slept. It's an attic loft at the far end of the house. Maybe we can do a quick search?"

Addie nodded excitedly. "Good, Mimi."

"There's definitely something going on there. We need to look at Barb closely."

"I don't know. Feels like a dead end to suspect Barb. She's had all kinds of opportunities to kill Jane and Matthew over the years, but she chooses to do it now, when we're stranded in a snowstorm with a house full of guests? It doesn't make any sense."

Mimi sat down. "You know, Addie, we have to be flexible. Learned that from years at the bridge table. You need to be ready to abandon your original thinking and adapt."

"Speaking of which, I've got a big Jim Towels–shaped bomb to drop on you. You're not going to believe it."

"What's that?"

"He's been laundering money. Towels Print Shop is a shell company."

"Towels? Shut the front door!"

"I know he doesn't seem capable, but look at this." Addie held up a piece of paper. "Matthew bought the shop from him. And there's a whole section of writing at the back of the ledger that's just about Jim. Money he's been paying Matthew, but also huge amounts of money he's been taking in. There's some tax paperwork in here too. It all looks really detailed and . . . carefully executed. Like Jim knows what he was doing. We definitely need to talk to him again. He respects you, Mimi. He might crack if we press him."

Mimi pointed to the items on the floor. "I see there's an issue of *Wine Down* magazine in there."

Addie nodded. "Yeah. I haven't had a chance to look at it yet. Not sure if it's anything."

Mimi paused thoughtfully. "There's stacks and stacks of those magazines all over this house. Why would Matthew hide away that one particular issue?"

"Hmm. I see your point." Addie picked up the crocodile-leather appointment book and leafed through its pages. "By the way, I've been looking through Jane's social commitments over the last year, and Kimiko is everywhere."

"Kimiko? Really? Doesn't she live in Japan?"

"Yes, but as recently as six months ago, they were hanging out all the time. Looks as though they were best friends." Addie held out her hand like a surgeon awaiting a scalpel. "Can I have the Murderbook, please?"

Mimi retrieved it and handed it to her, along with the Faber-Castell No. 2 pencil.

Addie referred to the suspect list. "We should try Kimiko next, now that it's a decent hour."

"Okay," said Mimi.

Addie went back to the Murderbook. A few moments of silence passed. The only sound in the room was her pencil scratching notes onto the paper. "I can't stop thinking about Woody."

Mimi raised an eyebrow. "I don't envy you."

"We need to crack him somehow."

"Dear, if this was your murder game, how would you guide players toward the solution?"

Addie sighed. A feeling of uneasiness stirred in her. "I don't know, Mimi." She jotted down a few more notes in the Murderbook. Suddenly, the pencil snapped. She groaned as she looked into the hollow end of the tip. The lead had broken off and the wood was splintered. She showed it to Mimi. "Don't suppose you have a sharpener?" she asked sheepishly.

Mimi shook her head. "Nope. Pencils are only useful for keeping score at bridge." She dug into her carryall and rose to her feet. Taking Addie's hand by the wrist, she placed her *Chicago Gazette* pen firmly into her palm. "Your thoughts will flow better with this. Trust those instincts of yours."

Addie stared down at the pen for a moment, feeling the substantial weight of its metal in her hand. She swept a wisp of hair out of her eyes. Maybe Mimi was right. *Perhaps it was time to start trusting herself.* She looked up. "Let's go talk to Kimiko."

"Okay. But I want to check something first."

TWENTY-SEVEN

Lies Lead to the Truth

C an you stand over there?" said Mimi, pointing off to her right, down the corridor leading to Jane's bedroom.

"Where?"

"By the bamboo palm," instructed Mimi, frowning in concentration.

Addie dutifully walked over to the spot Mimi indicated.

Mimi's frown intensified as she motioned for Addie to move a few inches back. "All right, good. Stay there. You're Barb, okay? Pretend to be . . . Barb-like."

Addie hesitated, then bent her knees and squatted down about a foot shorter to "Barb height." She pantomimed moving a feather duster across one of the paintings and watched as Mimi paced the length of the hallway.

Mimi approached, then walked around her in a circle and stood behind her. "Hmm," she said, unsatisfied with her reconstruction. "Very strange."

Addie rolled her eyes. "Mimi, if you're going to force me to be Marcel Marceau over here, can you at least clue me in on what you're thinking?"

"Sure," she said, walking back to where she was standing before. "This vantage point is where Barb told me she was standing when she saw Lillian leave Jane's room, but the angle formed by that wall and that pillar over there," she said, pointing at them, "makes it impossible to see Jane's door. Even if I move over here," she explained, moving a few feet to the side, "and I crouch down to trim a few leaves off this plant like Barb says she did, that pillar blocks the view to the entryway."

"Interesting. As Poirot says, 'Lies lead to the truth.'"

"She was a natural. Offered lots of detail," said Mimi, shaking her head.

"When lies are specific, they're more convincing."

"That another one of your Poirot insights?"

"Nope. That one's all mine."

Mimi turned in the direction of the staircase. "Kimiko's this way. Barb said she got the biggest room, at the end of the upstairs hall."

They climbed the stairs and arrived at Kimiko's door. Mimi knocked. The door swung open and Kimiko stood there, wrapped in a terrycloth robe. Her face was stern as she adjusted the pink glasses on her nose.

Addie took in a breath. "Hi, Kimiko. Sorry, I know it's a bit early. We just—"

Blam. Kimiko slammed the door in their faces.

Mimi turned to Addie. "I wondered when that might happen."

They turned around and walked back down the hall.

"Who else haven't we talked to yet?"

"Sebastián," said Addie.

They walked to the other end of the hall and approached his door.

"Who's taking the lead on this one?"

Addie shrugged. "Double act?"

They knocked. There was a pause, then the sound of rapid footsteps. Sebastián opened it and smiled at them. Wearing a black silk kimono, he raked his fingers through his damp hair. "Just got out of the shower, ladies. Come in."

They entered a sumptuous room decorated with silk damask wallpaper and buttoned furniture.

"The water heater in this place must run on gas, thank goodness. Make yourselves comfortable." He gestured to a small sitting area. The table displayed a crystal bowl stuffed with yellow roses and an unopened box of chocolate truffles.

"Looks like you got the presidential suite," said Mimi, leaning over to peek at his bathroom. "Ah, but still have the antiquated bathroom, I see."

Addie walked over to a dresser, which was lined with a variety of glass cosmetic bottles. All different shapes, sizes, and colors. Each one featured an elegant label that read *Silva*.

"What are these?" asked Addie.

He rubbed the back of his neck. "They're prototypes. It's for my new men's grooming line, Silva."

Addie raised her eyebrows. "When did you start that?"

"Still in early stages," he said, smiling. "I know every celebrity seems to be an 'entrepreneur' these days, but it's a serious endeavor for me. It's an homage to my late grandfather Alfonso Silva."

"How wonderful that you had such a loving relationship with your grandfather," said Mimi, looking to Addie. "Family is everything."

Addie smiled, nodding in agreement.

"He came from a time when how you presented yourself was a mark of your social status. He passed his grooming rituals down to me like stories. How to shave, how to dress, how to smell."

"The bottles are so unique," said Addie. "I love the design."

"They're inspired by his buildings," he explained, leaning on the dresser. "He was an architect in Argentina. His designs were very modern. People called them blocky, ugly. Historians say he was too progressive for his time. He was a maverick, a genius who influenced many of the greats, like Le Corbusier. Now his name has been lost to obscurity."

Addie fiddled with the sleeve of Jane's sweater. "Making games is kind of like architecture. You're in total control, but at the same time, you want the player to experience the space like it's fully their own."

He smiled so wide his eyelids crinkled. "I love video games. I play *Minecraft* with my daughter. It helps us stay close. She's back in Argentina with her mother."

Addie's face brightened. "I used to love *Minecraft.* I once spent weeks building a mega-base. It was a castle that had a moat with a drawbridge just like the one here. Had no idea I'd ever have to deal with one in real life."

He laughed gently, and they made eye contact.

"How old is she?"

"Eleven. Fernanda. Well, *Fernandita* is what I call her."

Addie smiled. "So many people think games are just for geeks playing alone in their basements. But they don't understand the social aspect of it."

"We really enjoyed watching the *Godfather* reunion special to-gether," Mimi chimed in.

"Thank you. It was my honor to host it. Things are on an upswing for me these days. It feels like there's even better things to come."

Sebastián moved to the center of the room and began a series of slow, graceful movements. Mimi watched him, confused.

"Tai Chi. It resets the mind," he said with a deep inhale. "Helps me deal with stress."

"Do you experience a lot of stress?" asked Mimi.

"Yes, I do, unfortunately," he said, outstretching his arms and lunging one leg forward. "I like the noncompetitive aspect of Tai Chi. But I work out seven days a week too. Part of the job."

"The television business must be cutthroat."

"It is," he said, with a barely perceptible shake of his head.

"Sebastián," said Mimi, catching Addie's eye, "did you notice anything that seemed out of the ordinary last night?"

He considered the question. "Jane seemed *really* drunk. I was a bit worried about her, but I also didn't want to embarrass her, so I just kept an eye out."

"Anything else stick out in your memory?"

He made a graceful motion with his arms. "Yes, I thought Lillian was acting strange."

"How so?"

"She kept leaving the ballroom and coming back all night. It was odd, given the auction was the main event. She seemed . . . I don't know, nervous."

"Do you two know each other?" asked Addie.

"Yes. She and my agent share some clients."

"Are you one of her clients?"

Sebastián laughed. "No. I don't need her services. But we sometimes cross paths. At parties and premieres."

"We're trying to create a timeline for last night's events, and we just wondered if you remember what you were doing from 9:00 to 9:15, during the auction."

The windowpanes shook as the wind moaned outside.

He continued his movements. "Well, I spent a while talking to Kimiko. I'm a big fan. She was sitting up on that stage for so long, not talking to anyone. Felt bad for her. Honestly, I was hoping to find out what film adaptations she has going on. See if there was a part for me. But she was kind of standoffish."

"So you act as well? I don't think I knew that," said Addie.

"Oh, yes. Hosting is my wife, but acting is my mistress."

Mimi rolled her eyes. "Do you remember anything else from the 9:00-to-9:15 time window?"

"I was chatting with Lillian for a bit. Also Veronique. She's been advising me on which incense to use for one of my Silva formulas. Then Jane went up to bed." He paused his movements and looked at them impishly. "Let's check the weather, shall we?" He disappeared into the walk-in closet and emerged with an old-fashioned radio. "Gus found it. Said I could have it."

"I have one of those at home too," said Mimi, turning to Addie. "Power outages are all too common here. That's why I keep my landline."

Addie shook her head. "You and the landline."

Sebastián set the radio down on the table in front of them and turned the dial. The signal crackled and then cleared.

"This snowstorm continues to clobber the region unabated. It's now officially been classed as a bomb cyclone. The National Weather Service's high-wind warning is still in effect. Travel is not recommended."

"Guess it's nice to know there's still an outside world," said Addie.

"Doesn't have your presenting skills, does he?" added Mimi.

Sebastián smiled, his cheeks and tips of his ears blushing.

Addie noted how his demeanor had softened. Perhaps the arrogance she'd detected earlier was a misread on her part. "Do you remember where Matthew was between 9:00 and 9:15?"

"He was up onstage."

"And where were you when you heard Gus scream in the cellar?"

Mimi thought she caught a flicker of interest on his face.

"I was helping Barb get firewood from a storage room. And at one point my agent called, so I took that."

"What did your agent want?" asked Mimi. "Isn't it a bit strange to call you on a Saturday night?"

"Ha," said Sebastián. "Clearly you don't work with agents. He wanted to tell me that Coppola is planning his next film. He liked me at the reunion special, so he wanted to give me a chance to read for a part."

"That must be exciting for you."

Sebastián smiled. "Would be a dream come true for me. But I don't want to jinx it."

Mimi cleared her throat. "Can I ask you, how did you know Jane, anyway?"

He averted his eyes. "We have the same agent."

"Why did Jane have an agent?"

"She occasionally appeared as herself on TV shows. A cameo as a socialite. Or a 'celebutante,' as they call them now."

They shared a smile. "What about Matthew? Did you know him well?"

His smile faltered. "No. The guy creeped me out, honestly."

"By the way, Sebastián," redirected Mimi, "did you hear any strange noises last night?"

He thought for a moment. "Don't think so."

"You didn't hear a clunk sound of any kind?"

His brow creased. "You mean like a thump?"

Mimi threw her hands up. "Thump, bump, clunk—take your pick."

The dining room gong sounded.

"Now I heard that," he said with a smile.

"Must be breakfast," said Addie. "Listen, Sebastián, we'll let you go. But could we ask you one final question? It's a bit delicate."

"Okay," he said as he walked over to the nightstand and poured a glass of water from a carafe.

"It's about the blackmail," said Mimi. "We know Jane and Matthew were extorting money from you."

He paused and looked down into the glass.

"Can you tell us why you were making the payments?"

His eyes fastened on them. "Listen, I'm a public figure. I can't tell you my personal business."

"That's just the thing, though, Sebastián," continued Mimi. "These days, rumors are enough to bring any celebrity down. Do you really want to be associated with this debacle? Help us and we can help clear your name."

Suddenly he appeared agitated. "Let's just say there are some things in my past that happened that I don't want made public, okay? I'm not proud of them." He drained the glass of water. "I paid the blackmail, but I'm not a killer."

"Listen, Sebastián," said Addie softly. "We know that you've been taking and making a lot of payments for quite some time. Tell us what you know, and we'll go."

He blinked. "Someone found out a secret about me. Something private and . . . embarrassing. They agreed not to expose me if I gave them the secrets I know about in return. Given what I do, I come across a lot of those. Between who my friends are dating and my agent's assistant liking to gossip with me, I have more than enough to trade on."

Addie nodded in understanding. Suddenly, she felt self-conscious. The connection they'd formed just moments ago over *Minecraft* was now nonexistent. His tone was icy and distant. In a way, he was just like Brian. Capable of shifting his entire personality based on what he needed in the moment.

"Can you tell us what the blackmailer has on you?" continued Mimi.

"Sorry, but anything I tell you could end up on Instagram. I don't need some silly scandal coming out that kills my chance at the Coppola movie. I'm launching my business soon. I'm close to hitting the next level." He walked toward the door and opened it for them. "If that's all?" he said, in a tone that clearly wasn't a question.

TWENTY-EIGHT

Breakfast

Through the large bay window in the dining room, they could see the trees swaying back and forth. Droplets of snow had frozen and mottled the glass. The entire front lawn had been leveled out into a vast carpet of white. Thousands of tree branches and sticks littered the snow as if they had been spun up in a giant blender.

Mimi sighed. "It's like we've been transported to the arctic tundra."

Addie walked toward a cheese platter and scooped up onto her plate a handful of crackers, along with generous helpings of Roquefort, Comté, and Camembert.

The service door opened and Gus entered.

"Good morning, everyone. We're fortunate to have a gas range, so our breakfast service hasn't been completely hampered by the lack of electricity. Jane always preferred a fresh and healthy start to each day, so we've got a buffet featuring scrambled egg whites, cheese and fruit, turkey bacon, wheat germ toast with sunflower-seed butter, gluten-free high-fiber muffins, vegan croissants, Greek boysenberry yogurt, and acai juice. Enjoy."

Woody blew out his cheeks. "Breakfast of champions."

Kimiko entered the room and avoided eye contact with the group as she helped herself to the buffet. Addie gave Mimi a nudge, indicating Kimiko's arrival.

Veronique approached them, looking chic in natural makeup. "What is that disconcerting smell?"

Mimi tilted her head toward Addie. "It's probably Frau Fromage over here."

"No, no. It is a strange, discordant smell."

"Might be the essential oils I got from Barb."

"Oh. No, no, no," said Veronique, shaking her head vigorously. "These oils are not suitable scents. You smell like roast lamb."

Mimi ran her nose along the length of her arm and frowned.

Addie lifted another square of Comté to her lips and closed her eyes as its flavor spread across her tongue.

"I'm sorry to interrupt your cheese-induced bliss," said Mimi, "but shouldn't we be chatting with people? Jim is over there. I want to confront him about his web of lies."

"Right," said Addie, reluctantly setting the plate down on the dining table. Mimi placed her carryall on the chair next to it to claim their seats.

They walked toward a sideboard where Gus had set up a coffee service. Jim Towels was standing in front of it, holding a plate piled high with fruit.

"Morning, Jim," said Mimi, pouring a mug full of hot water and dropping in a tea bag. She noticed how Gus had set out pats of butter and a stack of paper napkins, all carefully arranged and labeled with the ornate emblem of the Drake Hotel.

"Good morning, ladies," Jim said, gesturing to the tight-fitting *E.T. the Extra-Terrestrial* T-shirt he was wearing. "Wasn't planning to stay overnight, so I had to borrow some clothes. Think this was Alexandra's once upon a time."

Mimi looked at his plate quizzically. "Are you a fruitarian these days, Jimbo?"

Jim sighed and shook his head. "I've been plagued with a spastic colon for years. It could blow sky-high if I started in on all those cheeses."

"Listen, Jim," said Addie. "We need to talk to you."

He lifted a cherry by the stem to his mouth. "Why?"

"You lied to Mimi."

Jim froze mid-bite.

Mimi looked at him sternly. "We need you to tell us the *whole* story."

"Let's talk in private," said Addie, nodding toward the hallway.

He gulped. "Fine."

They stepped out together. Addie turned to him. "We know everything about the blackmail. Don't deny it again."

Mimi continued: "Towels Print Shop was being used as a shell company for the blackmail scheme. We want to hear it from you straight. What you knew."

Jim went quiet, looking lost in a cloud of torment.

Mimi crossed her arms. "Your store is always empty. Over the years, I've wondered how you managed to keep the lights on. Not to mention you own a nice house with an elaborate rose garden. Haven't I seen a personal gardener working there? And you recently had an addition built onto the house."

He fiddled with the fabric of his T-shirt. "That's my man cave."

Addie exchanged a look with Mimi. *Jim Towels has a man cave?*

Jim took a steadying breath. "Towels Print Shop was a stupid store name. Should have thought it through before we opened. Everybody thinks we only monogram towels."

"How and when did Jane rope you into this mess?"

His eyes darted back and forth as he grappled with his thoughts. "Jane didn't know about it."

Mimi frowned.

"Wait a minute," interrupted Addie. "Jane didn't know about the blackmail?"

"No."

"You're kidding, right?" said Mimi in disbelief. "So, it was only Matthew running the blackmail?"

"Yes. Well, no. Sort of."

"Jim," said Mimi firmly. "You're being more cryptic than Will Shortz on a Saturday. Help us out here."

"Look, I don't know that much, Rosemary. I really don't. He kept me in the dark about most of what was going on. I was just helping him cook the books."

"You really don't have anything else for us, Jim? Running the accounts means you know more than most. Nothing is coming to mind that can help us determine who killed Jane, or Matthew, or why?"

Jim flushed deep red. "No. I'm so ashamed. Matthew just caught me in a weak moment, okay? I have an addiction." He looked down at his feet. "I'm addicted to collecting. I have more than a hundred collections. Geodes, Beanie Babies, vinegar cruets, baseball cards. Well, you get it."

"I loved Beanie Babies," said Addie. "I remember trying to find Claude the Crab for weeks."

Jim brightened. "I've got Claude! Although one of his pincers is torn off. Still cost me $5,000. Anyway, I had the man cave built to store all my stuff. I'm ashamed to think how many times I maxed out my cards on eBay."

"I see how things could have gotten out of hand, Jim," said Mimi. "Sounds like you went deep into debt. Then what?"

"Matthew heard about my money problems from Jane. So, he approached me one day. Offered to help me if I'd launder the blackmail money in return. He didn't want Jane to know anything about it. He just told her he'd help me but didn't go into specifics. He swore me to secrecy and, honestly, I've been terrified to talk to any-body about it ever since." He paused and looked at them. "After a few weeks of showing him I could handle the laundering, that wasn't enough. He decided to start charging me extra 'interest' on my loan. It's all been extremely stressful for me."

Mimi was silent as she tried to absorb everything Jim had just revealed to them. It was becoming difficult to discern who was a victim and who was an accomplice in this whole blackmail scheme. All this time, she'd thought Jane was the blackmailer. Now it turned out she was innocent. Well, as innocent as a woman sleep-ing with her daughter's husband could be. *You never really know your neighbors.* She visualized Matthew's face and felt acid rising in her stomach. Anger fizzed in her chest like heartburn. *Or was that from all the Gibsons last night?*

Mimi put her hand on his shoulder. "Don't worry, we're not go-ing to report you to anyone. We know you're a decent fellow, not some underboss of the Mackinac demimonde."

"I'm a fraud, Rosemary," he said quietly. "Do you know what this means? If anyone finds out, they'll take away my Better Business Bureau Torch Award."

"It's going to be okay, Jimbo. It won't tear the fabric of Mackinac society."

"Look, you need to be careful, Rosemary. People have been . . . saying things about you. Both of you."

"Like what?"

"They just don't like you snooping around."

"Consider us warned. C'mon, let's go finish our breakfast."

"Okay," said Jim glumly. "I hope people haven't eaten all the cherries."

They reentered the dining room and helped themselves to the buffet.

"Mimi," whispered Addie, "do you think that last comment about 'snooping around' from Jim was a warning or a threat?"

Mimi shook her head, speaking quietly: "I agree with you that Jim is quite the *unusual* suspect. But he's no killer."

"What happened to your bridge-table advice? Didn't you say we need to adapt in the moment? Be ready to change strategies when the signs are there?"

Mimi smiled. "The student becomes the teacher." She took a seat at the table next to Addie. Looking around, she became preoccupied with the thought of her missing necklace. She lifted a forkful of scrambled egg whites and took a bite. "One of these yahoos took my necklace," she whispered. "I'm telling you right now, we're not leaving this place without it."

Addie took a gulp of her coffee and nodded. She looked around the table and tried to make eye contact with Kimiko, who averted her eyes again.

Mimi set her fork down. "I'm going to try something. I'll be right back."

TWENTY-NINE

Harmful to Your Health

Addie watched from the other side of the long dining table as Mimi sat down next to Kimiko. She couldn't hear a word they were saying, but she noted how Mimi had softened. Kimiko listened intently as Mimi spoke to her in a way that, from a distance, seemed maternal. Grandmotherly. She felt a sting of jealousy. Mimi never talked to her that way.

Sebastián cleared his throat as he took his seat at the table. "So, did anyone actually sleep last night?"

Everyone looked at one another.

"I did," offered Veronique. "I sprayed some calming lavender water on my pillow. Slept quite well, actually."

Lillian raised a skeptical eyebrow and took a gulp of acai juice. "I don't know how anyone can sleep right now. There's a killer among us, and we're all potential suspects in a double murder."

Woody tore a croissant in half. "Wonder which one of us will be next."

Mimi wrapped up her conversation with Kimiko and sat down next to Addie again.

Addie lowered her voice. "So, what was that about? What did she say?"

"It's a little theory I'm working on. Give me some time."

Lillian stifled a yawn and turned to Addie and Mimi. "How's your investigation coming along, ladies?"

A heavy silence fell over the table. Only the sounds of clinking silverware, pouring drinks, and throat clearing filled the room.

"Detectives don't usually brief others on their progress," responded Addie, taking a sip of her coffee.

Woody sniffed derisively. "Detectives. Ha."

"Did any theories emerge?" asked Sebastián, in a voice that sounded straight out of a *Dateline* episode.

"Yes, please, tell us. I'd love to know who you think murdered my sister and nephew-in-law," said Gus, leaning against a sideboard.

"Is 'nephew-in-law' a thing?" asked Lillian, eyes narrowing. "I don't think that's a thing."

Gus heaved a sigh as he began stacking dirty plates. "Well, I'm getting pretty sick and tired of this situation. Someone here killed my sister, and all this sitting around acting normal and polite like nothing's happened is really starting to get to me."

"Here, Gus, I made this for you," said Kimiko, getting up from her seat and walking over to him. She patted him on the shoulder and presented a drawing. "I know how much the stars meant to her."

He gasped and covered his mouth with his hand. "Oh, thank you, Kimiko. It's so . . . ethereal." He turned the paper around to show the group. It was a drawing of Jane sporting a halo and floating among the stars in outer space.

Everyone nodded and murmured variations of "Oh, wow," "You really captured her essence," and "Ethereal, indeed."

Lillian turned back to Addie. "Doesn't your little investigation concern all of us? I don't know about anyone else, but I'd like to know what you've learned so far."

"Yeah, wouldn't it help if we all discussed this together, rather than in little camps?" added Woody.

Addie rested her elbows on the table. "Honestly, it's important that we speak to each of you separately, not as a group. We don't want someone's memory of events to influence someone else's account."

"Well, it's *game over* for you two playing 'detective' once the police arrive," snapped Lillian.

"And when will that be, Lillian?" said Gus sharply. "When they figure out how to traverse the two-hundred-foot-wide moat, or when the wind finally calms down and one of the Keystone Cops manages to pilot an aircraft over here?" He snorted and shook his head. "You are all kidding yourselves if you think we're being rescued anytime soon."

Mimi noted how his demeanor had shifted from bright and helpful to more subdued, moody. He'd ditched the formality of his chef whites and was wearing a polo-neck sweater and chinos. His five-o'clock shadow had speckles of gray in it, aging him in the light of day. He looked less sun-kissed and more like a worn old leather saddle.

Addie looked to Gus. "Whenever the authorities do arrive, the clearer the information we can give them, the sooner we can all get out of here."

Woody sat back in his chair. "I'd like to remind you all that Granny Gibson over here is the one who had the murder weapon hidden in her room."

"That was planted," snapped Addie.

Veronique sniffed. "It is true that any one of us could be the killer. None of us seemed very friendly with Jane last night."

"I have to say, I think this is all deeply inappropriate," said Jim Towels. "I don't want to talk like this. Jane was my friend."

"That's not what I heard," said Lillian blithely, brushing croissant crumbs off her shirt.

The air was taut and brittle. Barb entered the room with a jug of juice. The group seemed grateful for the interruption.

Veronique got up from her chair and sat down next to Mimi. "Rosemary, these oils you are wearing, they are unstable, crude. Let me curate a bespoke scent for you."

Mimi smiled. "I'd like that."

Veronique pulled a cigarette from her case and cast a glance around the table. "Does anyone mind if I smoke?"

No one responded. Mimi caught Addie's eye and gave her a look that said, *Quiet.*

As Veronique lit up, Mimi reached into her carryall for a Pall Mall. "I'll join you," she said, as she pinched the cigarette between her fingers and raised it to her lips.

Addie shook her head disapprovingly.

Suddenly, Veronique gasped. She turned sharply to Mimi and smacked the cigarette out of her hand. It went flying across the room.

Mimi looked down at the cigarette on the floor and back up at Veronique in disbelief.

"Bitter almonds!" shouted Veronique, rising from her seat.

Everyone in the room froze in confusion.

"Wash your hands now, Rosemary. Do not touch your Pall Malls."

Addie's eyes widened in realization. "What? You mean . . ."

"Cyanide."

THIRTY

Lost and Found

Addie felt the sting of tears behind her eyes. Twenty minutes had passed since Mimi's brush with death. She replayed the entire breakfast scene in her head. How had someone gotten their hands on Mimi's Pall Malls without being noticed? They'd only been in the hall talking with Jim for a few minutes. The idea of losing Mimi was incomprehensible. What if Veronique hadn't come and sat down with them? The thought chilled her. The stark difference between murder as an intellectual puzzle and a nasty reality was hitting home.

She turned her gaze to Mimi, who stood over the powder room sink, drying her hands on a towel.

"Don't you think you should wash them one more time?" said Addie.

"I'd like to have some epidermis left after this. I've washed them ten times. I'm fine."

Addie pulled out the yellow rubber gloves from her clutch. "Let's make sure everything else in here is wiped down."

"Okay."

Addie busied herself digging through Mimi's carryall and

cleaning each item. "I just can't believe this. I mean, trying to frame you is one thing. But trying to *poison* you?"

"I know. And cyanide? I mean, what decade is this?"

"Actually," said Addie, polishing Mimi's Bicycle card deck, "cyanide is making a comeback. There was this whole article in *Wired* about it. It's fast-acting and hard to trace. In Canada, there was this guy who—"

"Never mind. I believe you, based on your encyclopedic knowledge of true crime."

Addie sighed. "I'm scared, Mimi. This is all getting a bit too . . . real for me."

Mimi tossed the towel into the wastebasket and turned to her. "We can't let this one feeble attempt on my life get us down. You need to focus on the immediate problem. *Who is the killer?* This is *real*, Addie. Your whole life has been building up to this moment. Where's that sleuthy kid who dreamed of transcontinental train rides ending in murder? You wanted Robert Stack to narrate your childhood. Well, here we are, right smack-dab in the middle of your very own *Unsolved Mystery*. Use all that passion and puzzling talent you put into your *Murderscape* game and help us get out of this mess."

"You're right," said Addie, admiring her grandmother's resolve. "But please don't leave your carryall *anywhere*."

Mimi straightened herself and rubbed some moisturizer on her hands. "What's next?"

"Lillian. We hardly got anything out of her last night."

"She strikes me as a bit woo-woo. Are you sure we'll get anything useful from her?"

"There's quite a bit of activity about her in the ledger. A year into making her payments, she got a huge discount. We need to find out why."

They left the powder room and went upstairs to Lillian's room.

Addie could see that the door was ajar. She gently knocked on it with her forefinger and nudged it open an inch. "Lillian?"

There was no answer.

Addie looked to Mimi, who nodded for her to go ahead. The door creaked open to reveal an immaculate room with high ceilings, garish egg-yolk-yellow walls, and ornate giltwood furniture. They stepped inside.

"Woman had no taste," said Mimi, shaking her head. "Half the rooms look like they belong in a funeral home, and the rest look like Imelda Marcos and Liberace were her interior designers. I just don't understand this place."

"Mimi, Jane's dead. Be respectful." Addie craned her neck to check the far corner of the room, ensuring it was empty. "Lillian isn't here. What now?"

"Let's have a quick look around."

"I'm not sure that's a good idea," said Addie. "She could come back any minute."

Mimi turned to Addie. "You told me to stop downplaying and get serious. This is me. Serious."

"Okay, you're right. Do you want to keep an eye out for her while I have a snoop?"

"Copy that."

Addie quickly tiptoed toward the en suite. She could see various expensive skincare products meticulously lined up along the vanity. Chanel. Tatcha. Chantecaille. She opened the medicine cabinet and scrutinized its contents. A bottle of Xanax. Some toothpaste and floss. Nothing interesting.

As she shut the cabinet, Addie noticed a shiny gold cap partially obscured by a plant on the windowsill. She walked over and picked up the bottle. The label, just a simple letter *V*, looked handwritten. She popped the cap and lifted the atomizer to her nose. The scent immediately transported her back to last night, when she'd first put on Jane's sweater. It was an alluring jasmine fragrance that she instantly recognized.

"Mimi!" Addie whisper-shouted. "I think Lillian took Jane's perfume."

Mimi called into the room from her sentinel post in the doorway, "Does it have a tonka bean drydown?"

"A what?"

"Never mind. Keep looking."

Walking back into the bedroom, she crouched down and peeked under the bed skirt, revealing a small suitcase.

"She has a suitcase under the bed!"

Mimi rolled her eyes. "You don't have to give me the play-by-play. Hurry up. I'm getting nervous!"

Addie grabbed the handle and pulled it out from underneath the bed. She tried to open it, but it wouldn't budge. There was a combination lock with three dials next to the handle. "It's locked!"

"Try all zeroes. It's the factory setting."

Addie raised her eyebrows, impressed. She tried 0-0-0. "No dice."

"Okay, I know another trick. Switch with me. Keep a lookout," said Mimi.

Addie marched toward the doorway and looked on as Mimi reached into her carryall. She pulled out a credit card and inserted it underneath each of the dials, fiddling with each one a little. Finally, the case snapped open.

"How the hell did you know how to do that?!"

Mimi shrugged. "Saw a video on YouTube. It's a standard TSA lock. I forget my combination all the time. Guess sometimes getting old pays off."

She lifted the lid, revealing an array of items. A clear plastic case containing Woody's saxophone cuff links and Jane's wedding band. The missing Lalique Venus, loosely wrapped in a pillowcase. An expensive-looking crystal dish. A box of those pretty little Claus Porto soaps that looked like candy.

Mimi continued digging through the case. A glint of gold underneath the Lalique Venus caught her eye. She lifted it, revealing a chain. Several other items were in the way, so she removed them from the suitcase and gently pulled the chain free. It was her emerald necklace. Pressing it to her lips, she squeezed her eyes closed.

"Your necklace!" exclaimed Addie.

Mimi's hands began to shake as an overwhelming sense of relief washed over her. Addie stared at Mimi in disbelief as her chin trembled, and a pair of tears chased each other down her cheeks. She couldn't remember the last time she'd seen Mimi cry.

Addie peered into the hallway to make sure no one was coming, then quickly walked over to her. "Are you all right?"

Mimi took a deep breath but didn't respond.

"I know you love that necklace, but you're the most unsentimental person I know. What's going on?"

Mimi leveled her gaze at Addie. Her eyes were red and wet. "This necklace was the last thing Peter gave me before . . ."

Mimi trailed off, then went quiet. Addie had never seen her grandmother like this.

"I . . . There's no way to say it."

"Please, Mimi. Tell me."

Mimi opened her mouth to speak. Then stopped.

"Mimi. Tell me. Now."

Addie studied her eyes. She could see the flicker of a deeply painful memory behind them.

Mimi looked down and bit her lip, then drew in a breath and spoke the words she'd been holding inside for over twenty years.

"I . . . I killed Grandpa Peter."

They exchanged a long, stunned gaze.

Addie stood motionless, trying to grasp the enormity of what Mimi had just confessed. "You . . . you what? I don't understand."

"When he had the stroke, it was a bad one. The doctors said he'd never fully recover. Brain damage. Paralysis. Pure hell," she said, fishing for an Altoid from her carryall and popping it into her mouth. Mimi continued: "At first, I couldn't do a thing. I couldn't think, I couldn't cry, I just stood there . . . staring down at him hour after hour. Then, one day, they told me he could go. That he'd be released to a nursing home, which one did I prefer? They'd have someone come by to show me our options."

Addie touched Mimi's arm. "Do you want to sit down, Mimi?"

Mimi shook her head. She seemed to have aged several years in the short time since they had entered Lillian's bedroom.

"Peter would have hated that. For him, that was no way to live. The doctor told me to go home and get some rest, but I didn't want to, so an aide brought me a pillow and blanket."

"Mimi. Are you telling me—"

Mimi's face contorted in pain, then nodded solemnly. "Yes."

"You took the pillow and—"

"Yes."

Addie felt her throat tighten and sat down on the edge of the bed. "Gosh, Mimi. All this time, you've been living with this."

"Twenty-three years."

"And this is why you're being blackmailed?"

Mimi nodded. "Maybe the doctor knew. Or a security guard saw it on a camera. I just don't know."

"I wish you would have told me before."

Mimi pressed a hand to her forehead. "Things were bad enough between you and me. Besides, it wouldn't have changed anything. I'm ready to let go of the life I have here on Mackinac. Send me to prison or shut me away in a retirement home. They both seem kind of the same to me, anyway. I give up."

"You can't talk like this, Mimi."

"I understand if you don't ever want to see me again."

Addie squeezed her hand. "Don't say that. I need you. I'm just shocked. Still trying to process it all."

Mimi shook her head. "I was selfish. What was his life going to be like, living like that? What was mine going to be like? I was afraid . . . for both of us."

"I understand."

"I could never escape the guilt," said Mimi, rubbing her thumb over the emerald pendant. "But I eventually found a life that I loved. Mackinac gave me peace. I've cherished my life here."

Addie nodded, looking into Mimi's eyes. They pierced her heart. There was a long pause.

"You know I love you, Mimi."

Mimi leaned in and gave her a hug.

Addie swallowed a hard lump, her arms frozen at her sides, unsure how to respond. "I thought we weren't a hugging family?" she said, her chin digging into Mimi's shoulder as she spoke.

"Don't get used to it," said Mimi, squeezing her tighter.

Addie closed her eyes and squeezed Mimi back.

They let go and Addie smiled warmly at her. "Let's get out of here. I don't like being—"

Someone behind them cleared their throat theatrically. They both jumped and turned to the doorway. Leaning against the doorframe with her hand on her hip, looking equal parts annoyed and unimpressed, was Lillian.

THIRTY-ONE

Auras

Lillian strode coolly into the room. "Find anything interesting, ladies?"

Addie took a deep breath and spoke to her in an even tone. "Lillian, we came in here because we wanted to talk to you."

"I've already told you what I know. What gives you the right to come in here and go through my things?"

Mimi squared her shoulders. "They're not your things," she said, holding up her necklace defiantly. There was a catch in her voice. "This is *mine*."

Addie put her hand on Mimi's shoulder. "Hold fire. Let me handle this."

"You don't think I noticed?" said Lillian blithely, ignoring Addie and looking directly at Mimi. "You were fiddling with that thing all night. You're obsessed with it. It's like an amulet or something."

Addie stepped in front of Mimi and stared Lillian down.

"There's priceless works of art and first edition Poes all over this house, and you're stealing Mimi's microscopic emerald?"

"Hey," grunted Mimi. "I prefer 'diminutive.'"

"I'm going to get straight to the point, Lillian. Talk to us, and we won't tell the cops you're a klepto."

"Maniac," added Mimi.

Lillian looked at her watch. "Fine. I'll give you five minutes." She walked over to the mirror that hung above the fireplace mantel. She looked at herself and adjusted her hair. "I'm not proud of it, you know. I've seen a therapist before. It's just that sometimes . . . I get stressed. And this is how I deal with stress."

"We know about the blackmail," said Addie firmly.

Lillian's eyes narrowed in the mirror and she turned around to face them. "That's a strong word. 'Blackmail.'"

"Call it whatever you want, but you were paying money to someone who threatened to expose your past of embezzlement and fraud to all your high-profile clients. Nobody wants a pricey 'life coach' who's a thief and a liar."

Lillian wrinkled her pert nose. "How exactly do you know about all that?"

Addie shrugged. "There's only so much you can bury in Google search results. I did a deep dive on you. Finally got some of your history around page eight or so."

"The deal was that you'd come clean, Lillian," Mimi chimed in. "If you don't, we might just have to tell Woody where his prized cuff links are. He doesn't strike me as the 'forgive and forget' type."

Lillian sat down across from them on the window seat and smoothed her skirt. "What do you want to know?"

"Why were you fighting with Jane last night?"

"She found out I was the one who leaked the story to Page Six. It humiliated her. She was furious. I did it because I wanted her and Matthew to break up once and for all, okay?"

"And how do you know Gus?"

"Gus? What do you mean?" Lillian said, saying his name as if it was a foreign word she'd never heard before.

Addie rolled her eyes. "C'mon, Lillian. He introduced you to us in the library, and you were arguing with him earlier. Obviously, you know him. Just tell us. Is he your client?"

Lillian pulled her shoulders back and lengthened her neck in defiance. "I don't like to reveal my clients. It's a private service, like being a doctor or a lawyer, and I have access to some of the deepest, saddest confessions of high-profile people."

"Is that how you managed to negotiate a reduction in your blackmail fees?" asked Addie.

Lillian went quiet.

"Look, we were able to access the blackmail records, and we noticed that a few months ago your fees went down by seventy-five percent. Is that discount because you were offering secrets to subsidize your cash payments?"

Her expression didn't change. A few seconds passed while she formed her answer. "I have three clients here. Well, four including Jane. The others are Gus, Sebastián, and Veronique."

"And you've been pretending you don't know them because your services are 'confidential'?"

She nodded. "People don't necessarily want to be associated with me. Given the services I provide. If you hire me, it usually means you're in some kind of trouble."

"What kind of 'trouble' are you helping them with?"

"I'm helping Gus and Veronique with reputational stuff. Building up their public images so they're untouchable if some of their past issues ever surface. Veronique, in particular, has some nasty rumors circulating about her in Paris. I've been working with her on a proactive strategy."

Addie arched an eyebrow. "Proactive how?"

"Catch-and-kill deals with the press. Bribes to a private investigator someone hired to follow her, that sort of thing."

"You really provide a comprehensive service, don't you, Lillian?" said Mimi. "Is there anything you don't do?"

"Not really, no." Lillian paused, then added, "I craft a persona for someone, and then I do everything I can to preserve and protect it."

"Why were you arguing with Gus?"

Lillian looked down. "He owes me money. He's in bad debt, I guess. His sister was supposed to bail him out, help cover the fees he owes me. Now I have to wonder if I'll ever see a dime."

"How much does he owe you?"

"Almost $50,000."

"What about Sebastián?" asked Addie. "What are you doing for him?"

"He's worried about a bullying thing that keeps getting bigger and bigger. His agent just dropped him because of it. NDAs are being nullified as we speak."

Addie frowned. "Wow, really?"

"Yeah. Don't let his charm fool you. He's always nice to me, but that's because he usually needs something. Apparently, there have been rumblings that he's not so nice behind the scenes. Bullying, harassment, tapes of him screaming at people. Ugly stuff."

Addie took in this information. Sebastián had already lied about not being a client of Lillian's. But that lie made sense. He was a celebrity, so he was protecting his privacy. His being a bully, however, painted him in a whole new light. Of course, it was also possible the bullying accusation wasn't true. Lillian could be making things up to deflect attention away from herself and onto others. In *Murderscape*, suspects used misdirection tactics all the time.

"Is somebody going to the press?" asked Mimi.

"Think so. Pretty standard stuff these days. There's a whole cottage industry for life coaches dealing with famous people in this situation. Nondisclosures don't mean much anymore. If anything, they invite scrutiny. Everyone's secrets are getting exposed. We have a saying in my business: 'You can't spell "scandal" without NDA.'" Her phone lit up with a notification, and Lillian looked down. "Listen, I've already told you a lot. I'm hired for my discretion, and here I am spilling the beans on everyone. I really shouldn't say more. Must be all the wine we had last night. My head still feels a bit swimmy."

"How did your affair with Matthew start?"

She shrugged. "Blame it on the wine. Jane flew me out to their Growing Concern vineyard for a week of coaching. She wanted to pin down her optimal speaking pitch so that she would continue to sound youthful. Women of a certain age often worry about wrinkles and hair color, but they forget to fix a croaky voice. I call it the Old Crone Tone."

"So you were coaching her when you first met Matthew? When was this?" asked Addie.

"Couple of years ago. We were sitting outside around a gorgeous firepit, watching the sunset, when along comes Matthew carrying a bottle of their wine. He hands us each a glass, and Jane starts babbling on about its angular pitch and anthracite afterglow. So I took a sip and it hit my throat like sixty-grit sandpaper. A bit too flinty for my tastes."

"Earlier you were asking for *biodynamic* wine, was it?"

"Yes. I like my wine how I like my people. Nontoxic. Anyway, I coughed and coughed. Matthew came over and rubbed my back to calm me down, and his touch was . . . oh my."

"Jane found out about you two eventually, right?" said Addie.

Her eyes welled up. "She might have had her suspicions, but she never said a word to me. I did love him. But Jane had some kind of magnetic pull with Matthew." She dabbed her eyes with a tissue. "I've always helped myself to whatever catches my eye, as you know. But he was the one thing I couldn't have. Anyway, when I started getting the blackmail letters, it was obvious they were from Jane. She was threatening to expose me. At first, she helped bail me out of my little embezzlement scandal. Lent me money to repay those debts and keep people from going to the police or press. But after

I became more successful, I guess she felt it was time that I repay my dues. Or maybe it was just payback for my affair with Matthew. I don't know."

Addie looked to Mimi and read her own thought in Mimi's eyes. *Should they tell Lillian that it was actually Matthew who had been blackmailing her?* She decided not to interrupt the flow they had going. "Can you tell us anything else significant that you remember from last night?"

"Nothing else is coming to mind."

"You didn't see or hear anything strange?"

Lillian's face briefly flickered with amusement. "You sure are pressing hard, aren't you?"

Mimi blew out an irritated sigh. "We've heard reports that you were seen leaving Jane's room right around the time of her murder."

"That's a lie!" exclaimed Lillian, rising to stand.

Addie tried to calm her. "We just want to eliminate you as a suspect. When you're evasive, it doesn't help us do that."

Lillian's jaw tightened. "I swear to you, I wasn't anywhere near Jane's room when she was killed. And I didn't hear a thing. I didn't see anything strange. All I did was try to be a good guest."

"Okay," said Addie. "Listen, we'll leave you alone in a minute, but we just need to ask one more thing."

Lillian looked at her expectantly.

"Your phone. We need to watch the raw videos you took last night. The ones you used to make the TikTok. In case there's any additional evidence there."

Lillian closed her eyes and drew in a weary sigh. "Fine. But I hardly have any charge left. Be quick."

Addie took the phone and went to Lillian's video library. She played the most recent videos from the last twenty-four hours in quick succession while Mimi watched over her shoulder. The videos of all the decorations and food they'd seen in the TikTok. Woody playing piano. Jane with her French 75 and Matthew behind her in his coat. Binky and Barnabas sleeping together on a rug. She toggled to the final, most recent video and hit play. It was Matthew and Jane standing by the door, announcing they were leaving the house for Drinks on the Drawbridge.

"Replay that," said Mimi.

They played the video again. Mimi nodded. "Got it, thank you."

Addie gave Lillian back her phone.

Lillian paused thoughtfully, studying her. "Why don't you let me use my powers to help you with your investigation?"

"Powers?" said Addie.

"I use visualization with my clients. It's a form of clairvoyance. I didn't even know I had a gift until I got into astrocartography. That's when I tapped into it." Lillian closed her eyes and sat back in her chair. She took in a deep breath, then exhaled theatrically.

Mimi turned and mouthed *Woo-woo* to Addie.

Addie mouthed back *Stop it.*

"I can see Jane in her bed," said Lillian. "She's lying on her back . . ."

Mimi looked to Addie again.

"Don't bother," Addie whispered under her breath, "too easy."

"And she's . . ." Lillian's breath quickened and her eyelids began to flutter dramatically. "She's completely shocked by the person who's standing over her. They're holding the knife. It's frightening." Lillian clutched her chest empathically as she spoke. "She's so upset. It's such a betrayal."

Taking this in, Addie looked to Mimi, then turned back to Lillian. "Go on."

"She knew them well. Whoever killed her. It was someone she'd never expect. Someone close to her."

"Well, everyone here knew Jane. So this doesn't help much," said Mimi.

"Wait!" Lillian called out, and sat up. "Now I'm seeing more . . . Jane is crying . . . and now she's reaching for . . . Damn, it's fading."

Lillian turned to Mimi. "Rosemary, could you move out of the way until I finish? Your negative energy field is blocking my reception. It's like a heavy lead curtain just dropped down."

Addie nodded for her to go. Mimi straightened her posture and walked to the back of the room.

Lillian leaned forward. "Sorry, my Third Eye chakra was giving me fits. Anyway, where was I?" She shook her head, then began to concentrate once again.

Addie studied Lillian as her mind whirred, realizing that she reminded her of a character in *Murderscape*: the Talisman. He, or rather *it*, was an invention of Brian's. A half-human thief that stole key clues and hoarded them away. It wasn't a killer, but it was evil. A malevolent force that subverted the game and worked against players—"dark play," as Brian called it. Their texture artist had spent days coloring in the vivid details of its secret lair, an elaborate cave system.

The supernatural aspects of the Talisman had been something that she resisted. *Murderscape* was about mastering your detective skills, so she wanted to stay focused on crafting the best mysteries possible. But Brian always seemed to be adding extraneous new elements, bloating the experience. There was a name for what he was doing: "feature creep." When they'd finalized the Talisman's design, she remembered shivering at the character's unblinking, soulless eyes. A sickly shade of yellow, pupils constricted into pinpricks.

It was around this same time that things got more complicated between her and Brian. Less intimacy, more rivalry. *Murderscape* started to change with each new episode, and the game gave her a feeling she didn't recognize anymore. But it remained popular, so Brian ignored her protests.

Addie's thoughts returned to the present. She sat transfixed, waiting for Lillian to continue. Uninterested, Mimi pawed through her trusty carryall, searching for her tin of Altoids.

"Jane is reaching for her telephone on the nightstand. Her head-piece is still on, but it's askew," said Lillian, straining to tune in to whatever "transmission" she was receiving. "She can barely get the words out: 'Alexandra, Alexandra, please forgive me . . .'"

She broke out of her trance and sat forward, suddenly lucid again. They made eye contact, and Addie felt the hairs on her arms stand up. Lillian's eyes were soulless too, like the Talisman's. Addie cleared her throat. "We appreciate you helping us, but we also need to know if there's anything else you *actually* witnessed last night. Not with your Third Eye, but with your real eyes."

"Fine. But I thought I already told you everything. What else do you want to know?"

"You said you saw Matthew wearing a coat around 8:30. He was talking to the guard. Do you remember anything else? Or seeing anything else before he died?"

She shook her head no. "Only that he was annoyed with the guard."

"Why?"

"He brought in a pair of walkie-talkies and was complaining that the batteries had run out. Said it was a security risk not to have them fully operational. Then Matthew grumbled something about him having an attitude and stored the walkie-talkies away in the foyer. That was it."

"Mmm-hmm. Well, this has been real helpful," said Mimi.

"You know, before you go," said Lillian, looking to Addie, "I just wanted to tell you . . . everything is going to be all right."

Addie looked around, confused. "What do you mean?"

"I can see your aura. It's brown, which means a lack of clarity and enhanced stress. But on the bright side, I see there's some red at the edges. That means you're smart and strong, so you'll figure everything out. Whatever it is you're going through, I hope you get through it soon."

Addie smiled and thanked Lillian as they made their way toward the door. "What about her?" she said, nodding in Mimi's direction.

Lillian hesitated, then laughed uncomfortably. "You know, it's the strangest thing," she said, looking at Mimi intently. "I can't see anything. No aura, nothing. It's just . . . blank. Never seen that before."

As they turned to leave, Mimi glared at Lillian. "Stop stealing people's crap, okay?" She shut the door behind them.

Walking down the corridor, Addie took out the Murderbook and jotted down notes in the margins by Lillian's name. "You lost your cool back there, Mimi. We had her talking and you put her on the defensive. Remember, we aren't supposed to reference what other witnesses tell us. And we know Barb's a liar."

Mimi fastened her necklace in place and gave it a loving pat. "Couldn't help myself."

Addie snorted and returned to the Murderbook. "You're just hurt about the aura thing."

Mimi stopped in her tracks. "It was rude!"

Addie shook her head. "Imagine being Matthew and blackmailing the same woman you're having an affair with. This thing is so complex. It's like we're making an Escher drawing on an Etch A Sketch."

"Can you picture her house? Stacked to the ceiling with all the loot she's palmed?"

"Mimi, I don't think those types of people can help themselves. You should feel bad for her. Be more open-minded."

"If you're too open-minded, your brain will fall out."

THIRTY-TWO

Walkie-Talkies

saw you looking pretty closely at that last video on Lillian's phone. Did you notice something back there?" asked Addie.

They were tucked away in a narrow alcove on the second floor, one of many nooks and crannies situated along the house's labyrinthine hallways.

"Yes. Well, sort of. I watched Matthew's hand while he punched in the code to the drawbridge. Tried to make it out, but I couldn't. Just watched his hand move seven times. It's a seven-digit code."

Addie nodded and made a note in the Murderbook. "Follow me."

"Where are we going now?" asked Mimi as they walked down the hall together.

"I want to get those walkie-talkies."

"Why do I feel like we don't really need them, and this is just some kind of wish-fulfillment fantasy for you?" Mimi grumbled as they went downstairs.

Addie surveyed the foyer to ensure that no one was coming. A mirrored console table, lined with vases, sat by the stairs. She approached it and slid open the door. Only a phone charger and some spare light bulbs. She took the charger and handed it to Mimi. "Put this in your carryall."

"What good is this going to do? The power's been out for hours."

"I want one in case it comes back on." Addie turned around and headed for a lowboy cabinet in the corner. She pulled open the doors. "Bingo!"

In one synchronized motion, she grabbed the devices just as Mimi opened her carryall again. Addie dropped them in.

"You'll be happy to know I have some extra batteries in here if we need them," said Mimi, patting her carryall. "Swiped a few from Barb's stash."

They headed back up the staircase.

"All these damn stairs would bring Rocky Balboa to his knees," Mimi sighed.

They hustled down the hallway and entered the east wing of the house, climbing another set of stairs before they reached the end of the hall. Mimi caught her breath and nodded toward the large grandfather clock.

"Are you sure this is right?"

Mimi gave a one-shoulder shrug. "It's what the woman said."

Addie gave the clock a once-over and then tugged on one side. It swung open like a door. Behind it was a hidden, curved staircase. She turned back to Mimi. "You keep a lookout. I'll be back in five or ten."

"Why do I always have to be the lookout?"

"If anyone comes, just press here," she said, pointing to a button on the device, "and say 'Salutations.'"

"'Salutations'?" said Mimi, frowning.

Addie looked exasperated. "Do you want to suggest something better?"

Mimi waved her off as Addie turned and ascended the steps into the darkness above. Mimi tugged on the clock, and it gently closed again.

At the top of the staircase, Addie stopped in front of a narrow door. She had the feeling that something behind it was very wrong. The skin prickled on her arms. Her breath held tight with fear, she pressed the walkie-talkie button. "Testing. Testing. I'm going in. Over."

Mimi rolled her eyes as Addie's voice crackled through her carry-all. She pulled out the walkie-talkie and pressed the button. "Ground control to Major Tom. Your voice sounds tinny. Repeat last transmission. Over."

Addie's voice came on again. "Testing! Testing! Hello? These aren't Bang & Olufsen speakers, Mimi. Can you hear me or not?"

"Copy. Roger that. Just hurry the hell up!"

Addie reached for the doorknob and slowly pushed the door open. It was a large attic space that had been converted into a loft. A hint of a fresh-paint smell gave her the sense the place had been redone recently. She entered and stopped to look around the room. An exposed brick chimney and a vaulted ceiling accented with skylights gave it an urban feel. The living room area featured the "Japandi" trend she had seen in many a hipster Chicago coffee shop. Neutral colors and Scandi furniture with Japanese accents, like a sake set and potted orchids, dotting every surface. A trestle dining table, large platform bed, and simple kitchenette completed the space. Something about it felt contrived and unusually clean. It did not feel lived-in.

One wall stood out as the focal point. From top to bottom, it was arranged with oil paintings in simple black frames. As she moved closer for a better look, the fine hairs stood up on the back of her neck. Each painting was of a dead bird lying on its back, legs up. She checked the artist's signature. They were all Millicent Barnstables, the same style of painting that Veronique had purchased at the auction.

The walkie-talkie crackled to life. Addie jumped.

"Clear sailing up there, Captain Cook? What's your 20? Roger. Over and out."

Addie grabbed the device. "Mimi! I'm the one who says 'Roger' when you ask a question!"

"10-4. Why is this taking so long? It's creepy down here all alone."

"I'll be done soon. Especially if you quit calling me!"

"Well, hurry up and be careful. Over. Rover."

Addie began a methodical search of the loft. She moved from the living room area to the bedroom corner, checking under the bed and mattress. As she riffled through a nightstand, she came across a well-thumbed paperback, *A Birder's Field Guide.* She dropped it back in the drawer and headed into the bathroom. After pawing through toiletries in various cabinets and drawers, she opened a closet door. She pushed aside some paint-stained clothing on hangers to reveal a tiny artist's garret. Her eyes widened. An easel, some blank canvases, an old wooden table piled high with paint tubes and brushes. She walked farther into the room, stepping over paint-covered drop cloths and rags on the floor. *Was Matthew painting under the pseudonym of Millicent Barnstable? Why?* She shut the closet door and headed back into the main living area.

Snooping around the kitchenette, she sifted through utensil drawers, dishes, and pots and pans. Nothing. She placed her hands on her hips. In *Murderscape,* the hiding place for a clue was always somewhere simple and so plainly obvious that you'd never suspect it. Her eyes fixed on the refrigerator. She swung the door open.

Her hand covered her mouth to stifle a scream as she staggered backward. There, neatly arranged on shelves, were at least a dozen dead birds. Rigid with rigor mortis, lying on their backs, spindly legs in the air. Little ID tags dangled from the claws of each one. *Barn Swallow. Cedar Waxwing. Red-eyed Vireo. Summer Tanager.*

A shiver ran through her body. She wanted to shut the door and leave, but she couldn't tear herself away from the sight.

She lifted the walkie-talkie to her mouth and pressed the button. "Mimi, Mimi! Do you copy?"

"What? I mean, affirmative. Yes. What?!"

"I'm in a Hitchcock movie up here. Matthew *is* Millicent Barnstable. *Was*, I mean. The dead-bird portraitist."

"Debrief me later. Finish your search and get back down here. Over and out."

Slamming the fridge door shut, Addie yanked on the freezer door, fearing what other horror might be next. Mercifully, it was empty except for a carton of vanilla ice cream. She closed the door and paused to think. *Something simple and so plainly obvious that you'd never suspect it.*

She opened the freezer again. This time, she reached for the rectangular white bin filled with ice. She rolled up her sweater sleeve and dunked her hand into the pile of ice cubes. At the very bottom, her fingers touched something. Bingo! She grasped on to it and pulled hard, extracting a white plastic bag.

After rubbing her hands together to warm them back up, she opened the bag. Inside was a manila envelope. The address was in handwriting she recognized. It was the same penmanship with dramatically looping *l*'s and *g*'s from Jane's letter to Alexandra:

> *Mendelsohn & Lewis*
> *100 N. La Salle Drive*
> *Chicago, IL 60600*

She knew this law firm. They were one of the global, prestigious ones that covered specialties ranging from life sciences to real estate and antitrust. She had considered meeting with one of their litigators before Sarah told her about Martin. She flipped it over, but the envelope was sealed. Maybe she could steam it open later in their bathroom.

Downstairs, Mimi stood guard in front of the grandfather clock. Leaning on one foot and then the other, she attempted to appear casual. Even though this wing of the house was quiet and deserted, she felt restless. What if someone came by and wondered what she was doing? She pulled out the walkie-talkie again.

She heard a whiffing sound and looked up. Gus was plodding down the hall in her direction. Mimi tensed and pulled her carry-all close to her body. The walkie-talkie was positioned firmly in her right hand, concealed behind her carryall.

"What are you doing all the way down here?" he called out as he made his way toward her.

There was an edge to his voice that Mimi found unnerving. She felt for the button on the receiver and discreetly pushed it. "Salutations, Gus!"

"Hello," he said, stopping in front of her.

Did Addie hear her up there? Mimi pressed the button again, hard this time. "Salutations to you too!"

Gus frowned. "Yeah, uh. Hello. Again. What are you doing all the way down here?"

"Shouldn't I ask you the same thing?" said Mimi, hoping her attempt at stalling didn't sound too defensive.

He smirked. "I'm getting an extra memory foam pillow from a storage cabinet in there," he said, pointing to a linen closet behind her. "Lillian asked for one 'to be delivered to her room.' I'm getting tired of her bossy attitude."

Mimi nodded as Gus went to the closet and retrieved a pillow. "You should do an inventory check before she leaves. Make sure you get that back," she said, nodding to the pillow.

He eyeballed her suspiciously. "You didn't say what you're doing all the way down here."

"Me? Oh. I'm just getting my ten thousand steps in. How do you think I manage to live on an island that doesn't allow cars? If I don't walk every day, I atrophy." She could almost see the gears turning inside his head, deciding whether to believe her.

An alarm sounded in her mind as a stain on the cuff of Gus's shirt caught her eye. It looked like dried blood.

Gus made eye contact with her. "You okay, Rosemary?"

"Yes, I'm fine," she responded. An awkward silence fell over them. She felt a knot of fear in her stomach. *Hadn't Addie mentioned she noticed defensive wounds on Matthew's hand? Was she standing alone in an empty hallway with a killer?*

"Where's Addie?"

Mimi tensed. "She's downstairs talking to a few of the others about what they remember."

He looked at her intently. "Rosemary, how long are you two going to keep this up? This feels . . . I don't know, disrespectful. Doesn't Addie understand that Jane and Matthew were real human beings made of flesh and blood, not pixels?"

"Gus," said Mimi, careful to sound calm and keep the walkie-talkie hidden from view, "someone made an attempt on my life this morning. You can't really expect my granddaughter to sit around and do nothing while somebody is trying to bump off her grandmother, can you?"

Her statement hung in the air for a while. His face softened. "Listen, I understand. If there's one thing I've learned in the last twenty-four hours, it's that you need to protect your loved ones, because you never know how much time you have left together."

Mimi held his gaze. His eyes were sad and weary. *Was it from grief, or culpability?* Her hand was starting to cramp as she clenched the walkie-talkie. At this point she was so nervous she didn't even know if she was pressing the button anymore. "You know, you're right, Gus. Neither of us seems to have much family. Before this party, I don't think either of us realized how much we cherished the loved ones in our lives."

Up in the attic, Addie held her breath. She was listening in closely to their conversation. Mimi was either subconsciously pressing the button or it was stuck.

Mimi felt nervous and shifted her weight. Best to keep the conversation bubbling on rather than appear that she was trying to get rid of him. "Anyway, I'm a big walker, so I didn't want all the square footage in this house to go to waste."

Addie raised an eyebrow. Mimi was tap-dancing as fast as she could down there.

Gus looked sullen. "I wish I could have spent more time with Jane. She and I were so different. But you know what? She was never unkind to me, even though I was a major screwup. And now I'm alone."

"It'll be okay, Gus," said Mimi, patting his arm, not knowing what else to do. She thought of Addie trapped upstairs. Trotting out a platitude didn't feel sufficient. "I'm truly sorry for you, but you've helped make something clear to me. That I still have time to make amends with my granddaughter."

He smiled. "You two have this way of talking to each other that I admire. There may be sarcasm or even anger, but it's obvious that, underneath it all, there's love."

Mimi nodded. "She drives me crazy sometimes, but I love her so much. I think she worries she's a one-hit wonder with her *Murderscape* game. But she's a brilliant kid. So much talent and creativity in that brain of hers. She's accomplished something amazing, and she can do it again on her own. In fact, I know she will."

Addie held the walkie-talkie to her ear. Her eyes welled up.

Gus gestured to the pillow. "After I deliver this to Her Majesty Lillian, I'm going to take a break. If you need anything, I'll be in the billiard room."

"Salutations!" said Mimi.

He turned to leave. "You know, you might want to retire that expression. I think my ninety-seven-year-old aunt uses it." He walked away and disappeared around the corner.

Mimi let a long breath of air escape. A few seconds passed, and she raised the walkie-talkie up to her mouth. "All clear. Over."

The grandfather clock opened and Addie slipped out, closing it behind her. She showed her the manila envelope. "I've got something."

They headed back in the direction of their room.

"Matthew had a whole Norman Bates thing going on. I'll tell you everything when we get back to the room."

Mimi sighed. "Pretty sure Gus thinks I'm a certified wackadoodle after our little chat. Oh, and I think he's got a dried bloodstain on his sleeve."

Addie gasped. "Really?"

"Yes, but I wasn't able to look very closely. I had to keep him talking so he wouldn't suspect anything."

Addie gave her a warm smile. "I know. I heard what you said."

"Meant every word of it, dear."

"Listen, Mimi," said Addie, slowing down her pace. "Do you promise we can talk about this . . . everything you told me about Grandpa Peter and all of the rest . . . sometime soon? Once we get the hell out of this place?"

Mimi reached out and squeezed her arm. "Yes. We can."

"All of it?" asked Addie.

"All of it."

THIRTY-THREE

The Last Will and Testament of Jane Ireland

Mimi blew air through pursed lips. "I don't understand. Why can't we just tear open the envelope?"

"Because," Addie called out from the bathroom, "the fact that it's sealed is part of this particular clue's story. We don't want to damage the evidence if we can avoid it." She emerged from a cloud of billowing steam and held up the envelope to show that the flap had steamed cleanly open. "It worked!" she said triumphantly, removing the documents inside. She read aloud: "*The Last Will and Testament of Jane Ireland.*"

They exchanged a look. Addie scrunched her eyes as she continued reading. She flipped through the rest of the documents, then paused. She stared at one page and reread it in dawning comprehension. "This is odd," she said, handing the papers to Mimi. "Jane wanted to give all her money away."

"Really?" said Mimi, taking it to examine:

I, Jane Ireland, residing at 1 Lilac Lane of Mackinac Island, Michigan, declare this to be my Will, and I revoke any and all wills previously made.

She scanned farther down the page:

I direct my executors to make this commitment as part of
the Giving Pledge. My pledge letter (attached) shall be
made public only after my death.

"What's the date on the letter?" said Addie, flipping through
Jane's appointment book.

"September twenty-first."

Addie leafed back through to August and found the entry she
was looking for: *Giving Pledge Zoom call w/BG!!* Her eyes widened.
"Oh, wow. Mimi, I think Bill Gates had a call with Jane about the
Giving Pledge in August. She must have changed her will right after that."

Mimi shook her head as she looked through the other papers.
"She's got a whole PR plan in here too. Wants her pledge published
in every major newspaper alongside her obituary. Even in death, the
woman wanted attention."

Addie rolled the *Chicago Gazette* pen between her thumb and
forefinger. "We need to start prioritizing suspects." She opened to
a fresh page in the Murderbook and wrote down Gus's name. "Let's
talk to Gus again. The dried bloodstain is one thing, but this Giving
Pledge thing . . . Maybe he partnered up with Alexandra to get the
money. If her inheritance was going to disappear, that's a motive to
kill Jane."

"I still think it's Woody."

"You've made your antipathy toward him clear. Just because you
don't like him doesn't mean he did it." She frowned in thought.
"And we still haven't talked to Kimiko, other than your mysterious
breakfast tête-à-tête."

"I told you, I'm working on an approach with her," said Mimi.

"Tell me more."

"Not yet. Still percolating up here," she said, tapping her temple.

"Okay. She seems low priority to me, anyway. She was onstage at the auction during the murder window. It would be impossible for her to have sneaked away to kill Jane between 9:00 and 9:15."

Mimi shook her head. "Haven't all those murder mysteries taught you anything? It's often the least likely person who did it."

Addie sighed. "What about Veronique?"

Mimi didn't respond.

"We know she's killed once before."

"She saved my life, dear," said Mimi. "Not a priority suspect."

"We can't let emotions cloud our analysis, Mimi. I think you want to be friends with her."

Mimi sat back and folded her arms. "Well, who do you think did it then? What about Mr. Square-Jawed Game Show Host?"

"I don't know. He's a rich celebrity, Mimi. He has more to lose than anyone else here. Why would he travel to a small island and murder someone in the middle of a blizzard? Gus said he saw him in the ballroom during the murder window, anyway."

"What's your gut telling you?"

She sighed. "Lillian definitely isn't sitting right with me. She has an alibi, according to Gus, but the whole klepto thing is just giving me a bad feeling. It could be fake. Maybe she's really taking those items to plant false clues." The image of *Murderscape*'s Talisman character flashed in her mind again. *Dark play.* "You know, she could easily be the person who planted the knife under the mattress to frame you."

They sat in a pensive silence.

Addie rubbed her forehead. Every time they unlocked a clue, things got more complex. The core game loop in *Murderscape* wasn't dissimilar. Players uncovered answers that increased their awareness and access to other spaces and clues. But that only led deeper into the mystery, and the bigger puzzle became even more challenging. In the case of Jane's and Matthew's murders, it was the same feeling. Only it was real.

"Listen, I've been thinking," said Addie, reaching for the ledger. "I noticed in here that the payments from Gus only started a few weeks ago. It's a little strange, because it's a very specific amount that repeats. It's down to the cent, and it's paid bimonthly. Almost like . . ."

"A paycheck," finished Mimi. "But didn't he already cover a lot in the kitchen with us last night? What more can we get out of him?"

Addie paused to think. "What if we get him into the ballroom for a bit? French police use this technique a lot."

"Really?"

"Yes, I learned it from a Netflix documentary. They take witnesses back to the place where they saw something, to question them, and it often sparks more accurate recollections. It's a better UX."

"Your neologisms do not impress me."

"'UX' means 'user experience.' It's about making things more intuitive. We'll just play-test this approach with Gus, okay?"

"Addie, my brain is not a trampoline for you to bounce around all your gamer guff."

"Play-testing is just what it sounds like. It's a process that allows you to look into the player's mind and revisit your assumptions so you can see the game in a different way."

"Naturally."

A heavy fog of cigar smoke wafted toward them as they entered the billiard room. Gus was playing by himself, aiming his next shot, with a thick stogie clenched between his teeth.

Addie shook her head, disgusted. "Is *everyone* here a smoker?"

Mimi sniffed. "Sorry we offend your Puritan sensibilities."

Barnabas waddled up to them, wagging his tail. Binky lay asleep on the floor, twitching her blond tail and growling in the throes of a dachshund dream.

"Barnabas can smell fear," said Gus.

"We're not afraid," said Mimi. "Just wanted to chat with you again, Gus."

His expression was unreadable as he moved to the other side of the table to set up for another shot. Mimi noted that he had changed his shirt. No more bloodstain.

"Always bugs me that they call this place the billiard room when all they have is a pool table," he said gruffly, sinking a striped ball into a corner pocket.

"Nice shot," said Addie. "We'll make it quick."

He gestured to a group of leather club chairs surrounding the fireplace, and they took a seat. "Jane was so damn particular about everything. Finicky. But she couldn't get something as simple as the name of a room right."

Addie lifted Barnabas onto her lap. "Gus, we noticed that Jane was wearing a wig last night," she said gently. "Was she unwell?"

The fire popped and hissed, filling the silence that followed the question.

"I suppose it doesn't matter if I tell you now," he responded, speaking carefully. "Jane had breast cancer. It was terminal."

Mimi cast a quick glance at Addie, who met her gaze. *Gus's reveal raised a bunch of questions, but could any of them be sensitively asked now?*

Gus leaned over the table and closed one eye, perfecting his aim. "Only the family knew. She didn't want anyone to pity her."

Mimi stopped listening and began to take a mental inventory of everything she had learned about Jane in the last few hours. Realizing not only that she was *not* the blackmailer but also that she had terminal cancer gave Mimi a twinge of something . . . Was it regret? Guilt? How would things have gone down if she had gotten the chance to confront her? Mimi shrugged. She had already tried to empathize with Gus about Jane in the hallway just a short while ago. Nothing more she could do now, even if she wanted to. Jane was dead. She turned her attention back to him.

"So, if only the family knew she was dying," said Addie, "is there someone outside the family who may have wanted to kill her?"

Gus rolled the cigar between his fingers. "I don't want to talk about my sister like this. Enemies and revenge plots. I've told you what I know."

"Remember what you said in the cellar, Gus? You wanted us to help find out what happened to your sister."

He looked up at them and made eye contact. "I do want your help. I'm just tired. Didn't sleep well last night."

Addie set Barnabas down. "Do you mind if we change scenery for a moment? We just want to jog your memory."

THIRTY-FOUR

A Better UX

Addie, Mimi, and Gus walked down the hallway together, with Barnabas and Binky marching behind them, heads held high.

"So," said Addie, lifting her voice as they arrived in the ballroom. "Can you show us exactly where everyone was standing when you came in the first time to check on the food?"

Mimi watched as Addie questioned him. Despite the utterly terrifying situation they were in, she was in her element. She was starting to see the glimmer of that strong-willed, bright kid who loved puzzles and adventure. Her moxie was back. There seemed to be something else there too. Self-belief.

"Yes," said Gus, positioning himself in the center of the room. "I checked the table over there. Everything looked okay. The auction hadn't started yet. Everyone was standing around, eating and chatting. I remember Matthew was over by the bar."

"What time was this again?"

"I'd say around 8:30."

"You know, Lillian showed us a TikTok she made around the same time. Matthew was wearing a coat in it. Do you remember that?"

"Yeah, I guess I do, now that you mention it," said Gus, making his way toward the well-stocked bar. Addie trailed behind him as he gestured to a marble pedestal on the countertop piled high with shiny lemons. "He was over here cutting a lemon. I did think it was a little weird that he was cutting a lemon with his coat on."

Mimi took a seat at the bar. "Strange indeed. Who does that?"

Addie shot her an irritated *You're overdoing it* look.

Mimi gave her a *Just trying to help* shrug.

"Anything else?"

Gus furrowed his brow. "Don't think so. That's really all I remember. I went back into the kitchen because I had so many things to attend to."

"And then, when you came back the second time, you said you refilled everyone's drinks?"

"Yes. At ten past nine. I topped up their champagne glasses."

"Who was there, again?"

"Like I said, Matthew was onstage, so I didn't need to top him up. But I wasn't really paying attention to what else was going on. Lillian and Sebastián were over there by the desserts table. Topped them up. And Woody. He was taking a break from playing the piano."

"And you said he slipped past you at one point?"

"Yes."

"But you didn't see where he went?"

"Nope, he just went down that way," said Gus, indicating the direction of the dining room.

He took a mixing glass down from the bar shelf and his shirt-sleeve slipped down his arm a few inches, revealing a Band-Aid on his right wrist. "Would you ladies like a drink? I know it's a bit early in the day, but what else are we supposed to do around here?"

Addie shook her head as Mimi nodded in the affirmative.

"Pick your poison," he said, catching himself and flinching. "Sorry, poor choice of words."

"Gibson," said Mimi.

"Two Gibsons coming up," he said, skewering three onions each onto a pair of cocktail sticks and placing them atop two martini glasses.

"I can see you know what you're doing over there. It's nice to have somebody around here who knows how to make a real drink."

He smiled as he poured the gin and vermouth into the mixing glass.

Mimi rested her elbows on the counter. "What did you do to your wrist, Gus?"

There was an uneasy silence as he stirred the ingredients with a weighted spoon. "Binky clawed me earlier. I was picking her up, and she doesn't like to be picked up."

Mimi nodded. Best not to press further, for now. They had other topics to cover. "So, can you tell us more about your nephew-in-law?"

"Not much to tell you, really," he said, shaking his head. "That whole situation was terrible. It tore our family apart."

Addie turned to Mimi and nodded subtly to indicate she should continue.

"How is Alexandra doing?"

"We aren't close, so I don't know." He handed Mimi her Gibson.

"Does she have any children?"

"No."

Mimi took a sip and looked at Addie, then back to Gus.

Addie looked up from making notes in the Murderbook. "So how do you know Lillian?"

Gus turned to her, curiosity piqued. "Lillian? What about her?"

"You were having a conversation with her in the lounge last night that looked pretty intense. We just wondered how you know her."

Gus cleared his throat. "She's been a consultant for me on a personal-branding thing."

"Were her services needed to fix whatever issues you were having? Issues that someone was blackmailing you for?"

Gus looked confused. "How do you know about that?"

Mimi raised the martini glass to her lips. "Let's just say we know a lot, Gus. And it's only because we want to find out what happened to Jane and Matthew. We're not interested in getting anyone in trouble for anything beyond the murders, okay?"

Addie watched the change come over him as he realized it was best to fess up.

"Matthew was garnishing my wages. He told me he'd get Lillian to help me if he could take my chef's salary for a good six months. Jane paid me, but I don't think she had a clue the money was going into Matthew's pocket." He paused to drink his Gibson. "I kept quiet because I couldn't bear the thought of disappointing her. Having her see that I let her down . . . again. I've always been the family failure."

Mimi observed the deep lines in Gus's face as he took out his phone. Imprints of a life full of disappointments.

"You see," he said, showing them the screen, "I had this dog surfing school that became a bit of an Instagram sensation for a while." He scrolled through several images. A chihuahua wearing sunglasses on the beach. Barnabas and Binky together on a longboard, ears blowing back in the wind. A terrified-looking whippet on a neon-pink boogie board riding toward the shore. "The narrow ones are the hardest to keep upright," he said, pointing to the whippet. "I admitted to Jane the dog surfing school was a sham. We had a green screen in my buddy's garage where we would show a video of the ocean. Then we'd put a dog on a surfboard and make it look like we were teaching him how to stand on the board while we jiggled it." Gus shook his head. "Demanded full payment from people who signed up, but they'd never hear from us again. We did have good intentions, but we were drunk half the time and couldn't pull it all together, I'm ashamed to say."

"So Jane told Matthew about this and he used it against you?"

"Yes, essentially. Jane had offered to hire Lillian to cover up the fallout from it. That way I could still get a job. But Matthew wasn't going to let that slide. He knew this wasn't the first time I had asked my sister to bail me out. Anyway, Matthew inserted himself into the conversation between Jane and me. He used my situation to line his pockets."

"Sorry, Gus. Listen, you've been a huge help. Is there anything else you want to tell us? Anything you've noticed in the hours since Jane's death?"

Gus furrowed his brow. "There is one more thing. I was upstairs in my room, taking a quick break before serving the late-night snack. It was just before eleven p.m., and there was a strange sound. Binky barked a few times. Odd since she's usually the quiet one."

Addie paused to consider this. "Was it a regular bark or an urgent bark?"

"Somewhere between the two. Kind of a *Hey, just making you aware of this* bark."

Mimi raised an eyebrow and turned to Addie. "We heard someone else mention this sound too. Around the same time. Can you describe it?"

"I'd say it was kind of a bump. Or a thunk."

"No idea what it was?"

"Nope." He made his way toward the ballroom's bar. "I figured it was just one of the 'ghost' sounds that these old houses acquire over the years. Listen, ladies, I want to get back to my game. I appreciate all that you both are doing to find my sister's killer." He nodded to them and raised his Gibson before sauntering back down the hall.

Mimi waited for the sounds of his footsteps and the dachshunds strutting behind him to fade. She grabbed Addie's elbow. "I think I've got something."

"What is it?"

"The Gibson. He made it with a bottle of Tanqueray. I didn't say anything because I didn't want to be rude."

"Hasn't stopped you before."

Mimi pursed her lips. "I hate Tanqueray. That's why I barely touched it at first. Except I took a sip . . . and it wasn't Tanqueray."

A wrinkle formed between Addie's brows. "So what? Gin is gin."

"I'm pretty sure it was Hendrick's. There were strong rose and cucumber notes. Tanqueray is all pine."

"All gin tastes like hand sanitizer to me."

Mimi shook her head disapprovingly. "Can't believe we share a branch on the family tree. Anyway, Lillian's TikTok said Jane's favorite cocktail was a French 75."

Addie tilted her head. "Yeah, so?"

THIRTY-FIVE

The Decoy

Your standard French 75 has four ingredients: gin, champagne, lemon juice, and a single sugar cube," said Mimi, taking on the air of a university lecturer. She was standing behind the ballroom bar facing Addie, her only patron.

"Okay," said Addie, taking out the Murderbook and pen.

"Last night, Barb was circulating with coupes of champagne. Gus told us he saw Matthew make a cocktail with a lemon here right in front of everyone. Presumably using a coupe from Barb's tray. For him to create a whole separate drink somewhere else would have been too conspicuous. He had his coat on, so that's our time stamp. We know it was around 8:30, when Lillian made her TikTok. And he made it here, in clear view of everyone. He was doing it performatively. Like when you're at the drugstore and you need to fish through your purse. You do it theatrically, so no one thinks you're shoplifting gum or Prevacid."

Addie frowned, then nodded. Mimi was making a lot of sense . . . for the most part. "So you're saying—"

"Before the party, he took a bottle of Hendrick's gin and poured most of it into an empty bottle of gin."

"The bottle of Tanqueray that Gus just used?"

"Exactly. He drugged the remaining gin left in the decoy Hendrick's bottle so everything looked normal when he made Jane's drink. He probably stowed it away in one of these cabinets so no one else picked it up, but it was easy to access. It had to be the gin because Gus saw him cut the fresh lemon. To drug the champagne would have been too risky and confusing, since everyone was drinking from matching coupes."

"What about the sugar cube?"

"I doubt he drugged a sugar cube. Seems complicated. Not to mention the danger of someone else putting it in their coffee or tea. No, he wanted the sedative in something he could hide away, quickly identify, and hide away again, something that looked benign."

"Okay, so if this decoy bottle of gin was used, did he toss it away? Where is it?"

"I'm sure it's here somewhere," said Mimi, crouching down to search through the trash. "If we can find it, that might help the police," she added, as she opened and shut several cupboards. "They can bag it up and—"

"'Bag it up'? Didn't know you had all the lingo."

"What? I've seen *The Wire*." Mimi crouched down. "Aha!"

Addie got on her tiptoes and peered over the bar to watch as Mimi reached underneath the sink cabinet.

"I've got something back here," she said, rising to stand.

It was a green plastic recycling tub. There was one single empty bottle of Hendrick's gin inside. Addie gasped in amazement.

"Knew it was Hendrick's," said Mimi, with a self-satisfied nod. "Such a distinctive flavor."

"You should work for their ad agency."

"We can tell the police about it when they get here," said Mimi, putting the tub back under the sink and brushing her hands together. "So there you have it. It was Matthew. With the decoy gin. In the ballroom."

Addie gave Mimi a soft round of applause. "I should get you a deerstalker cap and a pipe."

"It all makes sense now. Jim was saying how Jane liked to throw elaborate parties and that last night didn't feel up to her usual standards. The combination of the drugged drink, the subpar party, and facing Lillian was all too much. She was drugged around 8:30, so by 9:00, she could barely function. As far as she was concerned, the party was over."

"Was it ever," sighed Addie.

"So," continued Mimi, newly puffed up, "I've been thinking about how to get Kimiko to open up, and I have a plan. Let's go find her."

THIRTY-SIX

Remember You Must Die

Addie and Mimi stood quietly in the doorway of the conservatory. Kimiko was seated in a cane chair, surrounded by a cluster of trees and tall plants. Unaware that she was being watched, she gazed straight ahead with her hands folded in her lap. For a moment, Addie felt that she was glimpsing the real person underneath the reclusive-artist pretense. The feeling quickly evaporated as they walked in.

Kimiko sat upright. "What are you two doing here?" Her voice sounded hoarse.

"Are you feeling all right?" asked Mimi, looking concerned. "Do you want us to bring you some tea and honey? Something for a little throat coat?"

Addie retracted her chin into her neck. Mimi had never been so comforting and maternal in her entire life.

"No, thank you," said Kimiko.

"We just need five minutes of your time so you can tell us what you witnessed last night," Mimi continued softly. "We know all about the blackmail. You've been making huge payments, and we want to know why."

Kimiko stiffened.

She walked a few steps farther into the room. "We know you aren't the creator of *Memento Mochi*."

Addie turned to Mimi, frowning. Mimi looked back at her with a look that said, *Trust me, I know what I'm doing.*

"Do you want me to tell you what gave it away? I can tell you here, privately, if you talk to us. Or I can share my realization with the whole group over lunch, if you prefer."

Kimiko hesitated for a few seconds, then motioned to a love seat across from her. "Have a seat, then."

They sank into the love seat's squishy cushions. The air was fragrant with the smell of wet soil. Candles flickered from every corner, causing the room's greenery to cast eerie shadows on the walls.

Mimi tried to make eye contact, but Kimiko reached for a sketch pad on a table nearby and busied herself with a half-finished drawing. The motion of the charcoal pencil in her hand was frantic, nervous.

"First, I thought it was odd that you autographed the manga with your right hand at the auction," Mimi began coolly.

Kimiko froze. An awkward silence passed as Mimi's and Addie's eyes fell on her right hand, grasping the charcoal pencil tightly.

"Given that *Memento Mochi* famously features left-handed hatch marks, I thought it was strange. But I figured it was possible you were ambidextrous, so I didn't pay it much mind."

Kimiko pursed her lips. She remained focused on her drawing. "I didn't realize I was being watched."

Mimi leaned in, speaking in a confidential tone. "Knowing that I was going to be bidding on this work, you can probably understand that I wanted to learn every damned detail about it. Even surprised myself when I read the whole thing cover to cover on my iPad, and enjoyed it. I read the fanzines and the fanfic too. I read it all."

Though Kimiko kept her head down, there was a perceptible change in her demeanor, and her posture became more alert.

"So, when we briefly chatted at breakfast, I reminded you that I bought the manga at the auction, being the fan that I am. Told you how much the Indigo Wizard in particular resonated with me, and you thanked me for my kind words."

Mimi turned to Addie. "You see, *Memento Mochi* deals with themes of impermanence and mortality. The Indigo Wizard and his magical indigo mochi can transform a dead person back into a living being, giving them a second chance at life. The story really resonated with me. In fact, I think about it all the time."

Kimiko pushed her pencil harder against the paper, drawing more intensely. "What are you getting at? Everyone loves the Indigo Wizard."

Mimi turned back to Kimiko. "There is no Indigo Wizard."

Her forehead creased, and she looked up. She set the sketch pad aside. "What? Of course there is."

"I made it up. There's the Mango Wizard and, of course, the fan favorite, the Jelly Wizard and his elaborate neck tattoo that reads *Remember you must die.*" She turned to Addie again to explain. "Taken, of course, from the title's play on words with the Latin phrase 'memento mori.'" Focusing back on Kimiko, Mimi leaned forward. "When we spoke at breakfast, I watched your eyes when I said 'Indigo Wizard.' You didn't flinch in the slightest. If you knew I'd made a mistake and used the wrong term or simply made it up, you would have had a reaction. But you didn't. It was the practiced nonreaction of someone accustomed to deceit."

Kimiko sat back in her chair for a moment, in silence. The only sound was the wind rattling the windows. "What do you want to know?"

"How did the blackmailing start?"

In a small voice, she began to speak. "I come from an artistic family. My father was an opera singer, and my mother made pottery. But my older sister was the great talent. I can sketch and paint quite well, but I'm not gifted. When she was only seventeen, she was struck and killed by a motorcycle."

Addie flinched. The words "struck and killed" sent an electric jolt through her. Those same words had been used a little more than a decade ago to relay the message of her parents' deaths, just as she was about to return to college for her senior year. She swallowed her emotions down and went back to focusing on Kimiko.

"My parents went into deep mourning. That's when I found her storyboards and drawings tucked away underneath her bed. I took them as my own. I thought if I became a successful mangaka, my parents would stop mourning my sister and notice me." She took a breath and removed her glasses from her nose to rub her eyes. "After I got it published and it became a hit, I felt a deep, paralyzing shame, and I became a *hikikomori*."

"And what does that mean, exactly?"

"It means I withdrew from society."

Mimi nodded in understanding.

Kimiko plucked a leaf from a plant next to her chair and ran her finger along its edges. She looked up at Addie. "Your game is brilliant, you know. I play it all the time. I was nervous to say something to you earlier, thinking you might be a *Memento Mochi* fan. Gamers are my usual demo. Not your grandma here."

Addie smiled warmly. "Thank you. Although Mimi's a gamer too. Bridge, solitaire, crosswords."

"When my parents died, I felt like I could finally be myself again. I started to make small steps toward reentering society."

"Is that when you met Jane?" asked Mimi.

"Yes. Jane was in Kyoto with Matthew on vacation. Her agent reached out and asked if I would meet them because her daughter, Alexandra, was a fan. I was reluctant, but they explained that Jane had a lot of money and could fund my other projects. A patron-of-the-arts type. After we met, we became close. Jane knew a big ice cream company interested in doing a licensing deal with *Memento Mochi*. I told them I wanted no creative control, so I never even had to take any meetings. I just watched the money roll in. That's when Jane convinced me to move to Santa Barbara, close to their vineyard." She paused and a glint of a mischievous smile played at the corners of her mouth. "Everyone in California treats you like some kind of oracle or deity if you're a famous artist. I found it all a bit ridiculous. But I won't pretend it wasn't nice, sometimes."

A candelabra on the table flickered.

Kimiko's eyes grew distant and unfocused. "I'm ashamed to admit it, but I've only skimmed through the story once. I really only spent time studying my sister's drawing technique. Drawing has been my only comfort since I dishonored her."

"What was her name?" asked Mimi.

"Kazu. Her death has left an emptiness in me. She never got to marry or have children. Yes, her genius lives on, but in my name, not hers."

Addie looked down. A maze of thoughts swirled through her head. "Taking authorship credit away from artists happens a lot. It comes in different forms. People spread rumors that Mary Shelley didn't write *Frankenstein*, that it must have been her husband who wrote it. Andy Warhol was accused of plagiarism many times. F. Scott Fitzgerald took ideas from Zelda . . ." She cleared her throat. "I myself might just be another Zelda."

Mimi touched Addie's arm. "Maybe I haven't been as understanding as I could have been about all that."

Addie held her gaze. She thought of Mimi's words earlier. Maybe she was right. *Why didn't she trust her own choices, her own vision?* She'd always thought Brian saw more than she did. That he was somehow wiser, smarter. But in truth, he just exploited her weaknesses. She thought of that playful wink he'd give her whenever she got "moody," as he'd call it. Funny how he'd always try to lighten things up whenever she was in the middle of asserting herself. *It was control masquerading as love.* He twisted her sense of reality, took credit for her work, and then simply erased her from his life.

A few seconds of silence passed. She needed to redirect their line of questioning back to Jane. "When you started making money on the ice cream deal, is that when the blackmailing started?"

Kimiko gave a small nod. "Jane had been hassling me about creating a new manga. She and Matthew had come out to Santa Barbara on one of their wine odysseys. We were all having dinner at a little bistro when Jane brought up doing a new manga again. I blew up at her. Told her the real reason why I couldn't do it, and I took a taxi back home." She looked up at them with sad, heavy eyes. "That was the last time I saw her before this weekend."

"And that's why *Memento Mochi* was a stand-alone," said Mimi. "You never did another one because you . . ."

"Couldn't," finished Kimiko. "After the blowup with Jane, I realized I wanted to move back to Japan, for a quieter life. I didn't go back to being a *hikikomori*, but I mostly kept to myself. I've always been a loner. But I did miss Jane's friendship. We kept in touch for a bit . . . and then the blackmail letters started arriving."

"When was this?" asked Addie.

"About six months ago," Kimiko replied.

Addie nodded and flipped back through the Murderbook to the place where she had noted observations from Jane's appointment book. She jotted down a reminder to check if Kimiko's story aligned with what was in there.

"So, Matthew also knew about what you had done because the three of you were at dinner when you had your meltdown?" continued Mimi.

"Yes. And he put that outburst of mine to good use. He was angry because Jane had arranged the ice cream deal without taking a percentage. He felt that I was earning money that should have been his. Although why should he be entitled to any of it?"

Addie perked up. "Is that why you were arguing with Matthew, before he died?"

"Wow," snapped Kimiko. "You two really have been spying on me."

"I didn't mean to, I swear. I just happened to overhear you."

Kimiko sighed. "Yes. He was saying I owed him a percentage and trying to give me a guilt trip because Jane had just died. I refused and he flipped out." She looked down. "That money is mine. Well, more so than his, anyway. I'm no saint, though. I admit that when the ice cream money first came in, I was smug and selfish for a time. I thought I was so clever."

Addie felt her cheeks burning at Kimiko's words. She was describing the same smugness that she knew Brian must be feeling. She thought of the "Venetian Masquerade" episode of *Murderscape.* It had sprung completely from her original ideas, and she'd even drawn one of the Venetian masks in the Quoth the Raven notepad when they first conceived the game. Its imagery was what Closed Casket used in all the marketing materials. Besides the stiletto dagger, it was the one bit of iconography that every gamer recognized.

She'd also convinced Brian that *Murderscape* should be episodic, with a new, self-contained mystery releasing every two months. He'd initially wanted it to be open world, with more horror-style violence. Eventually, he relented as her vision caught fire and the game flourished. Giving it an ongoing structure was what helped to sustain its popularity. Brian had also wanted the game to be about competition among players, but she had convinced the wider team at Closed Casket that the game should encourage connectivity and collaboration. Friends played it together in small groups, and that's what made it memorable. The core aspects of what made the game special, and popular, had been hers.

Those years developing the game together had merged into one long, confusing memory of endless debates and deep self-doubt. He had intentionally implanted those insecure feelings so that it was easier for him to put his name on everything. Brian was working on another level. In game design, they had all kinds of names for it. Cheats. Hacks. Scripts. Exploits. *Dark play.* Studying the system in order to manipulate it. He had learned how she operated, then manipulated her. Saying they were an equal partnership every step of the way, but in reality playing a game she wasn't even aware of.

Sole credit for *Murderscape* was always his goal. She saw it now.

Kimiko continued sketching on her pad. Addie looked on as her pencil moved across the page. The drawing was of a crane. Her hand's movements were now calm and fluid. She caught Addie's eye.

"I see you use pencil," said Addie, admiringly. "Mimi over here's not a fan; she only uses pen."

Kimiko shrugged. "Why do they have to be pitted against one another? Like everything in life, they each have their pros and cons."

"What is it that you want to do next?" asked Addie.

As if she had anticipated the question, Kimiko pulled something from her satchel and handed it to her. "I want to make one-of-a-kind greeting cards. For unique occasions and gestures. Birthdays and anniversaries have become so generic and predictable. What about those times when you're face-to-face with someone and you feel something, but you struggle to form the words? I want to help people connect in the everyday moments in between."

The card was thick and soft; the paper felt handmade. On the front was an intricately drawn image of water flowing through rocks in a stream. Along the bottom was a message written in elegant cursive: *What is not said is what keeps us apart.* Addie swallowed, moved by the words. She opened the card. It was blank inside.

"You can keep it," said Kimiko.

Addie smiled and nodded thank-you. They got up to leave.

"Wait," Kimiko said. "There's something else I should tell you."

"Go on," said Mimi.

"It was something I noticed last night. In the powder room."

"Which one? When?"

"The one near the library. It was after Matthew died. I would have used the one in the lounge, but it was occupied. I was washing my hands, and I heard part of a conversation outside the door. I ignored it at first, but it started to get heated, so I got curious and put my ear to the door. I remember the woman's voice said, 'You can't change your mind now.'"

Addie jotted down the words verbatim in the Murderbook. "Anything else?"

"Yes. She got really insistent. She said something like, 'It'll take the heat off you!' But she was whispering, so I'm not exactly sure if that's what she said. And then I distinctly heard a man say, 'Keep quiet. Let's talk later.'"

"Thank you, Kimiko. We'll leave you be."

They left the conservatory and climbed the stairs back to their room.

"Bravo, Mimi."

Mimi shrugged. "Now that her ruse is over, she seems quite genuine to me. She's probably the most 'real' person here. Does that make her a player character?"

"That's exactly right," said Addie, grinning. "Spoken like a true gamer."

Addie's phone buzzed. She put the pen and Kimiko's card inside the Murderbook to mark her place, then set it down on a nearby console table.

"Your phone isn't dead yet?" asked Mimi.

"It's on its last legs," said Addie, looking at the screen. It was Brian. "Shit!" she said, reflexively.

"Oh, great. Let me guess. The Chinless Wonder?"

Addie hesitated as the option *Slide to answer* lit up the screen. If only it were that simple. She considered the sense of relief she might feel, just for a moment, if she picked up. So much had happened over the last twenty-four hours that it felt like she was getting a call from a different planet. She felt an overwhelming urge to tell him what was going on. With all that Microsoft money, he could fund a good criminal defense attorney for Mimi at the very least. She could take him through some of the clues, and they could test-drive a few theories.

The phone had been ringing for a solid five seconds now. Addie's finger hovered over the screen as she made eye contact with her grandmother.

Mimi responded with an affirming look. "You don't need him, Addie."

The words filled her with calm and courage. She looked at her phone again. It was her last chance. No. She slipped it back into her clutch and rolled her shoulders back.

Mimi gave her a warm smile and nod of approval.

Addie was silent for a moment. Her face cycled through several emotions before settling on a half smile. Although she sometimes didn't want to admit it to herself, it pleased her to make her grandmother proud. "Let's go back to the room. I've got an idea for a tactic we could try with Woody. Something that could help us understand his role in the blackmail once and for all."

"Clever girl."

"Don't sound so surprised. I did design a world-famous murder game."

THIRTY-SEVEN

A Tell

Addie flipped through Jane's appointment book. Kimiko's name appeared regularly, corroborating the details she'd just shared in the conservatory. *Skiing weekend with Kimiko. Pick up Kimiko at airport. Zoom catch-up with Kimiko.* Matthew, who she assumed to be the *M* with a heart drawn around it, was everywhere too. *M's Birthday. Date Night with M. Tennis with M.* In the weeks leading up to the party, Jane had a few doctor appointments: *Dr. Wagner. Dr. Marston.*

"I think Kimiko was telling the truth, Mimi."

Mimi looked up. She was seated next to her in the small sitting area in their room, leafing through the *Wine Down* magazine they'd found in Matthew's secret office attached to the speakeasy.

"Look at this," Addie said, holding up the appointment book for Mimi. As she started to point to one of the entries, a slip of paper fell out and fluttered to the floor. Addie reached down to pick it up. She looked closely at it, then her eyes widened. "Mimi! This is her password cheat sheet! She's written down all her passwords here!"

"Who? Jane?"

"Yes. Except they're hints." She squinted to study the writing. "It says *iPhone: Mom's bday* and *House alarm: Nelson's favorite food.*"

"Wow, impressive level of sophistication there. We'll have to call Bletchley Park."

"This is a huge discovery, Mimi. Look! It says, *Drawbridge: A's real name.*"

"Didn't she know you're not supposed to write your passwords down all in one place? Security 101."

"Wait a minute, wait a minute!" Addie raised a finger in the air. "Jane's apology letter to Alexandra said her name meant 'from the heavens.'"

Mimi frowned in concentration.

"And remember how you said the video on Lillian's phone showed Matthew's hand typing in a seven-letter code?! The password to the drawbridge is a seven-letter woman's name meaning 'from the heavens'! Mimi! It's just like a crossword clue!"

Mimi continued frowning.

Addie paused to think. "Angel? Aurora?"

"No," said Mimi firmly. "Angel isn't right, and Aurora means 'dawn.' Those aren't seven letters, anyway."

A few minutes of thoughtful silence passed between them.

"Wish my phone hadn't just died. We could Google it."

"No way, that's cheating," Mimi responded, with a disapproving shake of her head. "I'll keep thinking. We don't have power to get the drawbridge down anyway, so the code isn't much use to us right now."

"Won't the control pad operate on a battery?"

"Maybe, but that whole mechanism is definitely going to require power. You saw that big, hulking thing. Let's get back to the Murderbook. What do we need to do next?"

Addie opened it and clicked the pen. "Okay. Here's what I'm thinking. When I was doing research for the 'Ripper' episode of

Murderscape, I learned all about detectives in Victorian-era London. They patrolled their beats daily and were essentially walking criminal databases because they knew everyone in town, their traits and histories. Players love 'Ripper' because you have to rely on interrogation strategies based on human behavior to get to the truth."

Mimi set the *Wine Down* magazine on her lap. "Dear, I'm delighted you're feeling inspired, but I'm not a clown car for every game design thought that comes to you. We've got a murder to solve here. Can you get to the point?"

"Okay. So far, we've mostly been relying on rapport-based interrogation techniques, but those don't work with Woody. And Woody and Jim are the only ones we know for sure were in cahoots with Matthew."

"The fixer and the launderer."

Addie put the pen down and looked at Mimi. "What if we get them together in the ballroom? Ask them both what they were doing from 9:00 to 9:15, in real time? We ask them what they know about the murders and see if there are any tells. Maybe they'll trip over each other's words or try to cut each other off when one person is contradicting what they're saying."

Mimi drummed her fingers on the magazine's glossy cover. "You know, I might have something."

Addie looked at her. "What?"

"It only occurred to me just a bit ago. When I was questioning Jim in my room after Jane's death, he lied to me, as you know. He said he didn't know a thing about the blackmail."

"Okay."

"But thinking back on it now, I did notice something. His lip twitched. I can see it in my mind's eye, crystal clear."

"Seriously? It twitched?"

"Like Elvis going through caffeine withdrawal."

Addie's face ripened into a grin. "So we're going to use Jim as a sort of a human polygraph? That's pretty genius, Mimi. Okay. We'll get Jim and Woody together in the ballroom, and I'll ask the questions. You stay focused on reading Jim. We need to have a signal. Something subtle you can do that will tell me when he's lying."

"Sure," responded Mimi. "Maybe I could take a sip of a Gibson?"

Addie eyed her skeptically. "Probably not the best plan."

"Okay, what if I tap my nose, as in *Pinocchio*?"

"That's good."

"All right," said Mimi, walking toward the door. "Let's go find Leopold and Loeb."

"Don't really think that's an apt comparison. Didn't they have genius IQs?"

Mimi shrugged. "They got caught, didn't they?"

They made their way downstairs.

"What do you think about this 'clunk'?"

Addie shook her head slowly. "I don't know. Only half the people seemed to hear it. Not sure if there's any significance, really. In *Murderscape*, we often see players try to assign causality to every event. But sometimes events in the game are totally random."

"Just like in real life," added Mimi. "Not everything that happens can be explained."

They found Jim Towels in the drawing room, perched on the edge of a bergère chair, working an emery board across his fingernails.

"I can never get a perfect squoval," he said, shaking his head at his hands. "Damn weak nail beds."

"Jimbo, I've got a buffer here in my carryall if you want to sand down some of those ridges," offered Mimi. "But we need to borrow you first. Do you mind meeting us in the ballroom in five minutes?"

Jim looked dubious.

"Consider it a personal favor to me. And in return, I promise never to tell anyone about your illicit Towels Laundromat."

He nodded. "Okay, Rosemary."

Addie headed toward Woody's room, with Mimi walking closely beside her. They were finally starting to feel like a team. Hopefully, this next interrogation would get them some of the answers they'd been searching for.

THIRTY-EIGHT

The Polygraph

They knocked on Woody's door. After a few seconds, it swung open, and he appeared before them, looking groggy.

"Hey, Daphne," he said to Addie. "I was getting some beauty rest." He rubbed his eyes. "What time is it?"

"Daphne? Really? Always thought of myself as more of a Velma," said Addie. "It's 11:45 a.m. Can you come with us to the ballroom for five minutes? We need your help."

He leaned on the doorframe. "You know, this whole detective-duo thing is getting a bit hammy for my tastes."

Mimi stepped between them. "Cut the crap, Woody. We know all about the blackmail, and 'we've got the receipts,' as the kids say. Could really upset some folks around here if we told them you were Matthew's number two."

Woody's smile evaporated. He looked around in both directions, then wrapped his robe around himself and tightened the belt as he put on his slippers and stepped into the hallway.

Addie spoke softly. "We've got a lead on your cuff links. If you help us, we'll get them back to you."

"Good cop, bad cop, huh? You're really bringing out all the old chestnuts." Woody shook his head. "You know what? Fine. Let's talk. I have nothing to hide."

They went downstairs together in tense silence. When they arrived in the ballroom, Jim Towels was already there, seated at a table in the far corner. Mimi noticed Woody flinch at the sight of him.

"All right, gentlemen," said Addie. "We can't reveal our sources, but we know you two make up the nucleus of this blackmail operation, so we want to ask you a few questions. Assuming you already know each other? Since you're . . . colleagues?"

Neither of them responded.

"I'm going to pour myself a whisky," Woody announced, walking behind the bar counter.

"I'll call the papers," said Mimi.

Woody cocked his head, and a smile teased at the corners of his mouth. "You know, at first it bothered me that you didn't make even the slightest effort to hide your contempt for me, Rosemary. But I'm starting to appreciate you now. You're an acquired taste, just like Laphroaig," he said, holding up the bottle. "Want some?"

"No, thanks, I prefer not to drink my cigarettes."

Woody threw his head back and gave a laugh that turned into a wheeze. "That makes sense for you. I bet you like simple whiskies. Unchallenging. One-note."

"Guys," said Addie, holding up her hands. "Can we stop with the verbal fencing?"

Woody took a seat on a barstool and reached into a bowl of almonds.

"Jim, why don't you join us over here at the bar?" offered Addie, gesturing for him to come in their direction.

Jim stiffened. "No, thank you. I have a severe nut allergy."

"Okay," said Addie, clapping her hands together. "Look, we want to ask you what each of you saw. If you can just answer our questions as quickly and briefly as possible, we can wrap this up."

"Go ahead," sniffed Woody.

"Jim, please show us where you were between 9:00 and 9:15 p.m. last night."

Mimi observed Jim closely as he spoke.

"I was standing right over there," said Jim, pointing to an area near the dessert table. "I was keeping an eye on Jane." He looked at Addie. "I was explaining to your grandmother that she'd been up-set with me, so we weren't really talking. But I was worried about her. Earlier, Jane seemed to be her usual self, but then, at some point, she changed." Jim stood up and walked around. His answer was clipped, his voice rising an octave as his Adam's apple bobbed up and down. "I gave her the note to meet me upstairs, like I told you, Rosemary. Then I went to the bathroom and came out to all the commotion coming from upstairs."

Addie made eye contact with Mimi, who subtly nodded. No nose-tap.

"Okay," said Addie, jotting down a few notes in the Murderbook. "Woody, can you please tell us what you were doing?"

"Wow, you really know how to ask the hard-hitting questions." Woody dipped his hand into the bowl for another mouthful of al-monds, and they all fell into an awkward silence while his molars pulverized them to a swallowable size. "I was at the piano coaxing out some dulcet tones to soothe the madding crowd. And then I think at some point around that time I got up and took a break. I was parched. Could hardly get a damn drink all night. They need more waitstaff in this joint. So anyway, I went to the kitchen fridge to get a bottle of champagne."

"How long were you gone?"

"Only a few minutes. Then I went back to playing piano."

"Does that sound right to you, Jim? Do you remember Woody being in the room for most of the auction? Playing piano?"

"I think so. Yes."

She looked at both of them.

"Do either of you know anything about Jane's murder?"

"No." They both answered without hesitation.

"Do either of you know anything about Matthew's murder?"

"No."

Addie looked to Mimi again. No nose-tap.

She turned back to Woody. "Can we talk about the auction? You seemed to be placing a lot of bids."

Woody smirked.

"Did you buy something?"

"I did indeed. A marine chronometer from the nineteenth century," he responded flatly.

Addie leaned against the bar counter. "You don't sound too enthused about it."

"Oh no, it's just what I've always wanted. Now I'll know my exact longitude whenever I'm crossing the ocean by clipper ship."

Jim shifted in his seat.

"Jim," said Mimi. "What's going on? You're unsettled."

He inhaled a sharp breath. "I'm just upset, that's all. I gave Jane that chronometer for her birthday last year."

"Really?"

"Yes. It was one of the first ever made by Thomas Mercer, the father of astronomical navigation. It hurt me deeply that she would auction it off."

"I already told you that's not what happened," Woody grumbled under his breath.

Addie planted her fists on her hips. "Gentlemen, can you please explain to us what the hell is going on?"

Woody continued speaking to Jim as though they were the only two people in the room. "It was a mistake, okay, dude? That chronometer thing wasn't supposed to be one of the items. When Jane saw it in the program, she pulled me aside, told me to buy it and she'd cover the cost. She didn't know how it got in there."

Jim shook his head. "It still hurts my feelings. Obviously it wasn't that special to her if it somehow got mixed in with all that junk for the other patsies."

Mimi's face puckered into a scowl.

"Did you buy anything last night, Jim?" continued Addie.

"Why, yes, I did," he said quietly, "a beautiful set of pewter gravy boats once owned by Queen Anne. I've always coveted them."

Addie thought she detected a faint twitch and turned to Mimi, who tapped her nose in confirmation. "Okay, seriously, you two. *What* is going on?"

Jim began to stammer out an answer.

Woody held up his hand to silence him. "Let me cut to the chase since Mike Wallace over here isn't piecing things together. No, neither of us really bought anything last night because we didn't have to. We were just told to *look* like we were buying stuff and help drive up the prices. Me and Jim, we're just part of the staff. I collect secrets and payments, and Jim here runs everything through his shop and cooks the books. He's the Picasso of creative accounting. Makes Enron look like a crayon drawing on somebody's fridge."

Mimi shook her head in disgust. "We already knew that you two were Matthew's lead henchmen—"

"I prefer 'business partner,'" said Woody.

Addie held her hand up and cut in. Mimi's antagonistic drama with Woody was not helping them get anywhere. "What we need to know is what *else* you both know. Why was Matthew killed? Why was Jane killed?"

Both men shook their heads and shrugged.

"I don't know," said Woody.

Jim hung his head. "Sorry I lied to you again, Rosemary. I'm in deep. This thing is like *Chinatown*. I can't afford to lose my BBB Torch."

Addie walked toward Jim. "Since you two know each other so well . . . Jim, I assume you know that Woody is Aero Hart?"

Jim turned slowly to Woody. "Aero Hart? You're Aero Hart?" His mouth fell open. "I saw you tread the boards on Broadway! You played Alan Greenspan in *The Fed*!"

Woody heaved a resigned sigh.

"You were a terrific Greenspan. Really got into the soul of him. What was that great line? 'Fine, I'll raise the interest rate, but my estimation of you, sir—'"

"'—has plummeted,'" finished Woody flatly.

Jim frowned. "Wait a minute, you look different. Why don't I recognize you?"

"I just have one of those faces, I guess."

"Why are you using an alias?"

Woody huffed. "Look, I have nothing to hide, okay? Aero was my old stage name, and Woody is my nickname. My real name's Aloysius. Well, it's actually Sylvester Aloysius Pfefferkorn Junior."

"Aloysius?" asked Addie, Mimi, and Jim in unison.

"You can call me Al."

Addie turned sharply to Woody. "Who killed Jane?"

"I don't know!"

Mimi turned to Jim. "You really don't know either, Jim?"

"I don't, Rosemary. Listen, I have angina, and this whole thing is giving me a tightness in my chest. Can I go?"

Addie nodded. "Sure. Thanks, Jim."

Woody rose from the barstool. "Regretfully, ladies, I've become bored with this little kaffeeklatsch. Reached my max capacity for inane chitchat."

"Woody, don't go yet," said Addie. "Just hang out here for another second, okay? We want to chat with you for a few more minutes, and then we'll leave you alone for good."

He paused and took a gulp of whisky, ice tinkling in the tumbler.

"We don't think you killed Jane, okay? You threw the Baccarat vase against the wall because you were upset that she and Matthew were both dead."

"Your cash cow had just been sent to the slaughterhouse," added Mimi. "How many people did Matthew have working behind the scenes, anyway? Was it really just you and Jim? Or were there other bottom-feeders?"

Woody slammed his glass down on the countertop. "We're done here." He glared at Mimi. "You can judge me all you want, but I'm just trying to make a living." He turned back to Addie. "Sorry, Velma, but I'm done talking to Miss Marple."

Mimi frowned. "Miss Marple was a spinster. I am a widow."

Woody spun around. His eyes narrowed as they fastened on Mimi. They were empty and cruel. "Let's talk about why you're a widow, shall we?"

Mimi went very still.

"Our little Grandmother Superior here. Haven't you ever wondered how it came to be that someone knew your secret?"

Mimi felt a sweat sprout in her armpits as her heart started to pound inside her chest.

"And your nosy granddaughter here, strutting around the house like Nancy Drew. Spouting her righteous indignation about 'Mimi didn't do it!' and blah, blah, blah, like she's playing a game of Clue." He turned to Addie. "How old are you anyway? Twelve?"

Addie put her hands on her hips. "Well, Mimi didn't do it, you big bully!" *OMG. She did sound like a twelve-year-old.*

"Oh, but she *did do it* in another time and place, kiddo. Hey, Rosemary, remember way back in that Chicago hospital when you asked for a pillow and blanket to spend the night in a chair next to your husband? Who do you think brought it to you?"

A palpable tension enveloped the room, and they all stood in silence for a moment. Addie put her arm protectively around Mimi. She was shaking.

"I was the nurse's assistant working that shift."

"Wait a second," demanded Addie. "Why were you working as a nurse's assistant?"

"Acting gigs were drying up, and no one needed a full-time piano player, so I had to do something else to pay the bills. Not all of us have wealthy, attractive mothers-in-law to seduce. My mother-in-law looks like W. C. Fields."

"But after all those years had passed, how did you even know Mimi was living here on Mackinac?"

He ignored her and lit a cigarette. "Somehow I just knew what you were going to do, Rosemary. So I sneaked back into the hallway. You were hovering over the bed, and I watched." He winked at Mimi. "Wow! I didn't think you'd have the stones to do it. At one point, you were shaking so badly I thought I was going to have to step in and assist. If this lady wanted to off her pathetic husband, I was ready to lend a hand. But what a gal! You proved what a hard-boiled killer you really are."

Addie turned to Mimi, who stood motionless. No trace of her usual spunky self was visible.

He walked back around the bar and loaded fresh ice cubes into his glass. "Back to Daphne's question. Every once in a while, Matthew and Jane would tire of the cloying charm of Mackinac and take the helicopter to Chicago, where they could indulge their cravings to shop for spendy things on the Magnificent Mile. They always stayed at the Drake."

"Gus's hotel."

"Right-o. I played the piano there. Every so often I would notice this couple dining in a special corner where VIPs were always seated. Gus would come out of the kitchen in his chef whites and talk to them." Woody swirled the whisky in his glass. "Gus and I would sometimes meet for a drink after the dinner service was over. So I asked him about this couple. He told me she was his sister. He was having a tough time with the hotel management and was thinking about going to work for her on Mackinac."

"Then, one night, I was playing 'Fly Me to the Moon' when Matthew walked up to the piano and left a huge tip in the jar, explaining it was his companion's favorite song. Each time they came in, I made sure I played it for them. After a time, we became friends." Woody stopped to take a drink.

"Eventually, I agreed to help Matthew with his business dealings. I also played the piano for their social events and even occasionally did some side gigs at the Grand Hotel. So, I was at the hotel one afternoon when I saw a woman with red hair playing bridge with some other ladies. I instantly recognized her, even though she definitely had some age on her."

Mimi looked up at him. Her hand went to her clavicle and found her necklace. She squeezed the emerald so tightly her knuckles were bone white.

"I couldn't believe it. With a little of my own detective work, I soon figured out that she lived on Mackinac, so I filed this information away in my head," he said, tapping his temple. "I knew it might be useful one day. And what do you know, it paid off handsomely. Matthew had already started his whole blackmail scheme, but he was burning through a lot of cash. So, I told him how one of his very own neighbors had a secret so deep and dark he could surely get a little extra dough out of her."

Addie scowled at him. "I envy people who have never met you, Woody."

Mimi remained silent.

The dining room gong sounded.

"You snoops better get back to your role-playing games. Me? I'm going to have lunch." He strode out of the ballroom.

Addie turned to Mimi. "Breathe, Mimi. We need to stay calm and focused. Don't think about what he said."

Mimi drew in a shaky breath.

"C'mon. Let's skip lunch—we've got work to do."

Mimi scoffed. "You? Skipping lunch? This must be serious."

Addie smiled, relieved Mimi's Mimi-ness remained intact. "Let's go someplace where we can think."

THIRTY-NINE

In the Cards

Addie sat back in one of the aged-leather wingback chairs flanking the game room fireplace. She stared up at the ornate coffered ceiling with her arms folded in her lap, thinking. Mimi was playing solitaire at an octagonal-shaped card table, with a cigarette dangling from her lips.

Addie shook her head. "This place is going to smell like a casino by the time we get out of here."

Mimi took a long drag. "I'm happy to hear you think we're going to get out of here."

Addie turned to a clean page in the Murderbook and wrote:

MEANS. MOTIVE. OPPORTUNITY.

"How's that pen working for you?" said Mimi.

Addie smiled. "I do like it now."

Mimi slapped a card down on the table. "Any new theories coming together over there?"

Addie stared at the words on the page for a moment. "I don't know."

"I still think Woody's involved somehow," said Mimi, turning another card over. "From our little lie detector test, we know that Jim didn't know about the murder plot. But it's still possible Woody knew, and Jim didn't know that Woody knew."

Addie shook her head. "I don't think so, Mimi. This blackmail scheme was Woody's meal ticket. He didn't gain any advantage by killing anyone."

She stood up and walked over to a shelf that was lined with stacks of classic board games, some of them favorites she'd played with her parents growing up. Clue. Guess Who? Balderdash. Tracing her finger along the letters of each game's name, she stared at them as if they held the answer.

"Have you really considered every possibility?" said Mimi, frowning as she pulled a challenging card from the deck.

Addie paced the room and paused to admire a beautiful hand-carved chess set. She rolled her neck and shoulders as a thought came to her. "Wait a minute," she said, her face lighting up. "Maybe Matthew set up a way to get all the money. Yes! He faked signatures on a fake prenup, set up this whole party, had Jane killed . . . Then maybe he also orchestrated Alexandra's death at the same time, so he's the sole beneficiary. We've been cut off from the outside world for hours. She might be dead too, and we don't know it yet. He plans for both of them to die at the exact same time on the same day and then—"

Mimi shook her head and took a drag on her cigarette. "Who taught you how to sleuth, Rube Goldberg?"

Addie slammed the Murderbook shut and slumped back into her chair. "I give up. I think the killer's outwitted us."

"What would your friend Poirot do?" Mimi asked, turning over another card.

She leaned back in the chair. "His 'little grey cells' would have picked up on something by now. Some missing piece or false assumption that's been made. I'm afraid my 'little grey cells' just aren't good enough."

"Don't be ridiculous. Keep thinking."

She opened the Murderbook again and flipped to a clean page. She listened to the soft snaps and slaps of Mimi's cards on the table as she thought of the broken vase on Woody's floor. The bird graveyard in Matthew's fridge. The fleur-de-lis on Lillian's arm. Veronique's elegant perfume label. She chewed the inside of her cheek as she began doodling with her pen.

"You know," said Mimi, flipping a card over, "something from last night has been bothering me all day."

Addie finished drawing the fleur-de-lis and started to sketch Barnabas's sausage body and stumpy legs. "Do tell."

"The apple pie."

Addie's pen stopped. "Really? What about it?"

"Gus. The guy loves making food for us and showing off his cocktail skills. Tells everyone he was a chef at the Drake and even puts out the little butters and cocktail napkins to prompt people to ask about it. Such a proud guy, and then he serves us that gummy apple pie. It's just strange."

"I didn't think it was gummy. I gobbled it up," said Addie.

"That's not saying much." Mimi stood up from her seat and walked over to a walnut drinks cabinet in the corner of the room.

Addie watched. She was pleasantly surprised when Mimi poured herself a simple glass of water from a carafe. Mimi made eye contact with her as she took a sip. Addie averted her eyes and went back to doodling Barnabas. She tapped her pen against the paper.

"It feels like we're on the edge of it," said Addie, closing her eyes and replaying the entire evening in her mind. Still nothing. She rose to her feet and went over to the window, looking out at the shafts of wintry sunlight threading through the clouds. Turning away, she walked over to Mimi's table and sat down across from her. They sat together in silence for a moment, each with their own thoughts.

"What's been bugging me is how Gus said he refilled everyone's drinks when he went to check the ballroom. But when we talked to Woody, he kept complaining that he couldn't get a drink."

Mimi looked up from her cards.

"I mean, I know Woody's a liar, and Gus is a drunk. Both of them are unreliable witnesses . . ."

As Addie trailed off, Mimi's mind drifted. She turned her gaze toward the mantel clock. A few disparate thoughts blended together in her mind as she watched the pendulum swing back and forth. Then, something crystallized. She dropped her cards on the table and jumped to her feet.

"I've got something!"

Addie didn't look up.

"Dear, listen. Your play-test thingamajig. Remember how you said it allows you to see things in a different way?" She leaned over the table, trying to make eye contact with Addie. But Addie was staring down, trancelike, eyes unfocused. In a totally different place.

"Hello. Earth to Addie! Did you hear me? I think I have an idea."

Addie wasn't paying any attention. She was hovered over the table, studying Mimi's laid-out solitaire cards. "Don't make assumptions," she said under her breath.

Something in her mind snapped into focus. Her vacant stare ripened into a wry smile. She picked up the card she had been staring at, then lifted her head and met Mimi's gaze.

"I think I have an idea too."

FORTY

A Thunk

Okay, so remember the plan," said Addie as they ascended the back staircase together. "We can do our final checks after—" She paused abruptly on the landing and stared out the window.

Mimi stopped on the stair below. "What is it?"

Addie was fixated on the view of the observatory, an imposing structure situated amid the vast, deep snowscape. The sky above looked leaden and ominous, but the snow's intensity had lightened somewhat. Her face changed suddenly and she turned to Mimi. "Look!" she said, pointing out the window excitedly.

"What?"

"The observatory."

"What about it?"

"The dome."

"Addie, if you could give me more than a couple monosyllabic grunts, I'd appreciate it. What are you trying to say?"

"There's no snow. On the dome. But see how there's all those flat parts and ridges along the sides of it? And look, there's a little observation deck over there. All places where snow would accumulate . . . but there isn't any."

Mimi nodded. "So, you're saying it's heated?"

"Yes. Parts of it look delicate, like it's made of canvas. It probably can't support the weight of lots of snow. Gus mentioned Jane was funding some kind of special research, remember? Maybe there's a backup generator running in there to protect it."

"So . . . what now?"

"Let's divide and conquer. We need to hurry. I'll handle Barb, you gather up all the evidence for the drawing room reveal. After that, we'll check out the observatory together. If we can get the power back on and get the damn drawbridge down, the local cops can get here. I'll meet you back in the room in ten minutes, okay?"

"No," said Mimi firmly. "I don't want to separate."

"Mimi, we've almost closed the case!"

"But we left our walkie-talkies in the room. Can't we at least go back and get them so we can stay in contact?"

"Mimi, please."

Mimi heaved a sigh of resignation. "Fine. Ten minutes. You be careful."

They turned in different directions and left. Addie hustled toward Barb's room. The door was slightly ajar. She tapped on it and peeped through the crack. "Barb? Can I talk to you? It's Addie."

There was no response.

She nudged the door open. The fireplace was down to its last embers, and the room was freezing. A shiver swept through her as she stepped inside. There was a stillness to the room that made her uneasy.

"Barb?"

Something at the foot of the bed caught her eye. A fingertip. Addie held her breath and took a step closer. A body came into full view.

It was Barb. Her hair a dark mass covering her face. She'd been strangled with a tasseled curtain cord. Addie clasped her hand over her mouth to push back a scream. *A third murder?*

Stay calm. Examine the crime scene, she told herself. She scanned the body. Her eyes narrowed in on a strange outline inside Barb's uniform. Something was stuffed in her bra.

From somewhere deep within, a primal instinct told her she was being observed. She turned around. The room was empty.

Her gaze traveled to one of the curtains in the hallway. It was moving. She scanned the rest of the hallway from her vantage point in the room, then looked back at the curtain. It was now still.

A floorboard creaked. Every nerve in her body began to vibrate. "Who's there?"

Everything was silent. All she could hear was the pounding of her blood vessels. She paused, unsure what to do.

Out of the shadows, a figure stepped into a narrow shaft of light in the hallway. They wore a fencing suit, just like the ones that had been on display in the library. A black mesh mask concealed their face. There seemed to be no sound, almost like a silent movie playing out in front of her.

Her brain kicked in and began processing her options. *Run? Where?* The figure lifted a finger to the mesh screen, where the mouth would be. Addie stepped back. She felt rivulets of sweat run from the back of her neck down her spine.

Her heart hammered in her chest as she looked around the room for anything that could be used as a weapon. Barb's kitchenette had a block of knives. She moved toward them just as she caught the glint of metal at the edge of her vision.

The figure had a gun.

Addie's breath froze in her throat.

The figure raised the gun. She couldn't reach the knives in time.

As she dove to the floor, she saw a muzzle flash and heard a loud pop. The bullet broke through the window behind her.

She low-crawled toward a chair by the kitchenette. The figure fired again, and a large antique ginger jar exploded next to her.

"Help!" she screamed.

Adrenaline spread through her body and numbed her like an anesthetic. Everything felt distant and unreal, as if it were happening to someone else. She ducked behind the chair for cover. The figure fired again. Her hand seared with a sharp burning sensation.

THUNK!

The figure fell forward and the gun clattered to the floor.

Addie looked up. Mimi was standing behind the assailant, holding a fireplace poker like a baseball bat. Addie froze for a moment, stunned that her grandmother was able to exert such strength. The figure groaned, then started to get up.

"Mimi!" she cried out, her voice catching in her throat.

Mimi ran toward the gun, which had skittered over into the corner. At the same time Addie scrambled across the floor and reached for a large shard of porcelain from the broken jar. She charged toward the figure and drove the shard directly into their knee. A guttural groan burst from behind the mask as they shoved her away and she fell back onto the floor.

The figure scrambled to their feet and ran out the door.

"Where's the gun?" shouted Addie, frantic terror still pumping through her veins.

"I've got it here," said Mimi. She dropped the poker on the floor with a clang and ran to look down the hallway. It was empty. She crossed over to Addie. "Are you okay, dear?" Mimi said, trying to stop herself from shaking.

Addie blinked. Her right hand stung. She looked down in shock at the long gash running diagonally across her knuckles. In her entire lifetime of dreaming up murder-mystery plots and villains, it had never occurred to her that she would become the target of a killer.

"I'm okay, Mimi," she said, wrinkling her nose at the odor of burning gunpowder on her skin.

"The bullet grazed your hand, my God," said Mimi, wincing at the wound. "I saw a first aid kit in the kitchen. We'll get it fixed up when . . ." She stopped. Her voice was quavering. "I'm just so thankful that you're okay. This all could have gone so wrong."

"I can't believe you knocked them down to the floor. That was so badass. Why did you come back here? How did you know to find me?"

Mimi reached into her carryall and produced a white glove, holding it up. "I was heading for our room to gather the evidence and saw this lying on the carpet by the stairs. I knew it was from one of those fencing suits the minute I saw it. Knew I had to get to you. I grabbed a poker from one of the guest room fireplaces, and then I heard you scream . . ."

Addie put her arm around her grandmother. "I'm really okay, Mimi."

"If I had lost you . . . I don't think I could . . ."

"I'm here, Mimi. We're okay."

Relief flooded Mimi's face as she exhaled a slow, measured breath and looked down at the gun. She expertly opened the cylinder and removed the bullets. "Only two rounds left. I'll be in charge of this." She slipped the gun in her carryall and placed the bullets in a separate compartment.

Addie looked at her uncomprehendingly. "How do you know how to do that?"

"Took a marksmanship course to fulfill a college PE requirement. Never thought it would come in handy." Mimi turned back and nodded her head in the direction of Barb. "Poor Barb. She never got to launch her essential oils business."

Addie straightened and brushed herself off. "The killer is still in the house. We need to move quickly."

FORTY-ONE

Cracking the Code

The cold wind battered Mimi's face as she hugged her coat tightly around herself. She waded through the drifts toward Joan Rivers, who sat parked where she'd left her the night before. Parts of her lavender chassis peeked through the accumulated snow.

"Afternoon, Joan," she shouted, taking in a lungful of frigid air. She called out behind her, "You coming, dear?"

"How is my Pall Mall–smoking grandmother in better shape than I am?" said Addie, huffing and puffing as she trailed behind Mimi, high-stepping through the snow.

Mimi stopped and frowned. Joan Rivers was almost buried in a drift. "I hope you had your Wheaties this morning because we have to dig her out." She set to work brushing snow off the windshield and seat while Addie pawed away at the ground, vigorously scooping piles from Joan's back end and sides. Mimi went around to the front and began packing snow down in front of the skis.

Their faces were red from the effort and the stinging cold. "Try it now!" ordered Addie, brushing her hands together and stepping back.

Mimi climbed onto the seat and twisted the key in the ignition. Nothing happened.

"C'mon, Joan Rivers," she said quietly, trying it again. Nothing. She paused for a moment, took a deep breath, and exhaled. "We have a lot of people counting on you, Joan," she whispered to the dashboard. Then turned the key again. *VROOOOOM.* Joan purred to life. Mimi gave her a little love pat on her handlebars, then revved her engine to warm her up.

She smiled proudly at Addie. "Climb aboard. You better hold on tight."

Addie wrapped her arms around Mimi's waist just in time as Joan gave a big roar and they lurched forward.

Powering Joan Rivers through the snow and up a sloped incline, they progressed toward the west side of the house. Snowflakes hurled themselves into Joan's windshield, making it difficult to see the observatory's curved dome in the distance. To their left was the dizzying drop over the ragged cliff to the slate gray water below. She throttled the engine, kicking up powder behind them as they zoomed even faster across the snowy terrain.

"You okay back there?" Mimi called out.

"I think we just broke the sound barrier," Addie shouted back.

As they approached the observatory, Mimi could see a wall of snow, about three feet high, pressed against the entrance. She pulled up and cut the engine. The wind bit into her face as they dismounted and trudged through the knee-deep snow to get to the door. Despite the bitter cold, her determination acted as a protective shield. Addie crouched down to shovel the snow with her hands so they could clear a path.

Mimi tried the handle, but the door wouldn't budge. "I think it's locked."

"Let me try. It might just be frozen shut," said Addie as she twisted the handle and pulled it hard, bracing her legs against the doorframe.

"Good! Try it again!" encouraged Mimi.

Addie pulled with all her strength, but nothing happened. "Maybe we could break it down?"

"Sorry, I left my battering ram back at home."

Addie turned and nodded toward Joan.

Mimi grimaced. "No. I don't want to hurt Joan."

Gesturing toward the house in the distance, Addie asked, "Do you really want to go back there and wait for the power to come on again? We have to try."

Mimi thought for a moment. "You know, I might have just the thing," she said, as she unzipped her coat. Inside was her trusty carryall. She reached into it and pulled out a coiled black extension cord.

"How do you happen to have an extension cord in that magician's hat of yours?"

"These damned old houses never have enough outlets," Mimi explained as she handed one end to Addie. "Ever notice the miles of extension cords tucked behind all the furniture in these places? This one looked particularly long and sturdy, so I took it when the power went out. Figured we'd need it to tie up the killer or some such nonsense, so I tossed it into my carryall."

Addie smiled and shook her head as Mimi tied her end securely to a large metal loop on Joan's storage compartment. Addie tied the other end to the entrance door handle of the observatory.

Mimi gave a satisfied nod and climbed aboard Joan again, giving her a squeeze with her knees. "Sorry, old friend. I'll fix whatever breaks, I promise."

She gradually increased the pressure on the gas pedal as the extension cord was pulled taut, keeping the pressure constant and then increasing it more and more. A cloud of smoke began to pour out of Joan.

The observatory door flew open with a loud *thwack!*

"You did it, you beautiful broad!" Mimi exclaimed. She cut the engine and dismounted. She could feel the overheated motor underneath the chassis and gave her an apologetic pat. "Smoking isn't good for either one of us, is it, dear? We'll get you checked out, don't worry!"

As they walked inside, motion-sensor lights instantly came on, illuminating a magnificent circular room.

"We've got power!" said Addie, looking around in awe.

Facing them was an immense fenestration of windows overlooking Lake Huron. The words *Written in the Stars* were painted in different languages all around the sky blue walls of the sprawling room. Above them was an elaborate ceiling fresco swirling with galaxies, planets and moons. Mimi took a moment to study the room, looking deep in thought at the canopy of heavenly bodies overhead. She gasped.

Addie walked toward her. "What is it?"

"The code!"

"Huh?"

"It's 'Celeste'! Alexandra's real name. Seven letters, meaning 'from the heavens.' Celestial!" she said, pointing up at the fresco.

"Ah! You're a genius, Mimi!"

They high-fived and Mimi pointed at something behind her. "Look. Back there!"

To the right of a huge bookcase was an open doorway leading to a brightly lit stairwell. They approached it and descended the concrete steps into a deep, low-ceilinged bunker that buzzed like the engine room of a ship.

"Look at this place!" said Addie as they walked farther inside. They entered an enormous storeroom lined with shelves. Everywhere they looked, there were pallets stocked with canned food, bottled water, and what looked to be medical supplies.

"Over there!" said Mimi, pointing toward the back corner. They walked toward a row of large generators. The first one was labeled

O and looked different from the others, which were identical to one another.

"Do you know anything about generators?" asked Addie nervously.

Mimi shook her head as she studied each one carefully. "I think that first one with an *O* is battery-powered, since it's different-looking and came on automatically to keep this place running. The others must run on something else, probably gas."

"That looks like a circuit board," said Addie, pointing to a panel on a side wall.

"Shall we try those?" said Mimi, gesturing to a series of switches in the off position.

"We've got nothing to lose," said Addie. "Do it."

Mimi flipped all of the switches at once. Nothing happened.

"Hmm," said Mimi, walking toward the other generators again. She examined them more closely. One was labeled *Drawbridge and Exterior Lights*, and the others were labeled *House 1*, *House 2*, and *House 3*. She popped open what appeared to be the fuel tank of the one labeled *Drawbridge and Exterior Lights*. It was empty. She lifted a nearby red plastic canister, also empty.

Mimi sucked in a disapproving breath. "For a doomsday prepper, Jane forgot the 'prepper' part."

"Now what?"

Mimi looked around. "Over there," she said, pointing toward the shelves of medical equipment. "See if you can find anything in here with a long plastic tube."

They began opening boxes and moving tubs around.

"What about this?" said Addie, holding up a large wrapped circle of plastic tubing. "I think it's an oxygen tube?"

"Perfect," said Mimi. "Grab the canister."

They went back outside. Mimi unwrapped the tube and dunked it into Joan's tank. She adjusted the length so that it ran down to the snow and then came back up again, making the shape of a long U.

"I'm afraid to ask how you learned to siphon gas," said Addie.

"YouTube."

Addie watched intently as Mimi put her mouth on the other end of the tube and quickly sucked in. Then she pressed her thumb on the end of the tube and placed the tube over the canister. She released her thumb, and gas began to pour into the canister.

"Woo-hoo!" cheered Addie.

They carried the canister back inside and divided the fuel between the generators marked *Drawbridge and Exterior Lights* and *House 1* and turned on the power switch again. The machines whirred to life!

Addie clapped and reached out to give Mimi a hug. Mimi smiled resignedly and hugged her back.

They went back outside and could now see that the exterior lights had come on. The wind whipped the snow around them in tight, swirling eddies.

Mimi shuddered. "It's still so windy. Unlikely the mainland police can get here yet. But if we can get the drawbridge down, at least Pam's Sam and the local police can come."

Addie turned to Mimi. "Nicely done back there, Grandma."

Mimi patted her cheek. "Let's go tie up those loose ends, whaddya say?"

FORTY-TWO

The Show Must Go On

Addie drew in a confident breath as she paced the drawing room thoughtfully, head down with her hands behind her back. "Thank you all for coming."

It was 2:30 p.m. Everyone was seated in a semicircle around the fireplace. It glowed with crackling embers. The air was taut with expectation.

Mimi stood off to the side, ready to assist her chief inspector while also maintaining an ideal vantage point to observe everyone's reactions. Addie paused for a moment to look each guest in the eye, then began.

"This little weekend gathering at Jane's was described as a Jazz Age–themed party and a charity auction. But that wasn't true, was it?"

The group reacted with a mixture of grumbles and impatient frowns.

"It wasn't a joyous gathering of friends, no. You were all summoned here as part of a blackmail scheme. Then three murders happened."

"Hey, Poirot," Woody called out. "Can you skip to the whodunit?

We don't need the recap that plays before the next episode. We're all caught up."

"Fine," said Addie. "All of you in this room, whether victims, participants, or both, acted as the scheme's central nervous system. Most of you think Jane was running this whole thing. But Jane didn't know anything about it. It was Matthew."

"I don't understand," said Lillian, looking flustered and raising her hand like a student. "Why was Matthew blackmailing us?"

"He was desperate for cash. Growing Concern was being sued into the ground," said Addie, holding up the legal letter about the vineyard's negligence and the copy of *Wine Down* magazine. "Growing Concern had made false sustainability claims, and a leaked memo stating its wine contains carcinogens was featured in this issue of *Wine Down*. There was a class action lawsuit in progress, seeking compensatory and punitive damages. Matthew was facing massive financial issues and legal bills. But he concealed everything from Jane." Mimi took the letter and magazine from Addie and taped them to the wall, the beginnings of an evidence board for everyone to see.

"That tape's going to leave a mark on the wall," said Jim Towels disapprovingly.

"Thanks, Jim," said Mimi. "I'll make sure to let the cleanup crew know once they've mopped up all the pools of blood."

"But why didn't Matthew just ask Jane for money? Wasn't that the whole point of them being together?" asked Woody.

"Aha, good question," said Addie, who turned on her heel and walked toward the other end of the semicircle of guests. "They were on the road to a breakup. Our first indication of that, thanks to you, Veronique, was your tip about olfactory habituation. But we also learned that Jane had terminal cancer."

Reactions of shock and confusion filled the room.

"We have a letter to Jane's lawyer indicating she wanted to give all her money away. Show them, Mimi."

Mimi held up the Giving Pledge letter for the group to see, then taped it to the makeshift evidence board.

"It was part of her effort to redeem her public image. She was obsessed with leaving a respectable legacy behind, to the point where she hired an image consultant"—Addie paused to shift her gaze to Lillian—"who also happened to be jealous of Jane, and advised her to give away all her wealth and commit to the Giving Pledge."

A mixture of reactions rippled through the group.

"Huge Bill Gates fan over here," said Jim Towels. "Philanthropy is so cool."

"Philanthropy?" snorted Kimiko. "The height of vanity is wanting your name on a bunch of buildings."

Addie continued: "But all of this left Matthew in an impossible situation. He couldn't marry Jane. They were already on the outs due to his affair with said image consultant. Jane's daughter, Alexandra, who has no children, was the sole beneficiary of her will. Jane wrote a letter to her lawyer expressing her wishes to change the beneficiary to the Giving Pledge. But Matthew intercepted the letter. We found it hidden away in his private apartment in the attic."

Mimi held up the envelope with the letter inside. "No postmark. It was never mailed."

Addie scanned the room. She could see they were commanding serious attention now.

Sebastián cleared his throat. "Wait a minute. Wouldn't Jane have wondered why her lawyer didn't respond to the letter?"

Addie shook her head. "The letter is only dated a few weeks ago. Sadly for Jane, this letter gave Matthew an exact indication of her plans. We think it's possible Matthew posed as an intermediary and lied to Jane. Possibly even forging documents or emails to make her think that the changes to her will were moving forward. If you recall, Jane also didn't use email."

Jim's eyes lit up with a thought. "So, you're saying Matthew killed Jane?"

"No."

Jim's smile faded.

"Matthew couldn't kill Jane on his own," Addie continued. "This was a two-person job. It would be too easy to suspect him of Jane's murder because people always suspect the boyfriend."

"Son-in-law," corrected Gus.

"Whatever. He convinces Jane to host an intimate fundraiser, perhaps on the premise that it might be her last chance to see some of these people, given her illness. Mackinac is shutting down for the season, providing the perfect, isolated setting. But, of course, the auction was really just a ruse for him to collect more cash and gather a room full of people together to serve as potential suspects in her murder. People who had reasons to want her dead." She paused her pacing and stood to face the group.

"So he gets himself an accomplice, and that way he can remain visible, in plain sight, running the auction. An airtight alibi while Jane's murder goes down. Matthew made a big show of the weapons display in the library, enticing us with an array of easy-access in-struments of death. He figured someone was bound to become enraged at Jane for hosting this little extortion party. So he trapped us inside the house with the drawbridge and dialed up the stress of the auction by using a stunt bidder," said Addie, looking to Woody. "All in the hopes this pressure cooker would inspire one of the guests to do the dirty work for him."

Addie took a moment to catch her breath. The only sound was the loud ticking of the mantel clock nearby. "Matthew then drugged Jane's French 75 to make her woozy and therefore an easy target, but he miscalculated the dose because Jane had lost weight due to the cancer. By 9:00, Jane can barely function be-cause of the sedative. She goes off to bed early, without a soul taking the bait."

Addie took a dramatic pause. The audience was hanging on her every word.

"So they switch to their backup plan. His accomplice, the killer, slips away after Jane goes to bed. First to the library, where they grab the knife. Then they creep up into Jane's bedroom, through a secret passage we found that leads to her closet, and plunge the knife into her heart. Then Matthew claims to find the knife in our bedroom. He knew that whoever they framed, the others wouldn't come to their defense, for fear they'd get accused themselves."

"This doesn't explain anything. Matthew might have black-mailed us and tried to entice one of us into killing Jane at the party, but he's dead. We still don't know who killed him. Or Barb!" said Jim, rising to his feet.

"Don't get worked up into a lather, Jimbo," cautioned Mimi.

"I'm glad you mention Barb," said Addie. "She died because she saw something she wasn't supposed to see. Matthew took the gun from the library at some point during the aftermath of Jane's death and asked his accomplice to meet him down in the wine cellar. That's where Matthew tried to double-cross his accomplice. He wanted to kill them to cover his tracks and rid himself of any financial obligations to that person. Barb was in the cellar at the time, getting biodynamic wine for Lillian, and she stumbled upon this confrontation. This accounts for the broken wine bottle on the floor and the defensive wounds on Matthew's right hand. There was clearly a struggle before the accomplice overpowered Matthew and shot him."

"But if Barb witnessed Matthew's murder, why didn't she say something to any of us?" asked Lillian.

Addie smiled. "Because she saw it as an opportunity." She walked the length of the room and back again. "Barb offered her services to Matthew's accomplice. She would help spread lies to misdirect our investigation. All to take the heat off the real killer. But for a price."

"So, if Barb was blackmailing the murderer, then it follows that the murderer would want to kill Barb," said Jim Towels.

"Bingo, Jimbo!" said Mimi.

Addie held up a wad of cash. "We found this money stuffed in Barb's bra after she died. She was in the middle of accepting a pay-off from Matthew's accomplice when she met her demise."

"But why would Barb conspire with the killer?" asked Kimiko.

"Barb was an ambitious woman," explained Mimi. "Her employers were dead. Why not make some money out of this experience and use it to start a new life? She also needed help funding her little pill problem."

Addie held up the Murderbook. "I'll read this aloud because I wrote it down. Kimiko overheard a conversation in the hallway last night. We think it was between Barb and Matthew's accomplice. The voices said: 'You can't change your mind now. It'll take the heat off you.' 'Keep quiet. Let's talk later.'"

"*Cherchez la Barb*," said Veronique.

"I'm exhausted. Can we get back to who the killer is?" asked Gus.

"Isn't it obvious?" said Mimi.

"No!" came the chorus response of the group.

Addie smiled. "Then allow me to pause for dramatic effect while we wait for the answer. Just like . . . someone hosting a game show would."

Everyone's eyes widened in realization at the same time.

The confidence in Addie's voice silenced the room as she walked toward Sebastián, who sat completely still, his shoulders stiff and proud. A muscle in his jaw tightened.

"Matthew reached out to his old friend when he needed help. His classmate and close school buddy from the lacrosse team at Poplar Tree Academy."

Mimi reached into her trusty carryall and pulled out a photo from Matthew's study that she'd removed from the frame. She held it up to show the group, then taped it to the wall next to the letters and the article.

Addie walked to the photo and pointed to young Sebastián.

"Tell us, Sebastián," said Mimi. "What school yearbook award did you get? Most Machiavellian? Class Sociopath?"

"The species of poplar tree most commonly found in North America is the tulip poplar, also known as the yellow poplar. Most importantly, it has spade-shaped leaves." Addie held up the ace of spades from Mimi's Bicycle deck. "Last night, you were wearing a sweatshirt with a spade emblem from your school on it. But it occurred to me later that, being green, of course it wasn't a spade. It was a leaf."

The blood drained from Sebastián's face.

Mimi walked up to Sebastián and leaned down in his face. "Addie knows her plants. Never fuck with a phytophile."

The room reacted with gasps and a faint ripple of applause. Addie could see a vein protruding from Sebastián's forehead. His nostrils flared. He looked like an angry bull ready to charge.

Addie walked closer to him and stood next to Mimi. "You were about to lose work, possibly your whole career. Initially, I assumed that, among everyone in this group, you had the most to lose, but that assumption was wrong. You were worried about the bullying scandal that was about to come out in the press. NDAs that silenced people you worked with were being nullified, and someone was about to blow the lid off. We know this because your agent dropped you in anticipation of the firestorm."

Sebastián shot a look at Lillian, who averted her eyes.

"That call from Coppola? *Please.* You made that up. When you told Matthew your career was crashing and burning, you hoped that he'd either lend you money or have Jane talk to your mutual agent and convince him to take you back. But he had already started cooking up this scheme, and he realized he had found someone who was in a desperate situation and could help him. To make matters even worse for you, you'd already poured money into your start-up. Being a celebrity entrepreneur means you have to trade on the value of your name. So if your name loses its value, then what does that make you?"

"A bad investment," said Mimi. She looked to Gus, who was fuming, glaring at Sebastián.

Addie held the ledger in the air. "What confused us for a while were the letters *SP* in this ledger alongside the initials of everyone else here tonight. Why would Matthew be blackmailing Sebastián Palacios and getting payments from him right up until a few days ago if he was his partner in crime?"

"Because," Mimi chimed in, "*SP* was actually referring to the real name of one of the other guests here: Sylvester Aloysius Pfefferkorn."

"Junior," added Woody.

Mimi continued: "Woody was in the ledger because he was deeply embedded in the blackmail scheme. Taking payments but also making payments."

Addie directed her attention back to Sebastián. "When we asked you about the blackmail, you lied because you knew if it came out you were the only person *not* involved somehow with the blackmail, it might become obvious that you were the killer."

"You weren't in the ledger at all, were you, Mr. Palacios? You were just an accomplice. An old friend."

"Poirot said it best," said Addie. "'Every murderer is probably somebody's old friend.'"

Sebastián's eyes flitted around the room. "This kangaroo court is a joke. You and your geriatric stagehand are sensationalist liars."

"How is any of this really evidence?" asked Lillian.

"Yeah, I'm confused," said Gus. "I saw Sebastián in the ballroom when I refilled his champagne glass. He was chatting with Lillian, and that was right smack-dab in the middle of the time period when we know Jane was killed. How could he possibly have killed her?"

"Aha," said Mimi, who turned to Addie. "May I?"

Addie smiled and nodded. "Please, go ahead."

"Gus's recollection provided what seemed to be a solid alibi for several people, so we didn't suspect Sebastián for a while. But then something occurred to me. Just like when you're doing a crossword and early on you enter an incorrect answer, it throws off the whole puzzle. Makes a mess of the other clues."

Everyone leaned forward.

"The digital display for the clock and the timer on the kitchen oven are the same, and sometimes, when you look at it quickly, you can't tell the difference. It's happened to me before too. Veronique helped Gus take care of Barnabas and Binky while he was busy in the kitchen. She let them out a back door, which briefly set off some kind of motion sensor or alarm that beeped. It was loud enough for someone under the influence to think it was their oven timer going off. Gus told us he could account for several people being in the ballroom around 9:10. But really it was earlier when Gus checked on everyone. He wasn't reading the clock. It was the oven timer, showing nine minutes and ten seconds left on the pie bake. Gus, in his booze-shrouded haze—"

"Hey!" said Gus defensively.

"Gus, you're not fooling anybody," said Mimi. "You were intoxicated all night. You could barely keep your hands steady when you were slicing into that pie in the kitchen. And the pie is what gave it away."

"How do you know all this for sure?" asked Jim Towels

"Because the apples were crunchy and the crust was gummy. Underdone."

Gus's shoulders slumped in shame.

Addie met Sebastián's gaze. "Sebastián here is in prime shape. Works out seven days a week. Even does Tai Chi when he's stuck in a murder house in the middle of a blizzard. Easy for someone like him to take the secret passage we found leading to Jane's bedroom and come back to us without missing a beat."

Sebastián's mouth twisted into a sickening smile. Addie felt a cold sweat begin to bead on her skin. She was looking at an IRL killer.

"You still don't have concrete proof," said Lillian.

"You're right," said Addie. "Except, when we confronted the killer in the fencing suit, I stabbed them in the knee with a shard of ceramic. The killer would have a significant wound on their right knee."

Sebastián stirred in his seat and balled his fists. Suddenly, he jumped up and turned around to run.

"Stop him!" shouted Kimiko.

Jim Towels leapt toward Sebastián, tackling him to the floor. Veronique ran over and helped pin him to the ground as she pulled up Sebastián's right pant leg, revealing a crude bandage around his knee with blood seeping through.

The room gasped.

"Very Jean-Claude Van Damme of you, Jim!" said Mimi approvingly. She looked to Veronique. "Did you get ahold of the police?"

She nodded, holding up her phone. "*Oui*. I told them we can get the drawbridge down. They are on their way."

"Hey, Gus," Jim called out. "We could use some help here. I stopped lifting weights ever since irritable bowel syndrome put the squeeze on my colon."

Gus lumbered over and took a seat on Sebastián. Binky and Barnabas growled at him.

"Get off me, you dirt clods," groaned Sebastián.

Addie reached behind a curtain and pulled out the crossbow, aiming it at Sebastián. He registered the crossbow, and his body went slack.

"Have a seat over there, Sebastián," said Addie, nodding toward a chair in the back corner of the room. "We're not done yet."

He offered no resistance this time. Jim escorted him to the chair, and he took a seat.

Mimi walked over to a lamp table and yanked out two long extension cords from the outlets. "Here, take these," she said, handing one to Gus and one to Jim. "You boys tie him to that chair nice and snug." They followed her instructions obediently as she turned back to Addie. "Never realized how multipurpose those things are!"

Addie kept the crossbow trained on Sebastián. His eyes met hers. They were dark and hard. She felt a chill. "Why did you frame Mimi?"

He shrugged. "We needed to pin it on someone. Matthew picked her after she cut her finger on the knife, which was rather convenient for us." He paused to make eye contact with Addie. "It also didn't sit well with him that she'd brought her murder-mystery-expert granddaughter to the party, uninvited."

"How did you poison her cigarettes?"

"Easy," said Sebastián. "She set her bag down on a chair at breakfast when you two left to talk to Jim. Barb took it for me. She was running around this place cleaning up after all of you. Most of you barely acknowledged her presence. The whole thing only took a few seconds."

Addie kept the crossbow level. "Do you even have a daughter who plays *Minecraft*? Fernandita, was it?"

He smirked. "What do you think?"

"Look!" Lillian called out. "The police are here!" Everyone ran to the window. Two snowmobiles and an ambulance with flashing lights rolled toward the moat.

Mimi hustled into the foyer and punched in C-E-L-E-S-T-E on the keypad by the door. Outside, a low electric hum kicked in as the drawbridge began its descent. As the clanking and moaning of gears ricocheted off the mansion's outside walls, inside, the house echoed with cheers.

FORTY-THREE

Leaving the Scene

Yellow crime scene tape flapped in the breeze. Pam's Sam and another officer had handcuffed Sebastián. They were questioning him in the drawing room.

A sense of relief had settled in. Mimi could hear Lillian talking animatedly with Jim and Gus in the foyer, reliving the events of the last twenty-four hours. Woody was being uncharacteristically helpful, carrying dirty plates and glasses back to the kitchen. Veronique was feeding Barnabas and Binky from a cheese platter. Addie was talking with Kimiko, holding a piece of paper and smiling. She wrapped up the conversation and headed toward Mimi.

"What's that?" asked Mimi, nodding to the paper in her hands.

"Oh, Kimiko gave it to me," she said, proudly turning it toward her. It was a drawing of herself with a Poirot-style mustache against a detailed backdrop, entitled *Addie Solves the Mystery!* "She replicated a famous location in *Murderscape*. Isn't that sweet?"

Woody approached them and nodded to Mimi. "All right, Cagney and Lacey. Nicely done. You solved the mystery, and you also didn't expose the rest of us. I appreciate that. Although let's agree that it serves you to keep this blackmail business on the hush-hush too," he added, looking to Mimi with a smirk.

Mimi sniffed. "Glad to see the needle on your moral compass stopped spinning long enough to thank us, Woody."

"Hey, it's all water under the drawbridge," he said. "I still have one more question, though."

"What's that?" asked Addie.

"How do we know Alexandra isn't the wizard behind the curtain of all this drama? She had good reason to want both Jane and Matthew dead."

"We thought about Alexandra as a possibility," said Addie. "But she was only a red herring. From everything we can determine, she's tried to move beyond this horrible situation. She lives in California, which is a community property state. Matthew was set to get half of everything she owned if they divorced. There was no prenup. So, he needed to get rid of Jane before she could give away Alexandra's inheritance. And it was too risky to take the time to divorce Alexandra and marry Jane, even if he could convince her to keep the money. Jane was in a fragile state from the cancer."

Satisfied with their explanation, Woody nodded and walked away. Mimi hurried after him and gripped his arm. Addie looked on as Mimi whispered in his ear while she reached into her carry-all and handed him something.

"Uh, what was that about?" asked Addie, after she returned. "What did you say to him?"

"Oh, I'd rather not say," said Mimi curtly.

"Tell me."

"Well, it wasn't 'Merry Christmas.'"

"C'mon, Mimi, what did you say to him?"

"I convinced Lillian to give me his cuff links. I gave them back to him and told him I don't want him returning to Mackinac. Ever.

Now that all of this is settled, I just want him to leave us alone. Find another racket on somebody else's island."

Veronique approached them and tapped Mimi on the shoulder. "I have something for you," she said, presenting Mimi with a bottle emblazoned with a *V.* "It's my special formula, and I think it would suit you perfectly. An unimpeachable scent." She lifted the stopper and placed it under Mimi's nose. "The top note is sour. It can be off-putting at first. But it quickly settles down into a warm sandalwood base of great depth and impressive strength."

"Thank you, Veronique," said Mimi, taking a moment to appreciate her Veronique-ness one last time. So timeless and chic.

Jim walked up and joined them, sporting a bandage on his forehead.

"J. Teezy!" said Addie warmly, patting him on the arm.

"Who?" said Jim Towels.

"My man. Thanks for your help back there."

Veronique turned to leave. "Promise me you will throw the essential oils away. They frighten me."

"I will. I promise," replied Mimi.

Veronique gave her a little wave goodbye. There was a sadness in her eyes.

They turned back to Jim.

"Is that bandage from your tussle with Sebastián?" asked Mimi.

"No. It's the craziest thing. I went upstairs to get my things from my bedroom, and the showerhead in my bathroom fell off *again.* I picked it up and tried to twist it back on, but the thing is ancient. It's heavy as a tire iron. Last night it fell into the tub, but this time it hit my dang head." He touched the bandage with his hand. "I can tell you I saw stars."

Addie looked at Mimi. "The clunk!" they both exclaimed at the same time.

"Huh?" said Jim.

Addie laughed. "There was one clue we couldn't reconcile in this whole thing, and it was a clunk sound that some people heard. We decided it was a red herring, but we were never really sure what it was. Is that why you had duct tape in your pocket last night?"

"Yes, I tried to tape it. Didn't work, though. When it hit my head, I was so upset I used profanity."

Mimi clutched invisible pearls. "You, Jimbo? Profanity?"

Jim shook his head in shame. "My dear departed mama always said to me, 'Jim, don't you dare ever say—'"

"Move out of the way, folks." Everyone stepped back as a policeman escorted Sebastián, looking disheveled and dazed, out the door.

"I'll see you around, Rosemary," said Jim.

Mimi patted him on the shoulder. "Listen, after all we've been through, you can call me Mimi."

Jim nodded goodbye and left.

Tall and lanky as a flagpole, Pam's Sam headed toward Mimi and Addie.

Mimi looked up at Pam's Sam and smiled. "Hi, Sam. How's the oxygen level up there?"

"Are you doing okay, Rosemary?" he asked, his voice a deep baritone.

"We're all right. Just glad you're here. We have a wealth of valuable information to give you," said Mimi, nodding to the Murderbook in Addie's hand.

"Great stuff, Rosemary. Listen, you both look exhausted. Why don't you go home and get some rest? We'll come by your cottage in a few hours. We can get detailed statements from you then."

"Sounds good," she said, grabbing his arm and leveling an eye at him. "Listen, there's an empty bottle of Hendrick's underneath the sink of the ballroom bar you'll want to send to the lab." He nodded in thanks and walked away.

"I need a long hot bath and some clean clothes," sighed Addie.

Mimi looped her arm through Addie's and they stood together

for a moment, taking in a final view of Lilac House. Mimi tried to understand what she was feeling. Even though she abhorred this place, the thought that there was no one left to live in it was unsettling. She felt a strange sense of loss. *Only ghosts here now.*

"Let's go home, dear."

As they mounted Joan Rivers, Mimi hoped her body had enough reserves to get them back. Addie watched her closely. Mimi remained uncharacteristically quiet during the journey, looking around and taking in her surroundings as if they were parts unknown.

FORTY-FOUR

Moments in Between

The air in the cottage was still and quiet. Mimi woke up and looked at the clock, which was blinking. Thankfully, the power had come back on. She looked at her watch: 6:17 p.m. Even though it was still Sunday, and she'd only napped for a couple of hours, it was a deep, unburdened sleep that she hadn't experienced in many years.

She turned her body toward the window. It was already dark outside. Ever since the blackmail invitation had arrived, all the painful memories of Peter that had been locked away in her head had been brought out into the open again. She had felt raw, overwhelming sadness.

Sitting up, Mimi pictured him in her mind's eye. His kind smile. His affable charm. Not the skeletal man in a hospital bed who she barely recognized, but the curious, intelligent soul who loved people and travel. Tender memories spread over her like a warm blanket. She'd spent the last twenty-three years convincing herself that she didn't deserve his forgiveness. But now, she understood there was nothing to ask forgiveness for. He would never have wanted her to have a moment's guilt about what she did. *Dial down that worry machine of yours, Ro. It's gonna be okay.* She blinked back tears as she rubbed the emerald pendant of her necklace between her fingers.

"Power's back on," Addie called out from the living room.

Mimi got up and wrapped a blanket around herself. She shuffled into the living room. "I'm going to check the thermostat and make sure the heat is turned up."

Addie sat down at the kitchen table. Mimi returned to the kitchen, yawning and stretching. A smile hovered on her lips. The complexities and emotions of the last twenty-four hours were still hanging in the air.

"Gonna miss you, kiddo," she said, sitting down across from her at the table. "Can't believe you're leaving tomorrow."

"Don't worry. I'll be coming back to visit. You still owe me fudge at Ryba's."

"Pam's Sam should be here soon." Mimi got up and opened the fridge door. She gestured to a stack of boxes inside. "Why don't I zap us each a gourmet dinner from Emeril?" She retrieved two of them and held them up, "Do you want a *Bam! That's Good Lasagna* or a *Bam! That's Tasty Chicken Marsala*?"

"Lasagna for me, please."

"By tomorrow night you'll be back in Chicago, wondering if you dreamed all this."

Addie went over to the silverware drawer and gathered forks and knives. "I hope this hasn't soured you on Mackinac for good. I can't imagine you living in some Florida high-rise, stopping by the juice bar after Jazzercise."

Mimi waved the thought away as she placed the meals in the microwave. "Nah. I'm okay now. Besides, I can't leave Joan Rivers."

"Good," said Addie as she began to set the table. "It just feels right to me that you're here. You're my anchor, firmly in place. I want to feel tethered to something."

"Your metaphors are clunkier than Jim's showerhead."

The microwave beeped.

"And what about you, dear? Are you going to go through with the lawsuit?"

"Yes," said Addie firmly. "I think I will."

"Attagirl," said Mimi, setting the dinners on the table. "Sue the living daylights out of him and make me proud."

"I didn't realize litigation was the way to make you proud."

"Hopefully he finds a way to take it on the chin."

They shared a smile.

"You do have good instincts," said Mimi, blowing on a forkful of chicken marsala. "You saw through all that misdirection and deception."

Addie nodded. "See? I can take care of myself. Or, what is it that you call it? I'm a *doer.*"

Mimi smiled and held her fork in the air like a wand. "You know, I feel like we're having a *Wizard of Oz* moment here. You always had the power, my dear. You just had to learn it for yourself."

Addie smirked. "Somehow, coming from you, that doesn't really work. Wasn't Glinda the *good* witch?"

Mimi put down the fork and smiled. She walked over to Addie and pulled her up from her chair into a tight, spontaneous hug. As though it were the most normal thing in the world. Then they sat back down at the table and ate together in relaxed silence for several minutes.

"You know, I think things are going to turn out all right for you with this *Murderscape* stuff. I mean, look at you. Really, if I didn't know better, I'd say you're almost chipper."

Addie shrugged. "Murder does that to me."

Mimi smiled. "For a long time, I worried about you because you kept your childlike wonder alive. But now I know that's a good thing. It's why you're such a brilliant game designer. I think your life is going to be remarkable."

They both turned and looked at Big Phyllis. Addie walked over to her, feeling her brown-speckled leaves and checking her soil. "She's certainly sensed your distress over these past few months. Plants are highly attuned to their environment. They can sense more than we ever imagined. Life is going to be good again, and I think you're going to see her improve as each day passes."

Mimi nodded in agreement with Addie's diagnosis. "I think so too."

Addie gathered up the dirty silverware and empty trays. "The next time either of us gets sad, it might be nice if we talked on the phone. We could be sad together."

"You know, I keep an iron grip on my emotions because, on those rare occasions when I allow myself to think about Peter, and your mom and your dad . . . I can cry for days. It's not pretty. At my age, I can't afford to lose that much moisture." She sighed. "Grief like that gives you two options. You either become someone who needs help all the time or someone who shuts down and never asks for help at all."

"I've got something for you." Addie went to her bag and pulled out the handmade greeting card Kimiko had given her in the conservatory and walked back over to the table, handing it to Mimi.

Mimi opened the card and read what Addie had written inside:

I think what you did was a supreme act of love.
I'm proud to be your granddaughter.

Mimi looked up at Addie. "I needed this. Thank you." They shared a tearful smile.

There was a loud knock at the front door.

"Must be the fuzz," said Mimi.

Addie watched Mimi stand up and roll back her shoulders. As

she walked to the door, there was a familiar spring in her step. The spunky Mackinac-loving Mimi she knew was back.

She answered the door to find Pam's Sam and his partner standing on the porch, smiling at her. "Hi, Rosemary, can we come in?"

"You bet. Addie's just going to grab her Murderbook. Where would you like to start?"

FORTY-FIVE

Back in the Game

Addie wheeled her suitcase behind her as she passed through a cloud of a thousand clashing perfumes emanating from the duty-free shop at the Detroit airport. She couldn't help but smile at the thought of Veronique reacting in disgust. She made her way through the crowds and scanned the departures board. Her flight to Chicago said *DELAYED*.

She went to an empty gate ahead of her and sat down. The airport muzak was playing a familiar melody in the background. She tuned in to identify the song and realized it was "Somebody That I Used to Know," by Gotye. She repressed a smile. Brian felt far away now. Like the faint memory of a bad dream.

Even though it was only Monday morning, the weekend's surreal events already felt another world away. She took out her phone and clicked on a few articles that were already up:

TELEVISION HOST ARRESTED IN ISLAND MURDERS

MACKINAC MURDER MYSTERY?

SNOWMAGEDDON LEADS TO WEEKEND OF TERROR

She had a flood of text messages, but she'd deal with those later. Sarah's was the only one she opened.

> Edgar and I have both been so worried about
> you. We've gone through Tim Burton's entire
> oeuvre to cope. Come home.

She smiled as she texted Sarah back. Listening to music felt like a much-needed distraction, so she reached into the zipper pocket of her purse for her headphones. As she sifted through her bag, her fingers touched the edge of Kimiko's drawing. She'd have to frame it. Besides the Murderbook, it was the only physical reminder of the weekend's events.

Still searching for her headphones, her finger poked straight through a hole in the lining of the inside pocket and touched something thin and papery. She frowned, then pulled her hand out and opened her bag wide to look inside. There was a large hole in the fabric lining, and she could see something had fallen through the hole, into the bottom of her purse. She reached her hand in again and dug down, grasped on to it, and pulled it out.

Her heart leapt.

It was her Quoth the Raven spiral notepad! Her purse had been so stuffed with things from the move and travel that she hadn't noticed the tear in the lining.

Her eyes welled up as she held the physical proof of her authorship in her hands. She flipped through the pages of familiar notes, drawings, and ideas. The interlocking *P* logo with their signatures, the Venetian mask drawing—it was all there. She clutched the notebook to her chest, then carefully tucked it back into her purse and took out her phone. Martin was going to be thrilled. She tapped his number to call him, but she wasn't getting any service. She needed Wi-Fi.

She scanned her surroundings. Straight ahead was a bar that looked inviting, with big windows facing the tarmac. Gliding her suitcase behind her, she headed to the bar and took one of the leather barstools near the front. She logged into the Wi-Fi and texted Martin:

> Martin, you're not going to believe this, but I
> found the Raven notepad! It has Brian's
> signature on the logo and everything. I'm ready.
> Let's—

"Hi," she heard a male voice say.

She looked up. Mr. Bartender was cute. Martin could wait.

"Hi," she said, putting her phone down.

"Champagne?" he asked flirtatiously.

Addie blushed. "Sure."

He turned around and walked toward the refrigerator behind him. He opened the door and reached for the bottle.

"Actually," she said, leaning over the counter, "I changed my mind."

He paused and closed the refrigerator door, then turned back to her with a smile. "Sure. What'll it be?"

"I'll have a Gibson."

Acknowledgments

This book would not exist without my brilliant mom, Tracy Mullen. Thank you, Mama, for instilling a love of language and creativity in me from an early age. It has shaped my entire life's journey. You are my most trusted reader, sounding board, therapist, brainstorming partner, and cheerleader. While there have been many amazing aspects of this experience, the best part has been the joy we've shared in working on this together for the last two years. You're my best friend, and you are, hands down, the funniest and most creative person I've ever known.

The universe has brought me the two best editors I ever could have hoped for. Thank you to my exceptional UK editor, Emily Griffin. From our very first conversation, I knew you were going to be the right editor for me. I am genuinely awed by your eye-opening wisdom, passion, and kindness. Having you as my collaborator has enabled me to throw myself wholeheartedly into this experience and appreciate every moment. To Maya Ziv, my US editor, thank you for your laser-focused attention to detail, your humor, and your keen vision. I've learned so much from your feedback, which has made me a better writer, and your enthusiasm and thoughtful insights have kept me motivated and inspired.

The outstanding teams at Century and Dutton have made me feel so welcome and supported with their energy and ideas. At Century, I'd like to thank Sam Rees-Williams, Claire Simmonds, Olivia Thomas, Charlotte Bush, Rebecca Ikin, Amelia Evans, and the entire PRH foreign rights team, Rose Waddilove, Ceara Elliot, Jess Muscio, and of course, the inimitable icons that are Venetia Butterfield and Selina Walker. At Dutton, I want to thank Ella Kurki, Hannah Poole, Caroline Payne, LeeAnn Pemberton, Diamond Bridges, Mary Beth Constant, and Jeff Miller.

Judith Murray, you are the agent of my dreams. Thank you for always being so deeply supportive, intuitive, and kind. It's been a joy for me to watch you do what you do so brilliantly. Lucky for me, I get the added bonus that you are hysterically funny and also happen to know all the best restaurants. Thank you to Laura Williams and Mia Dakin for pulling me from the depths of anonymity— otherwise known as the slush pile—and into Judith's hands! To Imogen Morrell, Anne Clarke, Sally Oliver, and the rest of the fantastic team at Greene & Heaton, thanks for all your support in representing me around the world.

To my WME film and television agents, Nicole Weinroth and Carolina Beltran, thanks for all the heart and soul you've put into this. I still can't believe the fateful way we met. It was truly meant to be.

Chris Salvaterra, thank you for nearly twenty years of guidance and friendship. What the world needs now is more Chris Salvaterras.

Mackinac Island is a charming place that everyone should visit at least once. It's worth noting that I've taken some creative liberties for the sake of the story, but I hope that the essence of Mackinac still rings true to those who know it well. I am especially grateful to historian Russell Magnaghi for being such a generous and valuable resource to me during my research. For any readers who are curious to learn more about the area, his books *Prohibition in the Upper Peninsula* and *Classic Food and Restaurants of the Upper Peninsula* are both excellent.

I owe a huge thank-you to Dan Whitehead, Tom Harris, and Dave Lawrie for advising me on the gaming bits and for being such discerning readers in general. Any mistakes in this book are entirely mine.

Love and thanks go to my wonderful sister-in-law, Lindsey Mullen, who read each draft in great detail and gave me such astute feedback. Also, to my dad, Robert, and to my brother, Bradley, thank you for all your enthusiasm, suggestions, and support! Aunt Kris and Uncle Fred, thank you for always cheering me on!

A massive thank-you to the Novelry and especially Tash Barsby, Louise Dean, Katie Khan, and Amanda Reynolds. What you do for aspiring writers is simply amazing.

Bill Massey, thanks for your incredibly useful and honest editorial feedback. Those early drafts needed a lot of work, and you were hugely helpful.

I'm enormously grateful to Curtis Brown Creative for their writing courses, which allowed me to dedicate time and energy to my writing in a focused and professional environment. Vaseem Khan, thank you for your incredible mentorship and support. I can still hear you in my head, challenging me on some of those plot points— "That's not good enough!" You're the best. Simon Ings, thank you for identifying my strengths and helping me develop my voice.

Many of my CBC classmates read early drafts and gave me such helpful feedback and encouragement. I want to especially thank Timothy Ireland-Griffiths, Nola D'Enis, Emma Sibbles, Debby Taylor-Lane, Lauren Cluer, and Ali Boston.

Hugs and thank-yous to my friends Emily Fox, Elizabeth Bland, Phylicia Jackson-Jones, Steve Jones, Scott Troy, Kerry Ehrin, Tanya Colburn, Sarah Zumot, Jill McLain-Meister, Greg McLain-Meister,

Laura Greifner, Rebecca Rienks, Jordan Smith, Hannah Tucker, Rosie Dart, Dinara Bekmansurova, William Swann, Tony Hanyk, and Lindsay Jill Roth.

I would also like to thank my favorite Iowa schoolteacher, Phyllis Cadwallader, who passed away in 2018. She was a beautiful storyteller who always inspired me.

A portion of the proceeds from this book will go to three animal rescues: Dachshund Rescue of North America, London Inner City Kitties, and Croydon Animal Samaritans. If you have a soft spot for animals, please consider a rescue and not buying from a breeder or elsewhere. Most rescues around the world are bursting at the seams with loving animals who simply want someone to love them back. To all our rescues, past and present—Edgar, Wolseley, Agatha, Sooty, and Iris—thank you for bringing joy to our lives and for ensuring that writing isn't a solitary experience for me.

My wonderful grandparents greatly influenced me, and there is a little sprinkle of each of them within this story. For anyone who wants to enjoy a Gibson martini just like "my Mimi" would make, you can find the recipe on the next page.

Finally and most importantly, thank you to the love of my life, my husband, Philip. I truly could not have done this without you. Every day you found meaningful ways to support me, but one memory in particular sticks out in my mind. It was the night of the Rolling Stones concert in Hyde Park, when we were at that little Italian restaurant we can never remember the name of, and I grumbled over my spaghetti that I wanted to quit this whole writing thing. Finishing a book, let alone getting it published, felt so unrealistic, and I worried I was wasting my time. Then you took my hand and said the most affirming, motivating words I've ever heard. Your belief in me is what kept me going, and I haven't looked back since. I love you forever.

Mimi's Gibson Martini

INGREDIENTS

- 5 PARTS GIN
- 1 PART DRY VERMOUTH
- SPLASH OF COCKTAIL ONION JUICE
- COCKTAIL ONIONS

METHOD

1. Chill martini glass.
2. Combine gin, vermouth, and onion juice in a mixing glass filled with ice.
3. Stir for one minute.
4. Strain into the martini glass and garnish with 3 onions.

About the Author

Kelly Mullen has worked as a producer in Hollywood and a marketing executive in New York and London. During the pandemic she took online writing courses through Curtis Brown Creative and the Novelry, which reignited her childhood passion for writing. *This Is Not a Game* is her first novel and was inspired by a two-week stay at her grandmother's house in 2021.

As an executive producer, her credits include Academy Award–nominated *Trumbo*, starring Bryan Cranston and Helen Mirren, and AppleTV+'s *Dads*, produced with Ron Howard. Her creative work for brands has won more than fifty awards, including Cannes Lions and Clios.

Born and raised in Iowa, Kelly is now a dual citizen of the US and UK. She lives in London with her husband and their rescue cats.